Coincidences

Gloria Leister

Contents

Kai

Kai Winters

Kai Winters was born in a white wolf pack that was located on the mountain Mount Odins in Canada. The snow and cold doesn't bother white wolves at all because their hides are special. White wolves are rare, but not for this reason alone. There were only 50 white wolves in the world and they were all hidden in this mountain pack. Well, 51 actually.

His father was a huge dominant Alpha white wolf with red tribal markings that appeared during challenges or when their mate is found. His daddy was a slender white wolf that was a dominant omega. The two loved each other more than their own lives.

Tyran, Kai's Papa, and William, Kai's daddy, were playing in the snow together with their pup who was only eight years old. Unlike normal werewolves, white wolves can shift almost immediately into their wolf form (at birth or up to 2 years old).

Kai was practically swimming in the snow, chomping at it here and there. Kai's pup form was pure white, most getting their white coats when they're older. From his small size and shyness towards others, his parents assumed he was an omega; only time would tell if he was dominant or submissive. Not that either cared since Kai was their sweet innocent baby.

Kai heard his Papa chuckle at him, hopping in the snow towards the giant wolf. Kai suddenly disappeared before being lifted up by his scruff out of the deep snow by his daddy, who laid him on his Papa's head playfully.

Kai nibbled on his Papa's ear who licked and nuzzles his pup. Kai fell off his Papa before landing on his back in the fluffy snow, his little paws waving in the air happily. Will nuzzled and purred at his baby, the two scenting him happily. Tyran and Will feeling their hearts beat with joy for their only son. Male pregnancies aren't rare, but they aren't common either.

Kai yawned sleepily, snuggling into his Papa's chest, between his massive paws.

I think he likes you love Will giggled through the mind link, Tyran harrumphing at him. Tyran tugged on Will's ear happily before nuzzling and licking his mate, Will snuggling into his mate's side.

I love you Ty Will sighed, his head resting over Tyran's paws so his cheek was against their pup.

I love you too Will Tyran laid his head over his smaller mate's shoulders.

A howl rang out suddenly from a warrior meaning the pack was under attack.

Take the pup! Tyran yelled, running towards the pack grounds with Will on his tail; holding their pup by the scruff of his neck.

Stay in the house

Please be safe love Will begged giving a last nuzzle to his mate. .

.

Fire.

Fire was everywhere. The smoke alone was suffocating. A pup that shifted back into a child, lay crying in his bed; alone. His daddy, dead on the floor along with his Papa; the two protecting their precious baby with their last breath. Blood pooled onto the wood floor.

A large dominant Alpha rogue with cruel eyes handed the child to an omega following him in chains.

Kai was taken by a rogue pack whose Alpha was cruel and abusive. He was beaten daily for being weak and because he never shifted (at least not in front of anyone). The pack assumed he couldn't shift so he was deemed even more worthless. Kai was a submissive omega meaning: any orders from any ranking wolf or even a few humans, could command him to do anything they wanted. Only by the age of nine was he saved from their cruelty. Another rogue pack had invaded, trying to take down the dominant Alpha, wanting control.

Kai was grabbed by a girl who was 10; she belonged to the invading rogue pack. She was in rags but her eyes were the only kind thing he had seen in so long. One year of abuse still left too many mental and physical scars that no child should have.

A boy who was a little taller than her, skin and bones with dark black hair, was behind her. He had tear tracks, fresh bruises and cuts, and was wearing the same rags designed for the slaves in Kai's rogue pack. The pack house was a run down mansion that was huge, so it was likely the two never crossed paths; especially since Kai thought he was the only slave there. The thing that stood out about him was his left eye was scrunched closed, a deep scar running vertically from his hairline to an inch below his eyelid. It appeared to be an older scar.

"If we escape now we won't be hurt anymore. Please come with me. If we aren't alone then I know we can do anything"

Kai didn't know anything about this girl, but her eyes reminded him of how his parents would have looked at him.

Kai sobbed, noddind his head. The girl picked him up promptly since he was scrubbing the floor with a toothbrush while his leg was broken along with two of his ribs.

The three of them raced out of the rundown mansion, fleeing through the limbs and blood flying in the air.

The girl soon had to carry the starving boy on her back, Kai glued to her front, as she ran for days.

But they were free and Kai was going to follow the girl who saved his life, forever.

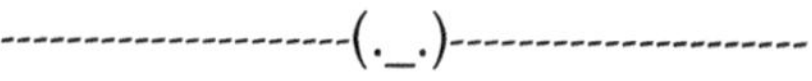

Amilya

I didn't know why my daddy and Papa were upset along with my two older brothers.

We were all in the car going back home and my daddy and Papa were whispering harshly to each other; we were coming back from pee-wee football! My brothers love playing that.

My Papa is really really tall with with dark black hair, tan skin and black eyes. My daddy is a head shorter than him with blonde hair, blue eyes, and pale skin.

My oldest brother is Car-Car. He has black hair, dark skin like Papa and blue eyes like daddy. My second brother is Co-co and has blonde hair like daddy and dark skin and black eyes like Papa.

My daddy found a little boy on one of his runs who was abandoned. He smells like he'd be an alpha even though he said his family got rid of him because they thought he was going to be an omega. He's super nice to me and a year older, and plays with my brothers a lot. He has dark brown hair, green eyes and two front teeth missing.

My name is Amilya! I'm ten years old. I love my family so so so much! My Papa is my bear and I'm his gummy! Cause gummy bears are my favorite!

I'm shorter than my brothers and I like to play quietly cause loud noise hurts my ears; my brothers make too much noise sometimes. I have black hair that's down to the middle of my back and I have black eyes like Papa and pale skin like daddy. Plus Papa and daddy love each other lots cause the kiss all gross, but daddy tells him no more kids for a while all the time which makes Papa pout.

I had snuck some gummy bears into my Papa's coffee this morning cause I couldn't find any sugar and I don't know why Papa likes coffee all gross tasting like that!

Gummy bears make things better anyway!

I was scared this morning though because this mean man was yelling at my Papa after I went to go get more gummy bears, daddy and my brothers in the room with Papa.

He was yelling about a submissy alpha or something, and how it makes a pack weak. I don't want that! I'll find this person and tell them to work harder or something.

Whoever the man was, was making my daddy cry silently while my Papa and his Beta were ordering the man to leave.

The man snarled as I scampered fast from the door and down the hall. I saw him walking my way, hoping he wouldn't see me.

His eyes snapped to me making me whimper, his eyes flashing red. That wasnt possible though cause only rogues had red eyes, right?

"You won't be here long," he whispered, almost snarling making me back up. The man soon disappearing from the pack grounds.

I tried getting my brothers or Papa or daddy to play with me. They all ignored me for some reason except for daddy who hugged me, before continuing to stress bake.

The morning and afternoon was really quiet and I had given my daddy and Papa my secret stash of gummy bears on their bed with a card that I drew before we had to leave so it's a surprise! I hope it makes them feel better.

We were leaving to my brother's football practice; usually Leon would come (the boy with the two missing front teeth), but he was sick today.

After the game we left, my daddy starting to cry again. I didn't know what to do and I wanted to give him hugs and kisses like he gives to me. I'll do it when we get home. Papa is holding his hand and I hope that makes daddy feel a little better.

Suddenly the car moved sideways, before tipping to the side. Everything went black.

I woke up slowly, my head hurting super bad with red stuff coming out. My brothers were crying and yelling since I could hear my parents growling and snapping for some reason outside the car.

Rogues! Echoed in my head from Papa, making it hurt worse.

My brothers started crawling out of the car while I struggled with the seat belt. I heard my Papa's friend the beta responding in the link, knowing the mean wolves couldn't beat my Papa and daddy.

I suddenly felt large hands grab me and tug me out of the broken window. I saw my Papa and daddy in their wolf forms fighting what little rogues were left; the rest of our pack headed towards us.

Wait... Then who has me?

I looked to see the mean alpha holding me, running away from my Dads.

No!

I screamed as loud as I could. I knew I must have done something to upset my family earlier, but they were still my family and would save me.

"Papa!!!" I screamed as loud as I could, crying, seeing my Papa's wolf head turn to the sound before he and daddy raced after the mean alpha.

I was screaming and struggling as hard as I could. The mean wolf hit me and everything was going black. My papa and daddy were so far away.

Please save me was my last thought.

When I woke up I looked to be in a damp cellar with a couple of old omega women.

"You're a worthless submissive alpha, girl. I can already smell it. You don't deserve to live, but out of the kindness of my heart you will do as I say. You were a burden to your family and pack for being so weak."

My head snapped up to the cruel alpha, his eyes blazing red. I was right! He is a rogue. A mean, nasty, smelly butthead!

Wait... I'm the submiss Alpha thing? Is that why papa, daddy, car-car and co-co were mad at me? Would Leon be mad if he heard too? I cried quietly, bringing my knees to my chest. Maybe I shouldn't go back if it made my daddy cry so much.

After several years, I was forced to be a Starter. A Starter is super illegal, according to the granny omegas I worked with.

No werewolf packs, rogue or otherwise, were allowed to have Starters.

A Starter is someone who has to fight the warriors of the pack as hard as they could, usually getting killed, so that the warriors were warmed up to go on raids.

I have two scars on my back that run diagonally from my left shoulder to my right hip and one scar from my right shoulder to the bottom of the left side of my rib cage. The other bruises, cuts and broken bones had eventually healed.

The only good thing about a Starter, in my opinion, was that I was getting dangerous enough that I couldn't be raped by the other wolves in the pack. That scared me more than anything because I was saving myself for my mate; I would kill myself if I was raped.

Anyway, the mean alpha (whose name I never learned since everyone called him alpha), said we were all moving out to take over another rogue pack.

My feet were bleeding since none of the slaves get shoes and aren't allowed to shift.

I see the warriors starting to attack people and I made a decision that my daddy had taught me a long time ago. Protect those weaker then you.

When I ran into the old mansion, there were two smells. They must have been weaker wolves or omegas since I knew what that smelled like. I ran to the back of the mansion seeing a black haired submissive gamma boy chained to a pole and beaten.

"Hello," I whispered, seeing him struggle in fear at me.

"I was taught to protect those who can't protect themselves and I'm a slave too. If we leave together I know we'll make it much farther. Will you come with me? I don't want to be alone or hurt anymore," I whispered to the boy.

The boy looked at me with one eye, the other scrunched closed; probably because of the scar I guessed.

The boy nodded, quietly crying as I fumbled with his chains for a second, breaking him away from the pole.

He pointed back to mansion, hugging himself.

"Someone else?"

He nodded as I held his hand, running into the house. I nearly froze seeing a little boy who had a broken leg and fresh bruises, cleaning. How inhuman and cruel could rogues be!?

I offered the boy the same thing, carrying the sweet boy with one arm, holding the starved boys' hand with the other, as we ran into the night.

Even though we were all submissive, I was going to be their Alpha, and protect them since I really didn't have anything anymore.

-----------(O_O)---------------(. _.)------

Amilya's Papa's wolf picture above!

Okay...so its longer than a 1000... But i couldn't help it >_< my fingers kept typing :P

Robin

R obin

Robin was born into servitude and sold along with his mother to a rogue pack.

It didn't matter what he did, he'd be beaten, spit on, trash thrown at him, and all around man handled. His mother was raped and killed in the rogue pack, leaving him to fend for himself.

He was allowed a single piece of bread every three days, knowing everything would get worse if he was caught taking more then that. He was the only submissive gamma, his mother telling him he was rare.

She also told him that she named him Robin because his voice was so beautiful even though he was so young. He was lanky anyways as a child before becoming skeletal because of the lack of food.

He had black hair and his left eye had a scar. He avoided almost all the pack, so afraid he'd be raped and killed like his mother.

He was fortunate enough to only get beatings, is what he'd tell himself. He could smell another scent that screamed omega, knowing this one was new to the pack. The other female omega was raped by the warriors and treated as a play thing for a few years before she committed suicide.

Robin didn't talk at all knowing it could draw attention, praying for anything to happen so Robin would no longer suffer.

It was years before anything happened. Robin was tied to a pole and beaten to an inch if his life by the warriors. They promised him that after the battle they were going to fuck him until he died because they were fighting in a battle and deserved a reward.

Robin sobbed, wishing for his death, before a girl with long black hair, offered to help him and free him.

Even if this is a trap, I will never get another chance after this battle

Robin nodded to the girl who helped him up, wrapping his arms around his chest, feeling his ribs under his fingers with each breath.

Robin motioned towards the house knowing that the only other weak member of the pack would get whatever was going to happen to Robin. Robin's mother taught him kindness, so he couldn't leave the kid alone. Especially since he smelled like an omega.

They found the boy in the kitchen who didn't look much better then Robin. The boy held onto the girl, Robin feeling warmth again from the girl grabbing his hand, the three of them running into the night.

Robin was soon carried on the girl's back, tears pouring down his face since he was finally free (at the moment) from the cruelty he had a known all his life.

He was going to follow this girl anywhere.

Tyler

Tyler didn't remember much of his life before he realized he was in a forest.

He knew he was a werewolf, but was left abandoned in the wilderness. For what reason, he didn't know.

He lived in he wilderness for years, hunting and surviving for as long as he could. He hadn't had any interactions with other humans or werewolves, always thinking he'd be alone.

Tyler's POV:

I heard a rustle a few yards ahead of me, bounding in that direction since I hadn't had anything to eat for days.

I snarled into the clearing, hoping it was a deer or something, before a small white wolf tumbled head over ass in fright.

I froze, never seeing another animal in the forest before (excluding deer, rabbits, and squirrels).

The little wolf suddenly howled in fear making me back up a little.

Does he have a pack? Was I trespassing? Is that a normal fur color? Why was that squirrel so stringy? No, focus

Suddenly, a slim black wolf with long legs and a scar over his left closed eye ran out fast, followed by a very large black wolf. The large black wolf snarled.

Alpha! Wait... Female? Submissive? I'm so confused! And hungry. So so hungry. But you are not a cannibal Tyler!

What do I do!? I don't want to be killed

I thought frantically before remembering a little from my Dad (a serious asshole). I bowed my head to the Alpha, whimpering, making eye contact with the white wolf who was hidden behind the other two.

I flopped onto my back, barking, rubbing my back on the ground, making my tongue flop out. The three of them looked at me confused, the little white wolf perking up.

The Alpha growled at him, moving closer to me as I bared my neck. I whimpered, feeling the she-wolf's breath before peeking open an eye. She was sitting on her haunches looking at me curiously.

I suddenly choked on my breath when the little white wolf bounced on my bared belly, the lanky black wolf sniffing me.

"Shift if you please," the pre-teen girl spoke gently.

My eyes nearly popped out of my head, seeing her naked and sitting cross legged on the ground. The lanky boy and white wolf matching her.

I slowly did the same, grunting at the change since it had been so long since I went into my human form. From what I last remembered I was blonde with pale skin and green eyes.

"You are a submissive Beta."

I was sitting on the ground, my shoulders hunching at the comment. I knew that was probably one of the reasons why I was abandoned.

"Oh, please don't be offended," the white wolf boy spoke gently.

"We have all been hurt and alone before we found each other. Perhaps if we told you our story you might like to join us? Wolves are creatures that thrive in packs. To sense you are so alone hurts us, you see."

I nodded at the girl. She sounded smart, seemed nice, and was pretty; even if she was covered in mud.

I learned all of their stories, telling them my own. It took a little longer since I couldn't remember a few words or how to talk for that matter.

They had even caught a deer and shared it with me. We were all starving but they were so nice to include me and it felt like a real pack.

No ones POV:

"Would you like to join us Tyler. Don't feel like you must say yes, alright?" Amilya tilted her head at Tyler making him slowly smile.

"Yes! P-Please," Tyler smiled shyly before getting tackled by Kai and Robin.

"Now our pack is even better!" Kai squealed making Tyler mess up his hair.

"Our dynamics has every level of wolf. Alpha, Beta, Gamma, and Omega," Robin spoke softly.

"We may all be submissive and unwanted by others, but accepting me as your alpha makes us strong and I couldn't be happier! I wouldn't even care if any of you were dominants, as long as we take care of each other," Amilya stood proudly under the moonlight. Kai the submissive omega, Robin the submissive gamma, and Tyler the submissive Beta, all bared their necks to their Alpha.

Tyler would follow them anywhere to save himself from the starvation and loneliness he suffered through.

------------(<_<)----------------------The last back story! A little timeline catch up in the next chapter!

Timeline

Lots of info here guys!

It has now been a few years, the four submissives having found one another. Amilya worked a few jobs to get a chunk of money for them to be able to eat real food every now and again, and share a hotel room with running water. Tyler helped out as well, Amilya teaching them all to read and write and do algebra. She also taught them about mates and bonding from what she overheard her Papa trying to teach her brother.

They made a pack decision to move to Michigan where there were vast forests, lakes, and places they could hide from rogues. Amilya felt it was a good place to start.

Descriptions:

Amilya is now 17 years old, about to turn 18. She has long black hair that goes to the middle of her back. She is 6 feet tall, 175 pounds, black eyes and has lean muscle. She wears baggy pants, big hoodies that hide most of her lethal form and a hospital mask to cover the lower half of her face. She does not want to be recognized.

Tyler is 18 years old. He likes his blonde hair to be beach messy and has green eyes. He likes to wear skinny jeans and bright colored shirts with his favorite coffee brown and black jackets and one of his many scarves. He is 5'9, 150 lbs, muscled (not overly so), and loves Starbucks. Well, coffee.

Robin is 18 years old. He has dark black hair and his one visible eye is also black. He likes to wear black and has a favorite lavender colored hoodie. He is 5'7, 140 pounds, and lean like a runner. He'd rather have tea than coffee any day of the week. His favorites are varying types of Earl grey teas.

Kai is 17 years old. He has dark black hair and grey eyes. He is full of energy and shy around anyone other than his family. He likes his skinny jeans, converse, and label shirts. He will eat as much dark chocolate as you can give him. He is 5'5, 110 lbs, and likes baby animals.

All wolves can find their mates at 16 and shift at 10.

All of them were scared to find their mates because it could separate their makeshift pack after being together for so long.

Amilya signed herself and her brothers up at a high school with fake credits. All of them in their senior year except for Kai who was a junior (it would be more suspicious otherwise).

Amilya had found some scent blocking soap for all of them to use so they would smell human to other werewolves.

What they found out though, was that being a submissive gave them something like special powers.

Powers! Say what!?

Kai realized he could heal others if he touches them in wolf form, allowing his power inti them; it was even more effective if he licked any wounds.

Wounds disappeared almost immediately and broken bones healed faster than a regular werewolf's healing time.

Robin finally told them that his left eye was cursed. When he opened it, it was violet in color with an outline of an hourglass shape in the middle. He could see fifteen seconds into the future when he opened it, though he has been training for years to get see that far ahead.

Tyler couldn't just shift into his blonde wolf, but could copy other wolves. For example, Amilya's wolf is pitch black and about 4'5 on all fours. Tyler could change the height, weight, and color of his wolf to look like an exact match to his opponent; pack link helps here so everyone can attack the right werewolf of course.

Amilya is able to swing up to a dominant Alpha power when there is extreme danger to her family, getting larger and more feral. Her body has the ability to become as hard as steel.

Now, the small family has moved into a town home close to the forest in Michigan, excited and scared for their futures.

----------(o-o) ---------------------I hope that caught everything up!

Coincidence!?

C arver's POV:

It sucks waking up in the morning. Especially after sitting through a three hour, boring meeting with your dad and brother late last night.

I got up, did my morning routine, and tried not to crawl back into bed.

I put on some jeans and a tight dark blue shirt to show off my abs and v-line. I had all the pack sluts drooling even though I wouldn't let those hoes come near me. I mean, pack sluts probably have something. I'm scared that them even breathing on me, will give me some kind if sexually transmitted disease, even though werewolves are resistant to them. I wasn't going to risk anything that would get my mate to hate me. I shivered at the thought, flexing and messing up my hair to give it a 'tussled look', before grabbing my phone and backpack, heading downstairs.

I'm 6'7, 200 pounds of muscle with black hair, blue eyes, lightly tanned skin, and am the future Alpha of the DarkIce pack.

"Rawr!" I felt the wind get knocked out of me, banging into a wall.

"Conner!" I yelled, dragging him into a noogie.

"Say it!"

"Never!"

"SAY IT!"

"Carver is masterful and a hella sexy beast!" Conner yelled before I dropped his ass on the floor laughing my butt off.

Conner growled, shoving me, as I ran after him to the kitchen.

I'm 18, soon to be 19. I'm in my senior year of high school along with my little brother and future beta, Conner. We were born 20 minutes after each other and werewolf pregnancies are six to seven months.

All future pack alphas and their betas must go to a training school in Alaska for a year, to learn the ins and outs to running, maintaining, and controlling packs. Once the elders agree that we are knowledgeable enough to run a pack, we can return home and accept our duties whenever, from the current pack alpha. Sometimes challenges are initiated for the title, but the title is usually passed down through family ties.

That's why I'm so old and still in school. Ugh. Conner was already stuffing his face with pancakes. He's 6'6, 190 pounds of muscle, and loves video games. He's also my best friend, I'd trust him with my life, and we are both on the football team at school; I'm the quarterback, cliché but whatever.

"Somebody got beauty sleep," my future gamma and my other best friend strutted in, trying to mess up my hair. We growled playfully at each other before Papa threatened us to not even start.

My gamma is named Raven and he is freaking smart and one Hell of a tactician. He came across our borders with his parents and a few other pairs when he was about twelve; all of them not agreeing to the rulings of their current alpha. We accepted them, after a few trials to make sure they were honest and truthful about why they wanted to join. We are very protective of our members.

Raven has helped our pack a lot by directing where our warriors should go when there were rogues attacking. My father, the current alpha, gave him a chance to prove himself when he first joined since Raven claimed he could drive back a recurring attack from several rogues, minimizing our own losses. Let's just saw, we became friends that day. He's awesome.

Speaking of warriors, my family and our whole pack are worried about our dearest family member and me, my brother's, and my gamma's best friend Leon. The head warrior of the pack. He's 21, about to turn 22, and he only has 4 years left to live.

I may be a 'big bad Alpha', but we grew up with him and have cried with him from the loneliness he bears and the depression setting in from not having a mate; my best friend is losing his wolf. My brother and family member, was dying and there was nothing anyone could do.

I sat down, eating my pancakes with Raven and Conner secretly throwing blueberries at each other.

I rolled my eyes at them.

"Good morning sweetie," My dad walked into the kitchen, kissing me on the head along with Raven and Conner, before kissing my Papa softly on the lips. Yes I have two Dads and they are amazing, caring, and don't put up with any shit. They love and know each pack member and make sure everyone is provided for. I love them.

My Dad whose name is Adam and Luna to the pack, gets depressed sometimes because he lost one of his babies. Our little sister was taken and he's never gotten over it. None of us have, or ever will get over it. All of us regret what happened that day. My daddy is 37 and my Papa is 38. They were both pretty young when they had me and my brother and sister.

"How are you today love?" My Papa whispered, holding my daddy around the waist while he was still sitting down.

"I'm okay honey," dad smiled softly, kissing Papa again.

"Now you boys go to school or you'll be late. I need to ravish someone," Papa smirked making me, Conner and Raven groan in disgust. We each kissed my Dad hurriedly on the cheek before grabbing our stuff.

Me and Conner kissed or fingers and pressed them against the picture that was hanging on the wall. It was a picture of our baby sister with the picture she drew of our family, the night everything went to shit.

We heard dad laughing making our hearts less constricted since his depression would make the whole house feel down since he is the Luna.

"Race you there!" Raven yelled, all of us stripping fast before running in our wolf forms. We stuffed our clothes in our backpacks, the straps in our mouths.

Don't you dare cheat Raven! Conner yelled through our link

It's called strategizing Raven cackled before we tried tripping each other, making it to school in record time. We panted while we redressed. The high school was 80% werewolves and 20% humans who were mates to the werewolves. The city limits were where the rest of the human population started. They pretty much left us alone since the city was more or less isolated from other parts of the state.

I high fived and punched some of my friends playfully. There were nerds with jocks and a couple of emos with some popular kids. No one really judged since mates were very important to us and bullying wasn't a loud at all.

"Hey sexy," Tiffany of the cheerleading team and the head pack sluts said, rubbing my shoulder.

"Don't!" I hissed at her, eyes glowing yellow to show my dominance. Tiffany pouted with a glare, stomping away to the table with her slutty cronies. I swear she tries to jump me around every corner. She even tried to grab my dick out of my pants one time! Almost broke her freaking hand and I had to shower again since I was walking out of the locker rooms from football practice. You have seriously got to watch out for her hands. Ugh. I think I gave my self the chills.

"Bro, I think I see the crabs on your shoulder," Conner laughed with Raven as I tried to shove my shoulder at them making them scream like girls.

We sat down at our table, with most of the football team around us, talking before class. Tiffany and one of her slutty friends were talking at their table, asses practically high in the air and bent over the table with their underwear showing. The other girls had their breasts nearly falling out of their shirts or legs spread apart while they were sitting. Some guys were drooling but I didn't see the appeal at all. I wasn't sure if I was gay or not, but I just wanted someone to love me for... Well... Me. Call me a romanticist all you want. Shut up.

"So when will Leon get here?" Conner asked, playing paper football across from Raven. Both of their noses were wrinkled in disgust too at the daily display from the slut table.

"He won't be here till after his birthday in a little over a month."

Leon had lost control of his wolf for about a minute, scaring most of the pack in a meeting before Conner and I had to tackle him with Raven calming him down. We knew he snapped because of the lack of a mate. My father gave him permission to leave to search for his mate.

"Maaan, I miss him and his ugly face!" Conner growled hitting Raven in the face with the paper football.

"Jerk!"

"Ass!"

"Bitch!"

"Fugly!"

"Slut!"

Conner gasped, hand over his heart.

"You wound me!"

I promptly hit my head on the table at the two morons I called my best friends.

"You don't want to lose anymore brain cells do you Carver?" Raven smirked at me, making me growl, about to lunge at him; everyone used to our antics already.

Ahem Papa was speaking through the pack link there will be four new students attending your school today. They are human and don't know about the existence of werewolves.

Everyone murmured at that seeing as that didn't make sense to have humans in a werewolf school. In fact, it didn't make sense to have humans anywhere near hormonal teenage werewolves.

If you are wondering why this is, it is punishment for the senior prank that was pulled. You will not shift in school, nor will your eyes glow for dominance stunts. Your Luna and the omegas took two days to clean up the school because all of you didn't even offer to help. Anyone disobeying these rules will be reported and sent to me for punishment. Is that clear?

Papa's alpha voice was harsh at the end, everyone immediately saying 'yes alpha!'

Their names are Kai, Tyler, Robin and Mila Winters. That is all.

"Well this sucks!" Conner grumbled along with Carver. We weren't even here for it or I would have forced the pack members to help clean since they all probably ran off for summer vacation.

Everyone was grumbling as well, a few of the guilty people saying sorry. Although I don't think it was really believable with the giant smiles on their faces.

There was still a few minutes until class with me longing to go home and back to bed. Papa said I could go search for my mate like Leon once I graduated. Sometimes I've felt more desperate then the others, but that wasn't true. I'd even get jealous of Papa and Dad, wanting the relationship they had, but I knew it was just my wolf getting anxious.

"Hey Carv, what are you thinking about?" Conner rested his head on my shoulder, him and Raven making faces at each other.

"My mate. I wonder what they're doing?"

Conner and Raven seemed to dream away too, wondering what their mates would look like and act like.

"I bet she'll be pretty," Conner smiled happily, batting his eyelashes at Raven who rolled his eyes.

"Puh-lease. She'll be as ugly as you!" Raven smirked, Conner growling at him.

"Dumbass"

"Whore"

"Skank"

"Bi-"

"Would you two stop it!" I yelled before laughing, standing up to smack both of them in the back of the head.

"Practice is at six tonight Carver!" One of the warriors and line backer of the football team yelled, most of the team heading towards the gym.

"Got it!"

"I don't care if my mate is a guy or a girl as long as I have a mate," I shrugged, stretching out my arms.

"Dude, you like guys?" Conner asked with shock, making me lift my brow at him along with Raven. I just shrugged at him, making him lift his eyebrow back at me.

"I think I'll just love my mate the way they are. I mean I've been waiting for three years to find my mate! I just want them in my arms already," I mumbled annoyed at the thought, slinging my backpack over my shoulder.

"I think I'd die if I didn't get pussy," Conner smirked making Raven and me gag at him. There were a couple of nice girls in the pack that weren't like the sluts, but they didn't peak my interest. I'm pretty sure my wolf won't even let me near anyone unless they're my mate since it literally grosses me out. Trust me, I've tried dating and kissing but regret it every time. Like a horrible pit in my stomach that won't go away.

"You've never slept with anyone! You know dad will whoop your ass if you don't lose it to your mate."

Seriously. Dad would beat our asses if we slept around, making the point that we wouldn't want our mates to have slept with a bunch of people. Pretty sure I'm gonna feel sorry for the person who'll be stuck with Tiffany.

"I'm just saying!" Conner grumbled. There were still fifteen minutes till class, no one really leaving the cafeteria yet, but we liked to hang out in the quiet hallways before it was ran-sacked.

I sluggishly made it to the middle of the cafeteria. How can Raven and Conner have so much energy in the mornings? I needed coffee but it ended up being taboo in the house; that's another story though.

I suddenly froze. All of my nerve endings suddenly on fire. I felt as if I was swimming in water. Was I floating or drowning? I could barely hear Conner and Raven freeze behind me, the entire cafeteria going deathly silent.

I closed my eyes slowly, breathing in deeply. Something smelled like chocolate. Chocolate that melts on your tongue before a burst of mint electrifies your mouth. I think drool just slipped down my chin.

"Mate," passed from my lips like a breath. The cafeteria was suddenly buzzing with pack members craning their heads around. No one moved from their seats. Raven and Conner were looking around just as earnestly.

In the School Parking Lot

"For the hundreth time! The soap allows for mates to find you still," Amilya grumbled since the four of them didn't have a car and the town house wasn't too far from the school.

"You bought it off of the black market Mils," Tyler rolled his eyes.

"You still feel like something is going to happen today Robin?" Kai whispered nervously, Robin nodding at him.

All four of them sighed, trying to remain calm.

"This is just a trial guys. We can make a run for it anytime, you know that. I won't stand for any of you getting hurt. I'll just snoop around for a month in the territory to make sure it is safe for us before making any further decisions, okay?"

The three boys nodded at her, fiddling with their clothes. Kai and Tyler finally convinced Mils to splurge some money so they could have a couple of cute outfits. Not that Mils could say 'no' to shoes... or cute shirts. Not that her brothers were any different.

Kai was wearing dark blue skinny jeans, a grey button down shirt that matched his eyes, and grey converse. He absolutely loved school supplies so he had an entire pencil bag filled with colorful pens, pencils, paperclips, highlighters, and anything Mils would let him put in the basket when they went shopping. His hair had some product in it, making it look soft and fluffy. Mils just couldn't let him out of the house without a cute gray bunny shaped bobby pin in his hair to pull back some of his bangs; a few pieces still escaping, making him look absolutely adorable.

Robin was wearing dark black skinny jeans, a button down forest green shirt and black sneakers. He had a black jacket and some black gloves on. It was chilly outside. He had a Starbucks cup with him filled with his morning tea. He got just as many school supplies as Kai, Mils and Tyler knowing they would be sharing color coded notes later.

Tyler was wearing white skinny jeans, a red sweater since it wasn't as chilly outside to him, and black sneakers. He had a white scarf wrapped around his neck, his hair styled to be a messy/sexy look he saw in a magazine, drinking Starbucks.

"You still look like one of those rich white girls that are brats," Mils chuckled, making Tyler scowl at her.

"It's called fashion bi-atch!" Tyler snapped his fingers, in a large circle making them all laugh.

Mils was in some loose faded jeans, a blue shirt, wearing a black hoodie. The hood was up covering most of her hair and she was wearing a black face mask to cover her face from her nose to her chin. She had a pair of black sneakers on as well.

"Do you think we'll meet other werewolves?" Kai asked curiously, his family shrugging at him. They stopped at the school doors, all of them breathing in deeply. Mil's nose wriggled at an array of scents, hoping she wasn't smelling werewolves right after Kai said that.

Mils brought them in for a group hug, pulling down her mask for a moment, kissing each of them on the head; her mask back in place.

"Use our link if there is trouble or a werewolf. Don't show any werewolf characteristics. Anything goes wrong, find me. We all have each of our schedules and we all have lunch together. I love you guys and be safe, okay?"

"We love you too," They said in sync, Robin opening the door for them. Amilya had decided it was time for them to get more of an education, knowing they wouldn't get far in the world without one.

The school was like most others. An open area that had different hallways going this way and that.

"Do you guys smell that?" Kai asked shyly, headed for the lunch room.

"Our first classes are that way," Robin shrugged his shoulders, everyone still on edge that Robin has a weird feeling about today.

Kai smelled something like the forest. It smelled like hot, strong, powerful man with a hint of cinnamon.

"Kai, slow down!"

Kai's mouth was practically watering, Tyler hurrying a little faster than Robin and Amilya since those two didn't want to make a scene.

Psh. What scene? No one is here! That little rascal is fast for having short legs! Tyler giggling to himself.

Kai's POV:

I turned the corner before freezing in my tracks.

Holy moon Goddess... Is this what wet dreams are made of!?

I could only stare at the god-like man before me. He was a good six inches taller than me with a lickable v-line and yummy abs evident through his tight shirt. His scent was intoxicating and my inner wolf was in a tizzy to bare our throat and get on all fours for him.

His beautiful blue eyes were like the ocean and he had midnight black hair. His skin was tan and he was tall. Although everyone is taller than my short butt. I could feel my mini me grow at attention, my cheeks warming in a blush.

For the love of all that is holy. Do. Not. Swoon. Oh my goddess is he checking me out too!? What of he doesn't like me? I know I'm super small...

Carver's POV:

My mate is beautiful. He's so small and adorable. His eyes are the color of storm clouds but look to hold playfulness.

My wolf was going crazy, instincts clawing at me to mark and mate with this angelic creature in front of me.

I felt two hands holding my arms, making me blink out of my stupor. I saw Conner looking at me in surprise and happiness along with my gamma.

Apparently I was walking closer to my mate without even realizing it.

I looked longingly at him, seeing him smile shyly at me, his cheeks tinting pink. He looked down at the floor bashfully, everyone in the cafeteria bursting into awes, coos, and giggles through our pack link. The actual cafeteria was buzzing with whispers.

Congratulations alpha! My pack screamed in my ear making me smile happily.

"Mate!" Conner whispered in shock, stunning me as well since I was not one for sharing... Or felt that way about my brother.

I snarled at him, feeling my eyes change color from my wolf taking over. I saw his eyes glaze over happily, but was looking passed my mate. Good. MINE!

I lifted my brow at my brother before an equally adorable blonde came running around the corner.

Conner gasped in shock as I saw his shoulders slump from shock or disbelief; I wasn't sure. His eyes were swirling with anger for some reason. Why was he mad? His mate was adorable, but not as sexy as my little mate. Biased, whatever.

"Conner," I spoke softly, touching his shoulder before he moved away, growling low.

"Conner, I don't see what the problem is," Raven whispered harshly getting a stony glare from Conner.

Everyone in the pack was whispering in shock at two mates being found the same day at nearly the same time. The overlapping voices increasing in the cafeteria in excitement.

"How can you move so fast with short legs?" I heard the blonde pant to my mate who scowled at him. I chuckled low at that, my mate looking at me with a blush before looking back down at his shoes.

Awe! Mate mate mate mate. Want. Mine!

I shook my head knowing my wolf was going absolutely crazy. His scent was mouth watering and I just wanted to bend his little bubble butt over and thrust my - No! Bad Carver.

I shook my head, freezing when my gamma whispered 'mate' with huge round eyes. What the shit snacks!?

No ones POV:

Another boy came around the corner. Raven just stared at the slim boy with dark black hair and an even darker black eye.

Wait, eye!? Raven looked harder seeing the boy with an eye patch over his left eye. His bangs seemed to cover most of it so it wasn't noticeable at first.

He's beautiful and looks mysterious Raven thought dreamily, smiling softly.

Carver gazed at his mate with love and adoration, sighing happily.

Conner looked at his mate with anger and shock.

"Why are they all looking at us?" The slim black haired boy whispered. All three of them suddenly looked scared at the pack that was openly gazing at them.

Carver's POV:

I growled low, not liking the fact that my mate was scared.

Sorry alpha! Everyone looked to move to their classes before freezing, since another person came walking towards our mates. This person, who I was assuming was the girl of the group since it was the only girl name my father announced, had a confident air around her. Everyone was looking around to see whose mate this person had, because Hell, I wasn't going to doubt it either at this point!

Her clothes shrouded her body and her face really well, that I don't think anyone could tell what she really looked like. The way she held herself made me think she wasn't someone to mess with.

The girl motioned her head, our mates following her like cute little ducklings. All of them had their heads down looking sideways at pretty much the whole pack who was in the cafeteria still.

Sorry alpha! They yelled, scrambling to get to their classes.

What if my mate is scared of me!? Frack! It hasn't even been ten minutes! What do I do!? Shit, shit, shit-

I caught my tiny mate looking back at me shyly giving me a tiny wave making my stomach flip flop. I think i had tunnel vision right there, sighing happily.

"You are so whipped," Jack, the running back for the football team, said with a smirk. I'm pretty sure my face was going to have a permanent smile because of my mate. The whole football team including the coaches came back from the gym to see who our mates were. Multiple mates being found on the same day, in the same place, spread like wildfire.

"Psh. Whatever," I grumbled at him getting a few congratulations from the team.

"Didn't know you were into guys," Jack winked at Conner who growled angrily.

"I. Am. Not."

"Geez, someone should turn on the heater," Robin glared at how cold Conner was being and I had to agree with him on this.

Jack held his hands up in mock surrender since Conner was usually so chill.

YOU FOUND YOUR MATES!?!?!

What the Hell! I covered my ears even though it was the pack link. Everyone else cringing in pain.

Daddy please calm-

I'm coming there right now! I'll go get Papa Dad squealing through the pack link.

"Okay, who told?" I crossed my arms, rolling my eyes at a few of my friends who raised their hands. All of them bowed their heads in apology. The cafeteria was nearly empty by now.

Everyone went to class since I knew daddy would just drag us out of class without a care in the world. Plus the teachers would let him do anything since he has one of the best puppy dog eyes I have ever seen, hands down.

"Conner... Shouldn't you at least give him a chance?" I suddenly remembered, speaking firmly, but with worry and confusion. I think my question just made him snap since his jaw ticked.

"I am not a fag!" Conner yelled before there was an audible gasp, all our eyes snapping to daddy who looked to be in tears.

"Daddy I-" Conner growling in frustration, looking legitimately sorry, before stomping off.

Papa arrived a second after daddy, looking shocked for a second, his eyes looking sadly at Conner's back. I was angry at my brother for being so upset. Finding his mate was supposed to be wonderful, and you didn't just go against the moon goddess.

Daddy looked crestfallen, eyes at his shoes, looking like he didn't want to come up to us after hearing that.

"Don't worry dad. We don't feel that way. Or at least I don't," I spoke softly hugging my dad tightly, feeling his tears on my shirt.

"Yeah... I don't care if my mate is a guy or a girl either," Raven nodded, daddy smiling at us, hugging him as well. He hurriedly wiped away his tears before Papa could hold him in a crushing hug.

"Well!" Daddy giggled, clapping his hands, "tell me everything!"

"I think he means congratulations," Papa smiled, hugging me, shuffling Raven's hair.

Daddy scowled at Papa playfully before pushing him off of me so he could hug me instead; sticking his tongue out at Papa. Papa harumphed, crossing his arms over his very buff chest.

Before they could start a fight I cleared my throat.

"He's adorable. He's about half a foot shorter than me with black hair and gray eyes. He has this cute bubble butt that I-"

"Nope!" Raven covered his ears with his hands, daddy's face red.

"Down boy!" Papa chuckled low, making me smile.

"One of the new transfer students I assume?"

I nodded at him, looking over at Raven, seeing him have an equally stupid smile.

"What do you think you're doing!? Win over your mates you dummies!" Dad gasping, pushing me and Raven towards the hallway, Papa laughing at that.

Daddy froze for a second, sniffing the air.

"What is it love?" Papa asked worriedly, daddy shaking his head. Daddy's eyes suddenly became dull, scaring all three of us. Papa, Raven and I lifted our noses, wondering what Dad smelled. I could smell something that was a softer mint scent than what my mate had in his own scent. Weird.

"Adam, honey what is it?"

"I-I thought I smelled..." Daddy shook his head, like he was trying to get the dullness to leave him.

"Go get em' tiger," Papa smiled a little at me and Raven, walking daddy back home.

"That...was weird," Raven whispered as I nodded.

"Let's go get our mates!" I smiled, fist bumping Raven.

"Hell yeah!"

No one's POV

"This whole school is a werewolf school! I am so sorry," Mils whispered, the others looking at her in shock.

"We found our mates, don't be sorry!" Tyler smiled cutely.

"What!? Who!?" Mils gasped, her alpha voice showing through a little demanding to know for curiosities sake.

"Mine had the black hair and blue eyes! He's so handsome and tall," Kai whispered, cheeks going red.

"Mine was the brunet with hazel eyes, black jacket and red tie," Robin smiled shyly, looking really really happy.

"Mine was the blonde with black eyes that had a scowl on his face. I don't think he likes me," Tyler whispered sadly, before getting hugged by Kai.

"Don't say that! You don't know!"

"But if they're all werewolves then I'm pretty sure he could tell I was his mate! He...didn't look happy at all."

"Just have hope. Don't go thinking negative things towards something like that," Robin said sternly, Tyler sighing out.

"You were right about something happening today," Mils nervously tapped her foot, crossing her arms over her chest.

"I'm sorry you didn't find your mate today," Kai said sadly, the other two looking sadly at the floor.

"I'm sure I'll find them soon. I mean I still got seven years left! Don't worry. Now. I don't want you guys revealing your werewolves yet. I know most mates usually complete the bonding almost immediately, but I want to make sure this area is safe for us. I'm not saying I will take you away from your mates, unless they are abusive, but I want you being werewolves kept a secret for just a little longer. Understand?"

"Yes Alpha," All three replied in sync.

"May we get to know them?" Kai raised his hand a little, all of them smiling at his cuteness. Kai is a submissive omega so it is always in his nature to question anything he is allowed to do since he can be easily dominated and abused by anyone who would want to overpower him. It wouldn't be so easy now since he had an Alpha and her word was higher ranking than anyone else's. So if anyone told him to do something, he could refuse a lot easier since his alpha hadn't commanded him.

"Of course Kai. I will not keep you from them. Just please be careful with your words and try to ignore any werewolf behavior. From what I could tell they think we're human so just roll with that. Now lets get to class and mind link me if anyone is being mean to you."

All three nodded, the four of them separating. Kai and Mils had the same first class together which was chemistry.

Amilya looked back to the cafeteria, the scent of Kai's and Tyler's mates seeming to remind her of something. Almost a memory. But that was ridiculous, right?

Conner's POV

My mate could not, COULD NOT, be a guy. I mean, I like GIRLS for crying out loud! At least most girls. I thought I did... I mean of course I do.

UGH! I hate this.

I froze suddenly from the smell of coffee with the scent of fresh made biscotti bread with chocolate chips.

His hair was a pretty blonde with these big gorgeous green eyes. He was almost as muscular as me and I'm a dominant Beta.

Shit! I. Am. a dominant. BETA! I can't be seen dating some guy! I mean that'll just start shit and... fuck I need to just reject this whole thing. The moon goddess obviously made a mistake pairing us up together.

I could feel my wolf clawing at me, whining almost pleading for me not to reject my mate. But this would be better for us! I know that mates are our other half and are supposed to help us with our flaws and make us better, but how could some cute guy do that?

I mean not cute. Not even slightly. No way. Not with that butt that swings a little when he walks or -

Hold the god damn phone! I did not just think that! Crap. Need to reject. Need to do this.

I saw the group of four split off after a lot of hurried whispering, the girl and Carver's mate leaving together, probably to the same class. Raven's mate walked a little ways with my mate, touching his shoulder.

Growl

I shook my head to stop my wolf from taking over. Crap, my mate was already making my wolf crazy and I was not going to lose control. Especially not over him!

I saw my mate, I-I mean the blonde kid, go to his locker. I tapped him on his shoulder quickly, knowing I wouldn't have the guts to do this later, or my wolf wouldn't let me. I could already feel my wolf clawing and gnawing at me, snapping and snarling at me not to do this.

Green. Like a vast forest of beautiful foliage. I couldn't help but stare. But to gaze so deeply into his eyes, trapping me.

I gasped, backing up, startling my mate, clearing my throat. He was smiling happily at me, cocking his head to the side cutely.

"I'm Tyler! Nice to meet you!" Tyler's smile widened, reaching out his hand for a hand shake. My eyes snapped down to his hand, gulping, before looking back at his eyes. I grabbed his hand, feeling sparks shoot up my finger tips, I held back my groan of how good it felt, before snatching my hand back.

"I-" I cleared my throat, my wolf nearly making my eyesight go white from his rage, "Conner Summers, reject you as my mate"

I squeaked out the sentence, running, never looking back. This was better. He wasn't my mate.

No one's POV

Conner ran fast from the hallway, his wolf howling in agony before growing eerily silent. Conner didn't stop running until he got to the forest. He couldn't shift though. His wolf only whimpered. Conner only ran faster. He was sure that his feet were bleeding but he didn't stop. He was going to ignore the pain. He was going to pretend that things weren't becoming gray. That this was for the best.

Tyler sobbed, falling to his knees, hand over his mouth to stop his cries from echoing down the hallway.

My mate hates me! He re-rejected us... Tyler didn't care anymore if he made it to class or not, but he couldn't have his family worrying so he tried to fix himself up so he looked relatively decent for second period. His wolf howled in misery, curling up into a ball, little whimpers escaping.

I hate my life Tyler could feel tears trying to leave him again, trying to concentrate on finding his class instead of the shattered pieces of his heart.

Kai's POV

I wish I had at least one class with my mate I was fiddling with my pen, doodling on my paper. I just couldn't concentrate in third hour since it was Trigonometry, yuck!

I could mentally see my wolf in my mind, my white wolf grooming itself, trying to make its fur look absolutely fluffy.

Don't worry, our mate will love us! I hope

My white wolf purred, mentally nuzzling me as I tried not to giggle. Our wolves were like our primal instincts. So they can only say a few words, but mostly don't talk; our bond was so close that words aren't needed.

The bell rang with me not learning a single thing, which was honestly going to suck later, before I ran around to find fourth period.

Oh no! I'm late! I think this is it!

I opened the door, hoping it was English, seeing everyone stare at me.

Mate! His ocean blue eyes bore into mine making me nearly swoon on the spot.

"I-I'm sorry. I-I got lost a little," The teacher smiled kindly at me, directing me to take a seat next to my mate *squeal*

"No worries Lun- ahem. What was your name?" The teacher asked politely. I could feel my cheeks grow pink, praying she wasn't about to say Luna because I don't think I'd be able to handle the position. Does that mean my mate was an Alpha!? I think I felt my heart drop into my stomach at the idea.

"I-It's Kai Winters," I whispered, everyone in the class smiling, saying hi back. I relaxed a little at that since no one made fun of me. I had read stories of how people get picked on for being small or looking like a girl. Being gay or something. I think I was gay anyway since I'd like the male model magazines more than the female ones. Ahem, sorry that was a little personal.

"You may sit Kai."

I nodded, walking shyly to the desk, sitting down. The teacher began speaking again about the syllabus, before I felt eyes on me. I knew they were my mates' and I could feel a shiver go down my spine.

Oh glorious man candy, please don't tempt me! My willpower is weak! If wolves could snicker I think mine would have by now.

I felt sparks hit my shoulder making me bite my lip to stop the moans from leaving me. I looked over at my mate seeing his blue eyes sparkle with happiness. My heart fluttered in my chest and my tummy felt weird.

"It's nice to meet you. My name is Carver Summers. You're new right?" Carver held out his hand and I shook it. My eyelids fluttered down on their own from the delicious sparks exploding in my body. I opened them to see my mate, Carver, with hooded eyes filled with lust. That was a good sign, right? He wasn't completely rejecting us on site at the moment at least!

I prayed he couldn't smell my arousal but I think my hopes were in vain because my pants were a little too tight to be comfortable. Not to mention I caught a scent of his own arousal which was not helping.

"I'm Kai Winters." I whispered, looking back at the board. I would have stared into his eyes but Alpha said to act human so I think this would have been a good reaction. Staring into someone's eyes just after meeting them and then presenting yourself right there over a desk, didn't exactly say 'human'.

I felt another tape on my shoulder, my wolf clawing gently at me to go to our mate. My wolf and I never fight and I think it's because we understand each other a lot and my status as a werewolf.

I smiled a little shyly at my mate, seeing that his smile grew wider.

I did that! Me! I made his smile bigger! My brain was gushing at this point.

"Do you need some help getting around the school?"

"Oh, I-I'm okay," I didn't want to get in his way already or seem needy. No matter how much time I wanted to spend with him.

"I don't mind at all. I like helping people," Carver rested his head in his hand, his smile glued to his face. He has such pretty white teeth.

"Oh, um, if it's not too much trouble. I don't like being late," I whispered.

"Then I'd love to show you around beautiful. I-I mean Kai!" Carver said a little too loudly. I could pretty much hear the whole class snicker at that, including the teacher, mostly because of my werewolf hearing.

My cheeks exploded into a blush at what he just called me. I bit my lip, fiddling with my pen again, looking down at my desk. I glanced over to see Carver nearly slam his head on the table. I had to hold in a laugh at that. He said I was beautiful.

Sad? My wolf whispered in worry, trying to claw a little harder out as I tried to calm him.

Don't worry. I think he thought he upset us by calling us beautiful My wolf preened at that, trying to make his fur look fluffier.

I was too scared to say anything else during class before the bell rang. Carver stood up immediately, as if to leave, making my heart nearly break, already feeling my eyes sting with the familiar feeling of tears.

"U-Um," I squeaked, seeing him freeze and nearly spin around fast. How did he not get dizzy? Plus, where the gravy did my confidence to actual speak out come from!? That alone was a little nerve wracking.

"I-If it's not...too much trouble, um, could you show me where the biology room is?" I was pretty sure I knew where it was, but I wanted to have my mate show me.

"Yeah! Come on!" He immediately perked up, as I could feel his wolf happily wagging his tail. I couldn't see Carver's wolf since we weren't mated, but I'd be able to once we were. I mean I hoped we would be. I bet his wolf looks amazing!

Carver grabbed my hand, holding it, as we walked through the school. I was having an internal war of whether or not I should get my hand out of his, since it wasn't a human kind of 'normal' with a guy you just meet, but I don't think my brain and body were in agreement at the moment.

No one seemed to comment and I think everyone was trying not to bow at us. Okay, he was definitely an alpha. But I mean, that didn't mean he would be in charge of the pack right? I mean I'm too weak to be a Luna, so I hope he doesn't reject me if he finds out I'm a submissive omega.

"This is the library," Carver pointed out, my eyes snapping to his yummy chiseled arm. I licked my lips, holding in my drool at this point, my cheeks exploding red when his eyes snapped to my lips. Uh oh. Bad puppy! Don't tempt me!

Carver took me all over the school, seeming to have forgotten that we need to get to class. Not that I was going to say anything since that would mean being away from him and my wolf and I were already getting attached.

I felt like I had known him my entire life. His voice was low and my mini me got a little harder imagining him talking even lower in my ear. His hand tightened on mine and I was pretty sure I was making this difficult on his wolf too. I was scared though. Submissive wolves were weak, unnecessary, and usually killed immediately. I... Couldn't tell him I was a werewolf too. Knowing that he would reject me immediately. At least that's what I heard all dominants do if their mate is weak or ugly or bad at sex or...

My wolf's ears drooped, not wanting my mate to be upset at us.

"So what do you like to eat Kai?" Carver asked, still holding my hand. His hand was big and warm and had a few calluses from fighting if I had to guess.

"Chocolate!" I nearly yelled, before looking away shyly towards my shoes. I am such a dork! I felt his finger under my chin, losing my voice when I saw little speckles of light blue in his eyes.

"What kind of chocolate?" Carver whispered, smiling softly.

"D-Dark chocolate."

"What!? How can you like dark chocolate? Milk chocolate is way better!" Carver threw his one hand in the air making me giggle, feeling some tension leave me, before I tried to scowl playfully at him.

"Nuh-uh! If you add caramel or fruit it makes it way too sweet, but with dark chocolate you can add whatever you like and it's perfect!"

"What! How could it be too sweet? Dark chocolate is like something you would drizzle on something, not eat whole!"

The rest of the period we were playfully arguing over chocolate. I think I was going to get a heart problem with how much it was aching for me to be claimed by my mate. I only hoped he felt the same. I only hoped he would like me as Kai before finding out I was Kai the submissive omega.

First actual chapter! What do you guys think!? Would love some comments :D

Date?

No one's POV

"Do you like chess?"

Robin turned to see his mate leaning against the locker right next to his, a tint of pink on his cheeks.

"Y-Yes," Robin whispered, hoping his mate wasn't going to bully him since most people thought chess was a nerd's game.

"Sweet! Come on!" Raven grabbed Robin's hand, sparks shooting everywhere with both trying to hold back their moans.

"U-Um, where are we going!?" Robin was a little nervous seeing that he was dragged into the lunch room to a table surrounded by football jocks. The weird thing was that there was a chess board on the table, not that any of them were touching it.

Raven suddenly stopped, turning back to look at Robin. Robin almost ran into his back, terrified, wondering if he should make a run for it.

"I'm Raven Hill, nice to meet you!"

Robin was suddenly tugged before he could introduce himself. He was forced to sit in front of the chess board. Robin bit his lip, half tempted to use his eye patch to escape. That would be a little more than evident that he wasn't human though. Especially since his eye was lavendar in color.

Robin saw Raven walking with confidence around the table, sitting in front of him, smiling happily; if not with a little giddiness.

"I-I'm Robin Winters," Robin never mumbled nor spoke loudly, but he wasn't monotone either. He just didn't like to speak up unless necessary.

"Well, Robin Winters, consider this initiation into the school!"

Robin lifted his brow skeptically, looking warily at the big jocks behind them.

"Ignore the meat sacks behind me," Raven chuckled, getting a few growls from them along with some playful punches against his arm, "no one likes playing chess with me."

Raven pouted so cutely that Robin felt his stomach flip flop, cheeks growing warm. His mate was cute... And playful. Nothing like himself.

"Why not?"

"Because they all think I cheat but the neanderthals just don't understand I'm just amazing," Raven laughed getting a few more punches to his arm. Raven chuckled, rubbing his arm, the football players seeming to go on with their own conversation.

Robin calmed down a little seeing no one was getting mad and he was pretty sure his mate was a gamma as well. The problem with submissive wolves was that they couldn't tell a normal or dominant status with any werewolves except for their alpha. He'd have to ask her about it later since she was probably already sniffing around the school.

"So what do I have to do?"

"You, cutie, have to beat me at chess. If I win you get to go on a date with me."

Robin just knew his face was on fire at that, his mate was really bold.

"Is this a ploy to make fun of the new kid or something?" Robin whispered, feeling his wolf whimper sadly, knowing the chances of a submissive being accepted was extremely low. He'd need more data from non-rogue packs to determine this though.

Robin suddenly realized the cafeteria was almost silent which freaked him out before feeling his breath get cut short. His mate Raven looked as though someone just died. It was heartbreaking.

"I'm not the kind of guy that does that sort of thing. I'd like to prove that to you," Raven whispered. Robin was shocked at that, the fierceness in his mate's eyes was stunning.

I guess... Taking a chance is a part of life Robin thought to himself. Robin nodded slowly, more of to calm himself down it seemed. The chatter slowly filled the cafeteria once more, Robin feeling like he could breathe again.

"So... You want to play chess? If I lose, we go on a date?"

Raven nodded at Robin, smiling widely. Raven loved the fact that Robin confirmed all the facts he was given before just bursting with an answer, "And if I win?"

Raven's eyes sparkled happily, wondering if this strategy of questioning would lead his mate to just leaving the table or accepting his challenge. His heart nearly stopped at the double entendre his mate decided to pick from his statement. Raven's wolf nearly tackling their mate to get him to understand he would never hurt him. Well maybe not literally tackle either.

"Pick your poison!"

"Anything?" Raven's one visible brow raising.

"Anything short of murder, yes." Raven chuckled, Robin smirking, rolling his eyes.

Robin looked around, a few people wondering what he was going to say since any werewolf that concentrated on someone else's conversation could hear it usually.

"You have to..." Robin looked around remembering that he saw a wolf statue outside representing the Ice Wolves Football team. He wanted it to be embarrassing. Maybe a little drastic and crazy to see if his mate would back out of the deal or not.

"Climb up that statue I saw outside-"

"Done-"

Robin lifted his hand, saying he wasn't done making Raven look at him curiously.

"Wearing a pink frilly dress singing I'm a little teapot with hand motions!" Robin smiled a tiny smile suddenly before the whole football team and a few others burst out laughing, Raven's jaw going slack.

"Oh my god I have to see this!" One of the football players said whose face was red from laughing.

Raven just spluttered for a second at Robin, like he couldn't believe what came out of those pretty pink pale lips.

"I hope you're good at chess. I haven't had a challenge in a long time," Robin smiled just a lite too cockily as if he said that the weather was nice outside. Robin had no idea where his burst of confidence came from, or the rise in his voice for that matter, but being with his mate was already making him so very happy. It was a little disturbing and a lot more excitement then he has experienced before.

"Well there's no way I'm losing baby so hold onto your hat!" Raven yelled, shoving the sleeves of his jacket up, slamming his pond forward.

The game was instense since it was timed chess, everyone looking back and forth between the two who were moving fast before eventually slowing down to concentrate. Everyone was impressed since no one could get passed a minute whenever playing Raven since he was an unbeatable tactician.

Robin suddenly gasped, head hanging, even though no one said check mate, confusing most of the people around.

"I just trap people, so I hope you've prepared yourself!" Raven laughed happily, making Robin pout at him. Raven almost forfeighted the game to declare Robin won just from the adorable pout on his mate's lips.

"Uh?" One of the cheerleaders raised her hand, "who won?"

Raven rolled his eyes knowing she asked that question for most of the audience.

"I did!" Raven winked at Robin making him give a tiny smile again, shaking his head. Raven was determined to get a full blown smile from his mate now.

"I was so sure you'd look good in a pink frilly dress," Robin giggled, Raven's heart thumping happily at the sound.

"You would look better in it though, totally your color!" Raven shot back playfully with a wink, Robin's cheeks turning a bright pink.

"But no one said check mate," A boy spoke up, Raven and Robin completely forgetting they weren't alone for a second.

"Beaten in three moves," Raven lifting up three fingers.

"Beaten in two moves," Robin saying at the same time.

Both men just stared at each other for a second.

"Three moves."

"Two moves."

"Three."

"Two."

Everyone was looking back and forth at the two, Raven looking at Robin seriously.

"Show me," Raven spoke sternly, Robin getting pleasant shivers from the tone. Robin breathed out slowly, feeling his lower half become interested in the sound of his mate's voice a little too much. Robin got his panting wolf to calm down enough to concentrate on the game board again.

Robin looked back at the bored, moving two pieces, saying check mate quietly.

Raven looked at Robin in shock and awe, before his eyes became hooded with amazement and happiness.

"Woah," One of the jocks whispered, the others talking quietly.

"The trapper huh?" Robin giving a small smile again, Raven softening at that.

"So," Raven grabbed Robin's hand, tugging him out of his chair, walking through the cafeteria. A chorus of 'you rock Robin!' was yelled behind him, Robin feeling that his cheeks were on fire from the attention. Apparently the two had sat through most of lunch. Kai was sitting next to his mate, with Tyler's mate sitting across from them and two other girls. They looked like cheerleaders and they were getting along really well with Kai it seemed.

Robin waved shyly at Kai, Kai giving him a cute wave back. Robin saw his mate look up quickly before seeming to calm down, holding Kai's hand, pulling him closer to him.

"How does a movie sound for our date?" Raven asked, both ending back at Robin's locker.

"Sure. What kind?" A deal was a deal after all and Robin felt an urge to find out more about his mate.

"Horror or Mystery!"

Robin giggled at that, liking how they both liked the same kind of movies. Of course the horror ones that had mysteries were fun since he tried to figure out who the murderer was.

"Is there another kind?" Robin asked, Raven smiling happily at that.

"Friday? I'll look up some movie times and see what's playing."

"That sounds good!" Robin's eyes got big, calming down immediately. Raven looked at him worried for a second before covering it up. Why was his darling trying to hold in his joy?

"So, uh, could I have your number?" Raven asked nervously, rubbing the back of his head. He looked absolutely adorable.

"Oh, um," Robin moved some of his bangs behind his left ear before it fell forward to cover his eye patch again. Raven looked worried at him again, Robin fiddling with his sleeve, his black eye looking sad.

"I-I don't have a phone," Robin whispered, hunching his shoulders, hoping his mate wouldn't be mad at him.

"Oh," Robin peeked up at Raven who looked like he was thinking.

"I'll just leave notes in your locker! Mine's 235 down that hallway so you can reply back! What do you think?"

Robin perked up happily at that, Raven trying to hold back and not hug his mate like a crazy person at how cute he was.

"I-I'd like that," Robin giggled a little, Raven becoming stunned at the beautiful sound, committing it to memory. Seriously. It was sweet and soft and made Raven feel like it was summer.

"Well I'd better get to class, don't want to get in trouble," Robin whispered, moving his feet a little.

"Oh, uh, yeah! Talk to you later! And don't forget about our date!"

"Never," Robin smiled, leaning in towards Raven who held his breath with big wide eyes. Robin giggled again, feeling bold and playful for a second, Raven nearly turning to jelly. Raven felt warm sparks on his cheek suddenly.

K-Kissed! Raven's wolf was howling happily, running in circles at being kissed on the cheek by his mate.

"Thanks for being so nice to me Raven," Robin whispered, Raven's fingers touching his cheek.

"Bye," Robin waved, turning before a huge smile that no one has ever seen before broke across his face for a second down the empty hallway, before calming down again.

"uh huh," Raven whispered dreamily before he was noogied by Carver. Although he didn't really care who or what was around him at the moment.

"What are you standing around like an idiot for? Didn't think you had it in you," Carver smiled, Raven pushing him.

"I got a kiss on my cheek sucker!" Raven stuck out his tongue, Carver's eyes bulging before laughing.

"Now whose wrapped around their mate's finger?"

"Us," Raven smiled along with Carver.

"We should have a double date," Carver smiled, both he and Raven knowing Conner was having whatever issues at the moment.

"Agreed."

---(._.)

Kai was the first one to walk back to the townhouse, knowing his brothers weren't that far behind.

I can't believe I found my mate and he actually likes me! Kai giggled, day dreaming away about his mate.

I wish we could run together so I could see his wolf at least

Kai's wolf whined at that, although both were very happy that they weren't rejected. Well for being a human, he wasn't rejected.

Kai hugged his books tighter to his chest, a goofy grin on his face. He went to his room, which could hold a bed and a dresser, setting his stuff down before he heard the front door open and close.

Kai skipped towards the living room seeing his brothers and big sister putting their stuff away.

Kai squealed, hugging Amilya who laughed at him, patting his head.

"Let's sit at the table, huh?" The other two nodded sitting down. Kai could hardly wait to talk about his mate.

"My mate's name is Carver! He showed me around school and held my hand," Kai giggled, "he's so nice and talks very softly to me, although he likes milk chocolate, I suppose I can forgive him."

Amilya chuckled at that, Robin nodding seriously with Kai.

"I-I hope he'll want to see me again," Kai whispered nervously, looking down.

"He will, so chin up," Amilya spoke a little louder, Kai immediately sitting straight up making his family frown.

"Just a saying sweetie, not an order," Amilya spoke gently, Kai looking down in embarrassment at the table.

"Your mate is a dominant Alpha by the way, Kai."

Kai paled at that, looking very scared before he was hugged and held by Amilya. Kai started crying quietly since dominants always commanded him and abused him, Kai having a huge fear of them.

"What about you Robin?" Amilya asked gently, rubbing Kai's back who was trying to control his tears.

"My mate challenged me to a chess game and would have beaten me in two moves," Robin pouted a little, all of them looking at him in surprise.

"Well, I suppose what they say about most gammas being tacticians is true since I haven't seen anyone beat you at chess before!" Amilya said surprised, Kai giggling shakily.

"Serves you right for beating us all the time," Amilya playfully scowling at him making Robin huff out a laugh at her.

"You'll just get better the more you play right?" Kai asked softly, Robin nodding. Robin was already daydreaming about spending more time with his mate anyway.

"We're seeing a movie Friday together," Robin whispered bashfully getting a chorus of awes at the table.

"Your mate is a dominant Gamma, and I'm glad for you baby bros," Amilya smiled before frowning with worry at Tyler who was unusually quiet since he was always bouncing and moving around at all times.

"Tyler?" Amilya asked softly, everyone looking at him.

They have mates that love them and mine just... Tyler thought for a moment before sobbing, all of them hurrying over to hug him, Amilya kissing him all over his head. She held him tight while Robin rubbed his back. Kai ran to make warm tea, hurriedly coming back with a full tea cup.

"He-He re-rejected m-me even th-though they think we-we're human!" Tyler sobbed, Kai immediately crying with him, Robin's face going white. That was what all of them feared more than anything. To be rejected by the one person who was supposed to accept you for everything you are.

"You know what I think Ty?" Amilya whispered, petting his hair, Tyler looking at her. The look in his eyes alone broke all their hearts. Their brother was hurting. He was in so much pain.

"I think that he's probably just in shock right now. I could smell it when I walked to you guys. I think he'll realize his mistake and soon you guys will make puppies everywhere," Tyler choked out a laugh before sobbing, pressing his body against Amilya's harder, not sure what to do anymore.

"How about we do some homework, unless you lucky ducks didn't get any, then have some dinner and play a game, how does that sound?" Amilya got nods from Robin and Kai, Kai handing Tyler some tissues.

They didn't have any electronics in the house except for a landline that came with the townhouse. They had a fridge and microwave. It was the cheapest Amilya could find. She went to a thrift store during lunch and found a hot plate that would act as their stove.

She also bought some board games since they didn't have a TV along with some books and magazines. She bought some light bulbs, instant soups, fruit, and cereal at Walmart. Everything ended up being about $50 and they had a budget of $200 or less a month.

She was glad they didn't eat too much, but was depressed that she couldn't provide more for their tiny pack.

At the Pack House

"My mate doesn't like milk chocolate! Who doesn't like that!? I mean I don't really like dark chocolate but still... Dad he is just too cute!" Carver smiled happily at his dad who was listening intently.

"You did growl when you thought someone was hitting on him though!" Raven laughed, Carver scowling at him.

"Carver," Papa warned.

"I didn't go all dominant Papa, I swear. Besides, Raven wasn't much better!"

"Listen, neither of you can shift or do anything until your mates are comfortable around you. We don't want panic," Chris, Carver and Conner's Papa, spoke sternly.

"We know."

"But Papa, it's like their already... how would you call it?" Carver looked at Raven who was nodding with him a moment.

"Like how other werewolves would have reacted when first finding their mates. I don't think they thought we were weird when we asked them out the first day we met them."

Werewolves normally mated within a week of meeting each other.

Carver nodded in agreement that it was weird, but they smelled human so...

"Just control your urges," Papa rolled his eyes, daddy giggling next to him.

Daddy's eyes got sad, looking at Conner who was pushing his food around on his plate. None of them knew when he got home exactly, nor did any of them see the state of his feet yet.

"You should eat your food honey," Daddy whispered, Conner looking very tired up at him, nodding. He slowly ate some peas, the food having no taste to him any longer.

"Honey, did something happen?" Daddy asked worriedly, Conner putting his fork down, pushing his chair away from the table.

Carver and Raven were looking at him with worry.

"Conner," Papa spoke sternly, "answer your dad."

"I rejected my mate alright!" Conner yelled storming away from the table, everyone's jaws going slack. Conner tried to hold back from limping, just wanting to lie in bed.

"I-I'll got talk to him," Adam whispered, Chris shaking his head.

"I think I better love. Keep eating."

Chris knocked on his son's door, not hearing a response.

"Conner, it's Papa, I'm coming in."

Chris saw his son laying on his side, back facing towards the door. He sat on the bed, Conner feeling the bed dip.

"Conner I know how you feel."

"No you don't!" Conner shouted sitting up, before looking away angrily at the scowl on his father's face.

"You listen to me Conner Summers. When I found out your dad was my mate, I freaked out and avoided him for a month solid. Then I realized I was destroying myself and my wolf in the process. I even thought how stupid I had been since I hadn't even talked to him. I just looked at him and ran, like an idiot."

"You never told me that," Conner whispered, his Papa sighing.

"Your dad get's mad when I bring it up since I get so upset about it when I remember. I can't believe I was so mean to my mate without even trying to get to know him. I mean I liked girls well enough, but mates are destined to us by the moon goddess, no matter how many people think their mates are a mistake the first time they see them. Just try to think about this before you get hurt even more. We don't want to lose you."

Conner nodded, knowing that his Papa's words actually made sense.

"Oh, and talk to your dad. He thinks you're homophobic or something," Papa rolled his eyes, sounding like he had been trying to convince his daddy otherwise for the entire day.

"Ugh, of course he thinks that," Conner grumbled, flopping down onto the bed.

"Night son, and try to eat breakfast tomorrow, okay?"

"Yes Papa, night."

Conner sighed out, not knowing how long he had been drifting. He had thankfully put on thick socks, washing the bottoms of his feet with cool water, resting on his bed again. The moon was high in the sky before Conner felt another weight in his bed.

"You're an idiot."

Conner grumbled, knowing that Carver was probably going to come up and talk to him eventually.

"Dad's been crying since you went upstairs."

"Dad's an omega."

"Don't be an asshole Conner!" Carver yelled, Conner whimpering at that. Carver sighed, laying down next to his brother.

"So...you on your man period or something?"

"Dumbass."

"Well you've been pretty bitchy since you found your mate."

"I've just never thought about a guy before like that! I mean it freaks me out Carver!" Conner rolled onto his back, swinging his arm over his face.

"You could have at least tried to figure out your feelings without rejecting him first," Carver mumbled, Conner sniffling.

"I know."

"Are you crying?"

"No! I have fucking allergies and you know it."

"Yeah, whatever," Carver rolled his eyes, smirking. Conner peeked under his arm, scowling, punching Carver's arm.

"Geez, and your abusive," Carver chuckled, rubbing his arm.

They were just lying together, both of them used to this since they would cry themselves to sleep when they remembered how they ignored their baby sister when they realized she was a submissive. That stupid alpha had put it in their heads that submissive wolves were horrible creatures.

"That month she was missing and the trackers couldn't find her," Carver whispered, feeling his eyes sting and throat close, Conner stiffening next to him, "we promised each other that it wouldn't matter who our mate was. Submissive, human, whatever. Remember?"

"Yeah," Conner replied, voice shaking a little.

"I'll try to figure out my feelings and be less of an ass about this whole mate thing, okay?"

Both fell asleep, Conner dreaming of soft green eyes.

Werewolves had three months to live after a rejection. They grew weaker with every passing day. Things would become tasteless or gray. Some werewolves wouldn't even make it to three months since suicide rates skyrocketed.

- (. _ .)

Conner felt like absolute shit, knowing Carver was already downstairs by now. Conner got up slowly, barely feeling the water on his skin in the shower, as he got ready for Tuesday.

Goddess, only Tuesday. This is going to freaking suck

Conner put on some jeans and a polo shirt, walking downstairs. Carver and Papa nodded at him, Conner grabbing a bowl of cereal. Daddy stopped in the doorway, the two making awkward eye contact, daddy going over to make muffins.

Oh no. Dad and his stress baking.

Conner hurriedly walked to his dad, hugging him. His dad stiffened before relaxing, hugging him back.

"I don't hate gays Dad. That's just stupid. I just need to figure out my feelings. Sorry that I made you cry," Conner said sadly at the end, before his daddy kissed him on the forehead.

"I just worry about you sweetie. I know you'll do what's best," Daddy smiled, Conner feeling even more like an asshole.

"Go eat your cereal honey or you'll be late for school."

Conner nodded, sitting down, getting punched in the arm by Raven.

Carver told you?

Yup

You going to tell me the same thing?

That you're a dumbass and meathead? Of course not

Conner glared at him, Carver chuckling between them. Conner saw his Papa smile, relaxing a little since his family didn't hate him.

Carver's POV

It's been two weeks and my idiot brother has been avoiding his mate like the plague. Me and Raven have gone on a double date with our mates which was super fun since neither of them have gone ice skating before. That was kind of weird sounding since they came from Canada and everything, but what did I know?

I walked into the school, my wolf growing more and more needy, wanting to claim our mate already. I mean I was getting regular hard ons from my baby and there have been some lonely and cold showers with my old friend; my hand.

I suddenly heard a yell, my wolf automatically knowing my mate was in distress. I ran to the hallway to see a few cheerleading girls trying to help my mate up, all of them scowling at Tiffany and two bitchy friends that were next to her.

"What. Happened?" I snarled, snatching Kai from the girl's hands, who squeaked before snuggling into my arms. Awe! No! Need to protect.

"Nothing," Tiffany hissed, the cheerleaders scowling at her. Most of them were really nice except for Samantha who was standing just as haughtily next to Tiffany along with Angelica.

"Speak," I used my Alpha voice knowing my papa would kill me if he found out, but my mate was shaking in my arms and that makes me pissed.

"The bitch pushed Lun- Kai into his locker with his back turned!" Mandy growled, her mate next to her. Both of the girls betas. The other cheer-leaders were growling at the slut squad, agreeing with the lead cheerleader Mandy.

"The lying skank doesn't know what she's talking about!"

"Don't call my mate a skank, witch!" Mandy's mate Leah snarled back, being held back by a beefy football guy who was her brother.

"Tiffany. You will go to the principals office. Everyone knows that bullying is not aloud."

If I find you anywhere near my mate again I will rip your head clean off and stick it on a post as warning My dominate alpha power freezing everyone in the hall with the level of anger and hatred I was showing.

"But baby, you should be with me! Not that weak little nobody!" Tiffany tried pouting but it just increased the lines in her face from how much make up was caked on.

I will never be anything more than this pack's Alpha to you, got it? I don't think I could recognize my voice at that point, my wolf baring his teeth.

"I suggest you move your plastic ass now," Conner growled, Tiffany running away with angry tears, her fellow Barbies following after her.

Bro, your eyes! Conner hissed at me. I closed my eyes quickly, feeling my mate's head move to look up at me.

"Carver? Are you okay? I-I'm sorry I caused trouble. I won't do it again," I snapped my eyes open, hearing my mate nearly in tears, shaking badly.

"Baby you didn't do anything wrong. Why are you apologizing? Hey, look at me," I cradled Kai's smooth china doll cheek, gently, Kai's big doe eyes filled with tears which almost broke my heart.

"Are you hurt anywhere?" I whispered, Kai shaking his head no. I sighed out at that. I rubbed my thumb along his cheekbone, Kai's eyes becoming less red.

"Thank you for standing up for me," Kai whispered to the cheerleaders who were smiling and talking about challenges for some reason; probably to embarrass Tiffany in front of the whole pack to get her off her high horse if I had to guess. Mandy smiled largely at me, gazing softly at Kai, Leah hugging Kai gently which made him giggle since it made Mandy pout at her girlfriend.

His voice is so sweet and soft. I love listening to it all the time. He's also so gentle and caring towards those who help him I couldn't help but feel pride towards my mate.

Kai's eyes found mine, making everything else fall away. I moved some of his hair behind his ear, making me sweet little love sigh out happily.

"Why are you so wonderful Carver?" Kai whispered, almost longingly it sounded like.

"Well I have my downfalls too baby, but you get the whole package," I motioned to my body making Kai's cute cheeks flush before he giggled.

Kai suddenly bit his lip before leaping up at me, so he could swing his arms around my shoulders, my baby on his tip toes I was sure. I laughed loudly, about to make a short joke to get him all ruffled. Mostly because he becomes even more adorable when he's ruffled.

My mind went completely blank however, when I felt power and sparks burst through my lips, my knees nearly giving out on me.

My eyes snapped down to my mate in shock, Kai looking at me shyly with a small smile.

He... he kissed me!

I smiled so widely I was sure my face was going to break. I moved slowly, giving Kai time to refuse my gesture, but my wolf and I burst with happiness when Kai didn't shy away from the action. I slowly bent forward, pressing my lips to his. His lips were soft and strawberry pink. I loved them. I felt sparks dancing across my lips, my tongue pressing against his bottom lip. I wanted to taste him. Taste how sweet he was.

Kai's little gasp let me move my tongue into his mouth exploring. His tongue was timid against mine but he tasted divine; my wolf was howling with pleasure. He tasted sweet. Oh so sweet. My hands moved down his back, unable to resist temptation. I gave his butt a squeeze making him whimper.

Dear moon goddess my dick twitched at that.

Kai broke away from the kiss first, his cheeks a dark red as he panted. I felt lust fill my entire being, wanting to see him panting as I fucked him over the edge and claim him as mine.

ALL MINE! Damn my hormones and my irresistible mate.

Hurt & Acceptance

- -

Okay guys I'm putting a trigger WARNING here. Prepare yourselves. I don't condone anything and suicidal thoughts are very serious. Okay, that's my speech.

Tyler's POV

Three weeks. It's been three weeks since I last saw my mate. I could see my blonde wolf, skinny and lying on its side, panting. I was sitting in the bathroom at 1:00 in the morning. I couldn't take this pain anymore. The agony of having a mate that won't even acknowledge my existence. It hurts. All I feel is pain. I can't eat or sleep anymore. The world was gray, tasteless, pointless.

Maybe my family was better off without me. Kai and Robin both have their mates and I'm so happy for them. They'd been abused more than anyone should in their life. But I guess, I'm cursed to remain alone. Just like how I was living alone in the forest. Maybe if I had stayed there I wouldn't be going through this. Although... I wouldn't have the closure I do now from finding out I have a mate.

I bit my lip hard, knowing blood was dripping down my chin. My teeth cut into my lip hard; pain was the one thing I could still feel. I held the razor blade in my fingers, watching it gleam in the light of the bathroom.

One cut. One deep cut and everything would be over. Just one cut. One cut. No more pain. No more tasteless food. No more being useless to my family and my mate. If he didn't want me than I would grant his wish and not be here anymore. One cut. Just one.

I felt tears dripping down my cheeks, putting the blade against my wrist. They made quiet plopping sounds in the silent bathroom. I could hear the ticking of the clock in the other room.

Tick.

It was teasing me.

Tock.

Mocking me.

Tick.

Telling me I couldn't do it.

Tock.

That I was wasting time.

Tick.

I should have ended this sooner.

My wolf whined sadly as I tried to hold in my sobs. The scent of Amilya's shampoo wafted up my nose. I do love the smell of rain. The way she'd twirl her hair and teach me to fight; then hug me. She gives the best hugs. I love Kai's dishes that he works so hard to make with the little amount of food we have. He can make anything yummy. I love having Robin tutor me and then show me his color coded notes. If only his wardrobe were that colorful we could actual share clothes. That boy has a problem with color I swear. He has, like, one color scheme!

A choked laugh almost left my lips, making me hold the blade tighter. I needed to do this. I gave nothing to this group. I was the weak link. I was useless. Unnecessary.

One. Just one.

I pressed the blade harder, blood dripping down. It... Kind of looked pretty against my pale skin. I never noticed it was so pale before. Maybe because red made it pop.

I pressed the blade harder, hesitatingly making a few shallow scrapes. A shaking breath. I slowly dragged it along my wrist, knowing I was about to finish this with one more movement. It'll go away. It'll all go away. All the dark thoughts. All the pain. I won't feel anything. I don't deserve to feel anything.

I breathed in deeply, feeling my body shake. I pressed down harder than I did before, about to cut fast; as if I was pulling off a band aid. Blood was already running down my arm, dirtying up the white tiles in the bathroom.

"NO!"

My head snapped up, Amilya diving onto the floor to where I was; not realizing when I had slumped to my knees. Before I could say anything, a lump already forming in my throat, she grabbed the blade from me and threw it as far away from us as possible. I heard it ping against a wall before I sobbed hard, crawling away to the last thing that could help me.

"Don't you dare leave us. Don't you ever do this again," Amilya sobbed, tugging me to her chest. I sobbed openly, holding onto her as hard as I could. I didn't deserve her amazing hugs.

"You are our family! Apart of our little pack! You are my baby brother and an idol to Kai and Robin. We need you. I need you. We can't survive if one of our family is gone. Do you understand that Tyler!?"

I sobbed, not knowing what to do.

"Y-You selfish asshole!" Amilya yelled, stunning me for a second.

"We need you more than anything! Your stupid mate is going to get his head out of his ass and see that you are amazing and beautiful and worth every second of every day of his life!"

I cried harder at that, something stirring in my chest at her words. I could live. I could live for them. For just a little while longer. I could live for my family.

I heard a soft gasp, peeking out from Amilya's chest to see Kai with tears pouring down his cheeks. My heart hurt seeing him in such pain. Kai crawled over, hugging me, making me shake harder against them. I don't know when Kai got up, but realized Robin had replaced where Kai had been hugging me, making me hold him tighter.

My wrist was suddenly grabbed making me hiss out in pain. I felt all of us just watching Kai wipe the blood away. His eyes turned blazing blue before licking my wrist, the deep cut slowly stitching itself back together. I knew there would be a scar there. Kai wrapped my wrist in gauze, not wanting anything to get into the wound while it was healing. Not that I minded.

I felt guilty now. Embarrassed even. I wanted to hide it away. The fog was clear for just a moment. What did I almost do? How could I leave my sweet little family behind?

"Y-You sh-shouldn't p-p-put weight on i-it, o-o-okay?" Kai wiped at his eyes furiously. I tugged him into our little circle again, nuzzling his head with my nose.

"I'm sorry... th-that was stupid. But it hurts so much!" I cried, feeling their arms tighten around me, almost knocking the breath out of me.

"We'll help you get through this, okay?" Robin whispered. I may have been a good few inches taller than both, and a beta, but I just wanted to huddle there with my family. The pain was becoming a dull thing in my chest.

"You aren't alone," Amilya whispered softly.

"We love you," Kai mumbled against me.

Our wolves were mentally snuggled together licking my wolf, which helped him feel better too.

For the first time in three weeks, I got a decent amount of sleep. My eyelids wouldn't stay open any longer.

No One's POV

Tyler had eaten breakfast with his family before the group walked to school, their wolves mentally nipping and playing with each other. Tyler's blonde wolf was a little slower but he was actually moving instead of just lying there. Amilya promised however, that tonight they would shift into their actual wolves since she didn't want anyone spotting their wolves without her finishing her check around the territory.

How are we today buddy? Tyler looked at his wolf who mentally nuzzled him before sighing.

Yeah... The teachers in his classes were just droning on it seemed. He didn't notice the worried looks from the other wolves and even the humans in his classes.

Great... Gym... Tyler thought morbidly. Tyler usually loved gym because he loved moving around.

"We'll have a free-for-all day," the coach blew his whistle, who was the coach of the football team; his name is Mike. He seemed to go back to his board that had football plays on it for an up coming game it seemed.

Thank the moon goddess Tyler scurried off to the bleachers. Throughout the day he would notice that he'd grab his wrist where a clean scar was now (even a little pink still). It reminded him that he still had his family to think about.

Tyler was sitting on the very top of the bleachers in the far corner. He was trying to concentrate on the last math problem he had. His books were spread out with highlighters and graph paper here and there. Tyler wanted to claim the spot so no one would sit down and bother him. He was wearing a dark blue sweater and washed out jeans today. Tyler kept fiddling with the sleeve where his wrist was bandaged, trying to not be obvious and happy he wore a long sleeved shirt. He couldn't concentrate for the life of him.

Stupid freaking math! Someone evil just had to put the alphabet, the Greek alphabet, and stupid numbers together to make stupid problems for stupid people to get stuck on them!

Dark black eyes were gazing up at the lonely blonde on the bleachers.

Okay, I can do this Conner whispered to himself. He was on the sidelines of the basketball court, not being able to concentrate while his friends played. He had been pacing, for a while, wringing his hands.

Here we go Conner's wolf was pacing, nudging him to go. His wolf was so weak and tired. He couldn't sleep, barely ate even when his daddy and papa tried forcing him to along with Carver, Raven, and a few guys on the football team. Even Mike, the beta to the pack alpha and coach for the football team, was telling him he needed to eat or he'd have to kick him off the team.

Conner slowly walked towards the bleachers, biting his lip, taking a deep breath before walking up the few rows. The fresh baked biscotti bread and chocolate chips scent of his mate made his mouth water, a punch hitting him in the stomach as reality was starting to dawn on him.

I've been a fool. He looks so tired There were deep bags under Tyler's eyes and he looked pale. So very pale.

I can do this! Conner took a deep breath before clearing his throat. Tyler didn't move so Conner cleared his throat louder.

Tyler snapped his head up before nearly scurrying off the bleachers, only to hit the metal bars on the sides (since he was at the end of the row). Tyler squeaked, falling off the seat of a bleacher. He had each of his arms propped on either side of him on a bleacher seat; he looked very cramped and huddled on the bleacher floor.

"Holy goddess! Are you okay?" Conner moved quickly to reach for his mate to help him up. Conner froze quickly though, seeing his beautiful blonde mate flinch hard. Conner's heart thudded with pain at that, feeling a familiar sting in his eyes.

"I-I didn't do anything. Please don't hurt me," Tyler squeaked out, holding his books to his chest as if they would protect him.

Oh, I would never hurt you. Never again Conner biting his lip hard.

"I'm sorry, I didn't mean to startle you and no. I won't hurt you," Conner rubbed the back of his neck, looking down at his shoes sadly. Conner took a step away from his mate, seeing the sweet blonde relax at that. Conner's wolf was howling in agony, Conner seeing all of his pack members in the gym flinch at the waves of pain that were probably coming from him.

Carver whimpered along with a few betas and cheerleaders who tried to look away fast when Tyler looked over. The gym was just a little too quiet at the moment.

Tyler blinked in surprise at his mate moving slowly (his wolf whimpering a little since he wanted his mate close) but the rejection was still hurting them. Tyler slowly uncurled from the half ball form he was in, moving to sit on the bleacher again.

"Um, I uh, also wanted to apologize for just randomly yelling at you the other day. That probably weirded you out, huh?" Conner whispered, shuffling his foot on the ground before seeing a graph sheet near his foot where it probably flew from Tyler's fall. Conner picked it up, fiddling with the paper's corner in nervousness.

Tyler nodded slowly, remembering that Amilya said to pretend to act human. He would do anything for his big sister and he still needed to protect his little brother's identities for a little while longer while he was still able; and breathing. His wolf was perked and listening to every word their mate was saying, wanting, begging, for their mate to not hate them. Tyler didn't want to be hated. He hated how much his heart yearned for his mate. Even his brain yearning for his mate. It was unfair.

"Re-Rejected," Tyler whispered out, his wolf taking over for a second, seeing his mate stiffen, Tyler praying his eyes didn't show his wolf since he was looking down. He felt the warmth leave his eyes knowing his wolf receded back into his mind.

"Oh yeah, that probably didn't make sense. Uh, listen. I was, I am, not good with this," Conner waved his hand between himself and Tyler who was looking at him in confusion.

Good with having a mate or good with having a guy as a mate? Tyler wondered curiously.

"I, Conner Summers, take back my rejection and accept you," Conner whispered, Tyler's heart soaring, his wolf howling with happiness, shaking on four legs. Tyler's eyes widened in shock, wondering what in the freaking world made his mate change his mind.

Tyler's mouth was dropped down in shock, grabbing around his wrist to make sure that this was real. Yup, shooting pain in his arm still.

"Um, I'm kind of slow with this so... could we start over?" Conner whispered, looking up with big black eyes that made Tyler's stomach twist in knots. His eyes were glassy, almost like they were broken. They screamed need, want, and desire. Tyler had only dreamed of such things but now that it was here in front of his face, he felt only fear. Would those eyes always look at him like that?

"I..." Tyler whispered, moving some of his blonde hair around on his head. Conner sat down slowly, keeping a three foot distance from his mate. Tyler looked at him and back at his books shyly, seeming unsure of what to do. Conner loved how green his mate's eyes were. The way his mate fiddled with the pages of his book with his fingers so delicately, absentmindedly; or the way he bit his plump pink bottom lip with his white teeth.

"Start over?" Tyler whispered, knowing his eyes were filled with tears, his heart feeling like it was beating again. Like he could see color again. He saw the way his mate's eyes lit up with hope and the way his blonde hair shined in the gym from nodding slowly at him.

Maybe this was his mate getting his head out of his ass like Amilya had said. Maybe... this was the chance he could grab if he wanted the loneliness to leave him. Maybe this was the one choice that decided if he would face his fear head on or watch his life crumble.

Tyler looked curiously at Conner, wondering what his mate would do. It felt like the room itself was holding its breath; or maybe that was just him.

"Hi, I'm Conner Summers," Conner smiled, stretching his hand out. Conner felt his stomach twist in knots, seeing horrible pain and anguish in his mate's eyes that made him shake and for his wolf to howl and whimper in guilt.

"T-Tyler Winters," Tyler shakily shook Conner's hand, the sparks alone making his tears nearly fall.

"So um, you need any help?" Conner asked hopefully. Tyler looked down at his math, seeing half finished problems, blushing a little. Tyler bit his lip, not missing the way Conner's eyes snapped down to his lips a moment which made his cheeks warm with hope. Maybe his mate actual liked his lips. Maybe enough to even... kiss him. One day?

"Y-Yeah, but you don't have to-"

"I want to! Here, let's see," Conner quickly flipping through the pages. Conner glanced up, Tyler looking for his pencil that had rolled somewhere, seeing that everyone was eavesdropping as best as they could on the conversation without looking too suspicious.

Carver lifted his thumb, cocking his head to the side, wondering if everything was okay.

Conner gave a curt nod, going back to the problem.

By the end of the school day, Tyler was in a little bit of shock and awe since Conner had walked him to his classes and helped him with his homework. He even talked about little things that made Tyler relax even further around his mate. It didn't hurt per se. He felt a little on edge, like this was too good to be true, but that was the fear he was trying to get passed; at least that's what he told himself.

Tyler felt pleasurable shocks on his shoulder, turning to see Conner smiling shyly; so cute!

"Hi Conner," Tyler spoke gently, which wasn't usually like him (since he's normally rambunctious and bouncy). Tyler just couldn't trust Conner yet; no matter how much his wolf purred and nudged him to go to their mate.

"Hi Tyler," Conner spoke excitedly, coughing, to calm himself down.

So cute Tyler giggled internally.

"So I know that it's Thursday and stuff and I was kind of wondering, do you like video games?" Conner bit his lip, seeming to look everywhere but at his mate. Tyler felt a little more tension leave him.

"Psh, heck yeah!" Tyler said loudly, surprising his mate who smiled at that. Tyler surprised himself since he didn't think he'd sound like his old self anytime soon yet.

"I hold the record at the arcade further in town for Snipers 3," Tyler said a bit more calmly, although there was some pride in his voice. Conner's mouth dropped down at that, guffawing at his mate.

"No way! I was the top score!"

"Is that envy I hear?" Tyler stuck his tongue out, laughing softly at how surprised and happy his mate was looking at him. This was nice.

"Well then this will have to get serious," Conner frowned, before smirking slyly at his mate, who lifted a brow at that.

"You, me. Saturday at 11. The arcade. We'll see whose better," Conner smirked, Tyler's eyebrows shooting to his hairline. It still felt a little fast but... Maybe this could be the chance for his mate to start proving himself again.

"I'd love to," Tyler smiled a little, Conner's eyes softening.

"Don't be late or I'll say you gave up your title," Conner tugging on a piece of paper that was sticking up between the pages of Tyler's book. Tyler's cheeks tinted pink at the playful and gentle manner of his mate.

He really doesn't want to scare me away, does he? Tyler thought a little giddy.

Both of their faces were close, green staring into endless black. Conner smiled playfully his shoulder bumping Tylers', who laughed softly at the action.

"I'll say the same thing about you!" Tyler playfully glared making Conner laugh, Tyler's heart thumping happily at the sound. It was low and sexy that it made Tyler's body heat up fast.

Conner walked down the hall backwards, making faces at Tyler who tried to stop smiling before Conner walked into a girl, making her drop her books. Conner scrambled to help the girl with her books who was glaring at him before walking away miffed. Tyler could fairly hear her muttering 'moron' and 'backwards' from under her breath. Tyler slapped a hand over his mouth to stop himself from full on laughing, Conner looking red faced and embarrassed. He looked up at Tyler, shuffling his hair sheepishly, before walking away quickly.

Tyler's heart ached at all the feelings that were flooding through him after Conner disappeared around the corner.

Maybe we finally have a chance Tyler whispered, his wolf purring and cleaning his fur with his paws.

How could I have thought this was a solution? Tyler thought morbidly for a second, tugging his sweater further over his wrist.

You guys ready to run!? Amilya shouted through the mind link.

My wolf has been bouncing everywhere! Kai giggled.

Mine as well Raven spoke calmly.

I'll see you guys at home Tyler spoke softly, wanting to surprise his family. That maybe things we're finally going to be okay.

Tyler walked quickly home after grabbing the rest of his books; a few people in the hallway smiling and waving at him. Conner politely smiling and waving back, not understanding why these people were noticing him now. Or maybe, he never noticed them before either?

At the Townhouse

"Would you two sit down? You're going to wear a hole in the floor," Amilya sighed, lying on the couch.

Robin and Kai were walking in circles around each other, waiting for Tyler to get home.

"I would like to go on a run together, but I hope it doesn't drain his wolf," Robin spoke with worry, Kai nodding.

"What if he-" Kai held in a sob, shaking his head.

"Don't think like that. I ordered him to never again, alright?"

Kai and Robin nodded, continuing their pacing.

Tyler walked through the door, sighing, glad to be home and that it was almost the end of the week.

"Tyler!" Kai and Robin nearly jumping the blonde at the door.

"Are you okay?"

"Why are you late?"

"Does it hurt?"

"Did you see your mate today?"

"Did you eat lunch?"

"Carver said Conner spoke to you in the gym."

"What'd he say?"

"More importantly," Amilya stood, stopping the endless questions from the two, thanks to Tyler's relief, "do I need to rip his throat out?"

All three of them had the look of 'what the hell' on their faces.

"Actually, I thought I'd surprise you guys on the run but," Tyler kept his face straight, trying to extend the suspense, "he took back the rejection and asked to hang out Saturday!"

Tyler's voice rising in excitement, nearly sobbing in happiness. Kai squealed and hugged him tightly, Robin sighing out in relief.

"I'm glad," Amilya patted Tyler's cheek gently, Tyler hugging her tightly.

"Thank you for stopping me Alpha."

"Always," Amilya whispered, "Told you he'd get his head out of his ass," Amilya smiled gently, Tyler blushing bashfully, tugging on his sleeve with a little embarrassment since they all knew the mark on his wrist was there.

"Now let's run!" Amilya shouted, getting Tyler's mind from going to dark places again until his mate could help with that.

Amilya lead the way into the forest, all of them stripping and folding their clothes by the tree line.

The sound of popping joints could be heard before four beautiful wolves appeared.

Amilya's wolf was pitch black with even darker eyes. Only her right front paw was blondish in color; here eyes would turn burning yellow if her wolf was in control. Tyler's wolf was a blondish white with green eyes; his eyes turning pitch black if his wolf was in control. Robin's wolf had very long legs and was a smokey black color, one black eye and his other eye closed tightly; the scar still evident in wolf form. His eye turned the same color violet as his cursed eye, even though gamma eyes turn bright green when their wolf is in control. Kai's wolf was a snow white color with grey eyes. His wolf's eyes would turn bright blue if his wolf was in control.

The four ran into the woods, chasing and nipping at each others heels. They ended up in a doggy pile, happily nibbling away like pups, Amilya looking at them with love.

Amilya sighed internally, her heart aching. She was invisible to everyone else and that was the way she needed it to be; no matter how much it hurt. The man who had kidnapped her said how much she looked like her Papa. She couldn't and didn't want to cause any more trouble to her family than she already has.

Whenever she saw Carver and Conner, something ached in her chest. Something painful. Neither her wolf nor herself could figure out what was causing that, or the lingering scent the first day she arrived at the school.

Every night, she thought about what her brothers were doing. What they looked liked. If they had their mates. If her Papa was still working late in his office with her daddy bringing him late night snacks. She missed them. She missed them so much. Did they remember her? Or did they forget about her entirely?

Kai nudged Amilya out of her morbid thoughts, whimpering slightly.

I'm alright pup. But we should head back. It's getting late and you are all grumpy when you don't get enough sleep

Awe!!!

Her little brothers complained, Kai happily jumping and pushing his brothers who were still playing.

A scent in the breeze caught Amilya's attention, Amilya standing up immediately, nose in the air.

Alpha? Robin asked softly.

Get back to the house now! Rogues! Amilya ordered. Kai was the fastest wolf with a lot of training from the others. Kai raced ahead of the group knowing he was in charge of locking everything down in their home once he got there.

Robin and Tyler were almost evenly fast, Tyler ahead of him in case he needed to increase his speed if Kai was in danger.

Anything gamma? Amilya was in alpha mode, nothing going to hurt her family. Robin's cursed eye was open, allowing him to see fifteen seconds into the future.

Nothing Alpha!

Amilya was behind all of them, knowing she could catch up to even Kai if she had to, but wanted to make sure that no one was following them since the rogue's scent was downwind from them. The special soap they had, blocked their major scents, so all a rogue could smell was that wolves had been in the area; not the type or sex.

A-All windows covered and l-locked, no lights on at all except the p-porch light since our n-neighbors have theirs on as w-well Kai's voice was shaky, all of them knowing he was automatically hiding in his closet. An old habit that they didn't bother breaking.

Good Omega Amilya praised, feeling Kai's wolf shakily calm down a little.

We grabbed our clothes Robin spoke quickly.

We're all in the house alpha. Tyler spoke firmly, guarding the front door, looking very dangerous if anyone happened to try to get through the front door. Robin was guarding the back door, the silence almost deafening.

Alpha! Dodge left! Robin yelled in fright mentally, able to see Amilya's silhouette from where he was in the house. Kai sobbed and cried in fear, needing his mate.

Amilya swiftly dodged the rogue wolf. His teeth dripping saliva, eyes bright red. Amilya faded back after a lunge from the wolf before instantly wrapping her jaws around its throat, snapping the rogue's neck.

Amilya dragged the body further into the forest and away from their home, not wanting any pack wolves to start investigating them.

Amilya hurriedly ran to the house, allowing the pack link to come back since she could concentrate better without feeling her little pack worry.

Amilya slammed through the front door before she was pushed harshly into the wall, both her and Tyler baring their teeth, before realizing it was the other.

Stand down Beta Amilya ordered, Tyler baring his neck.

Apologies Alpha

Amilya nodded, Robin hurriedly locking the door.

"Come on," Amilya urged, Tyler and Robin following her since they were all going to stay with Kai; knowing how gentle of a soul he was.

"A-Alpha, are you hurt?" Kai whispered, tears silently leaving him. His voice was small inside the closet, no part if him visible.

"I am alright pup. Come," Amilya opened her arms, Kai immediately cuddling into her, running from his closet. Only Kai's mate could truly calm him down, but having higher ranking wolves around a submissive omega makes them feel safer and stronger.

"Did you move the body farther away?" Robin asked quickly, Amilya nodding, stroking Kai's head. Robin sat next to the two knowing protective scents eased Kai down a lot.

"It will probably be found by the DarkIce Pack in a few hours, if Raven is in charge of patrols," Robin letting pride leak into his voice. Amilya and Tyler rolled their eyes playfully since Robin sounded like he was almost gushing.

DarkIce. DarkIce. The word rang in Amilya's head who grabbed her head at the pain.

"Alpha!?" Kai asked with worry, eyes glowing blue as he gently touched her forehead.

"Thank you," Amilya nodded, Kai's eyes going back to normal, whimpering a little.

"That has been happening to you a lot, hasn't it?" Tyler asked with worry, eyes sharp and daring Amilya to lie to him.

"Is that why we never see you at lunch?" Robin frowned, Amilya shrugging, trying to avoid the stare down from her three little brothers.

"There's something about this place that wants to draw up old memories that I don't particularly want to remember."

They all frowned at that. Not wanting to push their alpha, all of them ended up snuggling on the floor, listening intently to each others hearts and breaths. Ever so slowly they calmed down. Kai's body felt tingly and hot for some reason, almost enough to need a fan. The others were quietly talking to each other, the ambiance in the room gentle enough to stop Kai's wolf from shaking.

A howl was heard, Kai's eyes flashing between blue and grey.

"Carver," Kai smiled, all of them immediately covering their noses. Kai flushed scarlet, tears leaving him as he tried covering his bottom with his hands.

"If your heat has started then ours will as well. No school tomorrow and take your heat suppressants. You can go off of them soon."

"Yes alpha," All of them had red cheeks, leaving to their own rooms quickly, Amilya staying with Kai knowing he shouldn't be left alone. Submissive omega's would follow orders until they died, so it worried Amilya if he was ever left alone. Their heats usually synced up like female periods synced up. Omegas would also be more easily forced to submit, and with rogues recently near their home, Amilya wasn't going to take any chances.

Heats were... difficult. Since they were all submissive, they all got heats. Usually only females got heats, but that was another reason why submissive wolves were rare. Submissive wolves are either killed by other females, or raped and killed.

Kai handed Amilya the suppressants and a glass of water. They all usually got down to their underwear since its an unbearable heat, all of them wearing pads because of slick.

"We're like a matching gay band," Tyler chuckled, Robin rolling his eyes.

"I am a girl you know," Amilya sighing loudly, all of them chuckling at that.

"Yeah, but you have the same taste as us! Welcome aboard!" Tyler laughed.

Amilya could tell when each heat started, everyone's skin getting prickly because of the suppressants and no one touching at all. It was usually unbearable if it wasn't your mate. Amilya had to kill several rogues along with Tyler whenever one of them had a heat and they were on the run in Canada. Usually Kai's was the worst since omega's were normally considered breeders and so his was the strongest scent out of all of them.

"I bought us some ice cream earlier thinking our heats would start sometime Sunday," Amilya smiled, each of them purring at that. Their wolves would soon take over during their heats since the pain of not being knotted by their mate was excruciating.

"I'm starting to like it here. If everything goes well next week, I think I'll allow you to tell your mates," Amilya giggled, all of them immediately sitting up.

"Really!?" Kai squealed, jumping up and down.

"I think I'd like to shift in the middle of gym to surprise Conner," Tyler giggled, imagining his face.

"We should really think about this strategically. They are bound to ask why we hid it from them," Robin said.

Kai frowned at that, lip wobbling, not wanting his mate to ever know what had happened to him.

"They can know in time when you are all comfortable," Amilya spoke gently, Robin shrugging, getting comfy.

Kai snuggled on top of his blankets, shifting earlier into his wolf. It was easier to deal with heats while in wolf form if a wolf's mate wasn't around.

"Sleep. We will talk more after our heats."

All of them yawned sleepily, Amilya the last to fall asleep, the familiarity of the howl earlier, haunting her.

At the Pack House, earlier that evening

"Would you two stop pacing. You're going to wear a hole into the floor," Papa frowned, sitting on the couch with his arms crossed.

Carver and Raven were pacing, waiting for Conner to get home. Daddy was making cupcakes by the second it seemed.

Conner yawned walking in, freezing when he was nearly grabbed by his brother who was shaking him back and forth by his collar.

"What did you say?"

"How did it go?"

"What happened?"

"Are you alright?"

"How is your mate?"

"I need air!" Conner yelled, all of them snapping their mouths shut, Papa chuckling from the couch.

"I uh," Conner shuffled his hair, all of them looking at him in worry making him sigh for being such an ass to them.

"I took back the rejection and asked him to the arcade on Saturday," Conner said.

Conner flinched at the screech his daddy did before he was hugged by his family.

"Still. Need. Air!" Conner gasped, getting a noogie from Carver and a hug from his Papa.

"I'm glad you decided to try honey," Daddy spoke excitedly, Conner smiling at him, nodding. Conner looked down sadly, his daddy sighing gently, hugging Conner tightly.

"Well, since you're off your man period we can go on a run!" Carver smacked Conner on his back who growled at him.

"Man period?" Daddy murmured before flushing, "you two get out of here right this instant!" Daddy yelled, making a reach for the broom, Carver and Conner running for it since Daddy hit hard.

Of course Adam thought they were talking about heats. Daddy was an exception when it came to heats, even though he was a dominant male omega, half of omegas (male or female) can go into heats. He was still lovingly accepted into the pack, both Chris and Adam making it clear to their pack members that race, gender, and status didn't matter. Only actions and treatment towards others did.

Carver and Conner's wolves playfully ran together with a few of their warrior friends since they were on patrol. All of them froze when they smelled blood, Carver and the others crouching low before seeing a dead rogue in the forest. Its neck was snapped and appeared to have been dragged before the scent was lost in the forest.

I'll report to the Alpha Carver spoke sternly, the warriors nodding and going off to get rid of the body. Carver howled in warning in case there were other rogues lingering.

The two made it home fast, their Papa frowning at their report.

Most rogues were terrified to walk into the DarkIce Pack territory since it was well known that no rogues were treated well if they were ever spotted.

I want a second patrol out Papa ordered through the link, Raven seeming to be thinking.

"There isn't anything over in that part of the territory though. So why would a rogue go there?" Raven spoke quietly to himself, pacing. Raven would probably be thinking through the night about it since that is what he does.

All of them stayed up for a few more hours in case the warriors found anything. Adam was snuggled next to Chris who was a bit on edge. Carver was having Conner relay exactly what he said to his mate; Robin nodding at certain parts before thinking about the rogue again.

"Leon will be back home in about half a month," Papa spoke suddenly, "I had gotten off the phone with him when you all came back."

"I'll be happy to see his ugly mug," Carver smirked.

"I'll shove some whipped cream in his face like good ol' times," Conner cackled along with Carver; Daddy scowled at them.

"Everything will be cleaned up if you do anything with any food items, AND, you will not ask any of the omegas or gammas to do so for you," Daddy wagged his fingers at his sons who pouted at him.

"Yes Luna," They grumbled, Daddy satisfied with that answer. Papa chuckled, kissing Adam on the cheek; Adam snuggling against Chris' neck.

"I'll make him a cake though since it will be after his birthday," Daddy giggled, all of them sweat dropping from seeing the six towers of cupcakes on the table in the kitchen from the living room; an omega walking in before stopping and looking at the pile, hurriedly running back out. Everyone knew not to mess with daddy when they saw him stress baking.

Carver rubbed his chest suddenly, his eye brows pulling together in confusion.

"Carver, what's wrong?" Daddy asked worriedly, Papa, Conner, and Raven looking just as worried.

"My wolf is restless for some reason. I don't know why."

"You'll see Kai tomorrow so don't worry about it too much," Conner nodded, Carver trying to relax at that.

Carver and Conner went to their rooms later on, thinking of their mates. Raven left to go to the house where his parents lived; it was a little ways away from the pack house. There were houses for all the pack members who wanted to live closer to the pack house rather than living in the city further away.

Carver had a present for Kai when he saw him tomorrow, already wanting to give his mate the world.

Conner was thinking along similar lines, wanting to make his own mate happy and make up for the rejection.

Friday

It seemed like everybody was waiting for either Kai, Tyler or Robin to come into the school, but it was already lunch and everyone could feel the tension from their future alpha, beta, and gamma. Conner and Raven were already looking at phones to buy for their mates, getting the idea from Carver.

"Hey!" Conner yelled suddenly, since Carver and Raven were brooding at their lunch table, everyone cautiously away; even the slut Tiffany and her friend. Not that Tiffany didn't try spreading her legs at the table next to theirs making the three nearly gag; along with a few of their friends nearby.

Conner ran from the table, Carver and Raven confused before gasping, seeing the very mysterious and hardly ever seen fourth member of their mate's family.

"Hey!" Conner yelled again, jogging down the hallway. They stopped, seeing the girl talking to a teacher, head down, grabbing some paper.

The girl turned, freezing, Carver and Conner's hearts nearly skipping a beat when they saw a glimpse of the girl's dark eyes. They weren't able to see them clearly, but something made their hearts beat faster.

What the heck was that? Conner asked Carver confused, who shook his head, looking warily at the girl.

"Excuse me," Raven waved his hand, the girl pressing the papers to her chest, "um, sorry if we startled you."

Conner and Carver were just looking at the girl curiously, about three feet separating them from the mysterious girl.

She looks like she'd be pretty tall if she wasn't hunched over Raven noted suddenly.

She also smells... Pretty Conner agreed.

There was something about her eyes though Carver's voice unsure.

"Please," Carver whispered, the girl's shoulders relaxing at Carver's calm voice.

"We were wondering why our ma-... why Tyler, Kai and Robin aren't here today," Conner asked gently as well, the girl seeming ready to bolt at anything that even remotely sounded aggressive.

"A family matter needed to be attended to today. I am just collecting their homework since none of us want to get behind," the girl said.

All of their hearts skipped a beat, the girl's voice sounding beautiful. It was soft, gentle, and almost sounded like bells. Almost as sweet as Luna Adam's voice. But it was stern. Confident.

There's something Conner whispered through the mind link

To protect her? Or something Carver said with confusion.

She seems so... I don't know Raven whispered as well.

"Please excuse me, I must not be late," The girl bowed her head slightly, all of them moving instantly which shocked them after the realization. They were dominants and Carver was an Alpha to boot, and they just moved without hesitation for the girl.

They watched the girl leave, all the pack members watching her curiously.

"What-" Conner started.

"The-" Raven added.

"Hell," Carver whispered.

There was just something about the girl that seemed so familiar. Was that the right word to use?

Saturday

Kai's POV

Heat's suck. I get all yucky and I hate how much attention I attract from rogues if I do get my heat. It scares me a lot and I'm glad there are stronger wolves in our little pack.

I wish I didn't get scared so much, but I don't want to just be naive and think I'm safe. I'll never be safe.

Kai's heat was at it's low point, the heat itself lasting for four days, so they'd have to skip school on Monday too. Tyler went out on his date, his heat not going to come back for a couple of hours, as long as his mate doesn't trigger it early. Amilya is kind of spying on them since Conner did hurt our brother and since Tyler was still in heat.

Amilya is such a good alpha! I love my big sister and brothers! They treat me like a person and not like a pushover omega.

I had gotten out of the shower, getting a clean pad before dressing in loose pants and a hello kitty shirt. I've never seen the show but it looks so cute!

I skipped down the stairs, Robin still in his wolf form, sleeping away on his bed. He usually slept like a rock without moving for three of the four days.

There was suddenly a knock at the door. I shook and almost screamed in fear. What if it was a rogue? What if someone could smell my scent? Was the soap no longer working? I gathered my courage, not even a creek being made on the floor, gasping once I looked through the peep hole. It was Carver! Wait... how did he know where I lived? Well I guess he just knows where everyone lives if he's supposed to be the next pack alpha. I quickly fixed my hair and straightened my shirt, taking in deep breaths since I could feel my slick start to trickle out of me. I was sure my cheeks were already pink at that.

I opened the door a crack, Carver's gorgeous blue eyes snapping down to mine. He seemed to let out a huge breath before smiling.

"Hey babe," Carver winked, making me giggle shyly and open the door wider.

I was hugged immediately, strong arms holding me tightly with Carver's scent soaking into my brain and clothes. My wolf purred as I unconsciously rubbed my head against his muscular chest, scenting him.

"W-What are you doing here Carver?" I whispered, trying to get the fog to leave my brain. I could already feel my mini me harden and the slick increase from Carver growling low.

"You smell really good," Carver's voice was low and husky, my eyes rolling back at the sound. A whimper left me when Carver traced his nose along my neck as I bared my throat more. Carver bit and sucked on my neck, making me gasp and moan, biting my lip.

Carver seemed to snap back to reality, clearing his throat.

"I didn't see you at school Friday so I got worried and since there isn't really a way for me to contact you I got even more worried," Carver spoke quickly, looking me up and down before his eyes became hooded.

"I'm sorry for worrying you Carver. It was a family thing. I won't be at school on Monday either so..." I bit my lip seeing the questioning look in his eyes as if silently asking me to tell him.

"Here," Carver said suddenly, handing me a white and pink striped paper baggie making me giggle, grabbing it curiously.

I opened it before gasping, seeing a brand new spanking Samsung phone with a white case for it.

"Carver, I-I," I was at a loss for words trying to hand him back the phone while he just cupped my hands, kissing my fingertips.

"I get phones for free sometimes and I didn't really need one so, I want you to keep this baby. My phone number is already in there. It'll give me piece of mind knowing you have it," Carver said seriously.

I could feel tears leave me, Carver looking to panic for a second before I jumped on him, smacking my lips against his.

I moaned hotly, my pink tongue snaking into his mouth the way Carver usually does to me. Carver let out a moan that was husky and made my tummy tighten. He grabbed me roughly, pushing me against the wall as he took control of the kiss.

I could feel his hands reach down, cupping each of my butt cheeks. He groped and spread them; slick soaking my pad.

"You smell so fucking good," Carver moaned trailing kisses down my neck, licking and sucking where the mating mark was supposed to go. Carver lifted me up so my legs had to wrap around his waist.

"Carver!" I gasped, his tongue flicking my nipple that was still hidden by my shirt, before sucking on it, his other hand massaging my mini me through my pants.

"You like that baby? I want to take you and knot you," Carver's eyes flashing yellow as I arched into him, thrusting into the hand that was rubbing my sweat pant covered member. His wolf was out to play and really horny!

Oh moon goddess! Kai feeling his wolf almost taking over.

My cheeks felt like they were on fire, seeing Carver panting above me, just watching me thrust against his hand. My body had a mind of it's own!

I nearly sobbed when he rubbed where my hole was. I was sure my pad couldn't hold anymore slick. I choked on air, shoving Carver's hand away from my pant covered mini me, grinding against his own.

Carver moaned low at that, grinding even harder into me. I suddenly smelled another Alpha, whimpering with fear, before realizing it was Amilya. The fog left my brain for a second, knowing my wolf was about to shift and present. That would be bad. I don't think my actual brain was ready to handle having my butt cherry popped (a joke Tyler keeps making).

Please! We can't mate! My wolf whining, panting, and clawing at me, not understanding.

I tried to struggle out of Carver's hold which only caused more friction. My heat was on the peak of exploding along with my own orgasm, knowing I would right then and there drop my pants and present myself to my, dominant Alpha mate to claim and knot me with his massive cock. No! Bad thoughts! Bad!

I sobbed at the very image, begging Carver to stop before real tears left me in both fear and pleasure. He would only get hurt more, from me hiding this secret from him. Then he would be mated to a liar! I don't want to lie anymore.

"Please Carver! I'm scared!" I yelled, knowing that I would be in so much trouble if Amilya, Tyler, or Robin knew what was going to happen. What I wanted to happen at this very moment.

Distressed? Carver's wolf barked, making Carver look at his mate's face before freezing, seeing tears leave his mate, and not in a good way.

Carver gently put Kai back down, feet on the floor, taking in fresh deep breaths of air from the opened front door. Kai was like a drug and it was the hardest thing to step away from him. Carver reeled his wolf back in, painfully hard, moving his cock more comfortably in his pants.

"Baby? Did I hurt you? Are you okay? Did I do something wrong?" Carver was frustrated and that was an understatement. Most werewolves mated after a month of meeting!

"I-I'm sorry!" Kai sobbed, Carver calming down but frantically trying to console his mate.

"Hey. It's okay. It's alright. I'd never force you Kai. I promise. You were scared and I stopped. I won't ever force you," Carver whispered, reaching towards his mate who took a step away, Carver's wolf whining at that.

"I-It wasn't that Car-Carver," Kai hiccuped, Carver's heart twisting.

"Big Sissy will be back and you can't be here or I'll be in big trouble! Please," I whispered, Carver looking alarmed at me.

"What do you mean you'll be in trouble?" Carver asked with fear, horrible things running through his head. Not to mention anger. Well, hormonal anger, since a teenage wolf was being denied sex with his mate from an outside party.

"Please Carver. I'll see you on Tuesday. I-I liked what we did," I whispered, knowing my heat was a few seconds from starting again and my wolf and I wouldn't have the control to stop ourselves from attacking our mate.

"Okay baby, just.... just call me okay? If you want to, I mean," Carver whispered, gently cradling my cheek. I leaned into his hand, nodding, kissing his palm.

"Okay puppy," I slowly pushed Carver out the door who looked worried beyond anything, walking to his black SUV. I peeked out the curtain seeing Carver hit his head repeatedly on the steering wheel, almost making me laugh; although I did feel guilty.

I felt a brutal cramp in my belly, nearly making me double over in pain, racing up to my room, jumping in the shower.

Slick poured down my legs as I hurriedly thrust into my hand, sobbing when my heat hit me again. I came quickly, still hard, switching the water to ice cold. I don't know how long I was standing under the spray until my slick went back to a trickle again. My teeth chattered from the cold water and I was pretty sure I was turning blue.

I got out, drying, grabbing a new pad. I snuggled into my towel, freezing even more in the cool house. I was hugged when I walked out the bathroom door, sighing at the warmth before realizing I was in my undies and their hugs were uncomfortable right now.

"Guys!" I yelled trying to cover my parts.

"We smelled Carver was here. Did he hurt you, are you alright?" Amilya and Tyler fired at me.

"He-He stopped when I started crying cause I was scared I'd get in trouble since I knew you'd be able to smell he was here and you didn't give permission to tell our mates about being werewolves and I just thought... I didn't want him to find out this way," I whispered.

"Oh pup," Amilya sighed sadly, moving some of my damp hair behind my cold ear. Conner whimpered at that too, all of us hearing Robin groan in the room over, probably getting comfy again.

"You aren't in trouble sweetie. I was just... worried that he might-"

"He wouldn't do that!" I yelled, snapping my mouth closed in shock. Defiance. I was always taught that defiance from an omega was unworthy.

"Yeah. I think he's proved that," Amilya nodded with a chuckle, calming down my morbid thoughts. All of us went downstairs to eat ice cream since Tyler's heat was about to start again.

"So how'd the date go Ty?" I squeaked seeing him blush and fiddle with a stuffed wolf in his hands.

Tyler's POV

I was super nervous about the date in case Conner didn't come. Plus I didn't want to explain why I wasn't in class on Friday. I scrubbed my body extra hard with the special soap.

I gasped suddenly, my vision going dark, before my nose caught the delicious scent of my mate. Pine and fresh snow.

"Conner!" I giggled, poking hard into the body behind me, hearing a groan.

Conner looked hot. He was in new looking jeans that hugged his manhood nicely because holy yummy sauce he looked big. Crap. Can't think that or my heat will start.

His v-line looked so good in his tight shirt too and his hair was styled a little.

"See something you like?" Conner chuckled, making me blush and splutter.

"Come on!" Conner laughed louder, tugging me to the arcade. We played two person games and it was pretty even with winning. Some people even came to crowd around us when we were competing for the highs score in a shooting game.

"You somehow cheated!" I pouted, before feeling him tug me into his chiseled side. I could feel my cheeks warm at that.

"Awe, come on! Don't frown! You'll get a butt load of wrinkles."

I hit him in the chest making him cough and rub the spot.

"Damn you hit hard," Conner coughed.

"You're welcome," I stuck my tongue out at him before he rolled his eyes, grabbing my hand. I bit my lip, realizing Conner was giving me the choice to slip my hand out of his. I breathed a little shakily, tightening my hand around his. The sparks nearly made me cry in happiness, feeling my wolf get a little stronger.

We went bowling next. I didn't even realize it was next to the arcade and I had never bowled before. Not enough money.

I pouted again, getting another ball in the gutter, not understanding what I was doing wrong.

"When was the last time you went bowling?" Conner asked, eating one of the fries we ordered. It was so good and yet so bad at the same time somehow. It was greasy and delicious and Conner and I tried each one in the 20 sauces Conner brought over. Literally 20. Like, how can there be that many sauces in the world!? It was so hard to choose until I started mixing and matching flavors together.

"N-Never," I mumbled, rubbing the back of my head. I dipped a couple more fries in a sweet sauce. Conner blinked at me in confusion, getting in front of me.

"Big Sis doesn't usually-" I stopped there seeing confusion and worry in Conner's eyes, not wanting to seem suspicious, "I mean we just don't go bowling and there wasn't ever an urge to try I guess."

It was a lame ass lie, I know, and it seemed that Conner didn't believe me, but he didn't press the subject which I was thankful for. Conner just stared into my eyes and I felt my cheeks burst into flames from the proximity, my slick increasing when he smirked at me. I think I saw his nose wriggle for a second, but I'm just seeing things I'm sure.

"Well I'll show you then!" Conner smiled, grabbing a bowling ball.

Conner got behind me, my eyes fluttering at the contact. I could feel everything. Heats made everything super sensitive. I could feel each breath he took, how his chest pressed into my back. The way his groin rubbed into my butt. There was no need to get that close sir!

I bit my lip to stop the moan from leaving me, feeling my slick increase even more; my pad damp.

Sweet moon goddess I sound like a freaking girl! His hand covered mine as we swung the ball together.

"And release!" He commanded. I nearly came in my pants, the ball rolling down the lane, getting half of the pins. I felt a tightness in belly, feeling rock hard.

"Conner," I whispered, feeling his nose glide along my neck.

"Why do you smell so damn good?" He whispered, his tongue licking my neck, making me gasp. Conner turned me to face him immediately, my face going red before I nearly died. His lips pressed against mine.

Sparks erupted, his lips so warm and molding perfectly to mine. I wrapped my arms around his neck unconsciously, deepening the kiss, sighing out when he slanted his mouth more against mine. His hand slowly moved down my back, rubbing my lower back. I whined at that, biting my lip when I pulled away. I knew that our eyes both held lust and want.

Conner murmured a little, kissing me soft and slow. I could feel myself crumbling, gently pulling away before smiling softly. My wolf was keening and whining, clawing to escape and present ourselves. This... Was one of the things I dreamed of with my mate. I only hoped it would remain real.

"You're perfect," Conner whispered and my wolf jumped and spun on unsteady legs, puffing out his chest happily.

"Conner," I could feel my cheeks warm in a blush before we played a few more minutes; my bowling skills much better. I felt like Conner's eyes were on me, or at least my butt when it was my turn. That perv. Once the game was over, Conner beating me by 50 points sadly (although it was really fun), Conner grabbed my hand, leading me to a claw machine.

"I am the master of the claw!" Conner smiled as I giggled at him.

I looked to see what they had, smiling at a blonde looking wolf pup in the corner of the machine.

"That one," I pointed, Conner cracking his knuckles before starting. It took him a few tries and I was pretty much cheerleading him before he got it, holding it up in victory.

"I bow to the Master of the claw," I giggled, bowing slightly, practically seeing Conner preen at that.

Conner smiled, holding my hand again. My slick was still leaking out of me, kind of at an alarming pace.

I froze suddenly, seeing Amilya further away in the parking lot, slowly walking towards us. Alpha is super protective, not that I mind too much at the moment since Conner hasn't fully redeemed himself yet, but he was starting too. Not that I would have minded a few more kisses to get my wolf to calm down. She was silently telling me it was time to leave.

"Ty?" Conner whispered, before seeing my sister too (although she was still dressed up mysteriously).

"I have to go. But thank you for this Conner. I really like spending time with you," I whispered shyly, before I felt his hand on my cheek.

"I did too Tyler. Thanks for saying yes and giving me... This... Um, possibly us, a chance?"

I cocked my head in confusion before he grabbed my hand gently.

"Will you-" Conner clearing his throat, "go on a date with me?" Conner asked a bit shyly making me stunned.

"As in, a possible future boyfriend, kind of date," Conner whispered. I think I had to hold in my squeal of delight. This was more than I could hope for!

I nodded fast, laughing softly, seeing Conner looking at me in shock before relief seemed to sweep through him.

"You'll take care of him won't you?" Conner smiled, handing me the stuffed blonde pup. I giggled, nodding.

"Foxtrot will be well cared for," I smiled, hearing Conner groan at the name.

"You totally cheated for that game," Conner scowled. I bit my lip, Conner looking at my lips longingly. My wolf whined a little, and I wasn't sure if it was the heat or not. We kissed softly. Oh so softly. Shyly. He pecked my lips a few more times. I could feel myself turn into putty at the taste of his lips, my slick starting to increase soaking my pad a little too much. Oh boy...

"Conner," I whispered, seeing my mate's nostrils flare, his eyes flashing to a different shade of black; his wolf taking over for a second. Conner grabbed the back of my neck smacking his mouth against mine, his tongue claiming dominance. Everything was going fuzzy, my wolf howling to be claimed. I moaned and hummed into the kiss, tugging on his hair making him growl sexily.

"Mmm, later honey," I murmured, gasping at the nickname that just spilled out of my mouth. My stomach was doing somersaults in shock and happiness. Conner's eyelids were hooded and his obsidian eyes held dominance and want.

I felt my arm grabbed suddenly as I was tugged away by Amilya, Conner's eyes flashing dangerously in anger. I gave a sad wave to him, his eyes holding worry. My mate was definitely protective and I think I could finally tell myself that I could fall in love with him. That it'd be okay.

--(0_0)-----------------

Another chapter done :D

The Pack House

Kai's POV

Tuesday couldn't come soon enough. I wasn't able to text Carver all weekend because my heat hurt too much; but everyone was excited to have a phone in the house for free that wasn't the landline.

I have hated my heat ever since I got it at the age of 16. Amilya says it's supposed to be super pleasurable with your mate, and I was more than ready for that to happen. By the end of the week Amilya would tell us her final decision for our little pack, but she always took our opinions into consideration.

I sighed, hoping Carver wasn't angry with me. I kind of shoved him off of me when our making out got really intense. I mean Amilya would have probably killed him in the middle of our mating process and that would have been super bad. Amilya is really protective of us and anything she decides has usually been in our best interest.

I opened my locker, getting my books, my wolf whining in worry. I bit my lip, my heart aching since we haven't seen our mate yet.

I closed my locker, seeing Carver walking over to me, looking sad.

"Hi baby," Carver's smile not reaching his eyes.

"H-Hi Carver," I whispered, biting my lip with worry. It was an awkward silence. Like I was pretty sure people could hear my poor little heart beating like crazy.

"I-I'm sorry I pushed you away," I whispered sadly, looking at my shoes, but not without seeing Carver stiffen in my peripheral vision.

I felt his fingers under my chin, lifting my face to look up at him.

"I will never force you Kai. I love you too much to force you into something that makes you uncomfortable. I'm sorry I pushed you passed your comfort zone," Carver spoke sadly and I could see the worry in his eyes.

Wait. He was worried if I was upset with him? Before my brain went into overdrive. HE LOVES ME!?

"L-L-Love," I gasped, seeing Carver nod slowly with a tint of pink on his cheeks. I hugged him happily, tears leaving me, my wolf howling happily. Carver let out a big sigh, holding me tightly, running his nose along my neck. I giggled at that, knowing his wolf was wanting to scent us already.

I suddenly saw a small bouquet of roses in his other hand, blinking in confusion.

"I wasn't sure if you liked flowers or not since I never asked you and -" I put a finger against his lips, kissing him softly, feeling him instantly relax.

"I love flowers," I smiled, seeing him smile in return, handing them to me. There were three red roses that smelled lovely; probably freshly picked.

"Thank you Carver."

"Of course baby," Carver smiled, grabbing my hand, walking me to class.

"Could you show me how to use the phone?" I whispered, Carver looking at me confused before nodding.

"Sure!" Carver kissed my cheek, making me giggle since he had to lean down to do it.

"Thanks puppy. I'll see you at lunch!"

Carver smacked my butt, making me squeak and pout at him with a glare. The evil sexy man was smirking.

Lunch time came around super fast, me and my brothers and their mates all sitting at the same table.

I had been stealing some of Carver's grapes when I thought he wasn't looking before he kissed me hotly, going back to talk to Raven.

Tyler and Robin giggled softly at me, making me pout.

"So... we were kind of wondering-" Raven spoke suddenly, all of our mates looking at us.

"-If you guys wanted to come over to our house Friday night?"

"Meet the 'rents and stuff."

"Okay!" Tyler happily smiled, Conner nuzzling into his neck with a smile on his face too. Tyler blushed shyly, not used to such attention before.

"W-Will your parents like me? Us? I don't want to intrude," Kai mumbled, Carver kissing him softly, moving some of his black hair away from his face.

"I know they will love you baby. Daddy likes to bake and Papa may look mean but he is a teddy bear," Carver smiled, making me giggle, trying to relax.

"You have two Dads?" Robin asked suddenly as we saw our mates freeze at the question.

"Well they do. I have a mom and dad," Raven said quickly.

"Yeah," Conner coughed out, looking nervously at Carver.

"Yup. The best Dads in the whole world!" Carver smiled making me giggle. Them trying so hard to keep their werewolf identity a secret was cute. They really sucked at it though.

"Anyway, you want to come over?" Raven asked Robin who still had a lot of questions.

"You all live in the same house?" Robin lifted his brow, all our mates fidgeting. Carver looks so cute getting all nervous!

"Yeah, it's shared with lots of families since it's cheaper that way and it's easier with lots of people helping out."

Robin opened his mouth again to ask a question before Raven promptly kissed him, making me giggle. Looking back at Carver, my mate seemed to relax.

"So?" Raven asked softly, Robin giggling, cheeks tinted pink before looking shyly down at the table with a smile before frowning.

"We'd have to ask our sister first," Robin said quietly, all of us frowning; our mates frowning as well.

"Wouldn't you just ask your parents?" Carver asked, confused.

"W-Well it's a bit more complicated then that," I whispered, knowing we were being just as suspicious as they were. How any of us could keep a secret was beyond me.

"I'm sure she'll say yes though," Tyler said hurriedly, Conner lifting his brow up at that.

The bell suddenly rang, all of us heading towards our classes.

Carver's POV

Something bothered me about the way my mate talked about his older sister. Apparently I wasn't the only one who thought that since both Raven and Conner thought so too; once talking to our mates again.

It didn't make sense why they had to ask their sister for permission for anything. Now that I thought about it, they never talked about their parents either. Nor did they look that similar.

I was also worried about the dead rogue that was found. The only thing that was anywhere near where the rogue was found were the townhouses near the school.

It scared me to death that a rogue was that close to my mate. I couldn't have anything getting near my mate that would cause him harm. I wanted to tell my mate already that I was a werewolf, hoping to tell him Friday.

I needed him to know because my wolf was getting harder to control every day that he remained unclaimed without a mating mark on his neck. My baby had such a gentle heart that I was terrified I would scare him if he saw my wolf.

Carver

Hey Papa, what's up?

John said he smelled other rogues around the border of our pack. I'm having Raven switch up patrol locations just in case. Are we going to meet your mates yet? Your Dad is dying over here.

You guys will soon. Possibly Friday

Good! I want to meet the boys who are mates with my sons and best gamma.

Don't let Raven hear you say that Papa, his head might blow up

I heard Papa snicker at that saying bye.

I had more questions than answers about my mate and I wanted him. I wanted him more than anything. I ran a hand down my face at how stressed I was. I needed my baby in my arms since he could relax me almost instantly.

I guess we'll just have to wait till Friday to get any answers from our mates Raven piped in suddenly as I snickered at Conner's annoyed groan.

We just need to be patient guys. Friday is three days away

Oh like you're one to talk Mr. Self control! Conner snickered making me growl.

It wasn't technically my fault if my baby was irresistible, right? Right.

Friday

Kai put on some very tight skinny jeans that cupped his butt, Kai giggling in the mirror.

Carver has a weird obsession with my butt Kai giggled, his wolf shaking it's butt in the air happily.

Kai put on a cute light blue sweater that went down to his hands since it was a little big on him. Kai put on matching blue ear muffs, Kai twirling in the mirror, giggling.

"Mila," Kai whispered, handing her his light blue eye liner bashfully. Kai always thought Amilya's eyes popped and looked beautiful whenever she put on make up and he wanted to too. Just a little.

"Okay sweetie, sit," Amilya put it around his tear ducts, making it fade away.

Kai squealed, hugging her, running back to his room to make sure his hair looked okay.

"Alright, you three," Amilya had all three standing in front of her.

"Kai you look adorable," Amilya smiled, smoothing the fuzzy ear muffs he had on, Kai blushing happily.

Tyler had on tight skinny jeans with a dark green button down shirt that matched his eyes. He also had on a dark green beanie to match holding onto a video game case to his chest. He had one of his many scarves on, this one black with silver speckles.

"Tyler you look very cute," Amilya moved some of his hair around, Tyler smiling happily.

Robin had on black skinny jeans with a black button down top with a lavendar beanie and matching scarf. Tyler forced him to wear the beanie and scarf since Tyler claimed that Robin needed more color in his wardrobe. He had tried to style his hair so that it covered his eye patch without it looking stupid.

"Very handsome Robin," Amilya smiled, moving some of his bangs behind his ear.

"Call me when all of you get there. I'll be finishing up my patrol so call around 10. If you can, get them to drop you off here so you don't have to walk by yourselves."

"What if they don't drive us?" Kai asked shyly.

"Just bat your eyelashes and whisper sweetly to your mates that you don't want to walk ALL ALONE in the dark," Amilya bounced her eyebrows up and down making her brothers blush and giggle.

"Bye loves, be safe!"

All of them walked to the pack house, following the dirt road. Their wolves were practically bouncing off the walls wanting to see their mates. Tyler and Robin were getting a little skittish, seeing a few wolves running amongst the trees, but knew they were on pack grounds and the members were probably asked to hide their wolf forms.

"Woah," They all whispered. The pack house was a freaking mansion! It was made of cool gray stone and dark wood. It looked to be three stories tall and took up almost the entire open space before it became wooded again.

Kai's POV

Tyler and Robin walked ahead of me as I stayed close to them, seeing a few people peeking around the sides of the mansion at us or from the windows.

"I wonder if the doorbell is some kind of orchestral melody," Tyler asking with excitement, pushing the doorbell. It rang normally, Tyler pouting; Robin snickered at him. I tried to calm down my shaking, but people looking at me from around the pack grounds was making me nervous.

I grabbed onto the bottom of Robin's shirt seeing a few teens walking this way, looking at us curiously.

Calm omega. Our mates won't allow harm to come to us. Especially not on their pack lands.

The door swung open revealing a smiling Conner. I could hear running footsteps coming from inside the house, Carver's scent getting closer, making me giggle.

Tyler smiled at Conner happily, sticking his tongue out cutely, reaching slowly to press the doorbell again with Conner playfully glaring at him.

Tyler pressed it like five times before Conner tackled him, both yelling and tumbling on the ground, Tyler laughing happily, squishing Conner's cheeks together.

"Kai!" Carver yelled happily, promptly grabbing me, swinging me around in a circle.

"Carver!" I laughed, burying my head into his muscled neck, his scent intoxicating and making my tummy warm. My shaking slowly stopped now that my puppy was with me.

Carver pulled back smiling, seeing his eyes gaze into mine, or more of at my make up. I blushed suddenly, looking down nervously, hoping he didn't think I was really ugly with it on.

Carver ducked his head suddenly, his lips on mine, making me squeak and blush, sighing into the kiss. I wrapped my arms around his neck, feeling him lift me off the ground.

Beautiful mate. The moon goddess made me the luckiest man ever Carver thought dreamily. His mate's eyes popped with just the little bit of light blue eyeliner. He was absolutely adorable and his little hands were peaking out of his sweater.

Too freaking adorable! Gah, my heart Carver thought to himself.

I broke the kiss, giggling, seeing Carver so happy. My wolf proud for making our mate like that.

I walked in front of him, stopping from seeing the video game Tyler had brought, picking it up before hearing a growl. I peeked over seeing Carver staring at my butt, drooling. I giggled at that, shaking my butt a little trying to wipe off the "dirt" that was on the cover.

I stood up slowly, gazing back at Carver who was panting a little, my heart beating in my chest in excitement. Carver practically pounced on me, groping my butt, making me squeal and bite my lip to stop the moan from leaving me. I was half heartedly struggling out of Carver's hold before hearing Robin and Raven talking sweetly with each other.

"Sorry I'm late darling," Raven had hugged Robin quickly, kissing him softly, Robin smiling happily.

"Thank you for inviting us," Robin spoke politely, Raven kissing him hotly, Robin moaning into the kiss.

"Let's get in the house. Daddy said supper was ready," Carver whispered huskily in my ear. I giggled at that, feeling my cheeks warm since Carver hadn't stopped groping me.

I slapped his hands seeing him pout at me, making me get on my tip toes to kiss him softly. I slid my hand into his larger one, Carver interlacing his fingers with mine; the softest smile on his lips making my heart nearly hurt for making him happy with such a small notion.

Carver grumbled suddenly, grabbing Conner by his collar to stop the rough housing he was doing with his mate while holding my hand with his other.

Tyler laughed once Carver let Conner go when they were all in the house.

"My parents are going to love you," Carver whispered as I nodded shyly, frowning with worry. We were led down a hallway with beautiful wooden floors before seeing a huge living room with a cream colored carpet. There were coffee colored couches and matching chairs, some facing a huge flat screen TV while some were around a fireplace.

I could smell an array of yummy food, my tummy grumbling loudly. I flushed brightly, looking down, feeling Carver squeeze my hand gently. My big puppy was so gentle with me.

"If you start speaking whale again I might have to too," Carver laughed with everyone making me stick my tongue out at him.

"They'll love you," Carver whispered, kissing the side of my head.

I could feel Tyler and Robin's apprehension as well. We needed to act very human tonight and we had to be careful around the pack leader.

A large man suddenly walked into the living room, head held high and had this air about him that spoke of dominance; he looked very much like Amilya it was almost uncanny. I blinked rapidly a few times, since his scent was kind of similar to Amilya's too. Well the part where she smelled like mint sometimes.

I gulped, seeing him stare at me, making me hunch and hide a little behind Carver. I looked down at my shoes, hearing a few soft growls.

Papa be nice! Carver spoke sternly, his Papa pouting and crossing his arms.

I was just playing Papa grumbled, Carver rolling his eyes. Conner was nosing Tyler's hair, wanting his mate to look up too. Raven was whispering in Robin's ear, also wanting him to look up.

Why did you have to be so scary alpha? Robin stuck out his tongue, Papa growling, harrumphing.

Your Papa is sexy when he's like that Daddy came out of the kitchen before frowning at our mates looking at the ground; all of us frowning too.

Does he remind you of alpha? His presence is kind of suffocating I asked Tyler and Robin, trying to control my breathing. I held Carver's hand like it was my lifeline.

Yeah, like a lot.

Yup

I suddenly heard a smack, my head snapping up in fear before getting confused.

"You scared our guests!"

"Ow beautiful! I didn't do anything!" The large man pouted rubbing his arm, which made me giggle. He pouted like Carver.

"AWE! Look at them!" The blonde haired man with blue eyes shouted happily; the same blonde hair as Conner and blue eyes like Carver. His eyes looked so very nice and twinkled with happiness. He... kind of smelled like an omega, my body calming down a little at that.

"I'm Carver and Conner's daddy, Adam! That's my cuddly bear of a husband Chris!"

"Adam!" Chris shouted with pink cheeks, slapping his hand over his eyes. I giggled happily at that, Tyler and Robin relaxing and looking up again. Robin looked like he was analyzing the two, Tyler's nose wiggling at the array of scents since his nose was better than mine and Robin's noses put together.

"I've been dying to meet you all and Conner and Raven and Carver have been gushing about you guys so much which is so adorable-"

"Dad!" Conner and Carver yelling with pink cheeks, Raven spluttering trying to look anywhere but at his mate who was laughing softly at that.

"I hope you all aren't allergic to anything because I made a ton of stuff and others will be joining us if that's okay so you can meet everyone and I made some pies since I didn't know what you guys would like and I think -"

Luna's mouth was covered by the Alpha's hand, stopping the words from coming out of his mouth.

"Sorry, he gets super excited with guests," Chris said, playfully glaring at his mate who slumped. Chris gently released his mouth, lifting his brow.

"Nice to meet you Mr. Adam," I whispered, rubbing my hands nervously which didn't work out too well since my sleeves nearly covered my hands. Might as well break the ice.

"AWE! SO CUUUTTTEEE!" Adam squealed, running over before anyone could stop him, tugging Tyler and Robin into his arms with me squished in the middle. He was nearly swinging us around gushing everywhere.

"I could just eat them up! NOM NOM NOM!" Adam giggled. I felt so relaxed in his arms. He definitely acted like a Luna from the way Amilya described her own daddy; who she thought was the perfect type of Luna for a pack.

"Daddy!" Carver yelled, tugging me into his chest while Conner and Raven saved their mates.

"Awe..." Luna pouted, getting kissed softly by his mate.

"Well let's introduce you guys."

We were tugged into the kitchen, our mouths hanging down in shock.

There was so much food I think me, Robin and Tyler thought we were going to die.

"You'll catch flies babe," Conner laughed, tugging Tyler to sit next to him. I was sitting next to Carver who was sitting next to his father who was at the head of the table. Yup, definitely Alpha of the pack.

Robin and Raven were sitting across from us, Tyler and Conner sitting next to them.

Bowls of food were passed around the table, our mates placing food onto our plates for us. There was macaroni and cheese, salad, potato salad, pasta salad, mashed potatoes, gravy, sliced turkey and roasted chicken, green beans, broccoli, a tuna casserole. I had only read about half of the stuff in some cooking magazines, my mouth watering hungrily.

I was getting really dizzy from the amount of food on the table looking to see Robin and Tyler with giant round eyes like they didn't know what to do with the food either.

Chris looked at Adam who nodded, Chris kissing Adam softly, smiling. Their love was too sweet. I hoped with all my heart Carver and I would be like that some day. Although we kind of were!

"You may eat," Chris nodded, several pack members digging in, including our mates.

"So this is John, you've probably seen him at school," Carver said and he was one of the guys on the football team.

"Nice to meet you," John smiled as I nodded at him, Carver looking like he'd bite John's hand off if he offered it. I rolled my eyes, slapping Carver's chest, before shaking John's hand who smiled happily at me, going off about football. I tried following along but eventually left Carver and John to fight over state teams or something. I saw Luna Adam nodding approvingly, making me blush. Mandy started talking to me from across the table, making me relax since she was so nice. Her girlfriend was with her parents today.

Robin was talking to a few other people that were near him, Robin smiling gently when they were talking about a dare of some sort they would have loved to have seen; Raven was rolling his eyes.

Tyler looked like he was trying to be recruited by several of the other betas at the table, Conner laughing and nodding; though it looked like he didn't really want Tyler to join in case he'd get hurt.

Dominants. I tried not to roll my eyes since Tyler has taken down plenty of rogues.

We were also introduced to a few girls who looked to be omegas and a couple of big betas I hadn't seen at the school. I think they were some warriors for the pack grounds. The atmosphere was wonderful and happy and my wolf was calm; which didn't happen as often as I would have liked.

"Is something wrong dears?" Adam asked softly with worry, looking at our untouched plates. My head snapped down to the mound of food on my plate. I didn't even realize when Carver piled food onto my plate! It looked mouthwatering and delicious and I was so hungry.

"It looks very good Mr. Summers," Robin nodded politely, staring at his plate. His one eye was just as round and big as mine were at the moment I was sure.

Tyler was just staring at his plate not sure where to start or if he was allowed to touch it. His face pretty much saying 'this is mine? All this food is really mine?'

"Ty, you okay?" Conner asked softly, Tyler trying to blink away his shock.

"Yeah!" Tyler cleared his throat, "never seen this much food in my life," Tyler's voice cracked slightly, everyone looking concerned. I shivered a little, the room suddenly quiet.

I didn't blame Tyler. He had been starving in the forest when we found him. Amilya can't buy much food since we have to pay for electricity, water and gas and stuff. It was more food then we ever had when Amilya took care of us and this was just overwhelming.

"What do you mean?" Conner asked a little angrily, before Robin elbowed Tyler in the side.

"Oh uh, just hungry!" Tyler laughed awkwardly. Everyone looked at each other warily. If they weren't sure on believing that, I was pretty sure they knew we were lying now.

"You may eat," Chris said softly, almost sternly. I felt like that was more of a go ahead than earler before tucking into the macaroni and cheese. I could feel my eyes sting with impending tears at how good it was, never eating like this before. It was gooey and cheesey and so yummy!

I didn't realize I was hunched over my plate, so scared it'd be taken away from me; Tyler and Robin looking exactly the same, eating really fast. I didn't want the food taken away. What if they were done and wouldn't let us have any? Or maybe since we didn't eat right away they'd take it away cause Luna didn't think we liked it? What if we offended them by not eating with everyone else!?

I suddenly choked on some chicken feeling Carver's large hand hitting my back.

"Baby slow down!" Carver said softly, making me freeze and look around at the people at the table looking at us in shock. My plate was half empty and I just knew my eyes were red from both choking and impending tears of joy. I moved slowly away from my plate so I wasn't guarding it like I'd never see it again.

Tyler seemed to notice too, looking around awkwardly, trying to sit up straight. It looked like it was harder for him to do that, his shoulders still hunched over, gripping the table with his other hand. Robin whined softly, sitting straight immediately, eyeing his mashed potatoes hungrily.

All three if us didn't move, just looking at our plates, waiting for them to be taken away. I was shaking and I knew I was about to start sobbing. I was still so hungry.

Hush omega, it's alright Robin whispered through our link. I could feel Tyler calming down too, knowing he was just as high strung right now.

"You can still... Eat?" Alpha Chris spoke with confusion making me feel a little bad, since we were kind of obvious.

I calmly ate the mashed potatoes with some chicken, everyone glancing at us while they continued to eat. The atmosphere felt kind of awkward now, Carver seeming really tense.

What the fuck was that!? Conner yelled in the pack link

I don't know and I for sure don't like it! Carver snarled

It's like they've never had food like this Daddy whispered, sounding like he was close to tears.

Calm down. All of you. We'll just take this a step at a time Papa sighed sadly, the pack members whining sadly through the link. To have their future Luna and their new friends act this way around food was heart breaking.

"So where did you all move from?" Adam spoke softly, his voice shaking a little from sadness.

Okay guys, human answers! Robin spoke sternly.

"We were in Canada," Tyler nodded, happily eating a buttered roll, hunching a little like he was guarding it from being stolen right out of his mouth,

Conner looking at him with worry. Conner rubbed his hand on Tyler's thigh, Tyler relaxing a little.

"Oh, well I hear they have very cold weather up there," Luna nodded, looking at me with worry, when I glanced immediately down at my plate. I didn't want to see the motherly worry in his eyes that I've seen in Amilya's eyes when she wants me to tell her everything while needing to hug me.

"We have lots of sweaters," I whispered, Carver holding my hand under the table. His hand was warm and tight around mine.

"You look cute in sweaters," Carver smiled making me smile a little in return.

"We've traveled a lot, but we're hoping we won't have to leave," Robin said softly, Raven stiffening up significantly along with Conner and Carver.

"You'd leave?" Carver whispered, sounding angry and sad. My heart scrunched with the evident pain in our mate's voice.

"Well Big Sis-" I stopped seeing Robin glare, eyes glancing between us, "I-I mean I don't think we will. We really like it here and um... well you wouldn't be wherever we'd move to so, I wouldn't want to leave."

Carver gave a half lifted smile, kissing me on the cheek.

"How do you like school?" Daddy tried again which calmed down the conversation for the rest of dinner.

"What's that?" I pointed to a dish which was almost finished anyway.

"That's tuna casserole," Daddy smiled, Chris eating it happily next to him.

"What's casserole?" I asked, everyone just looking at me. Robin looked like he wanted to smack his forehead. Oops... I guess I'm being too suspicious.

"You've... never had a casserole before?"

I shook my head 'no' wondering why everyone was looking sadly at me.

"Is it good?"

"It's a pan dish that you cook food in and serve food out of," Luna whispered.

"Here babe, try some," Carver put a chunk on my plate as I dug in. My tummy was already near bursting, never eating so much in my life.

"You make the best food ever Mr. Summers," Tyler smiled happily.

"Oh you!" Adam giggled, blushing. Although I could almost see his hands wringing in his lap.

I rubbed my stuffed belly, seeing Carver looking lustfully and longingly at me when I did that. I blushed at the thought of me bearing his pups, my wolf going absolutely giddy with the idea.

"I brought a game if you'd like to play with me," Tyler said nervously, Conner nodding, dragging Tyler from his seat.

"I'll bring the dessert out a little later!" Luna Adam called as we were dragged out of the kitchen to the living room.

Conner and Tyler went straight to the game console, Robin and Raven going to play chess by the fireplace.

"Why don't I show you around love?" Carver asked softly. I nodded at that, his voice sounding off.

No One's POV

Carver was pissed off. His darling little mate looked so hungry and as though he were about to burst into tears. Tyler and Robin didn't look much better, their mates growing angry and worried with the rest of the pack members that joined them.

Carver showed Kai the kitchen, Adam refusing Kai's request to help him clean up dinner. The other girls were helping him already, Kai assuming they were omegas too. Kai was relieved that his mate's pack seemed to treat omegas nicely.

"And this is my room."

Kai giggled, looking everywhere, Carver watching him happily. Kai felt the wood the dresser and night stand were made out of, looking through Carver's bookcase and even going in the bathroom. Kai hopped onto the bed, never feeling something so soft beneath his fingertips.

Kai patted the area next to him Carver's cheeks warming in a blush before smirking, sitting next to his sexy little mate.

"I like your house Carver. It's very pretty," Kai smiled, Carver beaming at him

"Thanks! A lot of people work hard to keep it clean so I'll let them know you like it. They'll love hearing that."

"So how many people live here?"

"About 40 families or so. Maybe 600 people in the entire state, but not all of them are apart of out pack."

"6-600! Wow!" Kai gaped, Carver moving them so they were lying down, facing each other.

Kai snuggled into Carver's chest, Kai feeling his wolf go into a ball whimpering.

I know you want to see his wolf, but we will soon! Alpha promised that she'd give us an answer tomorrow Kai's wolf nodded at that, huffing (more like pouting).

"I don't want you to leave. You can't leave!" Carver said suddenly, looking angry. Kai whimpered, shaking a little. Carver held Kai tightly against him.

"I don't either. I want to stay with you," Kai whispered, Carver's eyes calming down as he relaxed his hold around his little mate.

"I can't lose you Kai," Carver whispered, Kai's eyes getting big, tears slipping down his cheeks. To have someone so desperate for him to stay, made Kai feel more wanted than he has felt in a long time.

"Oh baby," Carver sighed, wiping Kai's tears away. Kai grabbed his hand, holding it against his cheek.

Kai leaned forward, placing a small chaste kiss to Carver's lips, Carver sighing out. It was one of the boldest things Kai's done and he was super happy with the reaction he got.

Carver growled before Kai's lips were attacked, rolling onto his back with Carver over him.

Kai gasped when Carver's hand made it's way up his sweater (not under) pinching his nipple. Carver slipped his tongue into Kai's mouth, tasting the sweetness of his mate. Kai moaned happily, his hands gliding down Carver's back, going giddy at the flexing muscles beneath his hands.

"You're beautiful," Carver whispered, breaking the kiss, Kai panting beneath him. Kai shook a little, knowing that if Carver actually concentrated, Carver would feel the scars on his body.

"Carver," Kai whispered, rubbing his hand on his god-like mate's corded chest.

"Hm?" Carver hummed, leaving a trail of kisses down Kai's neck, licking and nibbling where the mating mark would go.

"I love you too," Kai whispered, Carver's head snapping up. Carver's face split happily, Kai relaxing, running his nose along Carver's neck. Kai's chin was suddenly tugged to look at Carver whose eyes spoke volumes with how he felt. Kai felt his heart skip a beat.

Carver's wolf was clawing at him to take his mate and to take him now!

We can't just do that right now. Our baby isn't ready Carver spoke sternly making his wolf whine. The large black wolf huffed, promptly turning his back from Carver, pouting.

Kai's wolf was just as equally clawing, wanting to run with it's mate, to cuddle in his fur, and to definitely bend over for them.

We can't. Not till Alpha gives us the okay. Of course that doesn't mean making out is out of the question Kai thought with a blush, leaning up to kiss Carver happily again. Carver was happy to reply groaning with little growls, completely devouring Kai's mouth who was whimpering happily. Kai's hands wove into Carver's black hair, his legs unconsciously spreading wider for his mate. Carver gave a low moan at that, laying more fully on top of Kai.

Carver's hand moved to explore Kai's body, about to slip under Kai's sweater, Kai breaking away quickly, afraid Carver would find the scars.

I'll be too ugly and he won't want me anymore Kai nearly panicked.

"It's alright baby, I won't go farther than touching," Carver whispered, smirking at the red tint on Kai's cheeks. That definitely wasn't the problem.

"Come down stairs love birds!" Adam yelled through the door, Carver groaning making Kai giggle. Saved by the Luna!

Carver promptly picked up Kai who was laughing happily, before they made it back to the living room. Carver was spinning him down the hallways, humming softly. Kai didn't think he was more in love than in that moment.

"Would you two put that down and get some dessert," Adam had his hands on his hips, looking adorable, Conner pausing the game he and his mate were playing. Conner grabbed Tyler from behind, lifting him up making Tyler yell happily, playfully trying to get out of his mate's hold.

All of them eventually made it to the table. Adam had to drag Raven from the chess board since Robin was smirking happily at a move he just played. The table was laden with small puff pastries, a few miniature breads, two apple pies and a custard tart.

"Open baby," Carver chuckled, feeding Kai like he was a cute baby bird. Carver grabbed one of everything, wanting to feed his tiny mate. Having the desire to make Kai round like he was pregnant -needy dominant were-wolves. Kai giggled, licking his lips happily. Carver was just too tempted, kissing Kai almost after each bite.

Conner wasn't much better, Tyler swiping his nose of the whipped cream Conner just put on it. Tyler sucked his finger, moaning softly, giggling when Conner growled happily at him. Raven and Robin were sharing a piece, playfully stealing the other's piece with something resembling a fork war with food.

Everyone suddenly heard a shutter sound, looking to see Adam gushing from taking their picture.

"You all are just so cute!" Adam giggled, Chris holding him around the waist.

Dessert finished quickly all of them heading back to the living room. Kai went towards the fireplace where there were a bunch of photos.

Carver was trying to steer Kai away from his baby photos since some of them were embarrassing. Adam would just drag Kai back, who was laughing at a few of the stories; Carver and Conner were getting more red faced with each picture.

"I'd like to meet your parents too," Robin whispered to Raven who smiled gently with a nod, kissing Robin softly.

"No baby photos!" Raven suddenly deadpanned, Robin stifling a laugh.

"You really think you can stop your parents?"

Raven scowled, crossing his arms, pouting away from his mate. Robin bit his lip to stop an impending smile, Raven cocking his head at him curiously. Why did Robin always try to be quiet when he looked like he wanted to laugh and smile just as much as his brothers?

Robin looked away quickly knowing his mate had the cogs turning in his head about something; having a deep suspicion it was about him.

"Whose that Carver?" Kai asked sweetly, pointing to a picture of a little girl on the wall since he was looking at all the photographs.

Carver froze instantly along with everyone else, awkwardly quiet.

"That's our baby sister. She was taken from us," Carver whispered sadly, Conner looking down upset.

Kai whimpered, hugging Carver as tightly as he could even though Carver was much bigger than him. Curse his short arms!

"I bet you were the best big brothers in the whole wide world," Kai whispered, Carver choking on a sob along with Conner, Tyler rubbing his mate's back.

The girl looked so familiar. Like Kai, Tyler and Robin had seen her before somewhere.

"Let's not talk about it now. You look tired beautiful," Carver whispered, moving some hair behind Kai's ear.

"Okay Carver. I'm sorry for bringing it up," Kai spoke sadly before yawning cutely. Carver awed at that, pulling Kai into his chest. Kai saw Adam quickly leave the room, eyes looking glassy, Chris smiling sadly at them before taking off after his mate.

Carver moved to lying on the couch with Kai on top of him since Kai yawned sleepily again, looking very much like a kitten. Kai rubbed his head into Carver's chest, loving that his scent was mixing with Carver's, Carver growling in approval, rubbing his hands up and down Kai's back. Kai was praying to the moon goddess that Carver couldn't feel his scars.

Conner and Tyler were playing their video game, Raven and Robin continuing their game of chess.

It soon became a few hours, midnight in fact, Carver passed out and holding Kai tightly, cupping his bubble butt with his hands possessively in his sleep. Kai just snuggled deeper into his mate, little snores leaving him.

"How could you miss that guy babe?" Conner whispered playfully since the other two were sleeping on the couch. His eyes softened, seeing his mate asleep on his controller.

"Goddess you're so cute," Conner whispered, pausing the game and turning off the TV, moving the controller gently away from Tyler's face carefully. Conner scooted over so he was laying next to his mate on the floor, wrapping an arm around his waist, snuggling into Tyler, laying half on top of him; he fell asleep almost instantly.

Robin was laying on his side, Raven behind him, holding him to his chest, the two spooning on the floor. The chess board pieces looking fairly even in number.

"Awe. Look at our babies," Adam whispered, Chris chuckling softly.

"I'm so glad our boys found their mates," Adam snuggled into Chris' chest, before saddening.

"I wish Leon could find..." Adam whispered, tears leaving him, Chris hushing him softly.

"He traveled around the world babe. There isn't much else he can do," Chris spoke sadly, Daddy snuggling into his mate's chest.

"Let's go to bed Luna," Chris mumbled against Adam's lips, kissing him softly.

"Yes Alpha," Adam sniffled cutely, the two quietly leaving their babies in the living room, dimming the lights.

--------------------------(*o*)--

Kai didn't know what woke him up, opening his eyes sleepily, seeing that it was two in the morning. Kai froze immediately, Carver tightening his hold around his mate unconsciously. Well squeezing his butt actually, Kai blushing red at that.

"A-Alpha," Kai whimpered, seeing Amilya outside from the couch, gulping.

None of you call and you just expect me to assume you are alright!? Amilya yelled, Tyler snorting awake, Robin blinking quickly on the floor before they realized what was going on.

I asked you to do one thing! To call me at ten to make sure you were alright! That's all I wanted! Amilya's voice was sad and it made their hearts ache.

Do you know this place Alpha? Robin asked out of no where.

What does that have to do with anything? And I'm not sure. My head hurts trying to remember

Robin frowned at that, Kai and Tyler wondering why he would ask such a thing.

Come home, now

Kai whimpered along with the others, Amilya rarely using her alpha voice on them. She was definitely mad. Kai wiggled out of Carver's hold, trying to hold in a giggle since Carver was pouting in his sleep.

Tyler kissed Conner on the lips a few times, holding in a giggle from Conner smiling in his sleep. Robin ran his nose along Raven's neck, smiling softly at Raven grumbling and grabby hands.

The three quietly made it out of the pack house, walking with their heads down behind their Alpha, headed back to their townhouse. Kai had grabbed a plate of food that was piled high with food, Adam insisting that they take food home tomorrow. Since they were going home now, Kai thought it best to grab the food right then.

It was quiet and awkward and none of them had intended to make Amilya mad. The one person who saved them and sacrificed everything for them to be safe. They felt horrible.

Did you all eat?

Yes Alpha all of them said in sync.

It was so much food I thought I'd pass out Tyler tried getting a sense of humor in before we felt a wave of guilt and sadness from their Alpha, their wolves whining. They saw Amilya eye the plate of food in Kai's hands, their hearts sinking further into their stomachs.

They all made it into the house, standing in the living room with worry. Kai quickly put the food into the fridge, getting an approving nod from Amilya who looked to have simmered down some.

"Well its Saturday, even though its 2 in the morning," Amilya spoke softly, her hood still up along with her mask which she didn't usually do when she was with them.

"You all may stay here," Amilya spoke softly, all of them growing excited. Kai and Robin hopping around holding hands, Tyler smiling happily.

"Thank you Alpha!" Tyler hugged her, saddening when she didn't hug back.

"A-Are we in trouble?" Kai whispered, all of them looking worried at that.

"No. But things will be different now."

All of them cocked their heads in confusion.

"Well... once your mates reveal that they're werewolves and you do the same, you'll be accepted into the pack."

"Alpha," Robin spoke with worry, Kai shaking, and Tyler looking just plain confused.

"It's alright. I've come to terms with it. All of you will be safe with your mates and taken care of much better than I ever took care of you."

"A-Alpha," Kai sobbed, hugging Amilya tightly. Him and Tyler both holding their alpha tightly.

"Y-You took care of us! Saved us!"

"You worked so hard so we could live with a roof over our heads and have food to eat."

"You were kind to us and didn't treat us like we were inferior."

Kai sobbed unhappily, afraid Amilya would disappear from his hands.

"It was never enough... not enough food to fill your bellies. Not enough to make you feel safe," Amilya sniffing hard, holding back tears.

"Bullshit!" Tyler yelled, scaring Kai and Robin.

"You gave us more than anyone did when we were all alone. You did your best and we love you for everything you've done. You're kind and beautiful and protect us with all your heart. So don't you god damn say that it wasn't enough because it was more than enough"

Tyler rubbed at his eyes furiously, trying to stop impending tears.

"You will always be our Alpha, no matter what. You taught us things we never knew and helped us feel that being a submissive didn't mean we were useless," Robin spoke softly, hugging Amilya too. All of them cuddled in her arms since she was a couple inches taller than them.

"I thought it would be best if I left. There would be no reason for them to accept me into a pack."

"You can't leave!" Tyler gasped.

"I-I won't let you!" Kai gasped, clawing his hands into Amilya's jacket.

"Your a great fighter and you are very kind."

"If they don't accept all of us then we won't be apart of their pack," Robin said sternly, the others nodding.

"We can always mate with them, but we don't have to be apart of their pack."

"You will be stronger with a larger pack " Amilya whispered, getting one of her hands free to comb each of their hairs with her fingers.

"But if it doesn't have you then we don't care at all."

Amilya let her tears fall, hugging and kissing them all on the head.

"Please don't leave. Please Please," Kai begged, crying.

"Hush pup. I won't decide anything now. But I don't wish to keep any of you from your mates any longer. It is safe here except for the occasional rogue siting."

A memory suddenly hit Amilya full force.

PAPA! Amilya remembering when she was a little girl, suddenly screaming for her Papa.

Amilya clutched her head, Kai gasping, eyes turning blue to help her headache.

"Amilya. Are you sure you don't remember anything about this place?" Robin whispered, sniffling.

"I keep getting flashes of my old memories. I don't know why. Years of fighting as a Starter probably gave me brain damage," Amilya giggled, the others whimpering at her.

"Why don't we go to bed?" Amilya sighed before Kai grabbed her hand, Amilya smiling. All four slept together on the floor with a few blankets and pillows, ending up in their usual doggy pile.

Kai's head popped out from under the blanket, his new phone buzzing like crazy.

"Hello?" Kai yawned sleepily before pulling the phone away from his ear.

"Where the hell are you!?" Carver yelled, Kai whimpering.

"Are the others there, do you hear them?" Kai heard Raven and Conner yell through the phone.

"Why did you leave? Where did you go? Are you alright?"

Kai was whimpering and shaking, Carver unconsciously using his alpha voice.

"Why the hell are you calling in the middle of my beauty sleep," Tyler grumbled, yawning. His green eyes the only thing visible under the sheets.

"Ty, we freaked out not seeing you guys! We thought something horrible happened to you!"

"Turtledove, I want tea," Robin sleepily blinked open an eye before Conner burst out laughing on the other end of the phone, Raven spluttering and turning red in front of his friends.

"Are they safe?" Daddy came in, being heard through the phone.

"Where are you guys?" Carver rolled his eyes at his Daddy before his Papa grabbed his shoulder to get his son to calm down a little.

"Big Sis wanted us home so," Kai whispered, shaking, hearing Carver whimper.

"I didn't mean to scare you baby," Carver mumbled, Kai sniffling.

"Your sister came and got you?" Chris came in through the phone shock in his voice.

"Why didn't we sense her?" Daddy mouthed to Chris in worry who became worried at that too. The border patrol would have caught her. So why didn't they?

"Yes. We forgot to call when we arrived at your house so she was a bit upset," Robin said sadly.

"What do you mean upset?" Raven asked stiffly using his gamma voice.

"W-We just had to stay home. That's all," Robin whimpered a little.

Breakfast guys Amilya spoke through the link.

"We have to go," Tyler spoke quickly, hungry.

"U-Um," Robin murmured, giving a quiet bye leaving Kai alone with the phone.

"Baby?" Carver asked softly.

"You're a grump in the mornings," Kai pouted hearing snickers on the line and a grumble.

"I'm not talking to a mean grump!" Kai huffed, hanging up, hearing Carver start to say something.

Don't worry, I'm just teasing him Kai giggled to his wolf who whimpered at hanging up on their mate, before barking happily, wagging his tail.

"Thanks for breakfast Mils," Tyler smiled, eating his over easy eggs and toast. Kai and Robin nodding as well, Robin boiling water for his tea.

"Turtledove," Tyler snickered suddenly, Robin going bright red, nearly spewing out his tea.

"That was just so cute," Tyler laughed with Kai and Amilya giggling.

"Jerk," Robin frowned, crossing his arms.

"I need to go to the store and get a few things," Amilya cleaned her hands before Kai grabbed her sleeve, whimpering. Tyler and Robin lookedvto stand up to as if to stop her, their conversation from last night coming to the forefront of their minds.

"I'll be back soon pups, promise. Don't go in the forest," Amilya wagging her finger at them.

All of them went to the living room to finish some homework before loud knocking was at the door.

"Stay," Tyler ordered, giggling when he realized who was on the other side.

"I don't know if Kai wants to see you," Tyler tried schooling a serious face, snickering at the worried look on Carver's face. Tyler put his hand against the door frame as if to block Carver from getting into the townhouse.

Carver looked down, clearing his throat, shuffling his hair; Tyler was holding back a laugh seeing Conner and Raven coming over, looking apologetic too.

"Carver!" Kai giggled, running under Tyler's arm and hugging Carver happily who was shocked for a second (considering he thought he was in trouble).

"Kai!" Tyler pouted, crossing his arms "it builds character if our boyfriends think they're in trouble"

"But puppy didn't mean it," Kai whispered, pressing his nose against Carver's who smiled sapily at his mate, practically purring.

"You're a little too devious babe," Conner grumbled, holding Tyler in a loose hug. Tyler saw Carver stick his tongue out a him, Tyler making a face at him back. Carver gasped playfully at that, Raven chuckling before walking into the townhome to find his mate.

Conner happily kissed Tyler (who was in the middle of a literal staring contest with Carver) before Conner twirled him around. Kai was trying to wriggle his way out of Carver's hold who was unconsciously holding him tightly to his body.

"Hello love," Raven smiled, smacking his lips against Robin who sighed out, being lifted easily from his sitting position on the floor.

"Morning Turtledove," Robin giggled, Raven having pink on his cheeks, softly kissing Robin again, hand sliding up his love's shirt. Robin moved Raven's hand from under his shirt, having his own fair amount of scars that he didn't like to show off either. Only Tyler and Amilya liked talking about wounds that got from fights.

"Behave," Robin mumbled against Raven's lips who chuckled.

"Never," Raven licked his way into Robin's mouth who moaned, knees going weak. Robin would have loved to feel his mate's hands on his body, but was still self conscious, both loving and hating that his mate's hands were only holding his hips at the moment.

"What are you guys doing here?" Kai asked softly, the pairs walking into the living room where Raven was practically shoving his tongue down Robin's throat happily.

"I felt bad raising my voice at you," Carver whispered, pouting, Kai giggling, kissing the adorable grown man's pout away.

"Let's go to lunch," Conner said happily, grabbing Tyler's hand and dragging him to the black SUV.

None of the submissives complained in the slightest to being dragged around town; which was still new to them. The three pairs got into the SUV, Kai in Carver's lap sharing sweet kisses.

Wooh. Kind of a long chapter there... oh well :D

You're What!?

One Week Later

Every time any of them get close to revealing their secret, they inevitably chickened out. No one wanted to lose their mate.

Kai's POV

I wanted to mate badly to Carver. Even without my heat I would trickle slick sometimes with need. That was embarrassing and I wanted to cry when it happened.

Robin had made a plan for us to reveal ourselves and today was the day. It was Friday and I was going to tell my Puppy. I wanted to. Needed to. I love him.

I was excited and scared all at the same time, my wolf cleaning himself all day wanting to look beautiful for our mate.

I walked to the field, knowing Carver and the others were there, practicing drills for football practice. I've been to a few of his football games and he is amazing! Sometimes I forget which number he is and I get scared when he gets hit hard by the other team. It doesn't seem to faze him though which makes me happy.

I saw Robin in the stands, doing some homework, Tyler on the field talking and jumping with the cheerleaders. I giggled at that, Tyler looking like he should be a football player but acted like a cheerleader.

I saw Conner looking at him with a sappy look, my heart happy that our mates were so kind. Conner especially seemed hooked to Tyler which made me relax. If Tyler ever had depressing thoughts again I knew that Conner would be there for him every step of the way. Raven seemed to be talking to the coach, probably about offensive and defensive positions (at least that's what Carver tried explaining to me -I think I just stare at his lips most of the time). Robin was gazing at him dreamily from the stands which made me giggle. Robin was always proper so it made me happy to see him getting more relaxed in his surroundings.

I walked over to the cheerleaders, most of them my friends since Mandy and her girlfriend Leah introduced me to them. I couldn't believe I actually had friends! They were all so nice and a few of the betas I met through Carver were too. The cheerleaders gave me some makeup tips that I told Amilya about since I decide to wear some eyeliner every few days.

I saw Tiffany still on the team, ignoring everybody except for her two minions that were pushing up their boobs and making their skirts even shorter.

I walked passed the field, Carver directing his team to take down their friends who were the bad team... um... not sure what that's called again. Anyway, I love the determined look in his eyes the most. He looks like he could do anything and I believe that with all my heart.

Tiffany suddenly smirked at me making me gulp in nervousness, my omega self wanting to run away. I breathed in deeply, trying to ignore her. I don't like confrontation if I can help it, but if she ever tries hurting me or the people I love then she will go down!

Tiffany suddenly ran across the field, doing cartwheels and some jumping with a couple of tuck rolls, landing with a smirk on her face. She was still in the splits, making a kissy face at Carver, pulling down her shirt, her nipple was starting to peak out. I growled low, but smirked when Carver and several of his friends had their noses wrinkled in disgust. Carver looked especially angry at her which made the jealously I had easier to extinguish.

"You'd think she wouldn't be flexible anymore since no one wants to fuck her," I overhead one of the jocks say.

My wolf was raring to show her up, though I didn't want to embarrass myself. I couldn't let her keep thinking she could flirt with my boyfriend. I wasn't a doormat and I somehow wanted to prove that I was worth more than she ever would be for Carver.

Cheerleading I thought suddenly. She was good at cheerleading. What if... I could show that I was just as good as her?

Then she wouldn't think she's such hot shit Tyler grumbled through the link.

Ty! Stay out of my brain! I blushed suddenly, Tiffany trying to get up from the ground in the most slutty way possible.

You were talking in the mind link Kai and I think that's a rather good idea. Show them that future Luna Kai likes a challenge Robin spoke with encouragement, making me excited. He was right!

Go ahead. I've seen you do flips in wolf form. Your mate will probably get a hard on Tyler chuckled waving at me.

I took in deep breaths, keeping my eyes off of Carver knowing he'd make me more nervous.

Ready I told my wolf who was snarling at Tiffany, shaking out his fur. I was not going to have Carver fight all my battles and this was my battle!

I looked at Tyler, seeing Robin nod at me. I breathed in deeply, hearing Tiffany cackle like a witch next to her friends, saying very mean things about me and what she was going to do with Carver once he gave up. I took off in a sprint because that made me really mad! (I don't know cheerleading stunts so please forgive me ><)

I jumped in the air doing a tucked roll, into a cartwheel, jumping into air splits, doing a forward roll when I landed, moving into the splits. I put my forearms on the ground, using my arm strength alone to lift my body up, keeping my legs in the splits while in a handstand, closing my legs and pushing off my hands to spin in the air, to stand straight. I went into an immediate back bend, slowly lifting my legs to scissor kick far enough to be in the American splits each time (my arms the only things holding me up). I leaped again, cartwheeling and doing a back flip, bowing to the cheerleaders who were screaming my name.

Your were awesome! Tyler screamed in my head, seeing Robin clapping happily.

I looked to the football players who took off their helmets, their mouths dropped down in shock. Carver looked like he wanted to eat me alive and there was drool down his chin. The other guys looked at me funny before Carver snapped at them, baring his teeth, making them run away from him.

I giggled at Carver whose head snapped to me, licking his lips. I waved at him, smiling when I passed by Tiffany and her friends who looked at me in shock.That's right! Weak little omega can do something!

"Oh my god I thought Carver was going to jump your bones," Tyler laughed hysterically before the cheerleaders ran up to me.

"You were amazing!"

"How did you do that?"

"You're so flexible!"

"I'm jealous!"

"Th-Thank you very much," I smiled, the girls complimenting me, showing me some of their moves.

"Okay ya' girls, practice is over," The coach yelled who was Mike the gym coach too.

Carver practically came running over to me making me giggle.

He smelled musky and of sweat. I fluttered my eyes closed when he kissed me hotly. I could feel slick leaving me, Carver's tongue gliding down my throat.

"Puppy stinks," I mumbled, Carver pouting at me, my nose wrinkling.

"You could give me a bath," Carver mumbled against my lips, I could feel my cheeks warm at the comment.

"You think I'll get wet for you Carver?" I whispered, shocked at my bold statement (double entendre insinuated) and for the fact that I was leaking slick at the moment. Carver panted heavily, eyes getting darker by the second.

"I'll make you wet for me " Carver's voice was low and husky, a shiver running down my spine making me whine, biting my lip. It was his alpha voice when his wolf partially took over. I gasped when he bit my lip in surprise and I swear I turned bright red, feeling something dribble down my thigh.

"Carver showers!" The couch yelled, Carver growling not looking away from me, grabbing my innocent little butt hard.

"Sis wants us home," Tyler yelled grabbing my arm, Robin joining him, tugging me away from my mate. I whined at him, looking back for a second to see him being held back by three betas including his brother.

"Calm your fucking ass " Conner growled, Carver snarling trying to take deep breaths, slumping slightly.

"I need to tell him Co-Co, I can't handle this anymore " Carver whined, dragging a hand down his face, "thanks guys."

"No problem alpha. Your mate is one hell of a cutie though," The beta laughed. Carver would have snarled at him if the beta didn't already have his mate. A human girl by the name of Carrie who went to the school.

"I know Carver and don't call me Co-Co," Conner looked both angry and sad at the ground, Carver sighing, hugging his brother.

"Sorry bro. Only sis is aloud to call us by our nick names."

"Man, you do stink!" Conner waved his hand in front of his nose, not wanting to talk about their sister, Carver growling and pushing him.

"Just helping you out!" Conner laughed, Carver heading for the showers.

At the Pack house

"Sooo.... you're chicken," Daddy asked, pouring Papa some tea. Papa didn't drink coffee anymore since it reminded him of his baby girl too much.

"Not. Chicken," Conner grumbled who was trying on a new outfit that he was going to wear for the date he was finally going on, to tell Tyler he was a werewolf.

"Chicken," Daddy pretending to cough into his hand, Papa chuckling into his mug.

"It's not like Carver is any better!" Conner snapped out loudly hearing several pack members laughing.

"I can hear you dumbass! And at least I have a plan!" Carver yelled from the stairs.

"I have a plan!" Conner pouted, Carver messing with his hair once he came down the stairs, making Conner growl before tackling him; the two playfully rolling on the ground. Papa and Daddy were just watching them lovingly.

"Yeah well mine will actually work," Carver smirked, everyone waiting to hear what it was but Carver was just ignoring them, Conner scoffing at that.

"Oh yeah, sounds freaking spectacular," Conner whispered, Carver growling at him. Conner fixed his outfit after the tussle with Carver. Conner was dressed up nicely, styling his hair and wearing a nice white button down shirt with black pants and shiny black shoes.

"You look so handsome," Daddy gushed, hugging Conner who tried to escape from the crushing hold.

"Papa!" Conner reached out, Papa just waving at him from the couch, "traitor!"

Carver just watched Conner being manhandled by their Daddy who was swinging him around before dropping his ass onto the floor.

"My other handsome baby," daddy yelled happily, Carver running in circles in the living room, not wanting to be caught by his dad.

"You are no help Papa!" Carver yelled, his Papa laughing his ass off with Conner crawling to the coffee table, dizzy as Hell.

"You pour souls," Raven chuckled, sitting next to the pack Alpha.

"Raven!" Conner and Carver yelled out, Raven rolling his eyes.

"Guess I have to use the big guns," Raven smirked, Chris lifting his brow up at the boy.

"Luna! Alpha says he's lonely without you!"

"That's just diabolical Gamma Raven," Chris crossed his arms before they were stuffed with his lovely mate who snuggled into his neck.

"Why don't you just strip naked and do it," Papa asked, running his hand through daddy's hair who slapped Papa's chest hard, scowling.

"I didn't mean it that way!" Papa laughed, Daddy's cheeks flushing bright red.

Carver sighed, putting a glass of cold water against his forehead. Running in circles was not fun after eating a pie; Conner looking green at this point.

Twenty Minutes Earlier

"Why can't I!?" Kai nearly cried, Amilya glaring at him.

"It's too dangerous Kai! What if you're attacked? They'll think you're a rogue for one thing!"

"Just because you're scared doesn't mean I'm going to be!" Kai yelled, tears rolling down his cheeks, never raising his voice like that to his Alpha. Robin and Tyler were watching with gaped mouths at the two, never seeing them fight like this.

"I'm not scared Kai! I'm worried about your mate hurting you!"

"He won't ever hurt me!" Kai starting to sob, "He proved that when I was in my heat!"

"If you didn't shower with the scent blocking soap he would have raped you!"

"You don't know that and I trust Carver more than anything!" Kai's face was red at this point along with Amilya's; Amilya's mostly in frustration.

"You are not just going to waltz onto their land in your wolf form Kai! You'll get hurt!"

"I want to be with my mate and you said you'd never stop me!" Kai's wolf whimpering and huddling down, never showing disrespect to an Alpha like this.

"I don't want you to go about it this way! Follow Robin's plan!"

"Just because this place is bringing back memories doesn't make it okay for us to hide with you! It's been weeks and my wolf is going crazy, I can't stand it anymore! We have our own lives to live and I'm scared my mate will hate me for hiding this from him for so long! I'm not some weak omega that can't do anything without help!"

"I never said that," Amilya whispered, calming down. Kai shook his head, sobbing, running out the door when Amilya reached for him.

"KAI!" Was yelled by all three, Kai ignoring them and shifting into his wolf once he got into the woods.

Kai didn't know how long he ran or where he was for that matter. He lied down, his chest heaving for air.

What if Carver rejects us when he finds out we're a submissive Omega? Kai thought sadly, his wolf whining softly.

That was the first time I raised my voice... especially at an Alpha! Kai gasped at the realization. Guilt suddenly overtook him, realizing he didn't just yell at an Alpha. He yelled at his Big Sister and friend.

Kai sighed, deciding to figure out how to get out of the woods, wanting... needing to apologize. Kai mentally smiled though, thinking that he was able to have such confidence because of his mate. Carver let him choose things on his own, letting him figure things out on his own. Carver gladly helped him with anything, but Kai loved how much room Carver gave him when he needed it.

Kai suddenly walked into a clearing, smelling wolves. Some of them smelling like the betas in the football team Carver had introduced him to. That was good but it could also be bad.

We must be on Carver's pack grounds! Kai thought with excitement, also nervous, not wanting to be mistaken for a rogue. Kai shivered at the idea, knowing Amilya was right about that. Kai started sniffing around the area, not sure which way to head.

Kai suddenly saw a big blue butterfly, fluttering passed him, Kai gasping, chasing after the pretty insect. It's not like he could get any more lost so might as well enjoy some outdoor fun.

At the Pack House

Carver, Conner, Adam and Chris were all in their wolf forms, getting some much needed family time in.

Chris' wolf was huge and black with pitch black eyes. Carver looked almost exactly like him except for his blue eyes. Adam playfully tugged on Chris' ear, the two lovingly chasing after each other. Conner suddenly pounced on Chris along with Carver, the three of them rolling and nipping at each other.

Adam sniffed the air, smelling something sweet, following it further into the woods. Adam knew a large clearing was ahead, wondering what the smell was. It smelled really familiar for some reason.

Luna, what are you doing out here? You escape? The older beta asked who was Chris' right hand man and the coach for the football team.

Hello Mike and yes, don't tell the warden Adam giggled mentally.

Sir! We saw some movement in the field! Mike's son, John (yes the same one Carver is friends with) came into view with three other warriors, Tom and his team are on the other side.

Rogue? Adam asked with worry, the warriors bowing their heads to him.

We couldn't see it clearly Luna, but whatever it is, doesn't really smell like a rogue which is weird.

Adam nodded, headed for the clearing, the warriors spluttering in shock since their Luna was too bold for his own good sometimes.

Oh hush, I'm just going to crouch here Adam rolled his eyes, the warriors crouching next to him.

All of them saw a rustle in a taller section of the grass that was about three feet high before it went down to normal grass again. All of them had their hackles raised before seeing a blue butterfly pop out, actually looking kind of flustered; which was weird. All of them blinked owlishly, before freezing, mouths dropping down in shock.

A beautiful white wolf popped out of the grass standing elegant and tall, glowing in the moonlight.

Wow and several murmurs of awe were heard before seeing the white wolf snap its head, all of them wondering what it heard. None of them felt aggression towards this wolf which was unnerving to say the least. The wolf was small, but bigger than a pup and it looked very fluffy and soft (which meant the wolf wasn't a warrior type).

They suddenly saw it race after the blue butterfly, snapping its teeth and twirling in the air before sticking its butt in the air, front paws flat on the ground. It shook it's butt playful, lunging at the butterfly that simply flew passed the pretty wolf. The little white wolf whined, pouncing happily after it. All of the warrior suddenly felt a need to play with the little white wolf instead of attacking.

AWWWEEE! I want one! Adam screamed, all the warriors cringing at the sound. That made them snap out of their daze to play with the wolf.

It is a very cute rogue Mike nodded, the warriors nodding in agreement.

But rogues are rogues father John said seriously, all of them sweat dropping when the white wolf ran over some of the taller grass, its hind legs swinging in the air, plopping onto the ground. The white wolf whined before shooting after the butterfly again.

Oh yes. Looks so vicious I'm shivering in uncontrollable fear Adam rolled his eyes, some of the warriors chuckling at that.

Adam! Where the hell are you? Chris growled through the pack link Adam giggling at that.

With the warriors. A rogue is in the clearing from where they were patrolling Adam cackling at the warriors next to him which looked super weird coming from his wolf form.

You're what!? Chris roared through the link along with Conner and Carver.

You are a trouble maker Luna one of the warriors laughed, Adam puffing up happily at that.

Chris popped through the trees in a rush a few minutes later, panting heavily, before crouching low next to Adam, grabbing the scruff of his neck. Adam whimpered licking Chris' chest as best as he could.

Oh love, can we keep him? Adam whispered with shining eyes, Chris about to give him a lashing before getting confused wondering what his mate was talking about.

The very ferocious rogue over there John rolled his eyes. Chris growled low before blinking owlishly, Conner crouching next to him, cocking his head in confusion at the scene. The wolf was beautifully stunning and the exact opposite of a rogue.

The white wolf stood still trying to find the butterfly, not realizing it landed on its tail which was perked in the air. The butterfly seemed to crawl lower on his tail, the white wolf turning his head before yipping very softly. It's little nose wriggled before the butterfly landed on his nose. The white wolf rocked its head gently side to side before the butterfly fluttered its wings, the white wolf letting out a cute little sneeze. The butterfly flew away, the white wolf staring up at the sky where it had gone; he whined sadly, getting all droopy.

So. Freaking. Cute! Conner gushed, Papa already nodding and aweing at the cute little pup. Adam was just freaking out wanting to just cuddle him and never let him go.

So... we can keep him? One of the warriors chuckled, Adam nodding eagerly with his wolf head at Chris who rolled his eyes, mentally smiling.

Carver, on the other hand, froze when he chased after his Papa and brother, nose in the air smelling chocolate and mint. His mate. Why was his mate there!? Carver followed the scent fast, rounding through the other side of the forest in case the rogue decided to run in that direction. Why was his baby there!? Was the rogue trying to use his mate as bait? What in all the heavens was going on!? Carver's breath caught in his throat once he slid into the clearing. His heart nearly stopping.

Beauty. The word alone couldn't describe the wolf further in front of him. It's fur glowed like the moon itself, shining like the millions of stars in the sky. Long legs that curved beautifully, showing off thicker thighs. It's fur looked soft to the touch, like a cloud. The wolf radiated elegance, tenderness, sweetness. Its eyes a cool gray.

Carver held his breath, realizing the beautiful wolf was staring straight at him, unmoving.

Kai was mesmerized. The wolf was a midnight black and a good two heads taller than him. He radiated power and dominance. His muscles large, looking strong and formidable. Yet the eyes had Kai drowning into the furthest depths of the blue ocean color they were. Those eyes nearly broke his heart, hearing his wolf howling to him in desperation.

Mate.

This was really happening. This was Carver's wolf. Kai could feel his legs shaking in happiness and fear.

He can smell it... Can't he? That I'm a submissive omega. Kai and his wolf both curled in on themselves slighty, seeing the black wolf tilt his head in confusion.

W-What did you say Carver? Adam whispered in shock, no one moving.

Carver lifted his nose in the air, taking deep breaths. It was Kai's scent. It matched perfectly to a T. It was intoxicating but that would mean... His mate, who he thought was human, was really a werewolf!?

Carver's jaw dropped a little in shock, seeing the gray eyes of his mate glancing from the ground to him every few seconds.

I... Don't understand Carver whispered through the pack link, utterly confused, hurt, and unsure.

Smell that? Conner whispered, everyone starting to sniff from afar before several gasps were heard.

A submissive omega!? How is that possible!?

What about him being a white wolf!?

Yeah! In history class they said white wolves were extinct!

I don't care about any of that! Carver snarled, realization hitting him hard. His mate was who the moon goddess paired him up with. He had already sworn that it wouldn't matter who his mate was. This was Kai. Somehow, someway, this was still the Kai he fell in love with. He needed to believe that. His heart and his head still trying to process everything.

This is my Kai... I know it. But damn it all I'm getting answers! Carver thought desperately, his pack and family whining sadly at him.

Kai whimpered, head bowed, backing up slowly, Carver freezing, whimpering back. Carver realized that snarling without context might come off as threatening.

My mate is beautiful and kind and sweet and he is MINE. I know he had a reason for keeping this from me... Whatever that is

Of course honey but I think you're scaring him Adam spoke quickly.

The pretty white wolf was shaking on his legs, head low, afraid to look up.

Carver moved slowly, laying on the ground in front of his mate whose head popped up in surprise; it showed weakness for an Alpha to lay on the ground so exposed.

Not that Carver cared. His mate came before anything in his life.

Safe Kai's wolf whispered in his head, Kai still shaking like a leaf, ready to bolt any second. Everyone was frozen in the field, waiting to see what Kai would do.

Carver... Do you think that's why none of them look entirely related? That maybe Kai was adopted or something and he turned out to be a werewolf? Conner asked curiously since his mate smelled human too the last time he checked.

I don't know Conner... But I need to get him to relax

Carver! I found your - A large chocolate brown wolf, almost the size of Conner suddenly popped out of the tree line, Kai yowling in fear, turning tail to run. Carver leaped up, snarling angrily at his gamma Raven, about to chase down his mate. A beautiful bleach blonde wolf dived out of the tree line, snarling angrily; almost in equal size to Conner and just slightly bigger than Raven.

Conner immediately snarled back along with Carver, his fathers coming out along with the warriors.

Mate? Conner gasped in shock, going stalk still with big round eyes, Carver nearly choking on air at that along with everyone else. Wolf jaws dropping down in shock.

WHAT!? A submissive beta! Everyone yelled in shock, snapping back to the situation at hand when the blonde wolf continued snarling. He was walking backwards, keeping Kai behind him.

Tyler its okay! Kai shouted through their link, Tyler protectively in front of Kai, hackles up and looking ready to strike any second, like a snake.

It's not okay! Mils and I ran out to find you and Robin is home alone in case you came back, if you were going to come back at all! We've never seen either of you fight before in our lives and we had no idea where you were or if you were hurt! Mils has been beside herself and blames herself Kai. Not to mention you've been locking us out of our mind-link!

Tyler spoke angrily, Kai whimpering sadly. Carver mistook that, snarling angrily at Tyler since no one made his mate whimper like that.

Tyler growled back before seeing a blonde wolf that smelled like pine and snow, exactly like the scent of his mate, snarl back at the black alpha who was currently growling at him. There was an equally huge black alpha who was older looking but didn't look any less formidable, standing next to the younger black wolf. An older blonde wolf was next to him, looking just plain shocked at the moment. There were about a dozen other wolves that were about the young blonde wolf's size that had mixed coat colors but weren't growling in aggression at Tyler which confused him.

Tyler looked stunned for a second, lowering his hackles from suddenly realizing where he was exactly.

Is that... Conner? Tyler whispered in shock, instantly falling in love with his mate's wolf. Conner's wolf was a dark blonde color, like sun kissed honey. Tyler's wolf was clawing to snuggle and play with his mate, the need to run with him almost overpowering his other senses.

R-Rogues Robin whispered through the link, Kai and Tyler freezing. Robin was all alone.

We need to go back Tyler's voice desperate, but longing to stay with his mate, Kai yowling at that.

Conner whimpered at Tyler, ears flat, trying to show he wasn't going to harm him or let anything harm his mate. Tyler whimpered back, his eyes full of grief, Carver stopping his growling seeing the look in the submissive beta's eyes. Tyler bowed slowly, seeing that that relaxed Alpha Chris some, Tyler turning his head high in the direction of the forest.

His mate cocked his head in confusion, moving very slowly towards Tyler, wondering what was wrong. Why was he so scared?

Tyler and Kai suddenly turned tail at the same time, running like their lives depended on it. Well their brothers' life depended on it. Kai and Tyler knew that their mates were following them along with a brown wolf that reminded them of Robin's mate, Raven.

Carver told his Dads and his friends to stay where they were, needing to do this on their own. Their mates would have to be brought back to the pack house since they had illegally crossed into their lands, but hoped their mates weren't running from them. From their bond.

Robin are you okay? Are the rogues close? Tyler asked quickly, Kai keeping pace with him.

Can smell them Robin whispered, Tyler pushing his legs hard knowing rogues couldn't be more than half a mile away from the townhouse.

We're almost there, run out in your wolf form when you see us Tyler commanded in his beta voice. Submissive or not it still held some power.

There, uh, might also be a different kind of surprise when you see us Tyler coughed out, knowing Robin was completely confused now.

Kai could feel his mate close to his tail, knowing Carver was going to stop him, which he couldn't let happen right now. He felt guilt swirling inside him from keeping this hidden for so long, but Robin was in trouble, so the truth would have to wait. Tyler and Kai ran out of the forest, the back door to the townhouse swinging open, followed by a lanky smokey black colored wolf who came running out.

Mate Raven gasped in shock, the scent of a submissive gamma shocking Conner and Carver . They wanted answers and they wanted them now.

Kai suddenly saw something in his peripherals, using his whole body to shove Tyler away before a black wolf slammed into his shoulder, Kai rolling on the ground hard seeing the wolf's eyes were red. Carver roared in anger, lunging at the rogue. The rogue swiped and evaded Carver for a moment, only a moment, before Carver lunged in, breaking the rogue's neck like a twig.

Carver ran over to Kai who already had Tyler and Robin nudging at him gently; Conner and Raven were whimpering near their mates, wanting to get close but were already growled at to keep their distance. Carver hurried over to his mate making Tyler and Robin move away a little. Carver stood over his mate protectively, nudging and whimpering at his beautiful white wolf. He buried his nose into the soft fur of his mate's neck, breathing in deeply. His scent was euphoric but it also told him Kai was alright. Kai blinked open his eyes slowly, gray gazing into blue, Carver physically relaxing, nuzzling Kai gently.

Kai purred at that, Carver licking his ear softly, rubbing his cheek against Kai's. His wolf nearly keeled over in happiness, his tail thumping on the ground. Kai went to stand shakily on his paws, Carver helping him stand.

Tyler was looking at the ground, tail drooping, ears flat, not letting Conner get close. Conner whimpered at that, taking baby steps towards him.

Robin wasn't any better, just watching Raven warily who was bouncing in excitement, Kai was sure. Kai suddenly felt a nudge under his neck, his heart thumping happily. Kai walked slowly, in front of Carver, pressing his nose against Carver's big black one.

Boop Kai giggled to himself, before heading to the townhouse, Carver nearly squished into his side. Robin came in after with Raven, who was less bouncy since Robin was pretty much ignoring him at that point. Tyler was the last to come in, droopy, Conner whimpering behind him. Kai went upstairs, Carver following his every step.

Kai was about to shift, turning around startled, seeing Carver on his bed, rolling around in the sheets. Kai giggled mentally at that, Kai's wolf preening that his mate was rolling in his scent.

Kai's POV

I growled softly, Carver's ears perking cutely at that. My wolf was getting giddy from seeing our mate scent the place where we sleep; the weirdo. I turned in a circle, indicating for Carver to turn his back. Carver's big wolf eyes rolled at that, but turned on my bed so his back was facing me. I looked around my floor seeing a pair of pants I could put on. I felt the usual burning pops of my shifting, the sound seeming to echo louder in my nearly empty room. I saw my favorite blue panties, grabbing to put them on, hearing similar popping sounds. I had tears running down my cheeks, slipping on the first shirt I grabbed, not wanting Carver to see the scars. All the ugly parts on my body.

I turned to grab my pants, hearing Carver gasp. I nearly froze before shakily looking up, my gray eyes meeting his blue. He was naked as the day he was born with the sheets thrown over his man parts. Carver's eyes were stern, beckoning me over with a single finger. I obeyed immediately, not wanting to upset my mate further.

"Hush pup," Carver's soft voice surprised me, making me hiccup. I flinched anyway when he placed his hand gently on my cheek. I opened my eyes slowly, so very scared, seeing his eyes sad. I felt his thumb wipe my tears away. He smiled sadly, yet softly at me, making the guilt feel like a brick in my stomach.

"I-I wanted-" I couldn't get the words out. Why wouldn't they come out!? My breathing increased in panic before muscular arms held me, Carver's head pressed against my chest, his head just under my chin.

"Calm mate, calm," Carver whispered. Why was he being so gentle with me? With a liar? With someone so shallow?

"Hey. We'll talk love, alright?" Carver whispered. I knew it was a command for me to tell him, but it was also open ended which made me feel less trapped.

"C-Carver," my voice came out wobbly before I felt his fingers against my lips. His eyes were sad and confused. I felt more tears leave me, seeing Carver huff out a smile.

"My wolf is going a little crazy right now Kai, and I need to know. Are you rejecting this? Running like that was-" Carver's voice was slowly rising in desperation, stunning me for a second. I quickly shook my head no.

"I accepted everything about you when I first saw you Carver," I whispered, seeing him calm down, his shoulders less tense. I suddenly felt his lips against mine making me sob, only to feel him hold me tighter.

"Shh love. Breathe," Carver whispered, grabbing a couple of tissues for me. I finally calmed down enough with his sweet nothings whispered endearingly to me; his blue eyes never leaving mine, no matter how much I tried to look away. He always tugged my chin back to look at him. I think he knew my thoughts were going to go in a million directions the second I stopped looking at him.

Carver smiled gently up at me, my breathing even and only tear tracks down my cheeks. Carver looked at my shoulder, whimpering, seeing a bruise forming from where that rogue hit me.

I ran my hand through his hair without a second thought, knowing that usually calmed Carver down. I suddenly realized my action, about to rip my hand away, not knowing where we stood. Carver suddenly grabbed my hand, kissing my palm gently. I felt my face flush and my heart leap with the hope that my mate wasn't completely rejecting me.

"You always calm me Kai," Carver whispered, making me smile; just a little.

"Maybe you should put on pants though," Carver chuckled softly, before I noticed his eyes flash yellow and look hungrily at my silk undies. Bad pervy puppy! I was about to scramble away before I saw his eyes go lower and darken angrily. I was about to move away fast at the realization that I still had a few scars on my legs too, really needing to put on pants.

"What the..." Carver's voice was that of disbelief. His one hand easily captured my wrist, keeping me in place. I whimpered when he traced a pale white scar that was on my thigh. It was long and jagged looking and I hated it. His eyes seemed to snap to my knee on my other leg, a wide scar on the inside of it. Carver's eyes were growing more and more angry. I could feel myself shaking.

I was ugly. Carver found me ugly too and now he was going to reject me! Carver's eyes seemed to snap back to my undies before I realized that I had a scar on my hip bone too. Carver snarled, moving to shove my shirt up before I sobbed, stumbling over my feet to get out of his grip.

Carver froze, but I was still struggling out of his hold, but I don't think I was doing much since he didn't even move.

"Please don't reject me! I-I know I'm ugly but I'm sure I can figure out a way for you to not see them! Please!" I knew I was nearly screaming before feeling Carver's full body pressed against mine. The sheet the only thing separating us. His hand was against my head and the other against my back. I sobbed into his chest, not sure what to do.

"Please please please," I was pleading and begging, having gone deaf to everything around me.

I felt Carver's hand grip my chin, nearly making the spots in my vision already, increase. I couldn't hear those words of rejection leave his mouth. I just couldn't.

"Kai!" Carver snapped, stunning me since he had never yelled at me before, I realized.

"I accept you. All of you. I would never reject you because I fell in love with you," Carver's warm callused fingers moved my hair behind my ear. My eyes went huge in shock, feeling my mouth drop down a little. Carver continued, seeing that my attention was solely on the words coming out of his mouth.

"And what's this shit about you being ugly? You're the most stunning and beautiful creature I've ever laid eyes on in my life. I wouldn't give you up for the world Kai"

I hiccupped, stunned. Carver thought I was, beautiful? Me? With all my scars? With my pointy hip bones and practically florescent skin.

Carver sat on the bed again with me still standing in front of him in shock.

Carver lifted my shirt again, making me nearly run and hide in a corner somewhere. Carver whimpered, his eyes flashing between blue and yellow. My breath caught in my throat when he suddenly kissed an ugly scar on my belly.

"You aren't ugly," a kiss to another scar, "you're amazing," kiss, "stronger than I could have imagined," kiss, "and I love you Kai."

Tears rolled down my cheeks, my heart absolutely aching. He was kissing my scars. It was like, he was making all the bad things they reminded me of, go away.

Carver moved to pull my shirt the rest of the way off, but I touched his hands gently, seeing his head snap up. His blue eyes looked at me longingly, and I knew that his words were true.

His fingers laced with mine before I leaned forward, kissing him softly. I whimpered into the kiss as though Carver alone was taking my pain away. This kiss was slow. Soft. Carver increased the passion slowly, making me sigh out.

He pulled away, but I kept my eyes closed, letting the last of the sparks dance on my lips. Carver's eyes were hooded, before he gently pressed his nose against mine, making me smile.

"Carver," his name alone made it seem like it would make all my nightmares go away. I rested my hands against his cheeks, my thumbs following the outline of his cheekbones.

Carver let out a breathy smile, nuzzling my neck. I giggle at the hair from his head, tickling my chin. I gasped, feeling Carver nip at my neck, seeing him playfully smile at me.

Carver gently pulled my shirt back down, running his hands down my body as he did so. My heart leaped into my throat, seeing his eyes looking at my body hungrily. That was another sign that he didn't see me as grotesque. My wolf was panting and whining. I could practically feel both of our wolves trying to nuzzle each other through our minds.

"Beautiful," Carver mumbled, his hand gliding down my belly before his nose repeated action.

"So fucking sexy with panties," Carver purred making me blushing ten fold once comprehending the words that just came out of his mouth.

"Oops, said that out loud," Carver chuckled. Carver stood, holding the bed sheet with one hand around his waist. We kissed a few more times and I felt as though I were melting deeper against Carver with each one.

"U-Um I'll go find you pants!" I giggled a little to breathily, since he looked a little too tempting to be strutting around with just a bed sheet. I turned before moaning low. Carver's hot and callused hand slowly dragged down my back before cupping one of my innocent butt cheeks, giving it light squeezes. I suddenly felt his very evident 'friend' against my butt, making me gasp, shivering almost violently.

"Not yet Carver," I smiled shyly, giggling at Carver's pout.

"I'll just tug around this blanket. I highly doubt you have anything my size here," Carver winked playfully, grabbing my hand. We slowly made it down stairs and I almost burst into tears again, realizing I still had my puppy with me. We got to the living room, seeing Tyler, Robin, Conner and Raven sitting down; the atmosphere felt tense.

Tyler was in light blue briefs. I couldn't help but giggle at the puppy boxers Conner had on that were tight on him since Tyler didn't usually wear boxers and they were slightly smaller than Conner in size. Robin wasn't any better since he was also in some black briefs, Raven having a pair of black boxers that were also too tight on him.

No Ones POV

Are you guys okay? What's happening? Everything alright? Adam was asking frantically in the link, Carver and the other two smiling a little at that. Kai cocked his head in confusion, Carver running his nose along Kai's throat for a second.

"Dad wants an update," Carver whispered, Kai nodding nervously.

"Baby, let's go back to the pack house and talk. I don't like that the town-house is so close to the edge of our territory where more rogues could sneak in," Carver spoke seriously. He eyed Kai's shoulder again where the bruise was, Kai snuggling against Carver's chest happily.

Carver had Kai tugged into his side, rubbing his hand slowly up and down Kai's hip. Kai looked at Tyler since he had the highest rank in their makeshift pack when Amilya wasn't there.

Please Tyler Kai asked softly. Robin was looking hopeful at Tyler too, Conner sitting close to him but Tyler had yet to allow his mate to touch him. The two hadn't talked yet and Tyler already had a few tears leave him when Conner started demanding answers when they went to Tyler's room. Conner immediately backed up with his dominance display, seeing it calm down Tyler significantly.

We'll have to tell Mils where we are, but I believe it will be safer if we are with our mates

Their mates were just watching the silent mind link that was going on. They didn't want to tell them that they would be forced to come anyway since they weren't technically allowed on pack grounds since they'd be considered rogues at the moment. Of course that would scare their mates so they kept that thought to themselves.

Tyler sighed audibly, nodding his head.

Pack your stuff. I highly doubt our mates will allow us to leave once we're at the pack house

Kai sighed in relief, tugging Carver back to his room who was happily complying. The decision between their three little mates obvious.

You mean they won't want us to leave. I'm sure they'll allow us to do anything Robin smirked, Tyler scoffing, shaking his head.

"I'll help you pack love," Raven smiled, grabbing Robin's hand, leading him to his room even though he had never been in the townhouse before. Robin was fidgeting in nervousness, trying to shroud his eye patch even more if he could.

"My, uh, room isn't much to look at," Tyler whispered, Conner perking up significantly since his mate was talking to him at least, but had yet to make eye contact with him.

"I don't care about something like that, honey," Conner smiled, following Tyler to his room.

Kai was hurriedly packing like he was running out of time, Carver just watching him amused. His little mate was stuffing shirts and pants and a few other knickknacks that were in the fairly barren room, into a suitcase or his backpack. Carver went to Kai's dresser, going to help his love pack since he was starting to look frazzled. His mate had a long day and he was probably already stressed out about the things they'd have to discuss.

Carver shook his head, seeing Kai nearly finished with half of his room already. Carver headed over to Kai's dresser, tugging open a drawer to help his mate pack.

Sweet moon goddess Carver wiped the drool from his chin. His eyes almost popped out of his head, picking up a pair of nearly sheer white lace panties.

"Carver!" Kai squeaked, bright red, snatching his undies from the man.

"You will wear those when we mate," Carver growled huskily, Kai shivering happily.

"Yes Alpha," Kai purred, getting on his tip toes to kiss Carver softly who moaned happily.

"Can't tear them though!" Kai said seriously hands on his hips. He quickly grabbed his other underwear, Carver craning his head to see them.

"Can't make any promises but I'll buy you more," Carver winked, leaning down to steal a kiss, Kai giggling happily. Kai yawned when Carver moved on to the next drawer.

Kai looked around at his suddenly very bare room, knowing it was kind of depressing that all of his stuff fit in a suitcase and his backpack. Kai yawned again, before smiling softly, Carver's scent wrapping around him along with his large arms.

"My dad Adam, who is Luna of our pack, is coming with a car to take us back to the pack house; I think he's too impatient to wait for us to bring you guys," Carver whispered, Kai's eyes getting droopy. Kai's exhaustion suddenly hit him hard, getting too tired to do anything else for the night.

"Carver," Kai whispered, Carver humming into Kai's hair, "please," Kai starting to nod off, "don't hate me," Kai suddenly had little snores leaving him, being held up by Carver's arms.

Carver's eyes became sad, sighing at that, lifting Kai bridal style in his arms. He picked up Kai's suitcase and backpack, seeing the others putting their mate's belongings into the black SUV; Adam looking like he wanted to say something to Conner and Robin but decided against it.

"I'll always love you my sweet mate," Carver kissed Kai's parted lips softly a few times, wanting so many answers.

Ready to go guys? Conner spoke softly, Raven looking longingly at his mate before Conner looked at Carver with grief. Carver hated that look more than anything on his brother's face, wishing he could do something more. They'd have to wait until morning.

"You'll always be with me from now on baby, because I will never let you go. You are my world," Carver mumbled, carrying Kai in his lap in the car.

- o (. _ .) o

Sooooo! Drama galore I tell you! Hope you all like it so far!!!

The Past

A milya's POV

Why? Why did that man seem so familiar? Amilya stood in the shadows of the townhouse. Her little pack carried out by their mates to a man with blonde hair and blue eyes, driving an SUV.

He was older and his skin still looked soft even though he had a few wrinkles around the eyes when he smiled. His eyes.

Where did I see something that blue before? When -

Flashback

"Would you like to make cookies with me sweetheart? Your brothers and Papa are being meanie heads and won't," a handsome blond man, with a bright white smile asked.

"Will they have gummy bears in them?"

Daddy's laugh sounds like bells. I love his laugh.

"Sorry sweetie, but they taste better with chocolate chips. Won't you help daddy?"

I nodded quickly. His blues eyes looked sad and I don't like my daddy sad!

"Yay!" Daddy squealed. I helped daddy make the dough and I liked playing with it when we were done cause it was squishy!

"Pat it like this honey!"

I saw him making it into a ball and I stuck out my tongue in concentration trying to match his.

"There! All done!" Daddy smiled happily, sticking the tray into the oven.

"Thank you for helping Daddy, Princess," Daddy kissed my forehead and cheeks and I couldn't help but giggle.

I helped Daddy clean the dishes, a ding going off on the oven. I clapped my hands excitedly, opening the oven.

"No no no, Amilya!" Daddy yelled, running over fast. I touched the pan by mistake, grabbing my hands. It hurt a lot! But I didn't want to cry or scream cause werewolves don't cry! A few tears left me though since I tried holding in my cry as best as I could. It hurt so bad!

"Chris!" Daddy yelled, Papa running into the room.

"What happened!?" Papa yelled, Daddy sitting me in a chair. Papa nearly ran over, daddy wiping my face with a tissue.

"Get the cookies out of the oven love," Daddy spoke softly, Papa looking miffed but nodded.

"Alright, let me see honey," I shook my head 'no' holding my hands to my chest.

"Now Amilya," Papa's alpha voice came over. I whimpered a little, showing my Daddy my hands. They were a dark red on my fingertips, Daddy looking sad. Papa came over with an ice pack, putting it on my fingers.

"Don't you touch something hot like that again," Papa spoke sternly, I nodded sadly, not liking when I made my Papa mad.

"We just made fresh cookies," Daddy smiled, Papa rolling his eyes, sitting next to Daddy with me sitting across from them.

I looked down at my golden cookie, not wanting to eat it since I made Papa mad.

"Princess, I'm sorry I yelled," Papa mumbled at me as I peeked up at him.

"Your Papa just yells when he's upset or scared," Daddy smiled, Papa spluttering at him, "now eat your cookie sweetie."

I nodded, eating my yummy cookie with the palms of my hands.

"We want some too!" Car-Car and Co-Co ran in jumping up and down.

I frowned at them, crossing my arms. Car-Car and Co-Co looked at each other, looking down at the floor.

"May we please have some cookies?" They asked as I nodded making them jump up and down, grabbing two each from the plate.

"That's my girl," Papa smiled proudly, making me giggle.

"Ugh, I can't wait till I finish the last of this coffee," Papa grumbled into his mug.

"I don't understand how this coffee is any different since its the same one you usually get," Daddy said confused.

"It just tastes weird."

"Put more sugar in!" I giggled

"I don't like coffee like that," Papa scrunched up his nose making me do the same, Daddy laughing at our faces; which were identical.

"But I keep putting gummy bears in it, it should be yummy," I crossed my arms, Papa's jaw dropping before Daddy burst out laughing, rolling on the floor, tears streaming down his face.

"I tried it and it was yucky so I added gummy bears!" I smiled, before looking confused at my Dads.

"If you two have been conspiring, so help me," Chris growled low at Daddy who was holding onto his stomach.

"That's my baby girl!" Daddy laughed happily, making me smile.

"Amilya, go play with your brothers," Papa put his fingers to his forehead, rubbing his temples.

"Okay Papa," I smiled, Papa ruffling my hair making me pout. Daddy was still laughing, kissing my forehead before moving some of my hair behind my ear, pushing my butt towards the living room.

"Definitely your child," Daddy smiled, Papa tugging him into his chest.

"Her deviousness comes from you," Papa grumbled, kissing Adam softly.

"She loves you so much you know," Adam smiling softly, Chris puffing up happily at that.

"Well she'll do anything for you when you frown just even a little," Chris smiled, kissing Adam softly again.

"Well you seem to be becoming immune," Adam pouted, Chris laughing happily.

"Like I said, you're devious," Chris mumbled against Adam's lips who smirked at that.

"Damn right."

(End of Flashback)

It hurt. Why did everything have to hurt! I clutched my head, my memories shooting to the forefront of my mind. When I lost my first tooth, when my brothers rough housed with me too hard and I hit my head. When I put gummy bears in everything.

"O-Oh, d-daddy," Sobs ripped out of my mouth, falling to my knees. The dirt moistening beneath me from my tears.

It's been so long. So many years. My heart led me back home and I wanted to leave. I wanted to run as far and as fast as I could. What do I do? Was I still a burden to them? Would they be in danger? Did they remember me? Want me?

I crawled into the townhouse, curling into a ball next to the couch.

Empty. Everything always ends up empty.

The Next Morning

Kai's POV

I peeked open an eye, everything fuzzy at first, I felt like I was lying on a cloud. I felt sparks along my back, an arm circling around my waist until I was tugged into a warm body behind me.

Mate! My wolf ran in a circle, jumping up and down happily.

I grumbled, turning on my back, seeing blue eyes gazing at me. Such sweet eyes. I loved them. Carver's cheek had a little stubble on it and I really wanted to touch it. I bit my lip, letting my fingers graze over Carver's strong chin and along his cheeks.

"It wasn't a dream," I realized, Carver grabbing my hand, kissing my fingertips.

"Morning love," Carver smiled so softly at me, my tummy filled with butterflies. I closed my eyes, his strong hand so gentle against my face.

"It wasn't a dream pup. Breakfast is ready downstairs. Your brothers are already there," Carver whispered. I nodded, biting my lip, looking at the sheets sadly. My stomach was still twisted in knots from guilt.

"Hey," Carver whispered. I felt his fingers on my chin, directing my face to look up at him. I didn't deserve his kindness... Or to have someone so wonderful as my mate.

I opened my lips, wanting everything to just spill out, but Carver's skilled lips softly pressed against mine.

"We'll talk, but breakfast first."

"Carver I-"

"Breakfast first love," Carver pressed his fingers to my lips. My heart scrunched into my chest seeing hurt in Carver's eyes making me feel like an even more horrible person.

I nodded, not wanting to start anything else, Carver getting me some clothes.

"We'll do some proper shopping a little later," Carver sighed, as I pulled up the jeans he gave me, again. I think he put my other clothes in the wash or something.

Carver grabbed my hand, leading me down the stairs. It was rather quiet in the kitchen which worried me. Actually, it was pretty quiet in the pack house. I took comfort in Carver's hand holding on to mine.

I peeked behind Carver to see Robin and Tyler not really eating their breakfasts, their mates looking at them with worry along with Luna Adam. Although, Alpha Chris looked kind of mad. I hope he would let us explain our side of the story and not just kill us.

"Oh! Kai! Please, come sit. I made enough food for everyone," Adam's smile seeming a little forced. I think it had to do with how strained Alpha Chris looked at the moment.

"Th-Thank you Luna," I whispered, nodding, not looking up from the ground. I heard Carver whimper a little, but saw a plate filled with food in front of me suddenly. Carver's hand rubbed my thigh encouragingly but it did little to ease my nerves at the moment.

I absolutely loved pancakes! And they even had chocolate chips! But... I was pretty sure anything I swallowed would come right back up.

Are they going to kill us for being submissive? I whispered through the mind link, Robin and Tyler looking quickly up at me in surprise, going back to pushing food around on their plates.

I hope not.

This is awkward, I hate it

D-Do you think I whispered through the mind link, knowing my voice was shaking Our mates will hate us after knowing...

Robin and Tyler stopped moving, putting their utensils down, hands in their laps with their heads down. I hadn't even touched my plate, afraid my shaking hands would just knock things over.

"We will take this to the living room," Alpha Chris spoke sternly, not quite using his Alpha voice since I could practically hear our mates seething if he did.

Robin sat on Tyler's left in the living room around a large oak table that wasn't there the last time we were here; I was on his right looking warily around the room. I looked tiny compared to them. Why did I have to be so short!? The couches were all moved against the walls making the living room seem even more empty and a little intimidating.

I suddenly sensed other werewolves coming into the room, feeling myself shake.

"This is my beta Mike," Chris spoke stiffly, all three of us nodding at him since we've seen him pretty often since he's the coach for gym and football.

"This is John and some of the warriors of the pack that I'm sure you have seen at the high school," we nodded again, all of them schooling neutral emotions on their faces. I wanted to say something to John or Leah's brother Charlie but thought better of it; both looked a little sad when I did that.

"Our head warrior will not be able to make it to this trial for another week or so, but everyone here is trust worthy and loyal. They are the voices of the families that live within the pack and I take their opinions very highly. The end decision will be mine, however," Chris finished tightly.

I was shaking already, my eyes having the familiar sting of impending tears. I looked down along with Robin, not realizing that each of our hands ended up in Tyler's. He was our rock at the moment. I knew my mate was standing behind his father. I was afraid to look up and see anger or hatred in his eyes. If I had looked up, I would have seen him being antsy, switching his weight from foot to foot.

"As the charges stand, you are all considered rogues. The only thing stopping me from putting you in the holding cells is that all of your mates are in this pack. However, you did not ask for permission onto this land and you lied to your mates for an extended period about being werewolves. These are very serious crimes."

I sniffled, wiping my eye with my free hand, trying to stop tears from leaving me. I wasn't sure if I was imagining it or not, but Alpha Chris' voice almost waivered, but I was probably just hearing things.

The room was silent except for a few of my sniffles. I felt like Carver was wanting to get close to me, but I didn't dare look up. Carver in fact was being held back by Conner who was looking longingly at Tyler. Raven had his arms crossed, looking stressed.

"Did you think I would care so much if my mate was a rogue?" Raven snapped out, Robin's head shooting up in surprise. Raven's eyes weren't on Alpha Chris though, the question was directed at Robin. Everyone was looking at the brunette in surprise since his tone was usually playful, unless rogues were attacking the pack grounds.

"Did you think I was that shallow?" Raven's voice low, taking a step closer to Robin whose one eye was round and large. I was shaking badly, Tyler's hand tightening around mine.

"Of course not," Robin whispered, Raven looking angry.

"Then why didn't you!? I've been trying to get answers out of you all night and nothing."

"I... We never asked to be rogues!" Robin stood shakily, Raven fully displaying his dominance. A few of the warriors looked nervous, probably because you don't piss off a master tactitian; even if he is a gamma. Chris sighed at the statement, Adam whimpering softly at his mate.

"And you think that's a good enough excuse!?"

Everyone was looking back and forth between the two, both seeming to forget they were in front of an audience.

"I'm not giving you an excuse."

"Could have fooled me."

"Did it ever cross your mind that it's painful to talk about my past? Or do you just want a robot spitting out facts?" Robin's voice raising a little, Raven only seeming to get angrier at Robin's rather calm demeanor.

"I'd like a mate who doesn't lie to my face!" Raven snapped, my own heart cringing at his words, surprised that Robin was still standing defiantly; even with tears down his cheeks.

"We are loyal to our alpha. She was making sure we were safe within this territory."

"Alpha?" Raven looking surprised, his anger going down to a simmer.

"I thought..." Raven looked at Tyler who was stone faced, "betas have been known to create pack links as well. I assumed it was formed easier between you three because you were all submissive."

Everyone looked confused around the room, not understanding who our alpha was.

"Wait... Your sister?" Raven asked quickly, Robin giving him a curt nod.

"We will need her here as well," Alpha Chris rubbing his forehead, Adam rubbing his mate's forearm.

Tyler and Robin exchanged a look while I just tried looking even smaller.

"What now?" Raven grumbled, Robin looking away with slight anger, another lone tear rolling down his cheek.

"If you wish to kill us, please get on with it. Reject me," Robin's voice shaking even though he managed to snap out the statement. Raven's eyes widened fractionally, before schooling his face again.

Robin took in a shaky breath, "A submissive's words have no standing nor do they have any merit within a pack; therefore, this meeting is pointless. Either kick us out or kill us," Robin continued making me sob quietly, feeling my shoulders shake. I heard a few whimpers making me confused. Shouldn't they have immediately agreed.

"Is it so hard to just tell me what I want to know you stubborn-"

"What do you think happens in rogue packs Raven!? That we all just sing kumbaya and get to run around like good little pups following their leader!?" Robin snapped getting a low growl from Raven in return. Robin shook, his wolf whining and showing his belly for being so defiant, in Robin's mind.

"Let's all settle down a little " Luna Adam tried mediating.

"I'm not stupid Robin! It still doesn't change the fact that you kept a main detail about yourself a secret for almost a month!"

"For good reason! I didn't think you'd reject me because I was a rogue. I thought you'd reject me because I'm a submissive. The lowest kind of werewolf there is. No one may say it outright but it's always the same no matter what pack! We're considered weak. Useless. Unnecessary."

"Stop it!"

"Only good for a fuck because we can't defend ourselves and must obey orders from a higher ranking wolf. Disobey an order and our wolf dies. And we ended up treated like objects for years. Years of being bruised, broken, beaten-"

"Stop!"

"Burned, starved, stabbed-"

"Just stop!"

"Threatened, scared, tortured-"

"STOP IT!" Raven yelled loudly, a few tears leaving him. Everything was so blurry though. I realized the crying was coming from my lips brokenly, blood pounding in my ears. I pulled my hand out of Tyler's to cover my face. The room was so very silent apart from my sobs. I couldn't hold them in though. Memories were spilling out and my body ached.

"You escaped from a rogue pack? Even I know a rogue alpha has to agree to any members leaving," Raven's voice barely above a whisper, but it was heard clearly in the almost dead silent room. Robin curled in on himself a little, shrugging.

"I was sold into servitude. The alpha didn't even bother accepting me into the pack so he kept me in chains instead. Since I was always surrounded by dominants I couldn't exactly leave unless I wanted to kill my wolf. Not that I was allowed to shift unless I was able to in secret," gasps of horror spilled thoughtout the room.

"It kills a person to not be allowed to shift at all," Chris spoke suddenly in shock and disbelief, Robin shrugging and trying to look small.

"Robin?" Raven's voice tight, Robin feeling his heart twist painfully. Robin slowly sat back down, looking at the table top.

"What kind-" Raven's voice going up an octave for a moment, "what kind of servitude?"

"If you're thinking sex slave, that was my mother. She was beaten, raped, and killed by the time I was five or something. Kai and I were just lucky there weren't any pedophiles in the pack. Not that, that stopped several dominants from groping us."

I couldn't help the whimper that escaped my lips since I was just trying to calm down my breathing at the moment. I knew I wanted to add my two cents worth into the conversation, but I'm pretty sure my words would turn into actual vomit.

I heard a large sniff, not seeing Raven angrily shove his hand into his hair, hearing him clear his throat. Everyone looked angry and shocked in the room, but it wasn't aimed at the three of us in the slightest.

"You asked how we escaped," Robin whispered, hearing that his mate had clearly settled down or at least had his anger directed somewhere else.

"Even a rogue pack will go after its members, no matter their standing," John whispered, Robin looking sadly away from the morbid eyes of the warriors who looked more like teddy bears that needed a hug.

"Another rogue pack declared war on our pack. That day... was both a blessing and a nightmare. The alpha of our old rogue pack was killed by the time we got away."

Robin stiffened, seeing Raven's hand on the table where his eyes were boring a hole into the tabletop. He didn't even notice his mate had gotten that close to him.

"I was tied to a pole in the back yard," Robin whispered, hoping his voice was too soft to be heard by any of them (but his hopes were in vain).

"It's where beatings usually happened but that night was different. Th-The warriors were going to rape me as a reward if they won the battle," Robin choked out the word, hoping he wouldn't start sobbing from the cruel memories.

Raven seethed, growling low, eyes blazing green from his wolf taking over. Other growls of anger joined him, making the three submissives on edge.

"A-A girl saved us though. She was from the other rogue pack that was trying to take over. She was my... our only chance to get out," Robin whispered.

"I-I told her that I smelled a-another wolf like me, since we hadn't ever seen each other b-before. I didn't want to leave an-anyone in that Hell hole. We headed b-back into the pack house towards the kit-kitchen finding Kai-" I knew Robin was looking at me as if for confirmation, but I don't think I could tell up from down or left from right at the moment I was so stressed. I wanted my Carver.

"Speak," Carver whispered brokenly, his voice alone making me remember all the scars he was kissing last night. His voice sounding broken.

"W-We found him wi-with his leg b-broken, cleaning the fl-floor with an ol-old toothrush," Robin growled angrily even though he was on the verge of crying, Carver's growl louder.

"He was hu-hurt...really bad," Robin sniffling, flinching when his hand was grabbed gently by his mate, the rest of him shying away; Raven whimpered at that.

"M-Mistress th-thought it wa-was fun-funny," I choked out, glad I didn't throw up.

"I would like a cool towel please," Tyler whispered sadly. I heard someone racing out of the room. A few growls later, I cried harder feeling Carver's hand against my neck with the cool towel. His arms wrapped around me, slipping me out of my chair where I was cradled in his lap. I eventually concentrated enough to notice sweet whispers in my ear from him. I hic-cupped, snuggling against his neck. I felt his hand on my belly where one of my scars was, his fingers tracing it.

"M-My parents we-were killed b-by the r-rogue al-alpha," I managed to get out, Carver tracing his nose along my neck. How did he calm me down so well? How could he even look at me?

"T-Took me aw-away. Don't re-remem-member the-their fa-fa-faces. B-Bad s-s-son!" I sobbed getting coos from Carver before feeling Luna Adam's arms around me too.

"Oh honey you aren't a bad son. I think you're amazing," Luna Adam's hands cupped my cheeks. I finally looked around seeing Alpha Chris, Mike, and the warriors sniffing hard and clearing their throats; eyes slightly damp. Conner was resting his head on top of Tyler's who was still unmoving but with a few tear tracks down his cheeks. Raven was holding Robin to him, whispering apologies to him, Robin shaking his head 'no'; probably not wanting his mate to apologize for anything.

"B-Beat us cause it wa-was f-fun," I whispered.

"Sh sh sh. Hush love. You don't need to explain anymore. You're telling the truth baby, I know," Carver whispered, but I needed to get this out.

"Cl-Cleaned... H-Hands bl-bled. Gl-Gl-Glass th-thrown. Br-Broken bones. Coul-Couldn't shift. Hurt. S-So b-b-bad. N-No foo-food. S-So hun-hungry. Sca-ared. Cha-Chained. Couldn't hi-hide."

"Please baby, stop. It hurts my wolf and I to hear this. I'm so sorry you had to bring it up again. I'm sorry you went through that. I wish they're had been something I could have done! I'll break their necks!" Carver's voice growing more angry and broken.

"P-Please don't throw aw-aw-away, p-please!" I sobbed harder feeling fully surrounded by Carver's hold, Luna Adam hugging me too with a whine.

"I will never let you go! You are mine! You are beautiful and kind and sweet," I felt my breath shutter, feeling him bury his head in my shoulder where the mating mark would go.

"It's alright little one. A pack dynamic is different from a rogues'. Our pack loves all kinds of wolves. We believe the more diverse a pack, the stronger the pack is," Luna Adam whispered. I felt his gentle fingers through my hair, peeking out from Carver's chest. I suddenly realized I was shaking horribly.

Alpha Chris was looking at us from afar, before gazing at Tyler and then Robin sadly.

"Maybe we could do a quick acceptance cause my wolf is freaking antsy," John spoke low, the other warrior wolves nodding.

"It'll be stronger in front of the whole pack," Chris mumbled. I wondered what they were talking about before concentrating on Carver in front of me who cupped my cheek. I nuzzled into his hand, sniffling, feeling only comfort in the room. It almost felt like a full pack acceptance right then and there.

Raven moved some of Robin's hair that went over his eye patch behind his ear. Robin shook hard when he did that, Raven whimpering when Robin held a back a sob. Raven cooed softly at him, kissing his left cheek softly. Raven held Robin's hand in place so it was against his cheek. Raven rested his forehead against Robins', wrapping his other hand around his mate's waist. Robin shut his eye tight, Raven rocking them gently side to side.

"You all got away cause of this girl? I would like to fully thank her for looking after you," Raven whispered, his lips fluttering against Robin's. Robin cuddled closer to his mate if possible.

"I'm sorry this was brought up Ty," Conner whispered, kissing the top of Tyler's head, hugging him while his mate remained seated.

"I... Wasn't from a rogue pack," Tyler whispered out, everyone quieting down from their angry whispers and plots to hunt down this rogue pack.

"Honey? What do you mean?" Conner pulled to the side, trying to make eye contact with his mate.

"Tyler," Conner spoke a little more sternly, Tyler wiping his eyes with his sleeve.

"I think I was from a normal pack," Tyler whispered out, rubbing his forehead as though that would help him call on his memories. Everyone cocked their heads in confusion at that.

I hated Tyler's story more than my own.

"It's just... Been so long," Tyler whispered, Conner kneeling so he could look in Tyler's downcast eyes, "I think I despised them for a long time. My parents. I think I hated them. Then I no longer cared."

Tyler looked far away, Conner getting more concerned by the second along with everyone else.

"I... I remember a car. I even remember dropping my plastic soldier between the seats. His grip was tight on my arm," Tyler's words being mumbled at this point.

"Whose grip?" Conner whispered, trying not to let the desperation leak too much from his voice.

"My fathers'. I know it was. I think I was frozen from fear cause I was dragged. Maybe I was crying or screaming. Dragged through the mud. That's right. It was raining. It was raining really hard. I was pushed? Or dropped? And the car was gone..."

The room was silent, on edge.

"Ty, honey. Baby look at me. Wherever you are, you aren't there anymore. You're right here. With me. With your friends and family," Conner's voice was so gentle, Tyler blinked a few times, looking around. He blushed hard, looking away with a few tears escaping him. Conner wrapped him up in his arms, whispering things that made Tyler's body become more relaxed. I wanted to go hug him too but I don't think Carver was going to let me out if his arms anytime soon. Not that I minded.

"What God forsaken pack-! What alpha would allow a member, a pup, to be abandoned and thrown away!? What-!" Chris started to yell, standing, shaking with anger. Adam kissed my forehead, racing over to hug his mate.

"Anyone weaker would have gone insane," John trying to express admiration towards Tyler who looked shyly at the other betas who looked ready to tear something apart.

"He was a bit odd when we met him, but he was starving and alone for a very long time," Robin whispered getting a half hearted pout from Tyler.

"Ha' m' wo'f," Tyler tried saying 'had my wolf', but his face was pressed against Conner's chest, sounding muffled.

"Sweetie are you sure your mate can breathe?" Adam spoke gently. Conner pouted, loosening his grip. Tyler moved his head a little before snuggling against his mate again.

"Who would abandon their baby?" Adam quietly sobbed into Chris' shoulder who was rocking his mate gently.

I think everyone felt the need to comfort Luna because his sobs hurt my ears and my heart.

"Alpha says it's b-bad if we try to figure out why evil p-people do evil things," I whispered out, Carver giving me little butterfly kisses and snuggles.

"Alpha and Ty have killed a lot of rogues who have tried to..." Robin whispered brokenly, Raven hushing him and combing his hand through Robin's hair.

"She kept us safe. Taught us to fight. We only had ourselves when we came across lone rogue wolves."

"Sh-She was taken from her family too," I whispered, looking up at Carver. They should know a little of Alpha's backstory so they don't think she's a threat. Carver pressed his lips softly to mine, releasing my lips, the sparks making me hum a little.

"Alpha wanted to make sure the area was safe for us which was going to take a month to do," Robin whispered, looking guiltily at Raven who smiled a little, kissing Robin shyly.

"W-We can't go against alpha and alpha promised to not take us away from our mates, but she needed to make sure it was safe here," my breath hitched, trying to explain, hating that tears were going to leave me again. I clawed my hand into Carver's shirt, desperate for him to understand, feeling his larger hands on top of mine.

"Hush pup. It's alright. I understand love. I'm not angry at you in the slightest," Carver cradled, my cheek in his hand. I shut my eyes tightly knowing a few tears of relief left me.

"Are you listening Kai? I love you. I knew you all had a reason to not tell us and that reason is painful and makes me so angry. I want to run and kill the people who hurt you. Kill every one of them that dared put a hand on you or didn't bother stopping the pain you were in. You know why I won't leave right this second?"

I looked up at him in surprise, shaking. I bit my lip, hope flaring in my heart at the passion in his eyes. I shook my head 'no', easing against his hand that cradled my cheek.

"Because my mate needs me right now and I will never leave you when you are hurt. Do you understand me Kai? I love you."

"C-Carver!" I sobbed, hugging Carver as much as I could with my little arms.

Conner cradled, Tyler's cheek in his hand, Tyler's eyes brimmed with tears ready to fall.

"My brave mate," Conner whispered, hugging Tyler, his hold becoming tighter from feeling Tyler shake badly in his arms.

Tyler was whispering 'so sorry', 'can't remember' every so often. Conner only covered him with butterfly kisses, soothing him. The room was quiet, Luna Adam and a few warrior leaving to get some more cool clothes and some water.

Carver dabbed the new cool cloth at my eyes. I could already feel how swollen and red they probably were; looking like a hot mess I'm sure.

"W-We didn't mean to trespass s-sir," Robin spoke nervously to Chris who waved his hand nonchalantly. Raven combed his hand through Robin's hair, nuzzling Robin's cheek with his nose.

"All is forgiven and cleared up. In fact I want more details about the two parties who have inflicted such pain, but at a later date. If you and your mates agree, you can see the pack psychologist who is a wonderful older woman. I think check ups from the pack doctor is in order as well and you don't have to be alone for any of it unless you want to be. Of course, that is, if you wish to join this pack," Chris' voice was gentle, still holding power with each sentence.

"Didn't you all know you were on a pack's land?" Conner asked confused.

"Submissive noses don't work so well. Can't tell if someone is dominant or regular and we couldn't recognize this pack's scent since we've never smelled something like it before," Tyler mumbled, his nose pressed gently against Conner's throat.

"Really?" Adam asked curiously since werewolves in general had a better sense of smell than most.

"You... would have us?" Tyler whispered, realizing what Alpha Chris just said, Conner harrumphing at him.

"Don't you listen blondie? We all want you here. We will never hurt you or treat you like-" Conner growled angrily along with Carver and Raven (and everyone else).

Tyler's heart relaxed, burying his head against the crook of Conner's neck.

"I-I would like to join," Robin whispered shyly, Raven kissing him softly again. Raven hugged him tightly as though that sentence eased all his worries.

"M-Me too," I could feel my cheeks heating up with a blush before warm lips pressed against mine. I hummed into the kiss, feeling want and need. I felt whole with Carver; with every fiber of my being.

Tyler nodded, whispering a 'please', Conner kissing the side of his head.

"We will have a ceremony then. All of the personal information you just shared will remain private. Only those in this room have heard what I have heard," Chris standing proudly, Adam by his side. Chris' hand was rubbing up and down his mate's back in comfort.

Mils! We got accepted into the pack!

They aren't going to hurt us!

They don't care that we're submissive!

This is the best day ever!

Amilya smiled sadly, still lying motionless on the ground at the townhouse.

"I would like to meet this girl who saved you," Adam asked excitedly before all three of us frowned, looking at each other nervously.

"Honey?" Conner whispered to Tyler who looked at him sadly.

"The reason why... we don't just... bend over when told," Tyler began everyone freezing at that, "is because Alpha is our leader and the strongest in our pack. Our wolves have the strength to refuse an order from someone higher ranking than us since we have an alpha. The only other person who can outrank Alpha are our mates."

"Alright...? What does that have to do with anything love?" Conner asked confused.

"If alpha doesn't agree, then technically, our wolves won't allow us to either, even if our mates ask us to. If we were fully mated, you would have higher standing than alpha, but as of now, you both are on equal standing," Robin whispered, Raven looking frustrated at that.

"I can fix that," Conner smirked, Tyler's cheeks a fire engine red at the innuendo.

"Down boy," Chris chuckled, the warriors joining him. Tension slowly leaving the room.

"Does she not want a pack?" Chris asked confused since that was rare for any wolf, including a rogue.

"She's been having a difficult time here for some reason, so I think we should give her some time," Robin nodded.

I breathed deeply against Carver, snuggling against him. His large hands slowly rubbed my back as he gave me sweet little kisses. Most of the weight and fear of being rejected by my mate and his pack, felt as though it was slowly lifted off of my shoulders.

I bit my lip, Carver's hand dragging down my chest towards my belly.

"You need to eat baby. You're too tiny," Carver mumbled against my lips.

"I'm not-" I was about to refuse, feeling bad for eating their food, before my tummy made itself well known in the room. I could feel the heat from my cheeks going up to my hairline.

"Breakfast is still on the table sweetie," Adam smiled, headed for the kitchen while ushering the warriors to grab a plate as well; Adam went to heat up the food. He let me help a little but Carver snatched me back so I was forced to sit on his lap. Puppy was pretty comfy so I didn't really mind.

I dug in happily along with Tyler and Robin since guilt wasn't clawing at us so badly. Tyler was hunched slightly over his food again, Conner rubbing his thigh and kissing his cheek every now and again. Tyler relaxed further after every few minutes.

"Wait a second," Carver said suddenly. My mouth was stuffed with a strawberry at the moment and I was really liking Carver rubbing my belly. I was trying not to giggle when he did that.

"Since she's an Alpha... couldn't she have... you know... I mean Alpha's get ruts, even females," Carver spoke with worry.

"Alpha is different..." Robin whispered, all of them wanting him to say more but knew he wasn't going to.

"Alpha bought us special soap so our heats don't attract," I added happily, not realizing what I just admitted to. Carver choked on his drink which scared the crap out of me, a few warriors choking on their food. I patted his back, confused. Adam did the same for Chris who was choking on his own drink. Everyone's faces were looking at us in shock.

"You get heats!?" Raven's voice going up an octave, staring straight at Robin who nodded shyly at him. Mostly because he caught the phrase our heats.

"Alpha was worried when she smelled you in the townhouse on Saturday, Carver. That week we didn't show up to school on Friday," I looked up at Carver who was still trying to breathe, "the soap masks our scents so no one can tell if we're werewolves, but our heats still get pretty bad."

I felt my blush increase tenfold, everyone just staring at us with their mouths open. Was it weird to have heats or something?

"Your scent was... so strong though," Carver whispered huskily in my ear. I felt a tingle go down my spine, feeling a bit damp down there; if you know what I mean. Carver groaned happily, gliding his nose down my neckline.

"Kai's scent is the strongest and most powerful since he is a submissive Omega," Robin clarified, an undertone of warning making everyone snap out of their shock. Tyler was looking everywhere but at Conner whose mouth was still dropped; his eyes an even darker shade of black it seemed.

"I can't wait," Carver growled low again and I accidently let a mew fall from my lips. Carver's large member pressing against my bum made me arch my back a little.

"Down boy," Chris growled, Carver grumbling and going back to rubbing his cheek against my neck. I whimpered a little before eating from my plate again, almost forgetting entirely that it was there.

"Alpha is a determined believer to wait for one's mate. She has stayed with Kai during his heats since his has attracted unwanted guests before," Tyler warning everyone at the table. Unmated wolves could be just as difficult to handle as rogues when a rut or heat happened.

I looked down sadly, hating that I've caused such problems. I felt Carver's fingers under my chin as we both gazed at each other. I love the blue color of his eyes so much. Carver kissed me hungrily, making me pant when he broke the kiss; far too soon.

"No one will touch or smell him again. He is mine," Carver growled. I couldn't help but smile softly at that, rubbing my nose against Carver's who chuckled. I loved possessive Carver too.

"Alright you two, lets finish breakfast," Adam wagging a fork at us, Carver rolling his eyes.

- (. _ .)

One week had passed and none of them could have been separated.

Conner was practically glued to Tyler's side, Tyler still getting used to the fact that he would always have someone. He was really trying to get used to not waking up alone. Having a constant warmth by his side always made him feel like he was dreaming. Conner would always sneak into his guest room in the pack house to cuddle. Not that Tyler minded since he was so comfy.

Tyler had a whole new level of hate towards Tiffany though. He had just gotten done with a shower, exploring the pack house. He was trying to learn about pack dynamics in a 'normal' pack since it mostly confused him. Tiffany had tried ordering him to do something the second she spotted him and realized he was by himself. Tiffany was a beta, but Tyler just flipped her off. Tiffany was using as much of her Beta dominance (even though she was a regular beta) to push Tyler over the edge so he could obey her. Tyler was shaking but could resist the commands she kept spewing off since he had a mate and an alpha; his wolf was on shaky legs though in his mind. A couple of football players from the school were being playful in the hallway, rounding the corner, Conner rough housing with them just as much.

"Get on your knees submissive," Tiffany snarled, eyes blazing black from her wolf taking over. She snapped her fingers in his face, Tyler flipping her off again before turning to leave. Tiffany grabbed his arm, Tyler pushing her easily. His arm felt like it was burned from it not being his mate's touch.

"You all saw that! He attacked me!" Tiffany pretending to cry. Tyler looked over shocked, seeing Conner and the other betas angry, who were stomping over.

"Con-" Tyler began hastily before he was hugged tightly, being pulled into Conner's side. Conner's head snapped to Tiffany who was shrinking down from the betas growling at her.

"How dare you try ordering a submissive. How dare you try ordering my MATE!" Conner barked angrily.

"Sorry, but can you take her to my Dad, Bruce? Max? I don't want her spewing lies and having you guys as witnesses helps."

"Yeah man."

"Course."

The two other betas lifted Tiffany easily by her arms, dragging her to the Alpha's office.

Conner kissed Tyler hard, once the betas rounded the corner, his tongue slipping between Tyler's pink lips. Tyler moaned softly, Conner's tongue dominating and claiming every inch of Tyler's mouth. Conner broke the kiss far too soon for Tyler who was panting heavily. Conner kissed and nibbled down Tyler's neck, sucking hard where the mating mark would go. Tyler keened in pleasure, growing embarrassingly hard. His legs were suddenly forced to wrap around Conner's waist. Tyler whimpered, feeling Conner's hard on press against his. Conner licked at Tyler's neck, a dark bruise forming as he continued to nibble it. Conner ripped part of Tyler's shirt open to leave hot open mouth kisses down Tyler's sweet skin, Tyler gasping, weaving his fingers in Conner's blonde hair. Conner pressed his forehead against Tyler's after a moment, both trying to catch their breaths.

"Conner, it's okay. Can't be ordered unless by my Alpha or you," Tyler smiled softly, Conner peeking open an eye, harrumphing.

"Damn right," Conner snarled, Tyler shaking his head before he was kissed again, deeply; moans and gasps echoing down the hall.

.

.

."Robin, darling?" Raven rubbing one hand up and down Robin's back who was currently folding clothes and organizing his guest room.

"Hm?" Robin hummed, sticking his shirts into a drawer.

"Love... I'm... I'm sorry for yelling at you without being given more information," Raven spoke sadly, hands clasped behind his back and looking down at his shoes; though his hands still wanted to continue touching his mate.

Raven's head snapped up when he felt a gentle finger caressing his cheek.

"I frustrated you and made you angry. It's just... Hard to talk about," Robin whispered, Raven nodding.

"I'm sorry I pushed you love," Raven cupping both of Robin's cheeks. Robin smiled gently, nuzzling one of Raven's hands. Raven kissed Robin hotly, Robin wrapping his arms around Raven's neck. The kiss was passionate, Robin whimpering a little. Raven broke the kiss slowly, biting where Robin's neck met his shoulder. Robin gasped, shaking with pleasure.

"Would you like a tour love?" Raven smirked at Robin's dazed look. Robin nodded numbly, his hand grasped quickly by Raven who tugged him out of the guest room.

Raven was showing Robin his favorite spots in the pack house and on the pack grounds. Robin's favorite so far was a little waterfall that had a stream that went deeper into the forest. Raven promised that they could return a little later.

Raven showed him the war room next, Robin inspecting all the maps and a large globe that was in the far corner of the room. In the center of the room was a large wood table that had 3D geographic landmarks on it along with symbols for different packs and such.

"This is my playing board, if you will, of the pack grounds. If there is an attack I can direct them best -" Robin kissed him softly, Raven surprised for just a moment before ravishing Robin's mouth, pressing Robin hard into the war table.

Robin always got hot and bothered when Raven would start explaining a tactic to defeat someone. The passion in his eyes turned him on to no end.

.

.

.

"Carver?" Kai giggled. He was straddled on Carver's lap, the two sitting under a tree.

"I have a surprise for you kitten, after the ceremony," Carver smiled, fingers running playfully under Kai's shirt.

"Not even a hint?" Kai kissing Carver softly, Carver smiling happily.

"Nope," Carver popping the 'p' Kai pouting so cutely.

"What a mean puppy," Kai grumbled, Carver barking out a laugh who turned so he was hovering over Kai, Kai laying with his back on the ground.

Carver licked down Kai's neck, nipping at his mate's collar bone. Kai whimpered, exposing more of his throat, panting.

Soon love, soon Carver thought to himself, knowing he was dangling on a thread at the moment with his self control.

.

.

.All three promised to meet with Amilya after the pack ceremony in a few days. She told them that they were allowed to accept the pack bond. All three tried convincing her to come and that the Alpha and Luna wanted to meet her. Amilya declined quickly, hiding back in the townhouse to all of their confusion.

"Carver I can't do this. What if your pack hates us? Hates me? I'm weak and -" Carver kissed Kai hard, growling low.

"You are the strongest and bravest person I know. To have dealt with all that shit and still survive, to keep going, it's the strongest thing I've heard. And you've showed that willpower Kai. Anyone, would be blessed, to have you as their mate, because I know I am," Carver smiled, wiping a lone tear from Kai's cheek.

"Why are you perfect Carver?" Kai whispered, Carver's eyes softening before smirking.

"Because that's the way the moon goddess made me baby," Carver smiled, smacking Kai's butt who blushed, covering his butt with his hands.

"Bad puppy!" Kai scowled, Adam laughing when he walked in.

"I'm sure I have a spray bottle with water somewhere," Adam laughed, Carver scowling at him, Kai giggling.

"They're starting. The others are already there," Adam smiled, Carver grabbing Kai's hand. Kai looked sideways at Carver. He seemed... on edge about something. Maybe it was about the ceremony.

"You can do this baby," Carver smiled, Kai nodding. All he had to do was swear loyalty into the pack and accept them.

Kai suddenly realized they were outside, a few people in their wolf forms and others standing in front of a stage. Kai didn't look up from the ground, feeling Carver's hand tighten around his.

Kai peeked up, seeing everyone staring at them.

I can do this. It's fine. No one will hurt us Kai whispered to himself, his wolf whimpering and curling into a ball.

"As you all know, we will be adding three new pack members. As Alpha I will answer any concerns you have before swearing them in," Chris spoke loudly, voice booming, making Kai and Robin shake a little, Tyler clenching his hand in a fist hard.

A few hands went up in the crowd.

"Why didn't anyone know they were werewolves?" Several nods went around the group, Kai visibly paling, Carver combing his hand through his hair.

"They needed to protect themselves. They had to know it was safe here before they made any other decisions. That is their right and they did not know these were pack lands," Chris nodding, everyone seeming to accept the reasoning.

"Will Kai be the future Luna?"

"He will be. He is the mate to Carver who is the future Alpha of the pack," Chris spoke sternly, everyone mumbling at that, Kai shaking, not wanting to look up.

"WOOH! LUNA KAI!" Mandy and her other cheerleading friends screamed out, Kai relaxing giggling. Kai waved over to them, some of the older members aweing.

"If there are no further questions-"

"Isn't it pathetic to have a pack with submissive wolves? Aren't they supposed to be extinct or something?" Tiffany piped up in a bored tone, Carver growling low along with Raven and Conner.

"Ms. Black. As you know a pack is stronger the more diverse it is. To have such rare, kind, and giving people in this pack is a gift. There will be no toleration for bullying, as you all know," Several wolves nodded, some glaring at Tiffany, "as a rule, no one is allowed to use their dominating voice to command any submissive. It is illegal and cruel, though it will have little effect if you try, I can assure you."

Chris glared hard at Tiffany who scowled, sitting back down.

"To clarify other matters, Kai Winters is the mate of Carver Summers. Tyler is the mate to Conner Summers. And Robin Winters is the mate to Raven Hill," Chris pointing to each pair. Yells and applause were heard in the crowd at the pairs.

"Let's move on with the ceremony," Chris turning to face Adam, who smiled lovingly at him.

"Tyler Winters, Robin Winters and Kai Winters. Do you swear your loyalty to this pack and to its Alpha, myself and future Alphas? Will you help when called upon? Will you aid those who can not aid themselves? Will you respect pack members without bullying or aggression? Do you accept this pack as yours?" Chris stood proudly, Adam standing just as tall next to him.

"Yes, Alpha!" All of them baring their necks in submission.

"I, Alpha Chris of the DarkIce Pack, accept Kai, Robin, and Tyler Winters into this pack!"

Yelling was deafening in the pack, Kai, Robin and Tyler feeling power fill them from having a strong pack, a mind link starting to work into their heads.

"I-Is this... what it's like?" Tyler whispered, looking at his hands before his cheek was cupped softly by Conner who smiled so gently at him. Tyler shook badly, being hugged by Conner who kissed his head, whispering sweet nothings to his mate.

"It feels kind of... warm," Robin whispered, rubbing at his chest, his hand grabbed by Raven who rested his forehead against Robin's.

Kai just smiled softly up at Carver who smiled just as gently down, moving some of Kai's hair behind his ear.

"POTLUCK!" Adam yelled, the crowd still freely screaming in happiness.

"Come on baby," Carver smiled, grabbing his hand.

Carver Kai whispered, before Carver stopped, eyes softening.

"I can hear you now," Carver smiled, kissing Kai softly who giggled at that.

.

.

.

It felt. Amazing! I felt strong! And I could talk to Carver through the pack link! Teehee Kai thought to himself.

Can everyone hear us if I talk to you like this? Kai asked curiously, Conner yelling a yes from across the room.

"We'll have our own links when we mate so no one will be able to hear you but me," Carver smiled, Kai blushing before grabbing a spoon of the yummy casserole.

"You like it baby?" Carver tried holding back his laugh, the two sitting in the living room which was packed.

Kai's cheeks were puffed out from all the food, swallowing hard, before nodding.

"Luna Adam makes the best food in the whole world!" Kai gushed, Adam aweing as he passed by, kissing Kai on the forehead.

Carver growled, tugging Kai into his lap, Adam rolling his eyes.

"The chicken is still in the oven love," Chris came over, Adam gasping, running to the kitchen.

"Thank you for accepting us Alpha," Kai whispered, head down.

"You're a good pup and I know you'll take care of Carver," Chris smiled, ruffling Kai's hair.

"Darling, Mike says he wants to put his observations in from border patrol before he gets some food."

Chris grumbled, Adam giggling, winking at Kai who giggled back.

"Kai, I still have that surprise," Carver smiled, Kai turning quickly to face Carver, straddling him.

"Now? When you said after I thought you meant in a few days. Not after, after," Kai cocking his head cutely.

"Yup! Let's go upstairs though," Carver smirked, his voice suddenly getting low and husky. Kai's nose wiggling before smelling Carver's arousal. His eyes became darker, Carver growling low. Kai's scent, shifted to like he was about to go into heat, making Carver's head spin.

Kai panted hard, cheeks flushing red.

I thought our heat wasn't for another week or so! Kai thought alarmed to his wolf who was panting hard.

Carver saw a few noses turn up at the smell, Carver carrying Kai up to his room, fast. His wolf was about to take over, daring anyone to challenge him for his mate while he tried racing to his bedroom. Carver didn't hear footsteps after them, proud that several members had such high self control. It was time to finally complete the mating bond. Their bodies had released the floodgates to their hormones, needing to claim each other, now.

Here you are lovelies! The next chapter is option to read. It is purely smut.

Smut ->Carver&Kai

- -

Okay guys this chapter is all smut. Literally... It's like rated R-21 or something. You have been warned, you may skip because there isn't going to be anything pertinent to the rest of the story here. No flames, flags or reports because you do NOT have to read this. Everyone else, enjoy you perves ;)

"C-Carver" Kai moaned breathy, Carver's pants tightening at that. Kai whimpered, feeling slick leave him against his will.

"You smell like when you were in heat baby" Carver panted, kicking open his room door before locking it. Kai wreathed in Carver's arms, slick suddenly coating his pants, Carver's eyes snapping down. The color of his eyes like a midnight blue, so dark. Kai felt his cheeks flush in embarrassment, his pants wet in the front and back.

Carver's nostrils flared at the smell, Kai knowing he wasn't using the special soap anymore since he had been wanting to mate with Carver for so long; he was dying to ask Carver to just claim him already.

"I-I think you triggered my heat early. It's stronger cause no ... soap" Kai panted, clawing at his clothes, Carver grabbing his hand.

"I'm sorry baby, I didn't mean to" Carver whispered, guiltily, Kai whimpering at that. Carver wasn't going to be a mindless knot-head, his Daddy called them. He was going to make sure Kai was 100% sure he wanted to mate.

"I don't mind Carver since you're here and will take care of me" Kai rubbing his nose along Carver's neck who moaned at that. Kai was shaking slightly, Carver's strong scent making everything in the room get fuzzy.

"This was part of your surprise and I guess now we can use it" Carver's voice was getting lower by the second, not sure how long he could remain sane.

Kai bit his lip, brows scrunching cutely in confusion. Kai rubbed his body hard against Carver's, wet spots appearing on Carvers pants from how much slick was leaving Kai. Carver was still holding Kai to him, Kai's legs wrapped around his waist.

"Look baby" Carver shook his head, not wanting to lose himself in his rut just yet; his mate had triggered his rut early as well and Alphas become rabid if they hadn't mated yet. Kai opened his eyes, not realizing they had closed. Carver slid the bookcase by his bed, over, a metal door behind it that had a scanner, "It will only accept my thumbprint or yours"

Carver grabbed Kai's hand that was almost too hot to touch, a beep resounding in the room when his thumb was against the scanner. The door swung open and Kai gasped. A huge bed was in the middle of the room with soft pillows and duvet. A sunk in tub was against the wall in the room that had a miniature waterfall and an array of soaps. Against the other wall was a mix of sex toys. A little kitchen seemed to be the furthest back.

"It's stocked with everything and anything. The only thing missing is you and me"

Kai had tears leave him, Carver kissing them away.

"I wanted to make love to you where it would only be me and you. No interruptions, no other smells, nothing. Our own little world for just a little while. I was going to ask you -"

Kai kissed Carver hard, Carver gasping in shock, before slamming the metal door closed with his foot. The room beeped again, a red light over the door. Carver took control of the kiss, his hand feeling like fire against Kai's body. Kai felt his much lighter body swing in Carver's arms, Kai being gently lain on the bed. Kai's body was too hot, ending up spread eagle on the satin sheets, head lolling around.

"It hurts Carver, please!" Kai whimpered, his hands shaking too much to get his clothes off.

"I'll take care of you baby. I'll always take care of you," Carver ripped Kai's shirt off, tugging Kai's pants off fast. He blinked slowly. If he wasn't completely hard yet, he certainly was now.

"You wore the panties," Carver growled, Kai licking his lips.

"You said to... Alpha. I was going to ask you too and hoped I'd be tempting enough," Kai bit his lip, humping the air with his sheer white lace panties soaked through, a spot of Kai's slick staining the bed sheet.

"Fuck" Carver snarled, his cock nearly ripping through his own pants.

Carver walked over to the desk, Kai whimpering, wondering where he was going. Carver grabbed an average sized dildo, walking back to the bed. Kai was panting hard, just watching Carver with haze in his eyes. Carver hovered over Kai who was whimpering and wreathing.

Carver breathed in Kai's scent, getting drunk off of it. Carver's tongue licked and nibbled down Kai's skin, leaving a trail of warm kisses. He tasted so sweet, Carver's head getting fuzzy, his rut taking over. Soon, both he and Kai would revert into their wolf minds. They would go in and out of their human consciousness until both of their cycles had ended. Sometimes mates could end up in their wolf forms, but that was only when cycles were completely in sync and the human consciousness was almost buried.

"O-Oh Carver," Kai whimpered, wreathing harder but stilled almost instantly, feeling Carver just stare at his very hard and smaller member. Carver's eyes drank in the sinful body Kai had, licking his lips and afraid to shift his hard cock in his pants in case that would set him off too early. Kai was going to push him away, no one ever looking there at him like that before. Carver smacked Kai's hands away, his large hand rubbing Kai softly through his lace panties. Kai's belly tightened, his entire body tense, breath hitching. Carver moved Kai's legs so his feet were flat on the bed, legs spread apart.

Kai froze nearly screaming, feeling Carver's tongue lick timidly at a dribbling of slick that was on the inside of his thigh.

"C-Carver!" Kai squeaked, Carver smirking, Kai feeling his belly tighten further with a burning need. Carver slowly slipped Kai's panties off and down his long toned legs, leaving a trail of hot open mouth kisses. He shucked off the panties and heard them make a wet splat on the floor.

Carver moaned low, Kai shaking, eyes becoming huge when Carver breathed deeply near his hole. His eyes were almost pitch black with lust, just staring.

Kai was going to shakily move away, his cheeks and body on fire, his omega side wondering if Carver was displeased. Kai's head threw back on the sheets, silently screaming when Carver pressed his tongue into his hole, lapping.

"C-Carver!" Kai screamed, moaning hot and low. Carver was groaning and growling heavily, eating Kai out, licking all the slick he could find like a man possessed. His nose pressed against Kai's cute sac, Carver's hands spreading Kai's cheeks further apart, licking desperately; Kai's slick was an aphrodisiac. Carver's eyes were nearly rolling back. The exploding flavor on his tongue making his mind scream at him.

"More!" Carver snarled, his dominant alpha voice making Kai see stars, feeling slick gush out of him, Kai's eyes rolling back in his head, Carver moaning and fingering him, wanting more of Kai's slick. Carver buried two fingers up to his third knuckle before adding another, scissoring Kai further. Carver was panting hard, not wanting a single drop of Kai's nectar to be wasted. His cock was burning and pre-cum was leaking out of him at a dangerous pace, feeling Kai's entrance squeeze around his fingers. Carver curled his fingers inside of Kai's hot chute, hitting something inside of Kai. Kai's mind went white. His seed shot out of him, making his body quake as he silently screamed, clawing at the sheets. He would have small, intense orgasms until he was finally claimed.

Kai was whimpering, trying to wriggle away from Carver's sinful tongue who was licking him still, holding his hips down tightly.

Carver's eyes snapped up to Kai's, which were a dark stormy gray at this point. Kai's penis became hard immediately, curving up his belly. Carver stood slowly, his muscles rippling. He had slick all over his lips and chin. A lone dribble was sliding down his chest to his sinful abs. Kai's eyes watching that dangerous drop, Carver gleaming with sweat and his slick.

Carver was licking his fingers, before leaning down to nibble and suck around Kai's cock. Kai whimpered, biting his lip, the need to be filled burning him. He felt his hole clench hard, needing his mate's cock.

"C-Carver" Kai whimpered, "hurts" Kai nearly sobbed. Carver growled, his fingers pistoning inside of Kai fast, who gasped loud, riding Carver's fingers, needing something more. Kai screamed, coming again when Carver curved his fingers inside of him, gasping in shock. He suddenly felt something foreign inside of him, whimpering pitifully to his Alpha's ears.

Carver had shoved the fake dildo easily inside of his Omega. Carver rubbed his slick covered hand down his pants and around his cock, watching Kai thrusting onto the dildo, not knowing what to do; he was going deeper into his Omega state.

Carver took pity on his little mate, bending down to lick around Kai's hole, Kai clawing at the sheets, head thrashing on the pillows. Carver shoved the dildo harder inside of Kai, swallowing Kai's cock hole. Kai came hard, filling Carver's mouth, who moaned hotly, sucking away all of Kai's seed. It wasn't as tasty as Kai's slick, but he didn't mind. He wouldn't be too greedy until later. Kai was still thrusting hard, Carver snarling a 'no' when Kai tried to touch the dildo.

"Yes Alpha"

Kai whimpered, the dildo being left inside of him. Kai couldn't be satisfied until he was knotted. Carver strapped the dildo around Kai's waist who was humping hard for more friction. Kai opened his eyes, seeing Carver undressing, watching him with hooded eyes. Kai whimpered, struggling to crawl over to him, watching as his mate's pants pooled to the floor, Carver standing next to the bed. Kai felt slick gush out of him, almost forcing the dildo out, his body ready for the huge cock to enter him. His mate's Alpha cock. Carver's body was gorgeous. A corded chest leading to washboard abs, with a yummy v-line leading to a huge, heavy, and big Alpha cock.

Kai timidly licked Carver's cock, holding it gently in his hands. He sucked on just the tip, Carver growling low. Carver's eyes became hooded, watching Kai's pretty pink lips travel on his cock. Carver wove his fingers in Kai's black hair, encouraging Kai's curiosity. Kai was exploring. He had never seen anything like Carver's member before. It was heavy and hot in his hands. It pulsed and was a dark red at the head. It was ridiculously larger than his own.

"Present, Omega" Carver snarled, eyes glowing yellow. Carver had enough and knew he was going to cum. He would be damned if his first orgasm with his mate wasn't inside his omega. Fucking him and knotting him; filling him. Kai's eyes flashed blue, scrambling to get onto all fours. He flailed for a moment, his body on fire. Carver was standing on the side of the bed that came up to mid thigh. Kai let the front of his body lay on the bed, his ass high in the air. His chest was heaving against the bed, Carver stroking himself harder. Kai slid his knees farther apart, moving his head to the side. His hands were above his head. Electricity is what was felt between them. Almost as though they would be burned alive when they touched. Carver rubbed his hand against Kai's hole that was stuffed with the dildo. Kai mewled at that, before Carver reached around to tug and flick Kai's pink perky nipples. Kai whimpered panting hard, rubbing his ass against Carver's abs, feeling the muscles flexing against him. Kai could feel himself filled with slick, knowing his body was practically swallowing the regular dildo.

Kai moaned heavily, Carver's cock bouncing against his ass, Carver smacking his ass hard several times until it was a bright pink. Carver licked at Kai's hole happily, Kai quaking in pleasure.

"You make me so wet Alpha" Kai whispered, hearing a low growl.

"Mine" Carver snarled biting and leaving hickies on Kai's ass cheeks. Carver had been dying to bite Kai's ass, loving how round and firm it was in his hands.

"Fill me Carver! I want your seed inside of me! Please I need you inside!" Kai screamed, desperate. Carver thrust the dildo a few more times inside of Kai before throwing it somewhere in the room. Carver devoured the slick that came out of Kai, moaning heavily. Several beads ran down Kai's shaking thighs, Carver massaging his hands against Kai's thighs.

"Don't. Move" Carver's wolf almost taking over. One eye blue, the other yellow.

"Yes Alpha" Kai whimpered, stilling, "Only wet for you... all for you. Knot. Wet. Knot now!"

"What a greedy knot slut" Carver purred, his hands running and groping Kai's bottom before slapping each cheek hard. Kai bit the duvet hard, Carver's large cock rubbing against his hole. Slick was freely pouring out of Kai, Carver's cock wet and glistening with his Omega's sweet slick.

"You want this my omega? To fill you. Breed you. To stuff you full of my seed and have you dripping it along with your slick? Is that what you want my omega?" Carver growled low, so low, hot and husky.

Kai mewled, thighs shaking.

"Need my alpha's cock!" Kai screamed before nearly sobbing, clawing at the sheets. Carver pressed the tip of his penis to Kai's hole, snapping his hips hard, the burn and stretch making Kai come instantly again.

Kai felt so full. Kai's hole was clenching happily, its needs finally being met. Carver moaned low and breathy, his fingers running around the edges of Kai's hole that was stretched beautifully around his huge dick. His body was meant for this.

Kai pressed his hand against his belly, sighing happily, shaking his hips a little, enjoying the heavy weight inside of him.

Carver pulled out slowly, moving just as slowly back in, his breath shuttering at the tight wet heat that was engulfing him. Pleasurable licks ran down their backs like fire.

"Fuck" Carver growled. He pulled out slowly, snapping his hips forward, Kai screaming happily.

"Omega likes?" Carver did it again, harder. Picking up the pace. Kai was holding onto the bed like a lifeline, Carver's scent drowning him. The stretch and heavy cock of his mate filling his every dirty desire.

Kai could see a blurry vision of a black wolf coming closer to his white wolf, before it was almost crystal clear in his mind.

Carver was ramming himself hard inside of Kai, his heart hammering and slick splashing out with every hard thrust. Kai's slick was running in streams down his pale legs along with Carver's thick thighs.

Kai was sobbing, Carver wrapping one arm around Kai's waist, his hand held tightly around Kai's member.

Kai was seeing stars, his body drenched in sweat and slick. Carver could see a white wolf in his mind that was beautiful and breathtaking.

"You are mine Kai. All mine. Every part. I claim every inch of you" Carver snarled. Kai was sobbing in pleasure, Carver scraping his canines against Kai's neck, his chest molded to Kai's back.

The white wolf was presenting itself to the black wolf, whimpering, the black wolf wasting no time in claiming his mate. Kai's eyes shot open, feeling Carver's cock growing heavier and thicker.

Carver snarled, pinning Kai with his body to the bed, knowing wolves instinctively try not to be knotted unless it was their mate. New mates did the same thing wanting to show they can't just be claimed easily. Carver was grinding hard and fast inside of Kai, pounding into the fluttering chute.

Kai snarled back, eyes blazing blue. He was clawing and drawing blood from Carver's forearms, baring his teeth at Carver. Carver growled, baring his teeth back, Carver pounding harder inside of Kai, his knot catching on Kai's rim.

"O-Oh" Kai mewled, back arching at the feel of the huge knot catching on his rim.

"Knot! Breed! Claim!" Kai sobbed, babbling at that point, not feeling his legs anymore. His alpha's knot was huge and he could feel his wolf struggling as well in fear at how large it was. It was too late though and Kai screamed to the high heavens.

Carver roared, shoving his knot into Kai's burning hole, Kai silently screaming back arching hard into Carver's chest who was like an immovable force above him. Carver came hard inside of Kai shuttering his load deeply into Kai's body. Kai sobbed and silently screamed, his seed shooting in ribbons up his chest and smearing onto the bed. Carver bit Kai's neck hard in that moment, feeling his alpha power swirl inside of his mate. Kai was beyond euphoria, drifting high on ecstasy.

Carver continued to cum, but it wasn't as intense; Alpha's cum for as long as they were knotted. Kai felt his belly pressed into the bed, feeling bloated from all the cum, a blissed out smile on his face.

Kai closed his eyes tiredly, feeling Carver move them carefully further onto the bed, everything going black. Their wolves would take over from there.

.

.

.

"mmm" Kai mumbled, eyes opening slowly, everything blurry for a second. Kai saw the sunken tub on the other side of the room, everything coming back to him.

Kai could feel that his face was on fire, suddenly feeling a large hand rubbing up and down his body. Kai whimpered when that hand stroked his penis, before rubbing into his hip.

"Hey baby. It's about five in the morning. How are you feeling?" Carver's voice was hoarse.

Kai smiled softly, tears leaving him.

"Kai!?" Carver looking at his mate's face, worry exploding into his mind. Kai gasped at the sudden emotions that he felt from Carver, their link being formed between them.

"I've always dreamed this would happen" Kai smiled, Carver relaxing that he hadn't really hurt his mate, smiling softly once the sentence made its way into his brain.

"Me too" Carver moved some of Kai's damp hair out of his face, going back to rubbing Kai's hip.

"Have you been with others?" Kai asked sadly, knowing an Alpha in a rut would fuck anything, not that females in heat were any better.

"No baby. My Dads would kill me if that happened and I really wanted my first time to be with my mate. I dated a few people who told me the ins and outs about heats, but I never..."

Kai sobbed, Carver freaking out for a second, rubbing Kai's back.

"I was so sure that you had been with other people! You're so wonderful and kind and handsome. All Alphas, besides mine, have talked about it while our group was passing through towns; they don't usually care who they are with"

Carver whimpered at that, wiping away Kai's tears.

"I'm not like that kitten. My brother and I made a promise to each other along with Raven to wait for our mates. I mean, we wouldn't like it if our mates were with someone else, you know?"

Kai nodded, sniffling, Carver kissing him softly. Kai moaned in the kiss, a low heat sparking in his belly. Kai wiggled his hips, Carver groaning, his knot having gotten smaller in the last few hours. Kai giggled, Carver biting his lip softly in punishment. Kai's heat wouldn't be back yet, so they had a little time.

Kai checked on his wolf, blushing scarlet, Carver wondering what he was thinking about before smirking. Both could see their wolves together now, clearly.

The white wolf was laying underneath a huge black wolf (almost hidden by the larger wolf's body), the black wolf laying happily on top of him protectively. The white wolf licked the black wolf's chin, the black wolf wagging his tail and licking the white wolf's ears. The white wolf was knotted to the black wolf, just as Kai was currently knotted to Carver.

"I need to mark you too" Kai pouted, Carver laughing low which made Kai's heart thump happily.

"Of course baby but maybe we should take a bath first" Carver winked, Kai's face heating up at that.

Carver sat up carefully, spreading Kai's cheeks apart, Kai whimpering at that. Both moaned low, Carver pulling out carefully. Carver's knot had almost fully deflated, at least safely enough to pull out of his mate.

Kai moved to sit up, knowing his lower back was already aching.

"Stay" Carver growled low in his Alpha voice, Kai freezing before his breath hitched. Carver massaged his fingers against Kai's hole, Kai feeling Carver's seed slip out of him. He looked down, seeing a little puddle of white forming, Carver practically purring in happiness.

"Fill me again" Kai whispered, Carver's eyes snapping to his face before kissing him hotly.

"Always" Carver growled, his tongue claiming Kai's mouth, Kai's vision becoming spotty from the lack of oxygen. Carver broke the kiss, panting, chuckling low at Kai's dazed look.

Kai shook his head to clear the fog, slapping Carver's arm who was smirking, Kai scowling at him. Kai shakily got on two legs, headed for the bath. Kai giggled, hearing Carver growling, Kai feeling Carver's seed slip down his leg. It was a hot mess down there.

Kai got into the tub that had steam coming off, carefully gauging the temperature, practically moaning at how it made his muscles relax. Kai got in, the tub getting deeper if he went further in, stopping when it reached his neck.

"Which one you want baby?" Carver walked over, Kai looking at the array of soap.

"That one" Kai smiled since it was lavender and honey. Carver smiled, pouring it where the waterfall was, Kai watching the bubbles and scent of lavendar and honey come towards him. Carver got in slowly, Kai slowly moving his hand around Carver's chest.

They explored, figuring out what little buttons triggered what. Carver left open mouth kisses on Kai's scars, tracing a few. Kai had a few tears leave him, feeling so much love between the. Kai found a few of Carver's scars, repeating the action. He enjoyed when Carver's muscles flexed under his little hands. Carver rubbed Kai's lower back, Kai's head resting on Carver's chest, whimpering a little.

"I love you Kai" Carver whispered, Kai's head snapping up before smiling happily, almost shyly at his mate.

"I love you too Carver" Kai kissed Carver softly who let Kai control the kiss, Kai never feeling strong like this before.

They had moved to the more shallow end of the tub, Kai's shoulders visible. Carver suddenly had only the tops of his shoulders visible (even though most of his chest was out of the water at Kai's usual height), Kai feeling around, feeling a stone seat.

Kai bit his lip, straddling Carver, Carver resting his hands on Kai's hips. Kai attacked Carver's lips, Carver happily moaning, loving the taste that was holy Kai. Sweet chocolate that just melted in your mouth.

Kai whimpered, a scorching heat burning up his body, Kai's pupils dilating, Carver's nostrils flaring.

Kai's hands dived into the water, before grasping Carver's heavy cock in his hands.

"Fills me so good Alpha" Kai whispered, Carver panting, feeling hard as a rock from his mate's little hands touching him. Rubbing, massaging, running his thumb over his slit.

"Kai" Carver mumbled against Kai's lips, Kai licking his way to Carver's thick neck, his canines scraping on Carver's shoulder. Carver held Kai's hips, thrusting in Kai's eager little hands.

Kai braced himself, grabbing the edge of the tub, feeling slick pour out of him, knowing his body was ready without needing his mate to stretch him first. Carver's cock was ready and at attention in the water, Kai grinding until he felt Carver's tip press against his entrance.

Kai slowly pressed down, head thrown back, falling with all his body weight, down onto Carver's cock.

Carver was panting, pupils blown wide, his hands rubbing up and down Kai's belly, one hand slowly stroking Kai's cock.

Kai whimpered, moving slowly on Carver's cock, before his heat hit its peak, Kai screaming when he bounced hard, Carver's cock hitting his prostate dead on.

"Fuck, baby, ride your alpha" Carver snarled, holding Kai's hips. Kai moaned, bouncing in Carver's lap, grinding and moving his hips in a circle, Carver's head thrown back in pleasure.

Kai's knuckles were white on the edge of the tub, moving as fast as he could. The coil inside of him was winding tighter and tighter, the scent of Kai's slick overpowering the scent of lavendar. Kai was wreathing, tears leaving him in pleasure.

"Alpha!" Kai screamed, needing more.

"Omega" Carver snarled, slapping Kai's ass hard, Kai mewling. Carver growled, Kai's thighs shaking, arms wrapping around Carver's neck.

"Harder!" Kai whimpered, Carver pistoning his hips into Kai who went limp against Carver's body. Carver spread Kai's cheeks apart, shooting his hips hard, fast and dirty into Kai's greedy hole. Kai was babbling and leaving mean scratch marks on Carver's back.

"Omega slut needs to learn some manners" Carver growled.

"Knot! Breed!" Kai screamed, his canines evident along with Carver's whose eyes turned a burning yellow, Kai's eyes an electric blue.

"You should be punished for commanding me" Carver growled, "let you wreath on my cock without knotting you"

Kai sobbed, wreathing on Carver's cock when he stopped moving.

"No please please! I need it Carver! Please!" Kai sobbed, Carver rolling his hips.

"Hush baby, I will always knot you" Carver murmured against Kai's lips who whimpered. Kai planted his feet on the seat, matching Carver's thrusts.

"Yeah, baby, like that" Carver panted hard, his knot growing heavy and catching on Kai's rim. Kai's back was arched, his nipples being nibbled and sucked on since they were displayed to their Alpha, the hot water and scent of Kai's slick nearly driving Carver mad.

"Breed me" Kai snarled, Carver roaring biting Kai's fresh mating mark in the same place. Kai bit as hard as he could into Carver's shoulder. Kai screamed long and loud, being lifted out of the water and slammed into the tub edge, cumming in hard ribbons all over his chest and just under his chin until he was just wreathing with dry orgasms.

Carver shoved his knot hard inside of Kai, locking them together, feeling his load shutter out of him, coating Kai's chute. He pressed his hand to Kai's belly, feeling it bloat in his hand from the copious amounts of his seed, filling his mate. Kai was panting hard under him, legs spread wide.

Carver growled hotly. His eyes blazed yellow, caressing Kai's flushed cheek before rotating Kai on his knot. Kai's small back was pressed into his chest now, Kai moaning at the change, panting hard.

Kai was bent over the tub's lip, blood dribbling out of the fresh bite wound. Kai sighed out happily, his heat calming down again. Carver's mark was a dark purple with a drop of blood running down his shoulder.

A knock was heard on the large metal door, Kai whimpering in fear, Carver snarling.

Carver stood up out of the tub, Kai dangling off of his knot, scrambling to press his ass harder against Carver's knot. His feet not touching the ground, only his forearms able to touch.

Carver roared in warning, eyes blazing yellow, grabbing Kai's hips, trying to thrust harder into Kai. Kai screamed in pleasure, Carver lifting his sexy little body so one hand was around Kai's throat, Kai's back arched and feet dangling off the floor.

Carver pistoned as hard as he could inside of Kai with what his knot would allow, Kai wreathing, coming hard with a shout. Carver moaned, burying even deeper inside of Kai, his seed stuffing his mate full. Kai was limp, passed out, Carver's wolf sniffing for danger while his canines were buried deep in the curve of Kai's neck. He laid Kai down on the bed, Carver sitting on his shins with Kai firmly in his lap. Kai was laying with his chest on the bed, his ass pressed firmly into Carver's hips even while unconscious.

Carver growled again, hearing a sliding sound outside; his hips spasming again, more of his seed spilling deeply inside his mate. Carver rubbed his hands on Kai's belly unconsciously, his wolf poised to attack if someone were to get close to his mate.

Carver's ears were perked at any small sound, knowing he wouldn't go to sleep for a while if his mate was in any kind of danger.

Carver's eyes were trained on the door, licking at Kai's neck, making the bite mark heal faster. Carver rolled his hips again, his seed continuing to fill his mate.

Kai was sleeping peacefully under him, Carver laying most of his body on top of him. His black wolf was mentally doing the same, picking the white wolf up by his scruff so they were in a comfier position, both also knotted.

"Our mate will never be hurt again" Carver growled, one eye yellow, the other blue.

Okay, my brain has finished with hardcore-ness.

Trouble

F ive days of hot and heavy mating and knotting. Kai was fairly certain he had a permanent limp.

"Mmm... Carver... no more" Kai panted. He was straddled on top of Carver, buried deep and knotted.

"Not my fault. You're too flexible for your own good" Carver smirked. Some of the positions Carver had Kai in, probably made it much easier for Kai to bend in that position from all the 'practice' they've had. Especially if Carver liked it, a lot.

"It'll only be for half an hour at most" Carver rubbed Kai's distended belly that was filled with his seed. When mates were knotted together, while both of their cycles were in sync (and they were always in sync for mated couples), a knotting can last up to several hours at a time. If neither of them were in their cycles anymore, than it was a much shorter time.

"You need to eat baby" Carver spoke sternly, Kai giggling.

"You made enough food Carver to last us those few days"

"Too few" Carver's eyes blazing yellow, "want you knotted and wreathing, filled for days"

"Bad puppy" Kai scowled, slapping Carver's chest. Carver grumbled, his hands rubbing up and down Kai's body, eyes returning to their gorgeous blue.

Carver was very, very pleased when he stuffed a butt plug in Kai when he had to cook food for his mate. When Carver was cooking his wolf wanted to keep him on his cock, becoming increasingly aggressive when his seed wouldn't stay inside of his mate.

Kai would waddle around funny, rubbing his belly. Carver and his wolf purring happily since the butt plug kept his seed in his mate and made his wolf keen at the idea of Kai being pregnant with his pups. Which was another thing they'd have to discuss. Normal wolves didn't usually conceive until their third or fourth heat/rut together.

Kai bit his lip, Carver's cock slipping out of him with a warm pop. Carver panted happily seeing his seed slip out of his mate and down his creamy thighs. Carver promptly carried Kai into the shower, both of them having moved back to Carver's normal bedroom since Kai's heat was over yesterday.

Carver washed Kai gently, Kai doing the same, their hands hardly away from the other.

"Out puppy" Kai scowled cutely, Carver kissing him gently.

"I'll behave" Carver pouted, his lips brushing against Kai's.

"That's what you said last time and don't you use those eyes on me!" Kai wagged his finger. Carver chuckled at Kai trying to be threatening. He licked Kai's mark soft and slow, Kai mewling at that.

"Be out soon or I'll come help" Carver winked, drying off before leaving to get some clothes on.

Kai shuttered, his heart thumping happily. Kai cleaned his poor and deliciously abused hole; his omega side needing to be clean down there when he wasn't in heat. Not that Carver's Alpha side would let him.

Kai sighed happily, feeling much cleaner down there, drying off with a fluffy towel.

"It seems Daddy bought you some clothes that'll fit" Carver sniffing at some clothes that were in a paper bag on the floor.

Kai squealed (promptly shoving Carver away from his new clothes) digging through, throwing clothes this way and that, hitting Carver in the face with some shirts.

Carver grumbled before purring happily, seeing Kai pull on a pair of light blue panties.

"Love those" Carver's voice husky, loving when Kai shivered happily who wiggled his cute bubble butt at him.

"Be-have" Carver ground out, Kai giggling. Carver groped and bent down to bite Kai's butt cheek from the part that was visible with the panties, adding to the marks that were already there. Kai mewled and shook his butt a little more, Carver slapping and groping him again. Kai giggled, scampering away from Carver's playful growl, pulling on some skinny jeans and a hello Kitty shirt.

Ready baby? Carver smiled, Kai happily gazing at him. Kai nodded, getting on his tip toes, kissing Carver's mark sweetly.

Carver repeated the action, both feeling sparks run down their bodies. They could speak through their own mind link now instead of the pack link.

Kai's tummy made a loud grumble of protest, making Kai blush in embarrassment. Carver laughed out loud, holding Kai's hand as the two walked to breakfast.

You sure you are feeling okay baby? Carver asked again with a twinge of worry in his voice. Kai smiled softly at Carver, nodding.

I'm sure puppy. You'd never hurt me Kai's heart thumping again at how happy that statement alone made him. Carver smiled in relief, leaning down to kiss Kai softly.

When they walked into the kitchen, everyone froze when they saw them.

"Kai!" Tyler and Robin yelled, promptly pushing Carver away who growled at them. They lifted Kai's arms and sniffed him, running around him in circles. Kai just stood their bored, knowing they usually did that anyway when they hadn't seen him for a whole day.

What was it like?

You have to tell us everything!

I'm so nervous when I'm going to mate

Was it romantic?

Do you remember anything?

Kai was overwhelmed, Carver feeling his mate's distress before tugging Kai to him. Kai relaxed, snuggling into his chest.

Awes resounded in the room, Kai giggling shyly.

"You still have your old link?" Chris said in surprise, before everyone looked confused at that.

"How is that possible?" Adam whispered, making breakfast plates for his son and Kai. He made chocolate chip pancakes with different faces for Kai.

"Let's wonder about that later" Chris shrugged, Carver pulling Kai onto his lap.

"Why does he get faces in his pancakes?" Carver pouted, Kai stuffing his face, not wanting his pancakes stolen since they were filled with yummy chocolate. Carver was definitely devious enough to do so.

"Because Kai was abused by you, you rough Alpha" Adam wagging a wooden spoon at him, making Carver roll his eyes; although a happy smirk was on his face. Kai was red faced at the innuendo, trying to concentrate on eating instead.

"Dude you look like a preening peacock when you do that" Conner snorted, everyone laughing at the table when Carver scowled at him.

Oh Kai! Tyler spoke suddenly through their original mind link.

Kai looked up, still happily eating his pancakes. Carver was adding syrup for him, the two already subconsciously knowing the others needs.

Alpha Mils wanted to talk to us today

Kai and Robin automatically felt guilty, not hanging out or even talking to Mils for the week they've been gone. They were kind of frozen for a second, before going back to eating their breakfasts.

"Honey?" Conner whispered to Tyler, grabbing his hand. Tyler blushed lightly, peeking over at Conner who was trying to get Tyler to face him anyway.

Kai felt his cheek cradled by Carver who had flickers of worry in his eyes. Raven was rubbing his hand on Robin's thigh, cocking his head curiously.

"You seemed worried about something all of a sudden" Conner's brows furrowing.

"Not to mention you three looked to be talking through your original link" Raven frowning slightly before Robin giggled quietly, kissing his cheek.

"Alpha wants to speak to us today" Kai nodded, "N-Not you A-Alpha Chris, the-the other-" Kai spoke nervously, Carver giving a huff of a laugh before kissing Kai softly who instantly relaxed.

"I understood" Chris giving a half lifted smile, relaxing Kai further. Adam rested his head on Chris' shoulder, looking sleepy.

"We'll only be gone a few hours at most" Robin finishing with his breakfast along with the rest. A few pack members greeted the group at the table before carrying on with their duties. Tyler, Robin, and Kai were getting ready to leave the pack house.

"Can't we come with you?" Conner frowned, pouting cutely at Tyler who laughed softly, kissing him gently on the lips.

"Yes! I would very much like to meet with her!" Adam practically bouncing in his seat.

"Alpha is..." Kai thought for a moment.

"Skittish"

"Wary"

"Rabid"

"On edge"

"Nervous" Kai finished with Tyler and Robin throwing words out at him, "around others who are 'new'. I think it would be best if it was just us for now"

"But..." Carver frowned, almost pouting. Kai huffed a smile, kissing Carver lovingly.

We can still talk through our link if anything puppy, okay? Kai smiled, seeing Carver relax a little.

As long as you aren't too far away baby, but that does help. My wolf and I just don't like you too far from us; we are newly mated

I know Carver, but Alpha is an important person in my life too. Maybe we can get her to come over?

Either way I want you back here in three hours at most. Or at least text me if you need more time. It isn't a command baby, I just worry Carver added quickly, Kai snuggling happily into his mate's chest.

"Awe! You two are so cute!" Adam squealed happily, Chris holding on to his mate from tackling the two.

"C-Carver" Kai whispered, with a cute blush on his cheeks that made Carver's heart thump happily. Tyler and Robin were whispering sweet goodbyes to their mates as well who were tugging them back for more kisses, wanting to come along.

"Yes baby?" Carver smiled softly, sighing happily.

"C-Could we run in our wolf form together when we get back? I'd like to actually meet and see your wolf. Plus his fur looks fun to play with" Kai smiled happily, seeing a black wolf in his mind puffing up happily, wagging it's tail. Kai's white wolf still sleeping away, curled up near the black wolf who licked the white wolf lovingly.

"I would love that!" Carver nearly shouted, lifting and spinning Kai around who squealed happily, laughing just as loudly.

Kai leaned in softly, kissing Carver gently who put his small feet back onto the floor. Tyler and Robin were getting their shoes and coats on, being constantly groped by their mates. Kai suddenly, froze, looking at the picture of the girl on the wall again. Still... so familiar. Almost hauntingly so.

Kai whipped around, hearing a low sigh, seeing sadness in Carver's eyes, the corner of Carver's lips lifting slightly. Carver wrapped his arms around Kai, Kai's small back pressed against his chest.

"I think I told you she was our baby sister?"

Kai nodded, getting his arm free so he could cradle Carver's cheek in his hand. Carver kissed Kai's hand gently, sighing sadly again; he knew that Kai deserved more of an answer.

"She was taken from us when my family and I were coming back from pee wee football. I don't think I could ever forgive myself for being mean to her that day" Carver whispered, looking down at the floor.

"Why were you mean to her?" Kai whispered, understanding that siblings fight. Kai turned so he was facing Carver, looking into those deep blue eyes that still held a sadness in them for his lost family member.

"Conner and I found out that she was a submissive alpha from this asshole who was yelling at my Papa and daddy about it. We didn't really under-stand what he was talking about, but we ignored Amilya anyways." Carver sighed.

"A-Amilya" Kai's eyes going huge, mouth dropping down in shock. That could just be a coincidence, right? That their alpha who was submissive and who was kidnapped as a child was named Amilya, and the weird fact that the daughter of the DarkIce pack who was also kidnapped as a child was named Amilya too. Right?

"Yeah... that's her name. She loved to help daddy bake and would stick gummy bears in Papa's coffee" Carver giving the saddest laugh Kai's ever heard, "she'd always want to rough house with me and Conner, even if that meant she'd get an owie."

Kai suddenly saw Adam freezing behind Carver, hearing Carver laugh like that. Tears automatically filled his eyes before he was hugged immediately by Chris who was rocking him side to side. Adam always knew when anyone was talking about his baby girl because it would always rip his heart apart and Chris would have to put it back together again or vice versa.

"My parents and pack looked for her for two years. We asked other packs around the country and a few out of the country to help, before we finally had to assume she... died" Carver sniffling loudly, Kai hugging him tightly, rubbing his cheek against Carver's chest before leaning up to kiss his jaw.

Conner cleared his throat, listening to the conversation while Tyler was getting his shoes and jacket on. Tyler wasn't paying attention to the conversation, but noticed Conner's change in mood having gone from playful to sad. Tyler hugged him tightly, feeling Conner's mood even out, wondering what was going on. Robin cuddled against Raven, since his mate was saddened by the conversation as well. Robin caught on to the conversation when the name Amilya occurred, looking just as shocked as Kai.

Their mates walked them out of the pack house, Kai biting his lip, a thousand thoughts racing through his mind along with Robin; Tyler didn't hear the conversation at all but knew something was wrong when seeing them around that picture of Conner's little sister.

"I'm sorry I made Luna cry" Kai whispered sadly, lip wobbling before he was kissed gently.

"It will always hurt when we talk about her because we will always love and miss her, but I thought you had the right to know about her since you'll always see her picture"

Kai nodded slowly at that, still looking guilty, Carver huffing out a sigh before running his nose along Kai's neck.

They just held each other for a moment, Kai not realizing how hard it was to leave until this very moment. Kai's wolf had woken up from feeling Carver distressed when he talked about his baby sister. Kai could see the black wolf tugging the white wolf back to him, whimpering softly, whenever Kai concentrated into his mind.

"We'll be back soon puppy" Kai whispered, seeing the black wolf whine loudly and unhappily in his mind. The white wolf cuddled under the black wolf's neck. Carver gave Kai little kisses, Kai slowly moving away.

"A few hours Kai" Carver spoke sternly, all three waving to their mates before walking from the pack house.

"You have to tell us everything!" Tyler jumped up and down when they were out of view of the pack house, trying to change the morbid mood.

"No!" Kai blushed red, knowing exactly what Tyler wanted to talk about, Robin and Tyler chuckling at that.

"It's a private thing Ty. Besides, we'll know once it happens to us" Robin lifting a brow at Tyler who was pouting.

"Did it hurt?" Robin blushing a little, wanting at least one of his own questions answered even though he just said it was a private thing. Kai giggled, shaking his head 'no,' his cheeks a dark red. The other two relaxed significantly at that since they heard horror stories of Alphas losing control whether they were mating or not.

All three suddenly saw the townhouse, running to it, opening the door before they were hugged happily by Amilya.

Amilya laughed (almost a bit brokenly) hugging them so tightly, feeling her heart calm at having them around her again.

Amilya's nose wiggled, suddenly sniffing Kai, poking his mark and sniffing around his body.

"That tickles!" Kai giggled, Amilya hugging him again.

"We did the same thing" Tyler smiling happily along with Robin who sniffed at Kai again too.

"Was he nice to you? Did it hurt? If he hurt you I swear -"

"He was very nice, it didn't hurt, and I love him" Kai smiled sappily getting resounding awes in the room from them. All of them moved to sit on and around the only couch they had. Kai naturally getting tea for all of them. They talked about school and whether or not they wanted to finish the semester. Amilya was adamant that they did since they were almost finished, and that they had a lot more knowledge about things now. The three explained the pack grounds and all the pack members they were becoming friends with.

"I know you all want to go back to your mates at the moment, even though it's been a few hours"

"Well we missed you too it's just... we lose track of time when we are with our mates" Robin shrugging shyly.

"I've heard of that and I'm not angry. It's just been... difficult for me here and I'm glad that all of you are happy and have your mates"

"Y-You promised you wouldn't leave, remember?" Kai whispered suddenly, Tyler and Robin stiffening at that.

"I know sweetie but..." Amilya gave a deep sigh, not sure what to do. The pain she was currently in was making things so difficult.

"We also still have our own pack link, even though we agreed to join the DarkIce Pack" Tyler crossing his arms, all of them not missing the way Amilya flinched at the word DarkIce.

"I gave you all permission to join..." Amilya frowning, although she had an inkling as to why their link remained.

"Alpha, they want to meet you" Robin whispered, knowing Amilya wasn't wanting to meet them in the slightest. He was going to press her until he got an answer.

OooooooOooooooOooooooOooooooOooooooOooooooOooooooOooooooOooooooOoo

Carver's POV

It's been three hours and my baby still isn't back. He texted me, saying that he would be back by dinner, but that was HOURS away.

I was pacing in the living room, my wolf doing the same in my head, wanting his mate with him again. I craved Kai. Like a drug. His scent, his voice, his warm little body pressed against mine.

My Papa and I finished some paperwork during the hours that my mate was gone. I think everyone could tell I was on edge until my mate was back in my arms. Mates didn't usually move away from each other when they mated for the first time; I was pretty sure Kai didn't know that. The only thing keeping me sane was that I hadn't felt anything bad happening to my mate, but I was still on edge.

Conner and Raven weren't any better than me either. Both were kind of working with the warriors, training, but it was obvious their minds were elsewhere. I was pretty sure they were on edge more than I was considering their mates hadn't been claimed yet.

"I'm sure he is fine Carver" Daddy smiled gently at me, sitting on the couch, "from how they described that Alpha, I'm pretty sure she is just as protective of them"

I growled softly, crossing my arms.

"Don't be short with your Dad" Papa walked into the room, lifting his brow at me.

"Sorry Dad" I grumbled, daddy just shaking his head.

"He texted you at least, right?"

"It's not enough" I sighed heavily, rubbing my hand down my face. Conner punched my arm playfully, making me scowl at him, Raven stretching before sitting on the ground.

"I still can't put my finger on that Alpha though" Conner putting on his thinking face.

"What do you mean?" Adam asked curiously, slapping Papa's hand away from his cookie.

"We spoke with her once. The Friday none of our mates showed up to school. She was... I don't know how to describe her" I spoke with frustration since all I cared about was having Kai in my arms again.

"It was like there was an undertone of power, even though she spoke softly"

"Her voice was pretty though"

I nodded along with Conner and Raven at that. Her voice was really pretty.

"I want to meet her" Adam pouted, crossing his arms, getting a soft kiss from Papa.

"You want to meet who?"

Everyone's head snapped to the entrance of the living room before resounding yells erupted. It was Leon. The head warrior and dominant alpha that was like our older brother. He has dark brown hair and beautiful green eyes. He has the same build as me except he has more scars on his body than I do.

"You ugly bastard" I yelled, smiling like a loon, trying to get Leon into a head lock. Leon was smiling just as widely, both of us trying not to be the first one forced to yield.

"You jerk face!" Conner laughed, hugging Leon around his body before going limp so all of his body weight was on Leon. A dead weight beta was not an easy werewolf to hold up.

"Someone needs a shower!" Raven smirked, jumping onto Leon's back whose arms windmilled before all four of us landed on the floor.

"Leon sweetheart!" Adam gushed, kissing Leon on the forehead, trying to avoid all the limbs sticking up in weird places.

"I heard you losers found your mates! Those poor, poor souls" Leon smirked, punching me in the arm before roughly shoving my head to observe the bond bite. We growled and snapped at each other playfully, but I couldn't help but preen at the bond bite on my neck.

"Why don't you guys have any bites? You too ugly or something?" Leon smirked before he was tackled by Raven and Conner who were rolling around. I laughed loudly at the statement, seeing Raven and Conner's cheeks turn red.

"It's complicated jerk-off!"

"Bitch!"

"Slut"

"Skank"

"Hoe!"

"Cumsh-"

"Language!" Daddy yelled, all of us freezing before laughing hard along with Chris. All four of us just rough housed, Chris and Adam looking at us so fondly. All four of us panted hard, calming down some. We were in a pile on the floor, Leon's wolf looking a bit more faded in our minds, but no one said anything.

"Leon honey, how did it go?" Adam had so much hope in his eyes it actually hurt to see it. Leon's smile vanished, shuffling his short brown hair, shrugging.

"I didn't find them anywhere. I swear I've looked everywhere..." Leon's eyes going dull which squeezed all of our hearts from the pain he was definitely feeling; or lack of.

I was about to say that he'd find his mate soon but... the words died on my lips knowing my best friend and older brother (not by blood) only had four years left to live. No. Three years. His birthday was last week. He's been waiting seven years to find his mate. Seven! Leon just came back from traveling the world to try and find his mate... but it seems that not a trace of them was left.

"I-If you're tired you should put your things away and go take a nap" Adam smiling kindly, his eyes filled with hurt; Daddy is a sensitive soul who loves everyone in this pack with all his heart. Several members howled in sadness for Leon's lack of success, others howling for joy at the return of their head warrior. No one was offended when Leon's wolf didn't howl back, knowing that his wolf was weak because of the lack of a mate.

"Okay Dad" Leon smiled, kissing him on the cheek. Conner, Raven, and I followed him up, helping him put his things away.

"I'm glad you guys found your mates" Leon smiled, and it was a real smile which made everything hurt even more.

"You'll find them man. I know it" Conner having a tear leave him.

"You are one of the best guys I know! You don't deserve to die so you won't!" I growled, hugging Leon tightly who was equal in size to me, his shoulders shaking.

"Maybe you'll find them when you least expect it" Raven whispered, rubbing Leon's back, the dullness remaining in his eyes for longer periods of time now.

"Maybe. Maybe! MAYBE!" Leon yelled before sobbing, all of them hugging their brother.

"It hurts" Leon whispered, his heart beating dully in his chest, "I'm scared that when it'll stop-"

"Don't" I snarled, my heart squeezing in agony at the very idea of my older brother dying. I knew Conner felt the exact same way, seeing his own shoulders shaking. Raven was looking down at the floor angrily; not at Leon but at the torment Leon was going through.

"You don't know how many times I thought about just ending it all" Leon whispered, knowing he couldn't say such things to Chris or Adam, knowing it would break their hearts.

"Don't" I whispered, Leon shaking harder when Raven and Conner hugged him tighter.

All four of us just stayed in a doggy pile, wanting to comfort our family member and brother; that was in so much pain and losing his wolf. I could only hope we were able to give him some kind of comfort.

OOOOooooOOOOooooOOOOooooOOOOooooOOOOooooOOOO

"I don't understand Amilya!" Tyler yelled. It was usually Tyler and Amilya that butted heads, rather than Robin or Kai butting heads with her. Tyler had taken over when Amilya slightly lost her temper with Robin's constant probing.

"It would just be for a little while! I wouldn't be gone forever!" Amilya snapped, crossing her arms.

"Amilya..." Robin whispered, both Tyler and Amilya snapping their heads towards him with anger radiating off of them. Robin shuffled nervously, Kai hiding behind him, peeking out.

"Did you know that the Luna and Alpha of the DarkIce pack had a daughter named Amilya too? They have a picture of a cute little girl with black hair and eyes along with a picture she drew"

Robin's eyes were sharp, almost like knives, Amilya turning her back to him, feeling her heart drop to her stomach. Her picture was still hanging in the pack house? Why?

"Mila?" Kai whispered shyly, holding onto Robin's sleeve. Tyler looked shocked at that, racking his brain from what they were talking about, before gasping, looking even more angry at her.

"Is. It. You?" Tyler spoke darkly, his beta voice coming through. Amilya's shoulders shook, knowing her secret was eating her alive. She thought she was too damaged though.

"Yes" Amilya whispered, the room dead silent.

"What the hell!" Tyler yelled, shoving the coffee table over, "You've had a chance to be with your real family and you've completely ignored it! Why the hell would you do something like that? Do you know the amount of pain we've seen in their eyes from how much they miss you!?"

Tyler was red in the face, panting. Amilya's shoulders shook, tears rolling down her cheeks.

"They knew I was a submissive Alpha and they were so upset... for years I thought if I ever found them again, I would stay away from them. I'd be a burden to them if I ever came back. For being something so... weak. I look just like Pa-" Amilya's voice hitching, "if anyone found me and recognized me, it could cause trouble to their pack. I was never going to put my parents and my brothers in danger like that ever again. Never again would I be the cause for them to be attacked. It's one of the reasons I've hid my face and body over the years"

Amilya didn't want to get into the other reasons why she wore baggy clothes and hid her face. Amilya turned partly, seeing Kai crying, Robin and Tyler with red rimmed eyes.

"You aren't weak" Robin rubbed his eyes, hoping his tears wouldn't fall. They never usually heard Amilya talking down about herself. She was their rock and the one to hold them up whenever they thought badly of themselves.

"Rogues are cruel and evil. Them attacking someone wouldn't be because a ten year old girl is a submissive alpha. They attack people because that's what they do. No rhyme or reason unless wanting to brutally hurt and torture others for their own amusement" Tyler snarled through clenched teeth, not bother to wipe away his tears that escaped him against his will. Over the years all four of them knew all about rogues.

"A-Alpha" Kai was hiccuping, hugging himself, eyes shut tightly to stop so many tears from escaping him.

"We've only brought up the subject twice about their daughter because the picture seemed so familiar. Just those two times Luna Adam has broken down" Robin spoke softly, voice hitching.

"C-Carver told me h-how everyone looked f-for you for two years. Packs from ev-everywhere!" Kai's voice rising because of his stress, "t-to see that pain still. I don't wi-wish to i-imagine how they were in-in the nine ye-years you've been gone"

Amilya's shoulders hunched over, face in her hands.

"I... I need to go for a run" Amilya whispered. The pain was too much. The words they were speaking to her, were to unbelievable to be true. She wasn't a good alpha. She couldn't even take care of them. She was ugly inside and out. Amilya couldn't take the squeezing in her chest, running out the back door, shedding her clothes.

"Amilya!" They all shouted, seeing Amilya's black wolf run out of the townhouse and into the forest.

"W-We need to tell Carver!" Kai sobbed, the others shifting fast to get to the pack house.

I'm following her. That way if they can't find her scent you can find mine Tyler ran out of the door, after Amilya. They knew tyler wasn't going to lose her scent. Years of living in a forest and you could track anything.

The other two ran to the pack house, needing to tell their new family and pack that they found the missing daughter of the Alpha and Luna.

oooooOoooooOoooooOoooooOoooooOoooooOoooooOoooooOoooOoooOoooOoooOoc

"Wow Luna! This is amazing!" Leon smiled happily, his lips turning blue from the icing off the cake. No one else was any better.

Carver was still worried that his mate had missed dinner, but knew that Kai would contact him right away if anything was wrong.

"Awe! You are so very welcome!" Adam smiled, pink tinting his cheeks, "It's never too late to celebrate a birthday!"

"He didn't make this stressed did he? Because if their are seven more of these, I'm running" Leon whispered to Carver, both looking at Papa who shook his head 'no', everyone sighing in relief at that. Adam cocked his head in question, before he was distracted by John; Mike coming to join them later.

"Woah" Leon whispered, getting up from the table. All of them turned to look out of the living room window too, Carver puffing up proudly. Carver immediately calmed down, seeing Kai headed for the pack house, just as beautiful as ever.

"That is my mate. The white wolf" Carver was preening, Leon's mouth dropped.

"They're both beautiful" Leon smiled, Raven preening right along with Carver. Leon playfully shoved both their shoulders, everyone watching the beautiful wolves heading towards the back door. Carver grabbed some pants by the door, Kai's old pair, Raven doing the same for Robin; now that their mate's clothes were clean.

Leon smirked, Carver and Raven growling playfully at him. The white wolf and smokey black wolf ran through the door, shifting, all of them surprised that the two shifted in front of other people. Kai automatically became a Koala onto Carver, Carver growling and covering (groping- let's be real here) Kai's butt so no one could see it. He tried to wrap the pants to hide some of Kai's scars since he knew his baby was really self conscious about them.

Raven growled at everyone too, holding Robin tightly to him so no one could see any part of his body either.

"Hi! I'm Leon! This idiot's brother!" Leon smiled, holding out his hand to Kai. Kai shied away, peeking nervously at him and then to Carver and back again. Leon frowned, rubbing the back of his head, not knowing what he did wrong.

"Kai is a submissive omega. He gets nervous sometimes" Carver whispered, finally able to relax, running his nose along Kai's neck. Kai mewled, pressing his nose against Carver's cheek playfully, both their eyes flashing to their wolves for a second.

Leon's nose wiggled, looking even more shocked, before looking at the brunette in Raven's arms.

"Both are submissive? Woah. That's so cool!" Leon smiled, Robin and Kai giggling at him. That wasn't a reaction they got very often.

"This is my older brother. He was adopted into our family when we were little and he's our family" Conner smiled, Leon shuffling his hair with a tint of pink on his cheeks. Kai and Robin awed at that, Leon harrumphing, trying to make his blush less evident it seemed.

"Baby, I'm all for you getting naked and all"

"EW!" Was resounded around the room, Kai burying his head into Carver's chest in embarrassment who was smiling happily.

"I want you to eat something before we run together" Carver spoke seriously, using one hand to rub up and down Kai's back, poking his rib. Kai was still too skinny for Carver's liking who wanted his mate healthier.

"Where's Ty?" Conner asked suddenly, looking around, immediately getting anxious.

Robin opened his mouth to say something before looking at Kai. Both looked worried and unsure.

"Baby?" Carver moved Kai's chin so Kai was looking at him.

"W-We didn't know C-Carver!" Kai sobbed suddenly, Carver not sure what to do, only holding Kai tighter to him, "I would have said something if I knew!"

"Please, we don't have much time" Robin said suddenly, Raven's eyes flashing to his wolf in worry for a moment.

"Where is he!?" Conner yelled, his wolf nearly breaking free.

Robin had grabbed a piece of Amilya's cloth for the wolves to track, the cloth being wrapped around his wrist in his wolf form, lifting it up to explain before everyone froze. Chris', Adam's, Carver's, and Conner's noses were in the air as though that scent reminded them of something so familiar. Something that made their hearts beat faster and for their stomachs to drop.

Leon's nose was in the air, inhaling deeply, walking closer to Robin. Raven growled low, holding Robin tightly to him, before Leon's nose buried into the cloth Robin was holding. Raven blinked in surprise, returning to holding Robin possessively to him. Leon snatched it fast, breathing heavily into the cloth, rubbing his face into it.

"Mate" Leon whispered, Adam full on sobbing, running to hug him. It smelled like mint and rain. It was warm and soft. Leon's wolf howled, the pain no longer stabbing at their hearts, his wolf finally standing on all four legs again; his head held high and feeling some of his strength returning to him even though every part of him was shaking.

Fire. Leon felt fire in his veins from the smell, his heart beating and feeling that the world was no longer gray. He could see the colors of things. To see beauty again.

"Where did you get this?" Leon's voice was low, his eyes yellow from his wolf taking over, "Where!?" Leon yelled, the desperation in his voice.

"Wait, your Alpha, your sister, is his mate?" Carver said in shock. Conner and Raven just as speechless.

"Where the hell is Tyler!" Conner yelled desperately, Leon's words jumbling with Conner's.

"You met them? They're an alpha? What are they like? Where are they?" Leon was firing off questions, his bones slowly popping. The need to shift and find his mate becoming too great.

"Alpha is Amilya!" Kai sobbed, everyone's breathing stopping.

"What?" Carver whispered, the confusion and pain swirling in his eyes. In everyone's eyes. They'd long given up hope that their sister/daughter was alive.

"She's your daughter!" Robin yelled, everyone's mouths permanently open.

"N-NO! Sh-She's -" Adam sobbed, not sure what to do. Hand covering his mouth, holding on to the top of the couch to hold up his shaking legs.

"She's your daughter! She couldn't figure out why this place was so familiar to her but she realized it was her old pack! She's running off to the border to leave because she thinks she'll bring danger to the pack by being here. Please we need to-" Robin was cut off before everyone shifted around him and Kai, all of them running out of the pack house. Robin and Kai looked at each other for just a moment, nodding, shifting and running after them.

--(*._.)

Do I leave it on a cliffhanger or what? Lots of stuff in the next chapter :D

Family

- -

Mike! I want all warriors except for two to go to the borders. There will be two wolves there. One will be Tyler, mate to my son Conner. The other will be.... our daughter. Amilya.

Gasps were heard throughout the pack link, everyone's voices overlapping.

Is it her?

Are you sure?

Everyone is heading there now

Chris saw Adam keeping pace with him, the pain and determination in his eyes matching his own. Their daughter. Their baby was alive. She was alive and leaving.

Chris Adam's voice was filled with so much anguish, he could feel everyone in the pack cringe at the pain they could hear in their Luna's voice.

We aren't losing our baby again Adam. Not ever again Chris' voice low and full of raw power that it shook all of them to the core.

A few warriors joined them. Kai was keeping up with Carver, Robin on Raven's other side who seemed to be making calculations in his head. All of them were following Leon who was ahead of them.

Leon wouldn't lose the scent. If he did, they all knew his heart wouldn't take it.

Amilya please. Your family is coming for you right now. They don't want you to leave. They thought their daughter has been dead. You can't hurt them like this. I won't allow you!

Tyler was blocking Amilya from crossing the border into no man's land, Amilya growling at him.

You don't understand! I can't put them in danger again! It was all my fault Amilya sobbed before her vision became spotty.

Alpha? Tyler whispered in worry, seeing Amilya wobble on her legs, When was the last time you ate something?

Tyler thought back knowing Amilya wouldn't eat for days if it meant saving up food for their little pack to eat.

Amilya whined, shaking her head to get rid of the spots that formed. Amilya's wolf suddenly froze, Tyler ready to fight, before Amilya's black nose went into the air.

It smelled like pine trees, lemon, and nutmeg. It smelled wholesome and clean. Strong. Amilya's wolf howled happily, Tyler's wolf jaw dropping in shock.

You can't leave now! Your mate is here! Somehow... Tyler didn't know if it was fate or luck, but if it would stop Amilya from running for the hills then he didn't care.

No, no I can't! They'll be in danger too! Amilya's wolf whined, clawing at her to take over, her eyes flashing between yellow and black.

A rustle came from the other side of the tree line, Amilya's wolf perking, ready to run to her mate. Three gruesome wolves snarled and snapped at them, insanity swirling in their red eyes.

Tyler stood beside Amilya, both of them snarling and snapping back at them. The rogue lunged at Amilya who rolled on her back before grabbing the rogue by the scruff of his neck, throwing him off.

Amilya saw spots again, hoping her vision wasn't getting worse since she was seeing doubles. Or maybe four more rogues came out. Either way, Tyler whimpered at her, knowing she wasn't at her best health at the moment.

Run Tyler. If you leave I can hold them off for a little while

If you think I'm leaving you, you got another thing coming Tyler snarled at her, his shoulder cut and bleeding.

A rogue lunged at Tyler's throat, Amilya shoving him out of the way, yowling when the rogue ended up biting her leg, a crack resounding. Amilay snarled, her wolf taking partially over, her jaws clamped down around the rogue's neck before another rogue jumped onto her back.

Tyler wasn't any better, fighting two rogues. He was about to shift into Amilya's wolf which was stronger than his, two other wolves dancing around them.

An angry roar came out of the tree line followed by a beautiful chocolate brown wolf, eyes blazing yellow.

Our mate's an Alpha... a dominant alpha Amilya swooning a little before realizing that this was not the best place to be day dreaming.

The large brown wolf tackled the wolf on top of her, their jaws pummeling against each other. Amilya snapped the rogue's neck that was still in her mouth, hearing another break of bone from the rogue the large brown wolf had tackled.

Amilya shoved him out of the way, seeing another rogue leap for her mate's neck.

MINE! Amilya's wolf roared, rolling on the ground with the rogue, her mate running to her when another rogue tried attacking her while she was on the ground.

Howls came out of the tree line, Amilya's eyes freezing in shock.

Papa... Daddy... Car-Car... Co-Co Amilya's memory shot into overdrive for her, Amilya shaking, yowling softly.

Conner and a few warriors leaped over to Tyler, nearly ripping the two rogues to pieces.

Chris, Adam, Carver, and Conner all felt their hearts skip a beat seeing a black wolf that looked just like Papa and Carver on the ground. Amilya felt the rogue that she was still wrestling with get thrown off of her, Adam ripping it away before Chris, Carver, and Leon ripped it apart. Amilya panted hard, lying on her side, the world going in and out of darkness.

Amilya felt noses and heads pressed against her, sparks shooting up her spine from feeling her mate against her. Yowls and howls were heard that were growing softer.

Amilya!? Tyler, Robin and Kai yelled in tears.

Forget to eat when you're gone Amilya whispered, passing out.

Leon yowled in agony, thinking the worst had come to his mate along with the rest of her family. Adam's sobs were heard through the link, snuggling around his baby along with Chris who was nudging her and whining. Leon's face was buried in her neck, whimpering.

Carver and Conner were nudging her and howling softly.

She-She hasn't eaten in a while so she p-passed out Kai whispered, Carver's big wolf head snapping up to him. Carver growled at him, Kai shaking, before Carver grabbed him by his scruff. Kai shook badly, whimpering.

S-Sam needs to l-look at her Adam spoke in tears. Sam was the pack doctor. Leon growled and snapped at any other wolves coming near his mate. He shimmied under her body so she was lying on his back, everyone hurrying back to the pack house.

Leon's POV

My mate. My mate was in my arms. Finally. After so many years thinking I was going to die and lose my wolf, she shows up. She shows up and is the girl I had a crush on when I first came to this pack! What the hell kind of coincidence is that!?

I placed her wolf form onto the examining table for Sam. I didn't want her out of my arms but she had several injuries and she was not going to be in pain. Her wolf was beautiful. Midnight black with her front right paw a creamy blonde color like Luna Adam's fur color. Oh how I wish to see her eyes.

Luna Adam was sobbing on the other side of the room. Chris had silent tears down his cheeks. Carver and Conner were standing with tears down their own cheeks, looking at her from afar. I wasn't ready to have them close to her yet, but this was their baby. Their sister. My wolf whimpered, laying down in my mind, both of us watching the slow and steady breaths of our mate.

She smelled so good. The mint and rain reminded me of summer rain showers. We played tag together in the rain one day. That was the day I got a huge crush on her.

I smiled softly, running my fingers through her thick black fur. It wasn't soft. Most warriors and Alpha's didn't have soft fur since fighting and training thickens our hides and fur to better withstand bites and scratches.

Amilya Her name was even beautiful. Everything about her was beautiful. I didn't care if she was covered in blood. I pressed my nose into her neck, breathing in deeply. I committed her sweet and pure scent to my memory, knowing I wouldn't be able to live without it.

I glanced my eyes up, seeing Adam shaking and looking at the floor. All of them were just looking at her like she was a ghost. And she kind of was. She was a memory none one could ever forget.

Luna I whispered, Adam's pain hitting me straight in the face. I moved my head slightly, telling him it was alright; my wolf and I were calm enough, knowing they would never harm her. I placed my cheek back against her neck seeing her family coming closer to us.

Adam's hand shook before sobbing when his fingers combed through her fur. Chris let out a choked sob, kissing her all over the head. Carver and Conner shared in hugging her, all of us having some part of us touching her. We needed her. She was the sunshine in this family.

"Alpha, Luna," Sam came in quietly, "I need to give her an IV drip."

I growled low, my wolf getting very protective.

She needs medicine I reasoned with my wolf who still bristled before I nodded at Sam.

Sam carefully put an IV into her shoulder, all of us pretty much quietly growling at him; he seemed to be used to such reactions since he ignored us.

"Future Luna Kai says he can help quicken the healing process," Sam whispered, Carver let out a broken sigh. Conner nudged his head against Carver, wondering what was wrong. Carver just shook his head, resting his head back against Amilya's side.

Carver's mate came in, looking down. He was very cute and seemed very kind. He definitely seemed perfect for Carver.

He shuffled over to me, Carver's eyes never leaving his little mate. I think they had an argument or something.

U-Um, Mr. Alpha Leon s-sir Kai whispered. He was definitely cute.

I-I can heal all of Alpha Amilya's wounds in an hour if you will allow me to. You can watch everything I do and tell me if you don't like something

An hour? I could look into my mate's eyes sooner? Hell yeah! Sam said she wouldn't be awake for a few days.

"She will be up?" My voice was low and deep since it was between my usual voice and my wolf.

She should be up and moving within a week Kai whispered, his eyes remaining fixed on the floor. He may have been been a werewolf with the lowest status, but he was a very brave wolf and I've met a lot.

"Please," I whispered. Kai nodded, shifting through the old clothes that were given to him. I saw Carver's eyes just love his little mate, even if he was upset about something. Kai bowed his head, hopping onto the bed. I growled a little, Kai shuffling nervously. Carver growled back at me, Kai glancing fast at Carver before looking down again. My wolf and I just huffed, watching the little wolf.

I stopped growling since I did want his help. Kai shimmied so he was curled into a small ball, pressed against Amilya's belly. He moved his head every now and again to lick where the IV was. His fur almost seemed to shimmer on its own, giving him an otherworldly look. I definitely wasn't the only one in awe at that. Even Sam was looking shocked at him. Carver was watching him in amazement, love so evident in his eyes.

I was happy for him. I was happy for my family and I was happy for myself. I had my mate, and I wasn't going to let her go. My future was healing.

--------------------------------------(^v^)--

It was the next morning, Leon barely sleeping through the night. Kai had finished healing Amilya, telling him that she should wake up soon. Everyone would come in and out of the room, either getting too depressed or too anxious.

Kai was currently in the bedroom he shared with Carver, tucked into a ball in the corner. Kai's little whimpers were barely audible, silent tears rolling down his cheeks.

Flashback

'How dare you keep something like this from me!' Carver snarled so angrily at Kai. Kai could feel so much hurt, coming off of Carver, his wolf curled in on himself, showing his belly. Carver's wolf was snapping and snarling, grabbing Kai by his scruff.

Kai nearly sobbed, thinking Carver was going to fling him to the ground, only for Carver to carry him back to the pack house with the others. Kai was shaking badly, Carver screaming at him to stay in their room.

'P-Please C-Carver! I would have told you if I knew!' Kai had shifted back into his human form, shaking on the bed, sobbing.

'Would you!?' Carver was panting, one eye blue, the other yellow. Kai just nodded, sobbing.

Carver was panting, trying to get his breathing under control, before his eyes widened in shock.

Of course Kai would have told him. Kai knew how much they loved their baby sister. How much Kai loved him. All the little things Kai did for him.

'Kai... I..." Carver realizing he behaved far too aggressively to Kai, never doing that to a pack member even. Scruffs were only grabbed if it was to make a mate submit (usually possessively because they were worried about their safety), or while they were mating. The other reason was to kill a rogue.

Carver stepped forward, hand outstretched to cradle Kai, before Kai flinched hard, curling against the bed frame, crying even harder. Carver's heart cracked in pain, a tear leaving him. Carver retracted his hand, shoulders slumping, slowly leaving the room.

'I'm a bad mate' Carver nearly sobbed, heading towards the hospital wing.

Kai was sobbing openly on the bed for what seemed like hours, hearing Sam through the pack link suddenly about Amilya's condition. He needed to help his big sister and friend. Even if that meant making Carver even more angry with him.

He couldn't be an even worse mate then he was now, right?

End of Flashback

Kai's POV

Carver and I haven't gone shopping yet. He told me there was this yummy food place in the mall that he wanted to take me too. Now I was just hoping he could at least stand to look at me. I tried wiping my tears away again, only for more to replace them. Carver had set a plate of food on the nightstand for me to eat, not saying a word. I didn't turn to see him, but I was pretty sure he knew I was awake on the bed. I had left the medical wing late last night, or was it early morning? I tried to get some sleep, but I was scared of having nightmares. Carver always made my nightmares go away.

I could tell that his mood had changed from angry to sad though; not that, that made my broken heart feel any better. My wolf was laying down in my mind, rolled onto his side, unmoving with his eyes closed. How could I not feel that Carver hated me? I just kept on lying to him. The sweetest mate in the whole world who loved me for everything I am. Who kissed my scars. Who made me laugh. Who protected me and loved me with all his heart. I didn't deserve my puppy. I didn't deserve anything.

I remembered Luna Adam telling me where the guest rooms were. I sighed bitterly, waving and trying to smile at the other pack members and a few rampant children. I traveled up another flight of stairs, seeing a few pack members bowing their heads to me again with encouraging smiles, making me feel even more horrible. I would never make a good Luna. I was pretty sure everyone knew that something was going on between me and Carver.

I bit my lip, thinking that it might be best if I just stayed in a guest room for a while. Just scope out the room for now.

Maybe that would make Carver hate me less I thought morbidly all of a sudden, my wolf whimpering. My wolf and I were really scared, only being picked up by our scruff like that when we were attacked by a rogue or when I was abused in my old pack while I was in my human form.

"I see Carver finally came to his senses to see how worthless you are," Tiffany smirked, leaning against a doorway to a room that was apparently hers.

Those words pierced right through me, praying I didn't just buckle then and there. I stuck my nose in the air, Tiffany scowling at me. Wrinkles showed up everywhere when she did that; what with the layers and layers of caked on makeup she had.

"T-That's Alpha Carver to y-you," I spoke softly, turning away to continue where I was headed. Skanky she wolf needs to leave me alone!

"Stop Omega," Tiffany snarled in her Beta voice, catching me off guard. I froze on the spot, my wolf unsure of who had ranking over us. Does Carver, even though he's so angry? Does Amilya if she is unconscious? I was thinking frantically, my wolf whining to obey and feeling pain start to crawl within us. I was so unsure if she had the higher power to do so.

"Hmph. So it's true. You submissives have to obey a higher ranking right?" I clenched my fist hard enough to draw blood. I was so angry and I wasn't going to give her detailed answers because she didn't tell me to. Not to mention it'd be used against me.

"Yes," I grumbled, Tiffany laughing like a hyena. Ugh.

"Then why don't you get on all fours and present to me Omega?" Tiffany smirked. My eyes widened, legs shaking.

"N-No," I whispered, feeling my wolf whining in pain. My hands were clammy and I was about to throw up.

Alpha Chris is higher ranking than her! But... Carver has higher ranking over me than Alpha Chris

I panted hard, feeling the pain in my chest increase from disobeying an order since my wolf and I couldn't figure out whether or not to listen to her. I shook my head fast, seeing the anger swirl in Tiffany's eyes.

"I said," Tiffany's hand came up fast, me being an unsuspecting moron, feeling my cheek sting. I lost my balance and ended up hitting the wall. I growled low at her, my wolf and I getting angry. I shouldn't bend for such a cruel person! Her eyes flashed black from not getting what she wanted.

"Spread your legs Omega,"

Tiffany snarled. I literally felt all the color leave my face. Sh-Sh-She was going to rape me! I thought frantically, about to shift into my wolf to run and find Tyler or Robin or anyone!

Help! I sobbed, not realizing I spoke through the pack link before opening my mind unconsciously so the entire pack could hear what was happening.

"You'll be the ugly whore now omega," Tiffany's eyes swirling with insanity, starting to unbutton her pants. She was about to push me down, my brain and body freezing in panic, my wolf trying to attack and submit. I was so dizzy and nauseous. Her pants slid down her legs, her scent making me gag and try to cover my nose.

The next second happened way too fast. A muscular bronze arm shot out of nowhere, Tiffany dangling against the wall by her throat.

"What. Did you say. To my Mate?" Carver had Tiffany held by her neck and lifted off of the floor, eyes blazing yellow. Tiffany was clawing at his hand, Conner and Raven snarling angrily behind him. Carver looked like he couldn't even feel his hand being shredded by her nails. I flinched every time I heard part of Tiffany's collar bone crack.

"How dare you order any mate of anyone's to present to you!" Conner roared in anger, considering she tried something similar with Tyler until

Chris gave her a warning. Carver was absolutely livid when he heard about it from Conner. As future pack alpha, having a pack member do something so cruel was inexcusable.

"You've had enough chances in this pack. Threatening the future Luna of this pack and others mates."

I saw two big betas from the football team come running around the corner. One being Leah's brother Charlie and the other his friend,

"Are you alright Luna?" They asked worriedly, making my eyes go round. Carver didn't call them? I nodded, seeing them relax before bowing to Carver.

"Take her to the holding cells," Carver looked proud at his betas before snarling, slamming Tiffany against the wall hard for good measure.

Are you okay Kai?

Where are you!?

Sweetie are you okay!?

Luna Kai where are you!?

Charlie and Tom are coming to help!

So many pack members were suddenly calling for me through the link. Raven, Tyler, and Luna Adam's voices were overlapping almost everyone elses, making me relax a little.

I-I'm okay.

My voice was shaky and I knew they wanted to ask more questions but I just closed our link off.

Several pack members were growling angrily and with hatred in their eyes at Tiffany who was crying and struggling out of the Betas holds. They all seemed to have run out of their rooms or from the hall. Did... I use the pack link? Were they coming to help me? But... I'd make a horrible Luna. Why would they help me?

"The Luna position should be mine! You should be mine! I should be in charge of this pack! ME!" Tiffany was screaming, people looking at her like she was insane while being dragged down the hall.

"Crazy bitch," Raven growled, Conner nodding next to him.

"Literally."

Carver's shoulders relaxed, his posture seeming to tell me he was calming down. I didn't know what to do but to look at the floor. I could see Carver's wolf whining. Why was he whining? Shouldn't he be walking away?

I think I caused more unnecessary trouble

My wolf whimpered at that, making me curl in on myself, seeing the black wolf wanting to get closer to my white wolf.

"Baby, are you hurt?" Carver asked softly, my shoulders shaking.

My chin was tucked into my chest, looking at the floor. I could feel all three of them looking at me, and I could already feel my tears ready to fall. I heard Carver's steps towards me, Carver moving so slowly; my heart hurts.

"Love, can we talk?" Carver whispered. If I looked up I knew I would see his hand stretched out towards me.

"I-I'm s-s-sorry I'm a ba-ad m-mate!" I sobbed, unable to hold in my pain any longer. I ran passed them fast, racing down the stairs, and out the back door. I was running blindly, before I was tackled by something, landing on the ground. Owie!

A huge black wolf with piercing blue eyes was above me. I was about to scramble away before shaking like a leaf. His head slowly moved down, his eyes never leaving mine. My heart was beating frantically in my chest and I was starting to see black spots.

The black wolf's ears went flat, laying down slowly, whimpering. That did little to ease me considering I knew how fast he was.

I didn't notice several other wolves and pack members watching us with concerned and worried eyes.

I'm a bad mate

I rubbed my eyes furiously from the tears leaving me, my eyes already feeling swollen and painful.

Wait. What? How could Carver ever think he was a bad mate? I was the bad mate.

"N-No!" I shook my head, weaving my hands into my hair, unconsciously getting into a ball.

I am! I lie to you and I make you angry and I've done nothing but be a burden to you. I'll never be a good Luna and I never deserved you and how much you take care of me. You're the best mate anyone could ever want. You're sweet and caring and playful. You ask about my needs or anyone's needs before your own! You care for your family and treat everyone equally. You make me feel good... Happy.

I sobbed, pressing my head against my knees, hearing a loud yowl which scared me. Why did it sound so painful?

Thats not true Kai! I let my anger take over. The truth is, I was scared of what was happening and I took it out on you. Worst of all... I scared you. I scared my wonderful, brave, kind, and smart mate. The one person that is my reason to get up in the morning. The one person who makes me more happy than anything else. The one person who is my reason for living. I know we've known each other for almost two full months, but I feel like I've known you my entire life. I love you Kai Winters. If there is anything I know for sure in this world, it is the fact that I never deserved you.

I sobbed even harder, everything getting spotty.

Deep breathes Kai. Come on baby, breathe Carver whispered as I followed his breathing.

That's it baby Carver scooting just a little closer to me on his belly; I was peeking over my knees at him. The spots were slowly going away.

Baby... Kai? I am so SO sorry I grabbed you by your scruff like that love.

I-It really sc-scared me Carver I whispered, almost instantly regretting it seeing so much pain in those blue eyes.

See... That's why I'm a bad mate. A mate should never scare you like that Carver sat on his haunches, his wolf whimpering.

You aren't a bad mate Carver I looked straight at him, wanting to do anything to make him forgive himself. Yes I was scared when he did that, but Carver was scared too. He let his anger cover up how scared he was. He didn't actually physically hurt me, just scared the living day lights out of me.

I'm sorry last night made you so mad Carver. I know you wouldn't ever hurt me. You're my sweet puppy and I love you.

The black wolf only howled louder making me frown. My heart felt like it was tearing. Carver was hurting. He was hurting so much because he scared me.

I unwound myself from my tight ball, crawling over to him. I felt my body quiver just a little, my wolf wanting out to comfort his mate. I closed my eyes, resting my head on Carver's large chest. The black wolf froze before I felt two massive paws trapping me into his chest.

"Please don't be sad," I whispered. I ran my hands through his tough fur, tugging on his somewhat soft ears, and running my hands down his back. His fur was thick and tough like Amilya's. He was so very warm and my body didn't feel so cold anymore.

I pulled away slightly, seeing blue eyes gaze into mine. He... Looked like he wanted something, but wasn't going to ask. I cocked my head in question before realizing Carver wasn't snuggling me like he usually did. He was just sitting there letting me do what I liked.

"If you're really not upset anymore, aren't you supposed to cuddle with me?" I blushed a little before letting out an 'oomph' from Carver's big wolf butt nearly laying on top of me. He slowly and gently nuzzled his giant muzzle against my neck. I slowly relaxed, knowing my puppy wouldn't ever hurt me.

"Carver... You haven't kept your promise to me," I pouted softly, seeing him looking confused at me and slightly anxious.

"Aren't we supposed to run together? My wolf would really like to meet your wolf too you know"

I laughed happily, seeing Carver's big black tail wagging a mile a minute before he got off me, jumping around. He had his front paws flat on the ground, butt in the air playfully, yellow eyes flashing. I giggled at his antics before he licked me gently. I kissed his cheek, making him let out a noise similar to a purr.

I was in my old clothes, deciding not to care if I shifted with them on. My wolf was already dying and howling for me to let him out.

I felt the familiar burn before shaking out my fur. Carver came over slowly as we both just let our wolves take over. Carver was holding me tightly in our minds, making me cuddle against him. My sweet loving mate.

No one's POV

The white wolf's piercing blue eyes looked down nervously and back up at the large black wolf whose eyes were a burning yellow.

The black wolf whimpered before laying down. The black wolf seemed to heave a great sigh before showing his belly. The white wolf blinked in shock, looking around frantically since that was a complete submission and Alphas never did that.

The white wolf slowly made his way over, whimpering, before carefully nuzzling the black wolf. The black wolf whimpered back before sitting up carefully. The two full on nuzzled and licked each other. The white wolf playfully nipped on the black wolf's ear, the black wolf pouncing on the white wolf.

The white wolf growled playfully before trying to tackle the black wolf. The black wolf pretended to fall down, nibbling the white wolf everywhere once he was in range. The white wolf's legs swung everywhere, yipping happily.

The two chased each other, weaving between the trees. The black wolf finally tackled the white wolf after playfully nipping at his mate's heels.

The white wolf was panting hard, getting nuzzled gently. The two lay pressed against each other, the black wolf resting his head next to the white wolf. Both just lazily gazing at each other. The white wolf suddenly felt something in his belly, feeling his body heat up.

The white wolf got up quickly, startling the black wolf. The white wolf looked around quickly, the black wolf wondering what his mate was looking for. He didn't sense any danger nor did he smell anyone nearby.

The white wolf panted slowly, the black wolf's eyes suddenly becoming dialated, nose quivering. He started to deeply breathe in the alluring scent.

The white wolf whimpered, presenting himself to his mate. The black wolf nearly lunged for his mate. The black wolf carefully and very gently started to mount the white wolf, grabbing him by his scruff. The white wolf only panted, not feeling an ounce of fear towards his mate. The two were not going to be leaving the woods for a while and their human's subconscious were cuddled together and deeply asleep in their minds. The turmoil greatly wearing them down.

OOOOOOOOOOOOOOOooooooooooooooooooooooooooooooOOOOOOOOOOOOO

Kai woke up slowly in the grass, realizing his hips and a certain area were very sore. He gave a sleepy yawn, a heavy arm on top of him, keeping him in place. Kai turned his head, smiling softly as sun filtered through the trees making Carver's hair glow. Kai yawned again before looking around, immediately sitting up, realizing that he was butt naked in the forest.

Kai squeaked, trying to shuffle out of Carver's hold. Carver was mumbling and trying to get Kai back into his arms before Kai slapped him on the chest. Carver grunted awake, looking quiet yummy all dazed and hair licked up in certain places. Kai tried not to drool before shaking his head to clear the naughty thoughts.

"What's wrong *yawn* baby?" Carver trying to get comfortable in the grass before realizing that he was sleeping on grass.

"Uh..." Carver looked at his surroundings before staring at Kai's hand motion that was currently rubbing his cute bubble butt.

"I think puppy got excited" Kai whispered bashfully before both of them saw Carver's black wolf preening happily in their minds, Kai's little white wolf tucked under him.

"What can I say? You're irresistible" Carver winked, placing his hands behind his head with a shit-eating grin on his face. Kai scowled, rolling his eyes, trying not to smile at the compliment. The two lazed away the morning under the canopy of the trees and the morning light. Carver lifted Kai up before they both shifted back into their wolves, heading for the pack house since Kai's tummy grumbled in protest at the lack of food.

Both kind of froze in the kitchen door way, seeing a plethora of baked goods covering every available surface. Carver only whimpered sadly knowing his Dad was very stressed right now about his sister. Everyone was.

"She'll wake up soon and you all can be a full family again" Kai whispered, rubbing Carver's bicep gently. Carver gave a half lifted smile, kissing Kai on the cheek, sighing softly.

OoOoOoOoOoOoOoOoOoOoOoOoOoOoOoOoOoOoOoOoOoOoOoOoOoOo

One week had passed, Amilya still unconscious. Luna Adam was baking like crazy or crying half the time. Both Adam and Chris would wait endlessly in her room, praying for her eyes to open. Almost all of the pack members came by to give flowers or their condolences.

Carver and Conner weren't much better, their hearts and wolves aching to see that their baby sister was okay. What they were most afraid of was that she wouldn't forgive them.

Leon never left her side unless it was to use the bathroom. Even then, it was a chore for Sam (the pack doctor) to get him to eat something. Leon didn't know if his heart was breaking everyday that Amilya's eyes remained closed, or if his heart was just overly joyed that his mate was actually here.

"Hey man, go eat something," Tyler whispered, walking into the room. Leon sighed, nodding, both of them hitting it off since Leon was a big gamer too. Conner would get a bit possessive though, leaving very evident love bites all over Tyler's neck and a few other places.

Tyler knew how difficult it was for Leon to leave his mate alone, but everyone convinced him that he should look healthy and well for his mate.

Tyler leaned back in a chair, hoisting his feet onto the bed.

"You pain in the ass. You need to wake up. Your family is waiting. Your mate is waiting," Tyler whispered, closing his eyes with his hands behind his head.

A minute or two passed, the single clock in the room seeming annoyingly loud for some reason.

A deep breath was heaved by the black wolf on the bed, eyelids fluttering open to reveal midnight black eyes.

Amilya's POV

Where...Where am I?

I would have flipped out right then and there if Tyler wasn't sitting back in a chair so calmly, relaxing.

How long have I been out for? Where the heck am I? Why am I -

I gasped suddenly, remembering that I was attacked by rogues. The memory was kind of fuzzy. I snapped my head back to Tyler, relaxing significantly, seeing that he didn't have any evident injuries; not to mention he was alive.

I breathed in deeply again before gasping. My mate. My mate was here! His scent is still thick in this room! Soft scents of pine and lemon and that little hint of cinnamon was mouth watering. His wolf was so handsome and I knew I would swoon once I saw his human form. My wolf yawned, nodding happily as we rubbed our furry cheek against a spot on the bed that seemed to have my mate's scent on it the most. But where is he!? My mind was going a million miles an hour before depressing thoughts started to swarm my mind. Did he... not want me?

I whimpered at that, afraid of the answer.

"Amilya! Praise the Goddess! You freaking moron! Don't pass out for that long ever again!" Tyler growled angrily before he hugged me tightly. I huffed at that, rolling my large wolf eyes at him.

"I don't even want to freaking hear it. You are getting lectured and that's final," Tyler growled, crossing his arms, taking a step back from me.

I huffed again, slowly sitting up, my joints popping as I did so.

How long have I been out for? I asked Tyler through our link.

"A freaking week you jerk," Tyler hissed making me growl softly back.

"Yeah whatever," Tyler turning sideways a moment, eyeing me.

"You should have told us you haven't been eating Mils," Tyler whispered. I whimpered softly, hearing his voice crack.

Tyler... I don't regret doing that. You all are my family and I love you. I'd rather you all have some kind of food in your bellies even if that means I don't

I hate that! I hate how you decide things like that!

I sighed, standing up on the bed, stretching each of my legs.

Where am I anyways? I had the sinking feeling I knew exactly where I was.

You know where. Your mate and Dads and brothers and every single pack member has stopped by, hoping you were awake. Everyone has been praying to the moon Goddess for your health. So try not to be a stubborn alpha and get it through your thick skull that you're wanted here.

I jumped off the bed, Tyler and I staring at each other. I turned away finally, shutting my eyes tightly. I wanted to believe those words so badly but... through all the abuse I've gone through, I can't help believe that the demented Alpha will come to attack my family again. It'll be all my fault again.

"Hey... you don't have to go through whatever this is alone, Amilya," Tyler whispered, placing his hand on my shoulder.

I had a sinking pit in my stomach and I was absolutely famished.

Tyler... I looked up at him, seeing Tyler with so much hope in his eyes that I'd talk to him about my fears, but I just couldn't. Not yet.

I'd... rather no one saw my body. Are there any clothes for me? My wolf is exhausted from being in this form for so long.

Tyler heaved an exaggerated sigh since I avoided his gaze. He rifled through a couple of drawers from the dresser across the room.

"They should see them Mils. See how strong you are. They should know why you fight so well," Tyler was putting together my usual outfit that consisted of dark colors and loose clothing.

Tyler turned his back to me allowing me to shift. I groaned in pain, nearly collapsing before Tyler held me up. I looked away from his worried gaze.

"'M fine," I mumbled, my voice scratchy from not using it for so long. Tyler looked away from me as I got into my underwear and clothes.

"You're beautiful Mils. You know that, don't you?" Tyler whispered, still looking at the wall across the room.

I sighed, shaking my head, before jumping back in shock. Tyler slapped my arm, growling.

"You are. I personally think your scars make you look bad ass anyway," Tyler grumbled, crossing his arms again.

I ripped a piece of cloth, wrapping it around the lower half of my face. Tyler groaned, head thrown back, throwing his hands in the air.

"You look like one of those desert assassins or whatever!"

"Tyler, dear, we need to talk about cutting back your game time," I lifted my brow at him, Tyler pouting like a little kid. I smiled a little at his child-like antics.

I tied my mid-back length hair up into a messy bun. I pulled my jacket hood up, relaxing a little since no one could see my scars now. I know scars show strength. All of us have discussed our own scars at one time or another, but my scars were ugly. Kai and Robin were lucky. Their bodies allowed for their scars to appear fainter than their fair skin; even if my skin was just a tad darker then theirs. You could still see them in any lighting where as Kai and Robin's scars could only be seen very close up, if you were looking for it, or if the lighting was just right.

I sat back on the bed, getting light headed all of a sudden, sitting cross-legged.

"Mils?" Tyler asked gently, "Duh Tyler!" Tyler shouted at himself.

"What the Goddess am I thinking!? Everyone needs to know you're awake! Plus you need food, since like six days ago" Tyler jumped up and down making me go into a near panic.

Tyler headed for the door fast and I was about to leap off the bed to tackle him, but my body felt like lead. The door swung open and I froze. My breath caught in my throat. I was staring into the most beautiful mint green eyes I've ever seen.

They were soft. Pale. Yet so warm. Like a pastel paint. I didn't even realize that he was directly in front of me instead of in the door way. When the heck did that happen!?

I could see love. It was so bright that my heart ached. My wolf was howling happily, but it seemed so faint in my mind. I was so concentrated on his eyes. Yet, as I looked closer, he had dark speckles of green in his eyes and had sun kissed skin. His jawline was sharp and he had a 5 o'clock shadow starting. His dark brown hair looked wind whipped. My heart was beating frantically at my handsome mate.

He seemed, so familiar. Like I had seen those eyes before.

I shuddered happily, my mate slowly smiling. His eyes crinkled and his white teeth made me swoon. I didn't realize his hand was reaching towards my cheek, before his fingers sent an electric shock through my body.

I gasped, panicking, jumping back from him before promptly falling off the bed.

"Are you alright? I'm so sorry for startling you," My mate's hands weren't sure where to go, flying this way and that.

His voice was warm. It was kind, yet strong.

I wasn't sure what to do, what to say, or how to act. I kind of just curled into a ball, looking nervously at him or back at the floor.

"Um-" I glanced up seeing him sitting cross-legged in front of me.

"I'm not sure if you remember me, but my name is Leon," My mate shuffled his hair before I straightened my back at the realization.

The boy I really liked when I was little! I leaned forward, seeing him smiling bashfully at me. Awe! How cute! Even from all the beatings I never forgot his smile. He was missing two front teeth before he got a cold, which was why he didn't come with us to the pee wee football game when we were little.

"You... have nice front teeth," I whispered before wanting to smack my head. Leon laughed loudly though, nodding.

"You remember that at least!" Leon smiled before reaching to grab my hands. His hands hesitated, but I bashfully looked down, jumping just slightly when he grabbed my hands. The sparks where our hands touched warmed my body.

We just stared at one another before he pulled me up slowly. I couldn't stop gazing at him. I could see things as beautiful and colorful, now that I found my mate. I had waited several years for my mate, not bothering to look for them, knowing they would only be disappointed to find out it was me.

"Are you and your wolf alright?" I asked worriedly, realizing that both the fight with the rogues and from not having a mate for so long was very dangerous.

"Yes" Leon smiled so warmly, his one eye turning yellow from his wolf happily letting himself out a little. I felt my wolf do the same. I felt a warmth in my cheeks, glad that my mask was hiding some of my blush. I looked down shyly before hearing a chuckle.

"Are you hungry?" Leon asked suddenly before dragging me out of the room without an answer. Not that I minded since my stomach tightened painfully at the idea of food.

Once we got to the kitchen I gaped at the piles of baked breads. I glanced at Leon seeing him giving a nervous chuckle, shuffling his short hair.

Seriously. Baked muffins were in piles on top of the microwave, along a counter top and part of the dining room table. Then there were different baked breads. Sweet breads, sandwich breads, glazed breads, nut breads, fruit breads, chocolate breads. Then there were danishes with different fillings, croissants, cookies, and miniature cakes. Thrown in were a couple of pies and tarts.

"So. Many. Carbs," I murmured, feeling Leon's hand tighten around mine.

"You will eat something," Leon lifted his brow at me. It wasn't in a challenging way because my wolf yipped happily.

I grumbled at that before realizing where this food actually came from.

"Dad..." I whispered suddenly, Leon nodding his head.

There was suddenly a flurry of footsteps coming from the second floor and several thumping paws from outside. My shoulders automatically bunched up. I looked around fast, not sure where the best place to run to was.

"It's alright sweetheart," Leon whispered. I searched his eyes, seeing only kindness and worry.

"AMILYA! MY BABY!" I gasped seeing my daddy sobbing. He looked so worn out and exhausted. I wouldn't blame him for baking enough food for an army.

He ran towards me and I nearly stumbled over my feet to move out of the way, but Leon had a tight grip on my hand.

Daddy froze in shock, whimpering, making me freeze and look at him again. He remained in his spot, tears spilling over his cheeks. His hands were clamped together against his chest as he sobbed.

I large muscled man who was older with tan skin and black hair came running in. He froze when he saw me. His stature screamed pack alpha and when I looked into his eyes, I thought I was looking into my own.

Papa.

"It's me Amilya. It's daddy," Daddy was bawling before several wolves came running in, followed by Carver, Conner, Raven; Robin holding Raven's hand. Tyler came running in with Kai on his heels. Tyler just had to run and get everybody, I swear.

Several of the cheerleaders from the school were there along with female omegas, beta warriors; most of which were on the football team. Other pack members who were peeking in from every doorway and window looked much older to me. Not to mention there were a lot more new faces than I anticipated.

I didn't realize I was holding Leon's hand in a death grip, probably looking like I was about to bolt; cause I seriously was.

"Honey? It's Papa. You remember Papa, don't you?" Papa whispered, moving very slowly towards me with his hands raised calmly. Tears were falling down his cheeks. He looked so very tired, dark shadows under his eyes.

"Amilya?" Carver whispered along with Conner at the same time, both in tears.

Why does it sound like they all think I have amnesia? I looked at Robin who tilted his head at me.

I thought you couldn't rememeber anything? That's what I told them anyway

I got some of my memories back when I first saw Dad picking you all up to take you to the pack house. Other stuff not so much

Well could you stop hiding behind your mate? You're freaking Conner out Tyler added in.

I blinked, realizing I was hiding half my body behind Leon, mostly because he didn't release my hand. His scent calmed me down and I resisted the urge to bury my nose into his neck.

I looked at daddy again, seeing him sobbing on shaky feet. I relaxed my hand slowly, Leon's brows furrowing, whimpering a little.

I gave his hand a squeeze, seeing him relax. I walked slowly over to daddy, feeling my heart hammering in my chest. My throat was closing up and I felt my eyes burn with impending tears.

Daddy looked at me with his blue eyes, swollen from crying. He was hiccuping, trying to breathe.

Daddy was about 5' 10 so I was barely a bit taller than him. His scent hit me in the face, a few of my older memories of my daddy playing tea party with me, popping up. I moved slowly until I leaned down, Daddy and everyone holding their breath. I pressed my head against his shoulder, hearing him hold back a sob. I felt his hands wrap around me, until my body shook suddenly.

"Don't cry," I whispered but that only seemed to make him cry harder.

I jumped a little before Papa hugged me too. He was still so warm. He was always my... What did I call my Papa?

"You're alright now Gummy," Papa whispered. I let out a choked sob, remembering that he was my Bear.

I smelled Carver and Conner next to me too. I shook harder, feeling all of them holding me tighter.

"I'm sorry we were such bad brothers!" Conner burst out, surprising me.

"We didn't mean to be so mean to you that day!" Carver added.

I looked up at them, seeing tears still leaving them. They looked so heart broken. Why would they feel bad? It's not like being a submissive alpha is a good thing.

I gave a shy smile, feeling a few tears leave me even though my mouth and nose were hidden by my mask.

"I'd forgiven you guys a long time ago," I whispered, hearing them choke back their cries before hugging me tighter.

"You, You remember us?" Daddy sounding like he was about to break down.

"I think I remember most things."

All of them sighed at that. I felt Papa and Daddy rub their cheeks against me along with Carver and Conner. I was pretty sure our wolves were dying to do a full family scenting again, but my wolf was still too exhausted.

I peeked out of the family hug I was in, seeing everyone sniffling or crying softly.

"Perhaps now would be a good time for lunch," Leon spoke suddenly before I was nearly tugged to the table that was laddened with food. Many of the other pack members started speaking over each other excitedly, some of them bowing to me.

I suddenly felt sparks in my hand before seeing Leon smiling softly at me. I shyly looked away before he placed me in a chair.

Everyone tried squishing at the table while others just spilled out into the living room. Several beef and vegetable dishes were placed amongst the plethora of bread.

"What would you like sweetheart?" Leon asked me gently. I looked at the food, feeling slightly overwhelmed.

It's been a long time since I've seen this much food and now I appreciate it more than I thought I would.

I pointed to a zucchini casserole. Daddy handed the dish to Leon immediately, Leon placing a chunk on my plate. Leon lifted his brow at me, making me grumble. I didn't need to be fat and ugly.

You're all muscle Mils.

We aren't having this discussion again.

I sighed heavily, Leon and a few others looking between Tyler, Robin and I.

I looked around again, pointing at the shredded beef and the toppings you could put on it.

Leon eventually stopped asking me since he said there was too little on my plate before piling food on my plate.

My parents and brothers looked like they wanted to talk to me, but Sam came in earlier saying he was glad to see me eating.

I stared at him a moment, knowing he was sure to have seen the scars on my wolf. He gave me a slight bow, leaving with a plate of food.

"You alright?" Leon asked quietly, eyeing Sam darkly. I held in a giggle at his protectiveness. So sweet.

"Yes Leon," I spoke softly, seeing him shiver at my voice. He smiled happily at me making me smile. I think it was evident behind my mask before realizing what all these people would see, if I pulled my mask down to eat.

"You should eat sweetie. You haven't eaten in a while," I frowned sadly at the crack in my daddy's voice. I patted his hand gently seeing him give me a shaky smile in return.

I kind of just stared at my plate. I wanted so badly to eat but I've hidden my face for so long.

I said it before and I'll say it again. Your scars make you look bad ass Tyler nodded making me roll my eyes.

They love you Mils Kai whispered, Carver cocking his head at me, seeing that his mate was talking in our link.

Besides, from what Raven has told me, your mate has a good number of scars too from being a warrior. The best, actually.

I couldn't help but smile sappily at that, preening for my mate.

"Okay, what the heck are your four talking about that's making her smile?" Leon pouted, crossing his muscular arms. So cute! And yummy.

"They are telling me you are a great warrior," I smiled shyly seeing his face turn red, fumbling for words.

Several chuckles were heard, making me bite my lip to stop my own laugh. He was being super bashful, sifting his hand through his hair and clearing his throat.

Several pack members had already finished their plates, leaving just my... family, at the table.

All of them kept glancing at me. I touched my cheek gently, hoping they wouldnt find me too ugly. Course that's my optimistic side coming out.

"Darling?" Leon asked gently making my hand snap back to my lap as I looked at him.

"We could leave if you like," Leon held my hand gently, his eyes glancing down to my mask before looking back up at me. I shook my head quickly, my intention not to cause trouble.

"If it means you eat then I'd rather do that," Leon grabbed my hand gently. I was about to nod my head before I felt a large warm hand on my arm.

I looked over, seeing my Papa kneeling down next to me. My older brothers were watching me in confusion, probably wondering why I didn't just take my mask off.

Daddy was wringing his hands, looking at me with worry and confusion. The silence was deafening and I knew they were waiting for some kind of answer. I was pretty sure they could hear my frantic heart beat. I... Wanted to lie. I really did. But they looked so worried and loving at me that I knew guilt would eat me alive; not to mention they probably wouldn't believe whatever lie I come up with.

"They said I looked like you," I whispered, looking down at my lap. Leon's warm breath was against my neck, his arm wrapping around my waist. Not that I minded. I loved his warmth and scent.

Daddy whimpered loudly, Papa's brows furrowing with anger.

"What. Did those. Vial. Wastes of space. Do to you?" Papa's voice was low and dark. I could feel everyone, including myself, shrink at the barely controlled hatred and disgust in his voice. Leon tightened his arm around me.

I lifted my hand to my cheek, as if to further hide it, before jumping, feeling Papa's hand cup mine.

"Let Papa see honey," Papa whispered making my eyes sting with tears. I missed his voice. He was my favorite story time reader before I had to go to bed.

I shook my head, feeling a tear leave me.

"Amilya. You will always be our beautiful baby girl, no matter what," Daddy spoke proudly, seeing him stand behind Papa. Carver and Conner came over too, surrounding where Leon and I sat. Kai, Tyler and Robin were smiling gently at me. It did little to stop the pounding in my heart or the clamminess of my shaking hands.

But... I was ugly. They shouldn't see.

Papa reached for my mask slowly.

They shouldn't see.

Papa gently grabbing the edge of the mask. Leon's hand tightening, his thumb rubbing soothing circles against my side.

They can't see it.

I ducked my head lower, but it was too late. Papa barely tugged at the makeshift mask, before it fell from my face.

I heard Daddy's barely held gasp. The silence was hurting my ears.

On the right side of my face, the first scar had the tip a few centimeters lower than the corner of my eye. It was about an inch long, going diagonally to my ear. A second scar was perpendicular to it. It started at my temple, some of it covered by my hair. It was longer, going straight down to my jaw. The third scar was about half an inch long, but it cut my lip vertically and it was a few centimeters in from the right corner of my mouth.

"I'll kill them. I'll kill them all," Leon growled darkly making me curl in more against him. Anger swirled in his eyes before he calmed down. His large, warm hand pressed against the middle of my back.

I jumped, my heart leaping into my throat. Daddy's gentle hands slowly followed the scars.

Papa, Carver and Conner were snarling and snapping in anger.

"Those bastards," Carver and Conner's eyes flashing to their wolves. Kai and Tyler were trying to calm them. Raven was seething darkly in the corner with Robin trying to calm him. Papa was deadly quiet. The malice held in his eyes made me look away fast.

"That's enough," Daddy stood suddenly, voice sharp, everyone snapping their head to him.

"Amilya honey, please eat. The rest of you. We will discuss this later but I'd rather get Amilya comfortable in her room and fully in the pack again," Daddy forcefully putting his foot down. Kai was observing, smiling at how much the Luna could control wolves that were getting out of control.

Papa and Daddy seemed to be having their own private conversation, Papa conceding to whatever it was.

"But Dad-!" Carver started before Kai placed his hand on top of Carver's.

"Not now Carver. Those rogues will get what's coming to them, but I'd rather enjoy the time we have together at this moment," Kai spoke gently. Daddy smiled at Kai happily.

I'm sure we could all see how Kai's kind nature and lovingness would make him a good Luna. I definitely could.

Carver grumbled, sitting down again.

"Finish your lunch Amilya. We will talk later," Papa grumbled, Daddy slapping his arm.

I smiled gently, feeling like my life wasn't falling apart so much anymore.

Woooh! That took me a while to finish but there it is! Yay :D on to the next

Surprises

"Oh... Ohhh.... OH! Carver!" Kai was screaming as he was being bounced on Carver's cock, before his back bowed. Kai's mouth remained open with high pitched whimpers leaving him as he came in streaks across Carver's belly.

Carver snarled before emptying his load inside of Kai, breathing heavily. His hips were completely flushed with Kai's ass. Carver rubbed his hand soothingly against Kai's hip who was currently panting. Kai's eyes were closed, still slowly rocking himself with Carver deep inside of him.

Carver let a pleasant growl escape him at the sight before blue eyes clashed with gray.

"Hi," Carver smirked, loving the pink that tinted Kai's cheeks.

"If this is what happens after I buy you panties at the mall, then we need to make more trips," Carver chuckling at Kai's adorable scowl. Kai slapped Carver's chest lightly, enjoying Carver's thumbs moving in little circles against his sore I.T. bands.

"We need to get to the training grounds for warrior practice," Kai completely skipping over any conversation about him and his panties.

"But Kaaaai," Carver whined, giving his lover the most adorable puppy dog eyes. Kai burst into giggles, kissing Carver happily.

Alpha Carver. Get your lazy ass down here! Carver grumbled at his brother's voice, knowing that Conner had been waiting impatiently for them to get downstairs since their submissive mates would be training as well today with the rest of the pack. Everyone needed to be trained to fight in their pack. The one thing that Carver's dad always reminded each member of their pack was that rogues don't care if you are a man, woman, or child. They will kill you.

Yeah Yeah I'm coming Carver grumbled, sighing as he slowly lifted Kai off of his spent cock. Both still loving the endless sparks that ran over their bodies. Kai whimpered a little before Carver gave him a very slow and hot kiss that made a little sigh escape from him.

Kai had a weird feeling in his lower belly again, one that had been happening for the past couple of weeks. In fact a lot of weird stuff was going on with Kai that he thought about the other night.

"I'll see you downstairs baby. You need breakfast before going out to train, okay? I don't care if you are super late because I need you to eat," Carver giving his love a stern glare, Kai melting at how much Carver cared about his health.

"Okay Carver," Kai chuckled, rubbing his nose playfully against Carver's whose eyes turned yellow, Kai's eyes turning blue; both of their wolves wanting to snuggle at the moment and not go train.

Carver shook his head, kissing Kai soundly, biting his plump pink lip playfully before hurriedly dressing. He didn't bother showering since he was going to get sweaty and dirty in the next 20 minutes anyway. Not to mention that he like having the scent of 'I just fucked my mate' all over him.

Kai sighed dreamily, flopping back onto the bed, smiling like a loon. He loved his life. His mind drifted back to what he had been thinking about last night. Amilya, Tyler, Raven, and Kai were now just taking their courses online since they only had a couple months left of school. They would work at least five hours a day on their school work so that their grades were at least decent, before spending the rest of the day with their mates and their family.

Kai, however, felt like absolute crap most days. He was nauseous. When he could eat, he craved the weirdest crap ever. But hey, it was delicious! He did lose a couple pounds though which he made sure not to tell anyone about.

He inhaled toast with cottage cheese and avocados like it was going out of style when nobody was in the kitchen; not wanting to seem like a freaking weirdo. He had been in absolute heaven eating chocolate shakes with french fries (and sometimes with ketchup too).

But besides food cravings, he'd get belly cramps all the time either in wolf form or human form; especially if he rough housed with Carver for too long or their friends.

He'd run to the bathroom sometimes to sob uncontrollably when he just watched a really sad commercial or when a sad episode of one of their favorite shows played.

He had calmly walked away from conversations other members were having before angrily stomping about in his and Carver's room, snapping and quietly snarling in anger for a few minutes before wondering why he was even mad in the first place.

His nipples hurt, his butt hole was like eight times more sensitive for some reason and he was sure he was getting fat. That's why he had agreed to go train with the rest of the pack, knowing he needed to start working out again; even if the scale said he had lost weight, he didn't particularly look it.

Kai sighed heavily, wondering what the fudge was wrong with him, before the nausea came back with a vengeance and he ran to the bathroom because the nausea now became a full on vomiting episode. Kai was in tears for five minutes as his stomach expelled everything he had practically eaten in the last week. Kai was panting, sloppily flushing the toilet, shakily standing so he could brush his teeth and get the taste of vomit out of his mouth.

Kai honey, Dad says you haven't come down for breakfast yet. If you're sleeping I will most definitely come and help you wake up Carver chuckled, Kai feeling the nausea ebb, hearing his mate's soothing voice.

I'm coming down! Kai trying to sound peppy but praying his stomach wasn't going to expel itself at this point.

Kai rubbed his face with a cool wash cloth and the back of his neck, before putting on Carver's clothes, knowing he'd be shifting into his wolf once he finished breakfast so he didn't need to wear anything special or cute that could be torn.

Kai carefully made his way to the kitchen, trying to hide his shaking hands.

"Kai dear! Here are some pancakes and I want you to wait at least 30 minutes before training, okay-" Adam speaking excitedly before seeing Kai's pale demeanor.

"Kai sweetie, are you alright?" Adam quickly putting the plate he was holding down, rushing over to Kai to feel his forehead.

"I'm alright Luna. Promise," Kai smiled, but Adam noticed it didn't reach his eyes, making him worry even more.

"Did Carver do something?" Adam started interrogating, making Kai giggle.

"No Luna," Kai giving a more real smile, making Adam relax just a little, "I think I'm just hungry."

Adam nodded nearly shoving Kai his fork, beckoning him to eat.

Kai would secretly put some of the pancakes onto the pup's plates (who were outside 'pretend training', who were going to be inside shortly).

Can't get anymore fat Kai thought solemnly, before a rush of pups swarmed the kitchen table, grabbing pancakes in their tiny fists.

Kai nearly shoved his pancakes at them, knowing that eating half a pancake was good enough.

"Kai would you like more?" Adam asked worriedly, knowing Kai couldn't really have eaten all of his pancakes that fast since he wasn't a particularly fast eater.

"Thanks for breakfast Luna!" Kai waved, running out the door to the backyard; Kai missing the suspicious look on Adam's face. Kai breathed carefully, his belly starting to ache again. Kai prayed he wasn't going to start throwing up. That's the last thing he needed. He especially jumped Carver as soon as he could, hoping Carver wouldn't notice his belly if he distracted him fast. Not to mention Kai got horny a lot faster and easier.

Kai concentrated on the groups in the backyard, smiling at how hard everyone was working. Carver had different 'rings' going, where an Alpha could be paired with another Alpha, Beta, Gamma, or Omega (dominant or regular). Only one person would shift from ring to ring so everyone got to fight someone new. Those who ended up paired with a warrior would be given fighting advise. Everyone would tell someone something positive they were doing and something negative they were doing. This had been going on for a couple of hours, a few people taking half hour breaks in between so they could rest, drink water, have a snack, before going back in. Chris allowed Carver some reign in pack dynamics since he would be taking over in a few years. Carver decided that four times a month they would work on fighting. Chris was all for the plan, happy his son was taking charge.

You jumping in Kai? Tyler easily avoiding his opponent who was a current warrior of the pack.

Luna said I should wait a few minutes since I just had some breakfast Kai's stomach nearly turning into knots with the idea of fighting. Kai wasn't really an offensive person, more defensive. He could dodge very well and tire out opponents, maybe leave mean claw or bite marks, but he didn't think he could ever kill someone or have the courage or strength to do so. When he lost control of his powers that one time... well... that was different. Kai quickly shoved that secret deep into the recesses of his mind, bile crawling in his throat at the very mention of being more of a freak than what his new pack knew about him.

Yeah, don't need you blowing chow Tyler chuckled, several others chuckling as well since they were both using the pack link. Kai wanted to snap that he wasn't going to vomit, but bit the inside of this cheek to stop himself from doing so.

Kai sat by the forest line, watching several sparring rings. Kai smiled happily, seeing Leon absolutely adoring Amilya since she was fighting each opponent beautifully, but was rough just enough to make a point that she could kill someone with a particular move if her opponent wasn't doing something well.

Kai doubted that Amilya shifted in front of Leon considering how self conscious she was of her body in front of anyone new in her life; even if it was her mate or her family.

Kai giggled seeing Tyler with his rear end in the air, back bowed, in something close to a downward facing dog pose in yoga, shaking his butt in the air playfully since his opponent was Carver. Carver rolled his shoulders skidding this way and that to try and catch Tyler who would almost bite Carver on a leg or arm, Carver doing the same with him.

Are you giggling over there Kai? Why don't you come over here? Carver challenged, Kai biting his lip to stop more giggles from leaving him.

Carver looked back at Tyler to continue fighting with him for another minute or so before Kai's belly hurt all of a sudden, Kai wrapping his arms around his belly. He pulled his knees up to his chest, taking deep breaths.

Why? Kai feeling his eyes fill with tears. Amilya stopped in her ring, stepping out, another opponent stepping in. Amilya snuggled under Leon's head, her mate nearly turning to putty as he let out a soft growl, licking Amilya's ear. Leon was tugged into another ring before Amilya headed over to Kai, seeing him in a ball. This confused Amilya for a second since Kai didn't usually go into a ball unless he was scared or in pain.

Kai honey? Amilya asked gently, speaking in their private link (no one sure why they still had their own link and didn't just merge with the pack link).

Kai looked up at her with watery eyes, Amilya immediately sitting down next to him, rubbing her head against his shoulder; she was large compared to Kai's tiny human form.

"My tummy hurts," Kai whispered, Amilya's eyes flickering with worry as she immediately sniffed at his neck near the bond bite since it usually gave off stronger scents than other scent glands on the body.

Amilya was confused. She sniffed a second time. A third time. The fourth time she breathed as deeply as she could, trying to place that particular smell. She knew she had smelled it before.

"Hey, you two coming?" Carver having shifted, crossing his arms over his chest, naked as the day he was born and proud of it.

Just a second Car! Amilya smiled, Carver seeming to get overly happy at the nickname before trying to scowl again but it wasn't working. Carver cocked his head in confusion, seeing Amilya nudge Kai a little ways into the forest. Carver would have bound right after them but tried to remain calm, wondering why he had been overly protective of Kai. Like way more than normal. In fact he hated it when any male even got near his mate. Carver shook his head, fighting against one of the omegas that regularly helped his Dad out in the kitchen.

"Am I sick, sick? Like bad sick?" Kai wringing his hands in worry, wondering what was wrong. Amilya could usually pinpoint whatever scent his body was releasing, but she just looked confused, concerned, and actually ... excited. Amilya shifted into her human form, both used to being naked in front of the other.

"Kai, sit please," Amilya trying to keep her Alpha voice from coming out, Kai noticing that she was more excited than displeased about something. Amilya knelt down, grasping Kai's hand, her eyes flickering with emotions faster than Kai could decipher.

"Kai, you know I am very good at sniffing out specific things in submissives, right?"

Kai nodded since Amilya could smell that Tyler was sick three days before his symptoms actually showed. Plus the time Raven's blood sugar was super low.

"Kai I don't know much about white wolves, but I do know that because you are a submissive and an omega..." Amilya led on carefully, seeming to find the best way to place her next words.

Kai was practically on pins and needles. If she knew why he felt like crap or weird most days (whether it was good or bad) at least he would finally have an answer.

"Kai I think, I think you're pregnant," Amilya looking anxiously up at Kai. Kai's jaw went slack a moment, blinking rapidly, his hand slipping out of Amilya's.

"What?" Kai's tongue felt thick and heavy in his mouth as though he had just walked through a desert.

"Under your usual scent, it's kind of hidden. It's kind of like 'new mother' or 'with child' kind of scent. I mean I've only come across a few omega females in my life who were pregnant so I could be wrong. Have you had any symptoms? Anything at all?"

Kai was still speechless where he sat, not sure if he knew what was left from right. Kai felt all the blood drain from his face, weaving his hands into his hair, curling into a ball again.

"Oh God," Kai whispered, tears falling quickly from his eyes as he began to rock.

Kai are you okay? Carver asked all of a sudden. Carver had been getting weird feelings through their bond sometimes for a couple of weeks but Kai continuously told him he was fine.

Yeah Kai said as quickly as he could, his mind still reeling, not wanting Carver to hear anything in his voice

"I can't. I can't do this. I-I'm barely able to take care of myself!" Kai suddenly sobbed, covering his mouth with his hand in case Carver heard him since a mate's senses were particularly high when it came to their mate.

"Kai I know it is a colossally huge step. But you won't be alone. You won't have to do any of this alone. You'll have support from everyone. Especially Carver," Amilya trying to quickly calm the omega knowing Carver could probably feel distress through their bond.

"I'm scared!" Kai shouted, tears wetting his knees, "I can't, I can't!" Kai rocking back and forth.

Kai! Are you okay!? Tell me the truth God damn it! Kai could practically hear Carver running from the training grounds to them.

Kai just wanted to run away for a second, just wanting the world to swallow him up for a few seconds.

Mates didn't get pregnant unless it was their third or fourth heat/rut together. It had always been that way. Kai only had one heat with Carver. Sure they had sex a lot, but a werewolf could only get pregnant during a heat since that was when the hormones in their body would allow a child to be created so there was some control with populations. When werewolves had sex while they weren't in a heat or rut, the sperm from the dominant would be seen as foreign and attacked before allowing a blastocyst to even form.

"Try to take deep breaths for me Kai," Amilya rubbing Kai's back gently, before every single warning sign went off in her head. Amilya stood, sniffing the air, her hearing and eyesight heightening. Amilya shifted back into her wolf form before shoving Kai hard. Kai yelped as his shoulder collided with a tree. Snarls came out of no where, Kai's eyes growing huge as three rogues popped out of nowhere, circling Amilya and Kai.

Amilya threw here head back, howling loud. Amilya got several howls back, both feeling their minds get bombarded by their friends, family, and mates.

Kai shifted into his wolf quickly, the clothes that belonged to Carver that he was wearing, being shredded in the process. Kai felt the hair on the back of his neck stand on end before leaping to the side just when a rogue lunged from behind him, pushing Kai deeper into the forest. Another rogue collided into him, biting his leg. Kai howled in agony before a deafening roar thundered, making everyone freeze for a second.

Carver was pissed off. It gave Kai just enough time to tug his front leg from the rogue before hauling ass, zig-zagging through the forest. The two rogues were fast on his tail, red eyes swirling and saliva dripping out of their mouths.

Kai was very fast though, losing one of the rogues on his tail who lost her footing, sliding down a sharp edge. Kai continued to run, the rogue snapping at his back legs. Kai was getting exhausted fast, his vision going spotty, his hearing going in and out of focus.

Kai's legs gave immediately out, the rogue not prepared at all for the stop, tumbling over Kai and into a shallow stream. Kai shook his head hard, running into the forest for several minutes. Mud splashed up his legs and was starting to cake his body, before hiding in one of the several dead trees in the open area he just ran in to. Kai breathed as quietly as he could through his nose, not wanting to be found by the rouge.

Crunch. Crunch. Snap. Crunch.

Kai's ears were flicking this way and that before holding his breath, seeing a paw at the opening of the dead tree he was hiding inside.

The rogue stood and sniffed the air hungrily before growling, finally running off, probably headed back to the heat of the battle. Kai thought it would be best to leave the tree after several more minutes before his adrenaline started to go down. His stomach thrummed in pain that seemed to spread throughout his body, a pounding behind Kai's left eye occurring.

Kai passed out in the dead tree, several miles away from the pack and his mate.

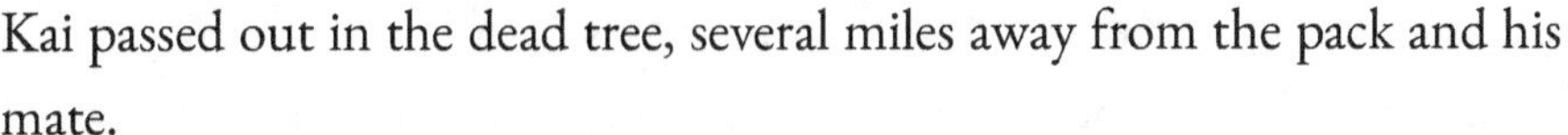

If Carver could describe his feelings for the last four hours, it would be insanity. His mate was nowhere to be found and his desperation was reaching its peak. Where the Hell had the rogues come from?

When the trackers had lost Kai's scent a few meters away from the small stream, Carver fell to his knees, pounding the ground with his fist until his hand broke. His Papa came over, holding him around his shoulders, lifting him to his feet once more.

Now, he was pacing a rut into the dirt below his feet that was near the stream. The last place that had his mate's scent on it. Carver tried to not let the bitterness of everyone comforting their mate get to him. His eyes would automatically zone in on couples, growls leaving him. His eyes flashing to his wolf several times. Everyone eyed Carver who looked two seconds away from snapping and attacking someone.

Conner was right next to Tyler who had a cloth pressed to his furry forehead, a nasty gash present. Conner was weaving his fingers through Tyler's fur, Tyler looking a little dizzy still while Conner stood next to him crouched and naked; he would growl at anyone who came too close to his mate except Sam, the pack doctor, who got less ferocious growls instead.

Raven's wolf was half on top of Robin who was licking his chin submissively, the two quietly discussing the possibilities and chances of where and what happened to Kai.

Amilya and Leon were sniffing carefully by the stream, working their way outward. Leon and Amilya's sides almost always touching as they moved together.

Chris was standing tall and stern, arms crossed, Adam standing next to him, wringing his hands. His Dad's small body partially squished against his Papa's side.

Carver. Couldn't. Take it.

"This is all your fault! What the hell were you two even doing in the forest anyway!?" Carver snarled, pointing at Amilya who froze, Leon giving a low growl at Carver.

"Carver, that's not-" Adam started sternly before being interrupted.

"No! If they weren't in the forest then Kai wouldn't be-!" Carver choking on the last word, balling his hands into fists, covering his eyes. His body shook with the cries that wanted to desperately leave his body.

"Why Amilya!? What was so God damn important!? Why did you risk my mate's life!?" Carver screamed, tears running down his cheeks. His heart was breaking apart, the world going gray.

Amilya's temper flared, hackles raised, Carver's eyes burning yellow in challenge at her.

Amilya took a calming breath, feeling the familiar sting behind her eyes.

We'll find him Carver Amilya's voice holding no room for argument.

What the Hell were you two doing!? Carver roared, shifting into his wolf as he lunged for Amilya but stopped short, a challenge.

Amilya felt herself mentally have tears leave her before a whole lot of brown fur ended up in her eyesight.

Leon snarled angrily, crouching low.

Back off Carver! I know you're scared for your mate but starting fights and blaming people isn't going to help! So what if they were in the forest? They didn't know rogues were going to be there.

Leon growled, Carver taking ragged breathes before sitting on his haunches. Amilya had moved away from the two, a scent catching her nose; and not wanting to be the reason why her mate and brother were fighting. Blaming her for Kai's disappearance.

Amilya breathed in deeply, smelling something like oatmeal and honey which was way different from Kai's usually chocolate and mint scent. Kai's scent was mixed in the forest, but it was hard to pinpoint it exactly.

What do you got Mil's? Tyler came over, sneaking away from his mate who was usually mediator between Leon and Carver when they had arguments. Amilya gave him a side long glance before sighing. She glanced at the cut on his forehead, glad it was almost healed. Robin came over as well looking sad and curious at her.

I know you've picked up a scent, need my help? Tyler asked hopefully, Amilya knowing he wanted to have the reassurance of being needed just as much as she did. Robin nuzzled under Amilya's head knowing she hated being yelled at.

Yeah...

I smell Kai's mint scent but if there was something more specific for me to catch than I could find him easier.

According to Amilya, Tyler was like a master trackman. Since he had lived in the woods for most of his life he knew how to find almost anything. It was an impressive skill and she didn't think most could match it.

Raven and I assume that he ran back into the forest since there were no prints found downstream.

Amilya sighed heavily, looking at her two dearest friends and baby brothers who looked at her like she had the answers to everything; and she wish she did.

Do you smell something like oatmeal and honey mixed with it?

Amilya knew that would give it almost immediately away about Kai. Oatmeal scents were a sure indicator that someone was pregnant.

Tyler and Robin blinked once, then twice, then guffawed at Amilya. Tyler started to snarl and growl at her, pacing a rut in front of her which attracted everyone's attention from the two alphas by the river. Robin just had his mouth dropped in sheer shock. Amilya was shifting loose soil with her front paw, looking like a reprimanded puppy.

Are you freaking serious!?

Tyler...

And the stupid idiot didn't even tell anyone did he!? Oh when I get my hands on him!

Tyler.

Goddess! No wonder Carver's acting like an ass! And probably why I saw Kai eating avocadoes and cottage cheese...

Tyler! Wait... He was eating what?

Never mind!

Tyler just huffed a breath as he looked at Amilya who looked beyond guilty.

Amilya it's not your- Robin started, finally getting somewhat over his shock.

Can you find him?

Tyler gave her a long look before they saw everyone looking at them curiously since they were probably acting super weird.

You're the best tracker I know Robin nodding, along with Amilya who was giving him the go ahead.

Tyler felt his heart leap at how proud they seemed to be before sticking his nose in the air smelling faint scents of chocolate and mint, but there was still an undertone of oatmeal mixed in. It was difficult though because of all the mud.

Tyler walked carefully, weaving this way and that, even turning in a full circle before continuing.

Tyler honey, what- Conner coming over, the three submissives allowing the pack link to invade their minds again.

Sh! Robin hushed quickly seeing most of the pack members following them out of curiosity.

Tyler is the best tracker we know! Robin spoke happily, Raven squishing up next to his mate. Robin was a few yards behind Tyler and Amilya; Amilya right on his tail.

He's the only tracker you know Carver harrumphed before getting bitten on the shoulder by his Papa to behave, Carver grumbling at him.

I-I know that Robin even stuttering in his mind which irked Raven since Carver was being such an ass. Raven was happy to see Carver look a little guilty at Robin.

But he's also the best because he's lived by himself in the forest for years so if anyone knows what to look for it's him.

Several of the betas and trackers, including the Alpha and Luna, nodded that he actually would be an excellent tracker because of that.

Block them out Ty Amilya whispered through their private link, Tyler nodding.

Tyler caught the scent of a rouge, following that as well since it seemed to follow Kai's scent markers.

That made Tyler rather nervous but he kept the thought to himself, for now. Amilya most likely caught the scent too, but both continued on.

Tyler picked up his pace, not wanting the scents to disappear and because he found a decent trail to follow.

Tyler started to trot, hearing several paws behind him before ending up in an open field with several dead trees and young baby trees.

The paws behind them stopped. Amilya walked out slowly into the open field, hunching down as she looked around. She heard several wolves do the same behind her, making a small perimeter within the tree line.

OooooOoooooOooOoooOOOOOOOOoooo

Kai opened his eyes slowly, smelling flowers, mud, moss, stagnant water, and dead trees. Kai struggled to open his eyes for a moment, feeling like glue was trying to keep them shut.

Seeing he was in the dead tree he had hidden in earlier, Kai whimpered, calling out to Carver through their link but got no response.

He's too far away Kai whimpered before softly yowling to himself.

Kai positively ached and he was starving. Kai slowly decided to venture out of the dead tree before the bark below his hind paw creaked and then gave out.

Kai howled in pain feeling his leg become wet, smelling blood. Kai tried lifting his paw back out but it only cause further agony. Kai laid back down, his front arm hurting from the rogue as well which was thrumming dully at the moment.

Carver please, I need you. We need you Kai crying mentally, his wolf's eyes damp. Kai fell back asleep, hoping help would come for him and not a rouge or other ravenous creature. Several hours passed in that cold darkness.

OoooooOoOooooooooOooooooooOoooOooooo

Amilya sniffed slowly before feeling Leon press against her.

Stay Amilya licking his muzzle making him huff before nuzzling her. He stayed hunched and ready to pounce as his mate moved through the meadow-like area.

Amilya could feel everyone's stares and tension.

Amilya suddenly smelled blood making her stop cold before bolting to a dead tree. She peeked inside before gasping.

KAI! Amilya yelled through the mind link seeing Kai bolt his head up in shock before looking around groggily.

Kai froze before whining, Amilya hearing sobs in her mind link.

A-Amilya! Kai cried, before freezing.

Carver! Kai yelled out. If Amilya was there then Carver wasn't far! He had to be! Amilya heard a rumble of paws before she pushed away from the opening of the log only for her place to be filled with Carver's wolf head.

Kai Carver breathed out in relief, his head barely fitting in the log. He could fit just enough to nuzzle and lick and rub his cheek against Kai's who was yowling and whimpering in sheer relief.

I'm sorry Carver! I just ran. I couldn't... I was... I just...

Hush baby, hush. Carver just wanted to breathe his mate's scent in but there were too many other scents in his fur and he didn't like it at all.

Come out baby Carver barely reaching Kai enough to lick his muzzle.

Can't Kai whimpered

It's okay love! All the rogues are gone.

I can't Carver... My foot is caught and it hurts.

Carver whimpered at that, not wanting his mate out of his site for even a moment.

Carver nuzzled Kai before backing out of the log.

Carver what is it? Chris and Adam came over along with a few members of the pack, all of them looking forlorn.

Carver shifted back into human form, kneeling by the log.

"Kai's foot is trapped and it could be badly injured," Carver was fluctuating between his wolf and his human self, desperate for his mate to be in his arms.

Several of the members shifted including Chris and Sam, the pack doctor.

"Kai, don't shift okay? You're wolf can heal your injuries better in that form."

Okay Kai whispered through the pack link, sounding exhausted. All of their hearts ached at the sound.

Carver and Chris, a few of their betas and Conner helped take apart the log with their bare hands. Some parts of the wood fell away easily while they worked from one end of the tree to the other so no part of the tree would collapse on Kai.

Kai's dirty head slowly emerged, Carver immediately nuzzling against him. Carver held Kai as the others continued to remove the dead tree.

Kai yowled, burying his face in Carver's chest when Sam gently took away the thicker pieces of wood from around his back leg. Carver hushed him, trying to gently comb his hands through Kai's matted fur, getting a nod from Sam.

Carver lifted Kai into his arms, running towards the pack house; almost moving as fast as a wolf on four legs.

OooooooooOoooooooOoooooooOoooooooOooooo

Kai didn't know when he had closed his eyes but when he opened them he was in the medical wing of the pack house and daylight was filtering in through the window. From the look of things the pink and purple hues reflecting against the wall indicated it was sunrise.

Kai breathed in deeply realizing he had somehow shifted back into his human form. That wasn't surprising considering his wolf was probably exhausted. Kai winced, his left wrist and ankle aching horribly before lifting the cotton sheets from his body. His left ankle was heavily wrapped in gauze, his left wrist lightly wrapped and almost healed; Kai guessed from the mobility he had in his fingers.

Kai sat up slowly before gasping, placing his hand on his belly. He let some of his power come out, his hair almost glowing an unnatural white, feeling the thrum of life below his hand. Kai wiped away the tears that left him, unsure of everything.

He hadn't even told Carver of his powers. None of the submissives in his group have told anyone anything of what they could do.

Now I'm... I'm pregnant.

Kai's head snapped up, the door opening, before Amilya walked in. She closed the door quietly before realizing Kai was awake.

"Kai!" Amilya hurried over, hugging him around his shoulders and practically shoving his face against her boobs.

Kai breathed in her scent, calming down for a moment before pulling back.

"Mils, does... does he know?" Kai could feel the sting of impending tears, placing his hand onto his belly. His emotions were a mess and couldn't even imagine how the conversation would go with Carver.

Amilya sighed before shaking her head 'no'.

"Tyler and Robin know of course, but it was inevitable for Sam to find out. He and I bathed you, seeing as how Carver was losing control and didn't let Sam tend to your wounds for a good half hour."

Kai let out a shaky breath, weaving his other free hand through his hair.

"How... How did they react?" Kai whispered, trying to hide the shaking that was evident in his hands. He clasped them together and placed them in his lap, avoiding all eye contact.

"Well, Tyler is pissed as Hell that you didn't say anything and Robin is practically gushing and wanting to touch your belly."

"Carver should have found out by now. It's not like he wouldn't be able to smell... it."

Amilya gave a heavy sigh, giving a long side glance at Kai before grabbing his hand.

"I told Sam how you acted in the forest before we were attacked and he agreed that you would be ready to tell him when you're ready. So we just used a strong soap to clean you with."

Kai had tears freely falling down his cheeks.

"I-I just thought that he found out so he wasn't here because of that. I'm scared Mils!" Kai sobbed, Amilya's heart dropping to her stomach at the sound.

"Oh sweetie. Carver has been here for you almost every minute. You've only been sleeping for a little over ten hours anyway. He just stepped out cause Luna demanded he eat something before refusing to move from your side again."

Kai took in a shaky breath, trying to calm his hormonal self down.

"Amilya I don't... I don't know what to do!"

"Just think about it. Think about everything. Weigh everything. Most importantly, decide if this is something you want. Okay? No one should give you any sway to what choice you should make. This is your life. Don't let someone else live it for you."

Amilya kissed Kai on the forehead, the little omega hicupping and looking a little calmer at her words.

Amilya smiled kindly at him, his big sister and the closest thing he's had to a mother, leaving the room.

Kai sighed again, leaning heavily against his pillow, his head slightly propped up.

His hand wandered to his belly again, his fingers seeming to itch with the need to protect. More tears left him before deciding to think and imagine his future. It actually got him to calm down better.

Just imagining a little baby with black hair and big blue eyes smiling a gummy smile at him made his heart ache and his wolf whine for the baby that was in his belly.

He couldn't get rid of it. It was Carvers'. The love of his life. The one person who had shown him every ounce of love and willingness to be with him for who and what he was.

Tears started to leave Kai in relief this time, knowing he wanted to keep this baby. Kai was so zoned out and ignorant to the world that he didn't see or hear his room door open.

Carver's heart leaped at the sight of his mate awake and clean and here. Carver had a plate of food in his hand, desperate to take care of his mate and ground himself with the knowledge that Kai was okay.

Carver almost let out a whimper seeing his little mate with tears down his cheeks. Carver stopped dead in his tracks when his sweet mate's voice spoke out.

"Don't worry baby, your Papa found us," Kai whispered, rubbing his belly. The crash of shattering ceramic hitting wood floor made Kai's head snap towards the door before his eyes widened in shock.

Blue gazed into gray before Kai became shocked as tears left his mate.

"Is it even mine Kai Winters!?" Carver yelled angrily, Kai shaking before his mouth dropped down in shock.

"C-Carver," Kai gasped out, suddenly not being able to breathe.

"We've only been in one heat together and everyone God damn well knows it's impossible to get pregnant in a first heat! Too many hormones and bonding initiations wouldn't allow a fetus to thrive in that kind of environment!" Carver was breathing heavily, one eye yellow the other blue.

Kai sobbed not understanding it himself but his heart shattered thinking Carver thought he slept with someone else.

Kai covered his hand over his mouth hoping it would silence his sobs better. Carver was seething in the doorway. Kai's wolf was yowling for his mate but even Carver's wolf held himself back from going to them.

"N-Never b-been with-with an-anybod-body! " Kai sobbed brokenly, his mouth feeling dry and tongue too heavy. His heart hammered in his chest.

"I will not care for some bastard child or some mate who thinks they can use me for my resources! I will not be used!" Carver yelled, tears falling down his sharp cheeks. He was breathing heavily, hands clenching into fists. Carver snarled before quickly leaving the room.

Everything broke inside of Kai. Every little thing. OoooooooOoooooooOoooooooOoooooooOooooo

Another chapter and ending on a cliffy. Comment please!

Scared

Kai didn't know how long he had been sobbing in his bed. He couldn't see straight, it felt like only the taste of iron was in his mouth. Carver had shut off their bond so they couldn't feel or talk to one another. It made Kai's heart curl into a vice, shaking uncontrollably, his lips feeling numb. Things were turning gray in his periphery. It seemed that Carver's scent was slipping away from him, through his fingers like water. The last words Carver saying to him feeling like shards of glass were being stabbed into his body.

Kai was rocking slowly on the bed, hugging himself. The world was going in and out. He lost his mate. Carver thought he had slept with someone else! Kai didn't understand how he was pregnant either but Kai's heart was shattered into pieces at the very thought that Carver thought he would do such a thing. Kai loved him. Trusted him. Needed him. He loved Carver to the moon and back and would die for him. Would honestly and truthfully die for his mate.

Maybe I should Kai thought morbidly, his wolf calling out to his mate. A call that was not going to receive an answer. His wolf didn't understand why they were rejected. He thought Carver would be happy with a pup. Now both of them were aching, Kai's heart being crushed with every beat it gave. The room was losing color. Gray was taking over. His breathing was ragged before his body shut down, limply lying on the bed. Kai's hand cradled his belly, his eyes half lidded and unseeing.

OoooooooooooooOooooooooooooOooooooooo

Carver was smashing and destroying everything he could find, his Dad running out of the kitchen. Carver's hands were flying everywhere, wanting to destroy everything. Glass and ceramic pieces were littered on the floor. Wood was splintered and crushed. Carver's eyes were hazed over in rage, hitting his Dad but neither seemed to care at the moment as Adam held Carver in his arms.

"Talk to me Carver!" Adam commanded in his Luna voice, Carver freezing before sobbing.

"It's not mine. It's not mine!" Carver's voice breaking, his knees buckling as Adam cradled him on the floor.

Before Adam could ask what he was talking about Carver interrupted him.

"Kai's pregnant! We've only shared one of his heats and he's pregnant and it can't be mine!" Carver sobbed, Adam feeling tears leave him as well. Adam tried to hold back his own sob seeing Sam walk in before the doctor gasped, leaving just as quickly. The doctor heard everything.

"M-Maybe-" Adam began, before Carver shook his head, pressing his head harder against his Dad's chest.

"It's not mine. Not mine. How could he do this! He was my mate! MINE! And he just-"

"Carver!?" His Papa came in before looking shocked at his son, hurrying over to them.

"I can't..." Carver said with so much bitterness it made his parent's hearts squeeze in anguish for their son. They held him tightly, not sure either of them knew what to say. Connor stood by the doorway along with Raven in shock.

The two had anger boil from within them before angrily storming away, determined to get some answers.

OooooooooOooooooooOooooooooOoooooooooO

Amilya was skimming quickly through a history book, hoping to find information on white wolf pregnancies. She knew there was something different. There was a part of her mind that tickled, like a memory that wouldn't come forward. Amilya rubbed her forehead in exhaustion before finding one sentence about white wolves.

"White wolves have unique pregnancies that are different from those of normal wolves."

Amilya re-read the sentence three more times before a memory shot forward of when she was a little girl and imprisoned in the rogue pack.

Flashback

"You are my second in command for a reason!"

"But sir, why attack another rogue pack that doesn't even have resources we need? It's a waste of time."

A low growl resounded in the room before a chair scraped across the floor. A prepubescent girl with black hair and recent bruises covering her face and arms was pressing her ear to the rogue Alpha's door.

"Our little spy in the other rogue pack has told me they took a boy from a white wolf pack some time ago but don't know what he is because he is forbidden to shift. We must get to him before they realize!"

"Another rare?"

"Exactly. Once I have all the submissives in this world I will breed them like the baby fuck machines they are until they are constantly bleeding from birthing and being fucked. Then we'll have an army that will soon grow in a few years to make us unstoppable."

Low humorous chuckles echoed in the room. Glasses clinking together.

"And the submissive alpha girl we already have?"

"Once she hits her period or heat, whichever comes first, I will fuck her raw before anyone else. Then, anyone who wishes can take turns with her."

The alpha smiled a cruel smile around the rim of his bourbon glass before sighing out in annoyance.

"We won't know when that is so we need to prepare to capture the white wolf within the month. If he truly is a white wolf and submissive, then I will keep him in my chambers until his heat hits. Unlike normal wolves it won't have to be a year after a third or fourth heat to get the submissive pregnant. I can just stick my cock in, have fun, and with a snap of my fingers he'll be pregnant."

"Of course sir. And, if I may ask, after the submissive is pregnant, may I use him after you?"

The alpha rogue waved his hand nonchalantly.

"Any submissive that carries my seed that catches are free to fuck. But, since you are my beta you can do what you wish with them first! I know how you like to use toys. Just don't damage the goods too badly, understand?"

"Thank you for your kindness sir!"

Heavy footsteps padded towards the door, the girl with black hair and bruises littering her body ran quickly down the hall and out of sight; as quiet as a mouse.

End of Flashback

Amilya gasped, standing up so quickly the chair she was sitting on rocked back onto two legs before slamming back down onto all four.

Amilya's head throbbed worse, trying to hold the bile that was in her throat down or she would truly vomit from remembering such a horrible memory.

Amilya took in large gulps of air before shakily running her hand over her face. Amilya quickly walked to Kai's medical room, needing to tell him what she remembered. She also needed to warn her family that there was a seriously deranged alpha rouge that had plans for submissives.

Amilya opened Kai's door quickly before freezing. Sam was bent over his still form, a stethoscope pressed against Kai's chest. Sam slowly removed the stethoscope buds from his ears before looking sadly at Amilya.

"I believe alpha Carver shut off his bond with Kai. Since he was already not feeling well, it shocked his system and his wolf. I'm not sure when or if he'll wake up."

Amilya's hand flew to her mouth, trying to hold back tears, before her eyes hardened.

"Take a sample from the fetus. I don't think my moronic brother will even believe me when I tell him the baby is truly his without substantial proof. Can you do this for me Sam? I'll watch over Kai."

Sam looked stunned a moment before nodding.

"How is it his? It isn't usual at all to get pregnant after a first heat," the doctor trying not to sound judgmental, but it was an uncommon phenomena.

Amilya opened her mouth to reply before Raven and Conner came into the room looking angry and determined. Both stopped once they saw the two other people in the room.

"We want answers. Now," Raven growled low.

"Do you know what you've done to my brother!?" Conner yelled at Kai, breathing hard, before slowly turning white.

"Kai...?" Conner whispered before looking towards Sam and then Amilya in shock. Raven caught on quickly, looking equally pale.

The room was silent. It seemed to go on forever. Sam didn't seem to know what to do for a moment either.

Amilya turned her back to them, heading for the bed before gently carding her hand through Kai's hair.

It could have been hours that the silence lasted. Amilya heard Sam's footsteps move about in the room, setting up an ultrasound machine so he could get a sample from the fetus. Amilya did not turn, so she didn't see Carver practically being dragged in by his Dad and Papa to the room. Dark bags already formed under his eyes and he looked sickly. There was such a sadness in his eyes that it was hard to look at him directly.

All three looked confused before freezing a few feet passed the threshold of the doorway.

"You can tell the moron that is my brother that Kai is loyal and would die loyal. Plus it doesn't even make sense on how he would even cheat on Carver when he is too scared to get close to anyone! Submissive omega with a mate, remember. He can't be ordered sleep with anyone. But since all of you seemed so quick to throw him away, I will not tolerate it. You will stay away from him. You will stay away from Robin and Tyler and once Kai wakes up we are leaving. I will not have any of us stay in a place that will turn toxic on you immediately if you do something wrong. If any of you had waited before shunning him, I would have explained that white wolves are special for many different reasons and this is one of them. But since reason is not a welcome course of action, you can all politely and quietly get the HELL OUT OF THIS ROOM!"

Amilya's voice boomed as she swiveled to see shock, guilt, and a dark sadness in all of their faces. Sam's head was bent to look at the ground, his medical supplies near him to do as Amilya requested.

"Sam," Amilya snapped. Sam cleaned Kai's belly before pulling out a long needle.

"Don't touch him!" Carver roared, eyes flashing yellow with brutal anger and horror.

"And why not!? You didn't want him when you thought the baby wasn't yours!"

"No! I love him!" Carver sobbed which stopped Amilya's tirade for a moment, "it destroyed me to know I wasn't good enough! That he wouldn't want to have my children!"

Carvers eyes turned to their normal blue color, tears rolling down his cheeks.

"You shouldn't have blocked off your bond with him," Amilya's voice still holding a twinge of anger.

"I-I can't lose him, please. I would have learned to love the baby even if it wasn't mine," Carver's hands shaking. Amilya's eyes flashed down to them before Leon came running into the room looking at her with fear.

Amilya kept eye contact for a moment before sighing, turning back to Kai.

"Amilya," Leon's voice shaking slightly making guilt crawl inside of Amilya for threatening to leave. It wasn't fair to him. To any of them.

Sam had quietly brought over the prepared ultrasound machine before looking at Amilya and then her Papa she assumed.

"What are you doing exactly?" Chris asked deadly calm, everyone's eyes darting to the needle that was near Kai.

"Continue Sam," Amilya spoke quietly. There were quiet gasps in the room before Amilya heard a scramble of feet before she felt Carver nearly slide into the bed.

"I won't let you hurt this baby!" Carver snarled, laying part of his body over Kai's looking ready to shift.

"We are not harming the child," Amilya spoke slowly, Carver still hunched protectively over Kai.

"Carver, Kai is in something like a mini coma because the bond was blocked while he just came back from a seriously stressful situation. Not to mention finding out about the pregnancy."

Carver whined at that, looking mournfully up at his unmoving mate.

"You've opened the bond again I'm guessing?"

Carver nodded, rubbing his head slowly against Kai's belly. A few tears plopping onto the exposed skin, Carver's heart aching like someone had an icy grip in his chest.

Carver whimpered before covering his hand over his eyes.

"Why can't I do this right?" Carver whispered brokenly, Amilya's own heart aching at the statement knowing she wasn't the only one who felt like that.

Leon's hand came to rest on Carver's shoulder, avoiding eye contact with Amilya.

Amilya gave a heavy sigh, crossing her arms over her chest.

"Carver. The only thing I can think of is if you lay next to him and continuously speak to him through your bond."

Carver nodded before moving to lay down next to Kai's small form. His head rested on top of Kai's before moving his hand slowly to caress Kai's chest and shoulder.

"Sam is getting a sample from the baby."

Carver looked up quickly before nuzzling into Kai's neck gently, leaving soft kisses. Sam continued his work, growling coming from all sides towards him. Sam took the blood sample back to his lab, the room completely silent.

Amilya was trying to reign in her temper still, angry at her brother and family. She glanced over to Leon who had his head bowed, looking at his bare feet. Just his presence had her calming down enough she wouldn't start punching people.

"Amilya..." Adam asked softly, Amilya cocking her head in his direction, letting him know she was listening but was still facing where Kai slept.

"You said you knew something about white wolf pregnancies?" Adam was wringing his hands, hating the guilt clawing at him for even thinking that Kai would cheat on Carver. He was the sweetest and kindest little thing he'd ever met. Looking over at Chris, he could see the same feelings in his mate's face.

"How I know, is a long story,"

"Then just the specifics would be helpful," Sam walking in with more gel he'd need to use for the ultrasound machine, wanting to do a complete scan on Kai and the embryo. Amilya reached over to the book on the night stand she had placed there when she walked in from the library.

"I found a single sentence in this book stating the white wolf pregnancies are unique compared to normal wolf pregnancies," Amilya flipping to the page she had marked so she could find it later. She showed it to Sam who nodded slowly, handing the book to Chris who had gotten closer to the bed, everyone looking over his shoulder. Chris handed it to Carver who sniffed hard, once reading the statement, placing it on the night stand again so he could continue to snuggle with his mate.

"That's when I remembered. A submissive white wolf in particular can easily get pregnant which is why the dominant has to be careful or the white wolf can lose their baby if the dominant doesn't bond right away with the child."

Quiet gasps were heard from each person, Carver stuffing his head against his mate's neck, shoulders shaking from the silent sobs leaving him. Carver felt his Dad's hand comb through his hair, hushing him gently.

Sam hurriedly set up the ultrasound machine, looking towards Carver to see him nod in permission to touch his mate. Sam place the gel onto Kai's belly, pressing the transducer against his stomach. Everyone held their breath, before Adam tucked his head against Chris' chest, seeing the outline of a fetus. Adam had done a very quick scan earlier in order to get a viable sample, no one paying enough attention to the screen from before and more towards the large needle he had used.

"Is it...?" Chris asked softly, feeling a lump in his throat knowing his son wouldn't be able to ask the question in his current state.

"The heart rate is a little low and the fetus is rather small but it is still alive at the moment. It looks a few weeks old, but we'd have to ask Kai when he started feeling ill or off."

Carver let out a choked sob, holding Kai tightly in his arms. Everyone could feel their wolves wanting to comfort him, but knew it would do little good since Carver honestly needed his mate awake right now. Everyone breathed in relief that the baby was still alive. No one was sure what would happen to the couple's mental status if Kai had, had a miscarriage.

"We should leave the two for now," Sam whispered, breathing out a sigh of relief that the fetus was still alive at least. Only time would tell if the embryo would survive.

Everyone slowly left, Adam kissing Carver on the forehead along with Kai, Chris giving his son's shoulder a squeeze.

"Keep talking to him Carver, it'll help," Amilya stated quietly, Carver look-ing to say something before Amilya quickly turned and left. The group was waiting in the hallway for her before Amilya stuck her chin up angrily, walking passed them.

_______________________□_______________________

Adam looked ready to burst into tears, finally getting his baby back only to have a rift tear them apart. Leon kissed his forehead before running after her, needing to speak with his mate.

"Sir," Mike briskly walking towards the pack alpha, "Tony from Blue Moon is calling for a meeting."

Chris nodded, kissing Adam soft and slow whispering that everything was going to be okay against his mate's lips. Adam nodded, hurriedly wiping away his tears, Chris giving him a sad smile before following Mike back to his office.

"Where are Tyler and Robin?" Adam asked suddenly, wondering where the other two were who were very much apart of the original makeshift pack.

Conner had the decency to look ashamed, crossing his arms.

"Ty and I had an argument. He got so mad that we accused Kai of cheating, asking if I'd think he would too, if he somehow got pregnant from his first heat with me."

"I don't even want to know what you said do I?" Adam crossing his arms, looking at Raven next.

"Robin ran off saying he needed some time alone. I... was also angry and said things."

Adam sighed, upset at all the disputes occurring in the pack house at the moment. Adam just shook his head, heading for the kitchen.

"Are you sure you don't want something to eat Mr. Winters?" Adam peeked into the kitchen seeing Tyler hunched at the table, shyly shaking his head no.

"It's Tyler, Kayla, remember?" Kayla was an omega who liked to cook all the time, Tyler getting to know her since he didn't know about a lot of foods.

"Yes, I remember Ty," Kayla rolling her eyes, hugging him and rubbing his back before leaving. Adam slowly walked in, feeling a grieving sadness coming from the blond.

"You alright sweetie?" Adam asked gently, Tyler's head popping up.

"Oh! Luna, er... I'm fine," Tyler shrugging, Adam's frown increasing.

"You want to talk about it?" Adam not liking the forlorn waves coming off the boy.

"What does it matter?" Tyler getting angry, Adam's eyes snapping down to Tyler's wrist where he was grabbing it tightly with one hand.

"I'm sorry... we jumped... I jumped to conclusions when I should have heard everything before deciding right away whether what we heard was true."

Tyler looked at him surprised, before frowning.

"Did something happen to your wrist?" Adam looking at it with worry, Tyler taking his hands off the table and hiding them in his lap.

"How are things supposed to work out with me and Conner if he doesn't even want to believe in me?" Tyler whispered, feeling the familiar sting of tears in the back of his throat.

Adam suddenly had an old memory hit him, looking down at his own wrist where a nasty dark scar was, looking as though it were very deep. He felt a lump of sorrow get stuck in his throat, something in his gut telling him Tyler would understand better than anyone.

"When I first found Chris, I had transferred from another pack to the same high school you guys go to. I thought he was the most downright sexiest, handsome, smartest mate I'd ever laid eyes on. Still is," Adam sighed dreamily. Tyler smiled a little at that, Adam still looking love sick.

"I knew he was my mate right away since I was already 16. When I found him, he was making out with some cheerleader in the hallway. My heart almost broke..." Adam's voice shaking, Tyler's jaw dropping.

"He what!?" Tyler hissed, Adam continuing.

"I had the naïve hope that maybe he just hadn't sensed me yet and that maybe that was his girlfriend or something. It's a common thing to date and stuff in the hopes they'll be your mate so I walked up to them anyway.

Right when I went up to him his head snapped over to me and I knew he could smell that we were mates. The cheerleader looked at me wondering why he stopped kissing her, probably."

Adam's hands started to shake, Tyler scooting closer to him.

"She asked what I wanted but I was just struck dumb by how beautiful Chris was. Chris had looked me straight in the eye and said he wasn't a fag, rejected me for being a useless omega, told me to fuck off and started making out with her again. My heart shattered," Adam whispered brokenly, wiping away a tear. Tyler whined, absolutely horrified.

"Luna..." Tyler choked out, his own tears falling.

"I had eventually become friends with Mike who was Chris' best friend at the time, still is, but I didn't know that. He helped me a lot since he ended up being my only friend in the school, Chris having told everyone to stay away from me. Mike had the good sense to wonder why. After I told him who I was, he was livid. I told him it didn't matter because my mate was happy, even if that meant he wasn't with me."

"I fell apart," Adam shuttering, sinking further into his chair, Tyler grabbing his hand, "I'd heard a rumor that he was going to marry the cheerleader whose name I found out was Linda. Her and her friends were the worst to me, telling me to die or leave. It was the last week of the third month. My wolf wasn't moving anymore. Sometimes I'd see a shuttering breath leave him, but nothing else. I feared I'd lose my wolf entirely, knowing by Friday he'd be gone. I couldn't do it."

Adam took in a much needed breath.

"Friday finally came and there was no reason for me to be there anymore. My only friend was Mike and he was already so popular I doubted he'd even notice I was gone. Since I hadn't seen him in a few days I assumed it to be true. I had one class with Chris and it was the second to last period of the day."

Adam's lips were scrunched together, Adam's tears flowing freely now.

"I packed up my things and left the school. Since I transferred, the pack offered cheap housing for students so I was in a small apartment a little ways away from the pack house. I remember everything in almost perfect detail. Where everything was in the apartment and that I wanted to find something that would make me feel something more than a razor blade could," Adam knew that saying those words would have an impact on the blond, seeing Tyler drop his chin to his chest, but he was still holding Adam's hand tightly.

"I found a paring knife in the back of the silverware drawer and headed up to the bathroom. If I had gone to class that day, I would have seen Chris and Mike and several of their friends with flowers; waiting for me. I guess when I never showed up, they started to worry. At least that's what Mike told me later. I..." Adam clearing his throat in an effort to keep his voice steady.

"It was probably the last period of the day by the time I had gotten back to the apartment. I decided that if my mate didn't come within the next five minutes that I wouldn't do it. I kept telling myself that for an hour before finally giving in, knowing school had gotten out by then. I took the knife and..."

Adam turning his hand over, Tyler blurrily seeing the ragged cut on Adam's wrist through his tears.

"I cut as hard and as deep as I could manage. Pain like nothing else was the last thing I felt. But I felt something and I was glad. I decided to curl up on the floor and I remembered being so cold. The floor started turning red and I was getting dizzy. I knew it wouldn't be long. Maybe a few more minutes."

Adam rubbed at his wrist, before trying to wipe away his never ending tears.

"I closed my eyes, wishing Chris all the happiness in the world. But then I heard a sound."

Tyler was quietly crying, seeing a very small smile on Adam's face.

"I heard feet rushing to me and shouts and it was all so disorienting. There was banging on the door and I peeked open an eye seeing my blood had leaked under the door. I closed my eyes again, not caring anymore. I could only see blackness then, faint sounds maybe."

"The next time I woke up I was in the hospital and my wolf was blinking and looking around in my head, seeming to be just as confused. Chris had opened the door an hour later and had rushed over to me in tears. I was shocked to say the least. Mike had hurried in too, standing next to Chris who was leaning over my bed and holding my hands. Chris had started telling me everything right away. How he had broken down the door and sobbed and begged me to come back, that he didn't reject me and that he was a stupid conceited asshole and Mike was adding things in and how he was trying to fix the biggest fuck up of Chris' life. I was stunned," Adam's tears finally slowing, Tyler still looking upset but in awe.

"Chris wanted to hold me and kiss me but the second his hand got close to me I flinched so hard. He had such a broken look on his face when I did that. I tried to tell him that I'd just need time but I couldn't. I literally couldn't. The doctor had come in at that point telling us that something in my brain made me selectively mute."

"You were mute?" Tyler whispered, trying to keep his tears at bay but it wasn't really working.

"For over a year. I eventually got out of the hospital and ended up back in school; reluctantly to say the least. My parents wanted to pull me back to their pack but I'd told them I'd decide later. Chris spent everyday getting to know me and down right bothering me. I mean my wolf was happy but I was still broken. Mike and his friends would hang out too as I got to know Chris and his true friends. I also found out that Linda was the one saying they were getting married, flashing a fake ring to everyone. Chris hadn't known either and had his father put her on probation in the pack. He told me that he'd broken up with her that previous week, Mike having gone to him and literally ripping him a new one for rejecting me. I was angry at what Linda did and I hate her more than anyone."

Adam snarled under his breath, Tyler joining him.

"After three months, with me going away for a few days each month for my heats, I think Chris was starting to think I was going to leave permanently or that I had someone else. I never told him I got heats like female omegas since I was a dominant male omega, but I ended up being a rare case. One day when I had come back to my apartment from one of my trips away because of my heat, he had hurried over and begged me to stay. To give him a chance to be his mate and lover. I had gotten to know Chris in the time I was mute, and all the time we spent together; I knew I was starting to fall in love with him for him. When he asked me to give him the chance, I think we both knew if he ever fucked up again I'd leave or..." Adam touching his wrist where his scar was. Tyler nodded quickly, understanding.

"I nodded yes because it's what I honestly wanted. I was absolutely terrified of getting hurt again, but when he kissed me for the first time I started to feel my heart starting to fix itself. And every kiss he gave me after that felt like a little piece of my heart was getting put back together. I think at one point he started assuming I was seeing a dead relative because it was better to assume that than assume I was seeing someone else. He'd get so possessive," Adam sighed dreamily, Tyler giving him a half lifted smile.

"I hadn't spent four of my heats with him after the year of being mute and graduating from highschool, the doctor telling me it wasn't good for my wolf, but it was up to me in the end since my mental state still had me selectively mute. I had truly fallen in love with Chris and finally took him off to the side. I had written down in a letter everything about my heats and why I had been leaving every few days in the month. His cheeks were so red when he got done reading. In fact he looked like a kid in a candy shop," Adam giggled. He didn't want to mention he had been getting hornier every passing day, but feared he'd have a panic attack during sex. He'd told Chris that, who nodded respectfully, Adam seeing the shattered guilt in his mate's eyes.

"Since my heat was during winter break, that's when we mated and I started to feel whole again. We've become so close and understood one another better than anyone else. He became the Prince I'd dreamed of my entire life and he loved me even though I couldn't speak."

Adam hugged himself happily, remembering the first time they ever made love, even during his heat, Chris was so careful and gentle with him it made his heart beat with so much happiness he thought it was impossible.

"When did you talk again?" Tyler smiling softly at Adam, his own heart stinging.

"Well, Chris and I had gone to college for a little bit by then; Chris bound to be alpha of the pack soon. By then, we had spent my next four heats together. I had been trying to talk again, my throat hurting from being so unused for so long. Chris's father had made him pack leader, traveling with his mate around the world. I think they're somewhere in Ireland this month. Chris had gotten into a good rhythm with taking care of the pack and we were both happy and completely in love; still very much are," Adam starting to giggle again which made Tyler happy, hearing the sound.

"Chris had gotten back from a meeting early and we had plans to head to the lake and hang out on the beach and run in our wolf forms. We could spend forever in each others presences. Anyway, he came home and kissed me everywhere."

"Luna!" Tyler whined, Adam cackling a little, "and finally, finally, I spoke out loud for the first time in over a year. The first thing I said was 'Chris' and he stopped dead in his tracks and looked at me with wide eyes. I couldn't believe his name came from my lips and I don't think he could either. Feeling a strength in me again I continued and said 'I think I'm pregnant' and he went down like a sack of potatoes. Mike had come running in, looking at Chris in shock who was on the floor. I said Mike's name out loud too and he had to go sit on the couch because he was so shocked. I tried shaking Chris awake who finally popped up, looking around all confused and adorable. When he looked at me that day though, I felt everything from him, that I started to tremble. He asked me to say it again," Chris had cupped his cheeks, looking desperately at Adam.

"I said, Chris, love," Adam playfully having his lips flutter against Chris's, "I think I'm pregnant. And he started to cry into my shoulder and I held him so tightly," Adam's eyes watering, remembering Chris sobbing so hard into his neck before scooping him up and carrying him to Sam who they had been friends with in high school who was currently an apprentice to another pack doctor out of state. They found out he was indeed pregnant but it was too early to see that he was carrying two pups.

"I told you this story because I thought it was a good example of life giving you hard ships and experiences to learn from. That it takes a lot of courage to face things you're scared of. That fighting with your mate or having something hard happen, makes us grow as a person and understand. Does that make sense Tyler?" Tyler sniffled, nodding slowly, his other hand squeezing his opposite wrist that hid his own scar.

"When Conner had eventually told us he rejected you, I was so upset and so was Chris because we lived through something similar. We were both terrified for him and you because we are destined for one another."

Tyler got up from the table quickly, looking torn.

"Thanks for telling me Luna. I... um, I mean it really helped," Adam nodded, seeing Tyler heading for the back door, "I'm gonna go for a walk if that's okay?"

"Sure," Adam standing too, "I know it's not really my place to tell you what to do, but maybe you should tell Conner. It might help," Adam's eyes flicking to Tyler's wrist, Tyler flushing for a second before shrugging, hurrying out the door.

"You never told me that," Chris whispered, stepping into the kitchen, effectively making Adam jump.

"Chris..." Adam patting his chest before hurrying over to his mate who looked broken hearted for a second. Adam whined a little, wondering what was wrong.

"You never told me they told you to die or leave or that you went looking for the paring knife," Adam bit his lip, knowing Chris would think about his suicide attempt sometimes. Especially after they made love and he'd feel Chris finger the scar on his wrist.

"It's not like you told them to," Adam knowing that for a fact when Mike had grilled Chris for everything he had done or said to Adam back in high school, "and I didn't think... I don't think that it mattered what I used to..." Adam looking down sadly before his chin was lifted.

"It matters to me. I have nightmares of not getting to you soon enough. About not having this life with you. I'd be empty without you," Chris whispered before Adam hugged him, kissing him passionately.

"You have me and we have our babies. All of our babies."

"But because we lost one we couldn't have anymore because of the depre ssion..."

Adam bit his lip knowing his heats hadn't been that intense since they had lost Amilya or he wouldn't get one at all; Sam telling him it was a common reaction to losing a child for both the dominant and submissive.

"Now I'm too old to have a baby," Adam shrugging. He longed to have a large family since he had been an only child growing up.

"Adam," Chris rolling his eyes, "you're only 36. You're too young to be a granddad already you know?"

Adam blushed, looking bashfully up at him.

"But we have three babies in high school! It'll be too large of an age gap!"

"But I want to make a baby with you," Chris whined before swooping in to kiss Adam hotly who moaned loudly. Chris slipped his tongue into Adam's mouth, Adam feeling a heat low in his belly and a sharp shock of electricity zing through him, suddenly feeling himself trickle with slick. Adam gasped, pulling away, slick never having left him again since Amilya went missing.

"What's wrong love?" Chris looking confused at his mate with a slight pout at the kiss being broken. Adam blushed red, grabbing Chris's hand before sliding the large callused hand down his back slowly and into his pants; Chris's breathing went ragged, completely turned on.

Adam whimpered, spreading his legs as he pushed his front against his mate, rubbing his cock torturously slow against Chris'; having to get on to his tip toes to do so, feeling his alpha's cock jumping to attention. Chris's finger naturally slid to his mate's entrance before feeling something warm and wet. Chris blinked in confusion before his eyes snapped down to his mate's gorgeous half lidded blue eyes.

Chris started panting hard, easily slipping his finger into Adam's entrance, Adam throwing his head back in ecstasy. Chris snarled, his eyes blazing yellow, lifting Adam up with his other hand easily, his finger still in his mate's soaked entrance. Adam moaned, wrapping his legs around Chris's waist, trying to ride Chris's finger before a second finger joined the first. Neither had gotten so hard so fast since Amilya had been kidnapped. Chris was thrusting his fingers in and out of Adam's entrance, both suddenly looking down to see Adam's crotch area completely soaked, the scent driving Chris mad.

"O~h!" Adam whimpered, grinding helplessly on his mate's long, thick fingers, an ache growing for something larger to fill him.

"Chris!" Adam gasped, Chris biting Adam's shoulder, "Fuck me. Please, please!"

Chris snarled, slamming Adam against the counter, shoving Adam's pants down so they were scrunched around his knees before he ended up ripping half a pant leg off. Adam kissed Chris fiercely, the kiss filled with biting teeth, bruising lips, and saliva dripping down their chins. Adam sobbed, feeling the head of Chris's cock press against his entrance, Chris snarling before fully sheathing himself into his mate's hot tight entrance, slick dripping out of Adam; some slipping down Chris' thighs.

Chris pounded hard into his mate, Adam keening and moaning, head thrown back, hands woven into his mate's thick black hair. Chris's sack slapped against his ass, Adam's slick dripping off of them.

"Fuck! Mmm, Yes! Oh yes!" Adam crossing his ankles around Chris's lower back, one hand scratching up his lover's back.

"Chris!" Adam crying out, Chris licking and nipping at Adam's mating mark. Chris' one hand had Adam's hip in an iron grasp, before tilting Adam's hips up slightly.

"Oh fuck me!" Adam screaming out, Chris hitting his mate's prostate dead on, Chris snarling feeling a burn at the base of his cock. Chris hadn't been able to knot his mate either due to his own depression with losing their daughter.

Chris's thrusts were getting erratic and extremely rough, the alpha losing control.

"Fuck your knot into me Chris," Adam snarled, baring his teeth in challenge. Chris roared, shoving his knot brutally into his mate, biting Adam's mating mark hard. Adam bit Chris' mark in return, both yelling into the others skin. Adam's belly was streaked with his come, getting rubbed into both of their bellies from Chris grinding his knot into his mate. Chris shuttered hard into his mate, holding Adam's quaking legs around him as his seed filled his mate's hot fluttering shute.

"Take me to our room," Adam's wolf eyes blue like ice, Chris's bright like gold.

"I have silk bindings I've been dying to wrap you in."

Adam whimpered, Chris carrying Adam back to their room, neither caring if anyone saw their pack alpha balls deep inside his mate; Adam's hole stretched erotically over a huge knot.

"Fuck my way inside of you so you'll feel me for days after. Days of my seed spilling from your hole. Unable to move as I fuck my way inside you day and night. Your ass high and presented to me like the naughty little omega lover you are."

"Yes!" Adam hissed, moaning with every step his mate took up the stairs, his cock coming back to life. From the feel of Chris inside him, Chris was hard as a rock.

"Either hurry your ass up or you fuck me raw on the stairs," Adam growled, Chris growling back, loving when Adam got demanding.

"I'll fuck you as I please, when I please," Chris thrusting hard with what his knot would allow, Adam squealing in delight before moaning at the stretch.

"Demanding little thing," Chris indeed hurried to their bedroom, the door barely closing before fucking his mate over every available surface. He'd have to wait for his knot to deflate before tying his mate up in the silk bindings he promised. Neither had felt like that since Amilya was little and Chris had been wanting to have another baby along with Adam when Amilya was still a toddler. Now they would have to see if this turned into an actual heat, Chris feeling all kinds of randy again.